ROYAL DECOY

Praise for Heather Frost

"This is a story that completely captured my attention from the very beginning and didn't let go the whole way through ... I've been craving a book like this."
- Aimee, Getting Your Read On (*Royal Decoy*)

"Blackmail. Betrayal. Romance. Frost expertly combines them all with political intrigue and characters you can't help but fall in love with. The next book can't come fast enough!"
- Rebecca McKinnon, Author (*Royal Decoy*)

"This book has just about everything! ... The intrigue is fantastic. This is a series that is worth reading. I will anxiously await the next installment to see what happens next."
- Bookworm Lisa (*Royal Decoy*)

"You know what I love? Fantasy. You know what really thrills me? When a story like this one works its magic on me in a way I still feel its power after finishing it. ... Full of action, conspiracies, exciting twists and turns, charismatic characters, and heart-warming moments—I demand my own Grayson!—this first installment is a fantastic opening."
- Silvia, Darkest Sins (*Royal Decoy*)

"This book was superb. ...Well thought out story that was action packed ... It was amazing ... a fantastic read that made me read it in one sitting. Heather Frost will be an author that I keep on my radar from now on. Can't wait for book two!"
- Stacy, A Court of Coffee and Books (*Royal Decoy*)

"If you are looking for a good read with royalty, mystery,
intrigue, spies, war, and romance, this book has it all. Heather
Frost certainly delivers a great read with Royal Decoy."
- Sheila, Why Not? Because I Said So (*Royal Decoy*)

"Frost has written a magnificent young adult fantasy romance
that readers will absolutely love. The turn of every page is
jam packed with fast paced, thrilling and adventurous twists
and turns that will keep readers guessing and wanting more."
- Sydney, Singing Librarian Books (*Royal Decoy*)

"An amazing first book in a series! The premise of this
novel was so interesting! It's something that I'm fairly
certain I haven't read before in other books."
- Caitlin, Chapters and Pages (*Royal Decoy*)

"Super unique ... The story flowed and [...] was well-paced and
didn't end off in a cliffhanger. I totally recommend this book
to everyone especially those who want a fresh royalty read."
- Thindbooks (*Royal Decoy*)

"*Seers* is a really good paranormal read mixed with a great
romance, and a some really fun characters."
- Mundie Moms Blog (*Seers*)

"Heather does an amazing job of keeping the story rolling,
fast paced and full of intrigue and suspense."
- Cindy C. Bennett, Author (*Demons*)

"You won't be able to stop until the last page is turned.
... 5 out of 5 stars."
- Min Reads and Reviews (*Guardians*)

Also by Heather Frost:

The Seers Trilogy:
Seers
Demons
Guardians

Asides: A Short Story Collection

Royal Decoy

FATE OF EYRINTHIA · BOOK 1

Heather Frost

Copyright © 2020 Heather Frost

Map Design by Kevin Frost

Cover and Interior Design by K.M. Frost

Summary: Kitchen maid Clare Ellington is blackmailed into becoming the princess's decoy, to ensure a tenuous peace with an enemy kingdom.

Hardcover: ISBN 978-1-7348919-0-4
Softcover: ISBN 978-1-7348919-1-1

Kimberly, this one is for you.
You are my sister and my best friend.
This book—like many other things in my life—
would not have happened without you. Thank you!
I love you. Forever and ever.
PS: You will always be Grayson's first fan.

PRONUNCIATION GUIDE

Demoi	*de-MOY*
Desfan	*DES-fawn*
Devendra	*duh-VEN-druh*
Devendran	*duh-VEN-drun*
Duvan	*DOO-vahn*
Eyrinthia	*air-INTH-ee-uh*
Iden	*EYE-den*
Julne	*JOOLN*
Mortise	*mor-TEES (rhymes with geese)*
Mortisian	*mor-TEE-shun*
Ryden	*RYE-den*
Rydenic	*rye-DEN-ik*
Saernon	*SAIR-non*
Ser	*SAIR*
Serai	*sair-AY*
Serjah	*SAIR-zjaw*
Serjan	*SAIR-zjan*
Zennor	*ZEN-or*
Zennorian	*zen-OR-ee-un*

*Note: zj is a French "J", as in Jaques

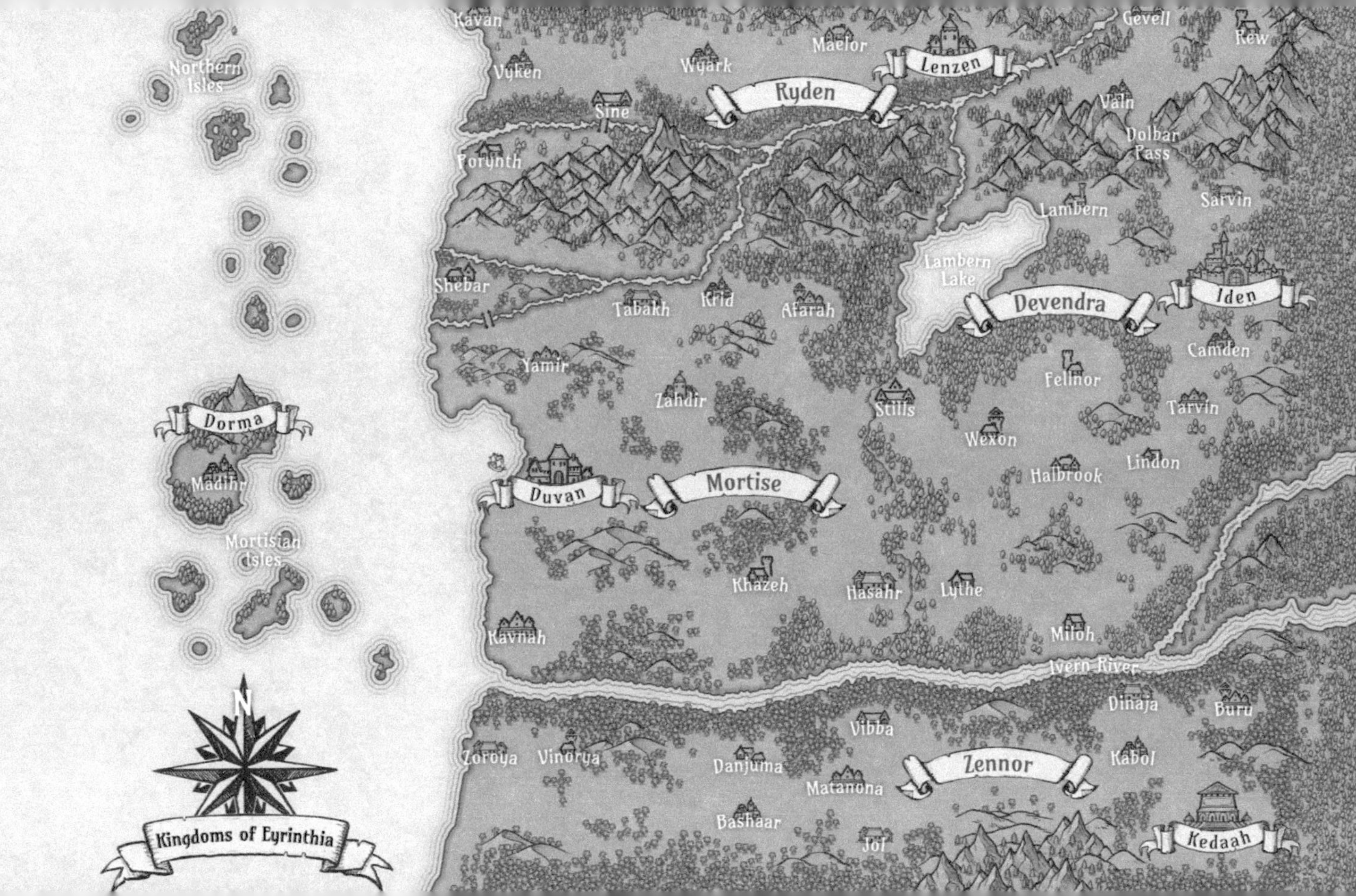

Kavan
Northern Isles
Vyken
Wjark
Maelor
Gevell
Rew
Sine
Ryden
Lenzen
Vain
Dolbar Pass
Porynth
Sarvin
Lambern
Lambern Lake
Shebar
Devendra
Iden
Tabakh
Krid
Afarah
Camden
Yamir
Felnor
Zahdir
Stills
Tarvin
Wexon
Dorma
Halbrook
Lindon
Duvan
Mortise
Madihr
Khazeh
Mortistan Isles
Hasahr
Lythe
Kavnah
Miloh
Ivern River
Dinaja
Buru
Vibba
N
Zoroya
Vinorya
Danjuma
Zennor
Kabol
Matanona
Kingdoms of Eyrinthia
Bashaar
Jof
Kedaah

CHAPTER I

CLARE

CLARE CALLED A FAREWELL AS SHE LEFT the castle kitchen, a fire still dying within the scorched hearth. Cook Towdy gave his usual grunt, hunched over the thick wooden counter, his apron dusted with flour. He didn't look up from tomorrow's menu as he made final adjustments. Clare was the last maid to leave; even after working under Towdy for ten years, she still felt like that eight-year-old girl with too much to prove.

The heat of the castle ovens clung to Clare's skin as she entered the deserted corridor and stretched her tired arms. Errant strands of brown hair brushed her cheeks, her long braid swinging against her back. Her aching feet didn't relish the long walk to Lower Iden, but she was anxious to see her brothers.

Silence reigned in the servant's passage this time of night, the quiet scuff of her worn boots the only sound aside from the guttering torches. Flames leapt in the evenly spaced iron sconces, forcing the shadows to dance back, forever a servant to the light.

Clare knew how the shadows felt.

Somewhere down the hall a door slammed open, wood thudding against stone. Clare's head jerked up, though she couldn't see anything around the hallway's bend. Rapid footsteps clipped against the floor and a male voice drifted around the corner, his tone wry. "Perhaps you want to slow down."

"No." The woman's deep voice was sharp with annoyance. "If you'll recall, I wanted a private walk in the gardens. That means *without you*, Bennick."

"I'm sorry I couldn't accommodate, Princess."

Clare froze, stomach dropping. *Princess?* Fates, kitchen maids weren't supposed to be seen—especially not by the royal family. She fell back a step, eyes darting to the nearest door. She grasped the cold handle, but it caught.

Locked.

Clare pressed her back against the closed portal, cheeks burning as she ducked her head. Her palms skated over her stained apron and she hooked loose curls behind her ears before her hands fell, fingers twitching at her sides.

When the princess and her three bodyguards stepped into view, the princess's cutting gaze caught Clare in an instant.

Even with a scowl, Princess Serene was beautiful. Sheathed in a dark purple gown that brushed the floor, she walked with regal grace, her chin lifted. Her dark brown hair was twisted into a braided bun at the back of her head with loose curls styled artfully around her face. The nineteen-year-old princess was half-Zennorian, her skin a rich and beautiful brown. It was a shade darker than Clare's, but their deep blue Devendran eyes were nearly an exact match.

The princess was well-loved in Devendra for her charitable

work, but everyone in the castle knew of her legendary arguments with her father. Even tonight the kitchen had buzzed with talk from the servers who claimed Serene had stormed out of dinner while the king yelled after her. Gossip had been so consumed with the dramatic scene that no one had even mentioned the Mortisian emissaries who had been the focus of rumor since they'd arrived at the castle a month ago. They'd been sent by Serjah Desfan Cassian, who currently served as regent since his father, the serjan, was reportedly ill. A chill raced over Clare's arms whenever she thought about the Mortisians living in the castle, and she knew she wasn't the only one uncomfortable with their presence. Rumor had it Serene herself was quite upset about it.

Seeing the princess for the first time, Clare could easily imagine her being upset with all four kingdoms of Eyrinthia. Her frown was severe, her eyes hooded, and her steps deliberate as she stalked forward. Her bodyguards only added to the intensity of the moment. Two walked in front of the princess and a third was behind her.

The bodyguard in the lead noticed Clare first, his long strides continuing easily even as his sharp gaze assessed her. His spine was stiff, his brown hair brushing the collar of his dark blue uniform. He looked to be about thirty and had a thin scar slicing over his right cheek.

The bodyguard behind him was easily twice as wide as anyone Clare had ever seen, and he stood head and shoulders above the two other guards. As if the man's hulking stature wasn't distinctive enough, a dozen or more pox scars dug across his rugged face. He was probably in his late forties and everything about him was hard, from the stern cut of his mouth to the steel-gray hairs at his temples.

The third and youngest guard strode behind the princess.

He was probably about the same age as the princess he guarded, which meant he must be highly skilled. Broad shoulders strained against his fitted uniform while his hands hung relaxed near the hilts of his sheathed weapons. There was controlled power in his gait, a surety and confidence in each step. Torchlight flickered on his golden skin and caught the sand-colored hair curling over his brow. Stubble lined his angular jaw and his strong nose was slightly bent, as if it had been broken once. When his crystal-blue eyes found Clare, she was surprised to see warmth there. The corner of his mouth lifted, curving his lips into a half-smile.

She was staring.

The tips of Clare's ears burned as she dropped her gaze, fingers knotting in her skirt. What had come over her? She knew better than to draw attention to herself.

It had been a long day. That was the only explanation.

She kept her head bowed, eyes trained on the gray stone floor until the moment the princess and her guards passed and she could escape.

Clare had only taken two steps when the click of a lock disengaging made her look over her shoulder. Her eyes briefly caught crystal-blue ones as the youngest bodyguard also twisted to track the sound.

The door Clare had been leaning against burst open and six men exploded from the room, long knives spinning in their hands and catching menacingly in the torchlight.

Clare stumbled back, fear strangling the cry in her throat as the men crashed into the princess's guards. Even surprised and outnumbered, the three bodyguards leapt instantly into action. Grunts, hisses of pain, and angry snarls filled the corridor. Fists pounded flesh. Steel clashed against steel. The tang of blood flooded the air, changing the space completely in a matter of seconds.

Adrenaline shook through Clare and throbbed at her temples. Her muscles twitched, but she was unable to move. Sweat coated her palms and her lungs locked. She'd lost sight of the blue-eyed bodyguard, the pox-scarred one taking up most of the space in the narrow hall as he shoved into two of the attackers, pushing them back with his dominant size. As he plowed them into the wall, Clare finally saw past him.

The princess stood in the middle of the corridor, eyes narrowed on the fight, a long, thin dagger clenched in her hand. Where had that come from? Had the princess been carrying a weapon in her own home?

Someone yelled for the princess to run—the guard with the scarred cheek?—but Princess Serene ignored him. She was searching for an opening, a place to join the fight.

Was she insane?

Clare could ask herself the same. She should be running. If not for safety, then for help. But before she could move she spotted an attacker creeping behind Serene, the princess wholly unaware as he lifted his knife.

Clare reacted without thought, diving around the scarred giant and running for the princess.

Serene's eyes rounded a second before Clare slammed into her, shoving them both against the wall. Clare swore she felt the whisper of the assassin's blade as it flew past her neck, barely missing her.

Serene's breath rattled out, her eyes burning Clare with a mix of fear and rage.

Before Clare could even open her mouth, a strangling hand caught her upper arm, shooting pain all the way to her fingertips. She cried out as she was ripped away from the princess, her shoulders cracking against the wall a second before a hand grasped her throat.

The pox-scarred soldier glared down at Clare, his hot breath searing her face. Fury blackened his fierce gaze and a muscle in his rigid jaw flexed as he squeezed, pinching off her breath.

Clare scratched the hand that crushed her entire neck. She kicked him, but his body was as immovable as the castle wall biting into her spine.

Her vision wavered and blood roared in her ears, muting the crash of steel that still filled the hall.

"Wilf!" the princess shouted. "They need you!"

The grip around Clare's throat clenched fiercely, lancing pain through her neck and down her spine. He was going to snap her neck.

Through watering eyes, Clare caught sight of the blue-eyed soldier as he looked up from the body sliding off his long knife.

The young bodyguard's eyes widened. "No! Wilf!" He lunged toward them, but it was too late.

The giant drew back a fist and knuckles as solid as stone hit Clare's temple.

Clare shivered awake, blinking against the pain in her aching head. The left side stabbed with agony. She swallowed, but that only made her cringe at the burn in her throat. She reached to feel her bruised neck and chains rattled, dragging at her wrists.

They were shackled in front of her.

Her heart stopped. Her eyes cut over her surroundings, her pulse tripping as she realized she was in a small cell. Torchlight flickered over the glaring emptiness. There wasn't even a chamber pot. The stones were grimy and an unpleasant moistness clung to the air.

She was in a prison cell.

Horror washed over her as memories crashed into her. The ambush. The fact that she had slammed the princess into the wall. It would have looked like an attack, not a rescue. Especially if they hadn't noticed the attacker sneaking up behind the princess.

Clare trembled, the cold stone floor leeching all warmth from her body. She needed to speak to someone. To tell them what had happened. That she was innocent.

She had no idea how long she'd been unconscious, but it had been long enough. Her brothers would be worried. Thomas was barely thirteen and Mark only ten. They might even go to Eliot's barracks, and her older brother couldn't afford to be pulled into this.

The cell door grated open and the lone torch guttered. Clare hitched to her feet, nausea rolling in her gut as pain sparked in her head. The chains swung from her bound wrists and she stumbled from the dizziness that hit her. She leaned against the wall, jaw clenched and head pounding as she watched three men file into the cell.

The man in the lead had a gold rope on the shoulder of his uniform, marking him a commander. His lined face was indistinct in the flickering light, but Clare thought he was middle-aged. His hair was light brown with silver strands sprinkled throughout and his eyes cut to Clare, hard and cold.

Her stomach dropped.

The two men behind him fanned out on either side of her, raising the hairs at the back of her neck. The cell door clanked shut and she swallowed thickly. "Please." Her voice cracked and she cleared her throat with a wince. "There's been a mistake."

The commander's thick brows slammed down. He jerked his chin and the two men grabbed Clare's arms. They hauled her toward the commander, putting them a mere pace apart. He towered over her and her breath stuttered but she bit back a whimper. She didn't want to reveal her fear, even though she was exploding with it.

"You were the lookout, I presume." His hard voice was chillingly quiet. "Once the princess passed, you gave the signal and the other rebels attacked."

"No, I—"

He backhanded her and pain burst across her cheek, radiating through her aching head. Hard fingers dug into her arms, holding her upright as the commander glared down at her. "Don't waste my time with denials."

Clare blinked against the tears stinging her eyes. "I swear to the fates, I was only trying to save the princess. There was a man behind her with a knife. Just let me talk with her and—"

The commander grabbed her chin and forced her head back so their eyes met. "You'll never get close to her again," he sneered. "You failed. Your accomplices failed. So tell me everything about your friends."

"I'm not one of them!"

His jaw flexed. "I have the power to make your death swift or agonizing. Now, answer me."

A tremble shook her, but Clare tried to remain calm. It was hard with the commander breathing down on her, fingers digging into her chin, while the other two soldiers held her firmly. She swallowed hard but her voice still sounded too thin, too ragged, as it came up her abused throat. "I had nothing to do with the attack. I'm not a rebel. I work in the kitchen—I've worked there since I was a child. Ask Cook Towdy. He'll tell you who I am."

The commander's face was unreadable as he studied her. Then, without warning, he shoved her face away and she would have stumbled if the guards hadn't been holding her arms.

The commander took a step back and Clare would have felt relief, except for the darkness swimming in his eyes. "Very well. I will test your story." His eyes bored into her, and she struggled to keep breathing as he continued. "I'm going to learn everything about you, girl. And you're going to regret ever stepping foot inside this castle."

CHAPTER 2
CLARE

TOO MUCH TIME HAD PASSED. CLARE'S anxiety rose with every pacing step she took in the small cell, the clink of her chains only intensifying her anxiety. It should not have taken this long for the commander to question Towdy.

The fear that something had gone wrong was all-consuming. Her mouth was dry and she couldn't stop fingering the bruises around her throat, even though the iron manacles weighted her wrists. Panic spiraled, exploded, and then she forced it back down—only to have it return moments later, a relentless tension coiling her body again and again.

The silence was horrible. All she heard was the thin gutter of the torch, her own stuttered breaths, and the unsteady leap of her heart. Despair stabbed at her when she thought of her younger brothers. Thomas, who wanted to be a soldier like his older brother, and Mark, whom Clare had raised since infancy.

If Towdy could not convince the commander of Clare's innocence, she would never see her brothers again.

Footsteps thudded beyond the door and a key jangled. Clare trembled with exhaustion, fear, and something horribly like hope.

The cell door swung open and the commander swept inside, a cloaked man striding in behind him. The door closed with a heavy, fatalistic thud.

The commander's eyes were cold, but not as angry as before. He stared at her, his eyes carving over her face. Studying. Evaluating. His expression gave away nothing.

Clare blinked under his scrutiny, biting her tongue even though she was desperate to ask about his conversation with Towdy.

"Your name is Clare Ellington," the commander said at last. "You've worked in the castle kitchen since you were eight years old. You begged for your mother's position while she was on her sickbed, heavy with child. Cook Towdy obliged, with the condition it would revert back to her when she recovered. But she never did. She died in childbirth."

Clare exhaled shallowly. She didn't know why the commander was telling her about her life, but at least he wasn't condemning her to the gallows. Yet.

The commander lifted his chin. "You helped raise your brothers because no one else stepped forward—probably because your father was a traitor. He sided with Ivar Carrigan in the civil war and was executed two months before your mother's death."

Clare gritted her teeth against the memory his words sparked. Screams had ripped up her throat as she'd clutched her father's hand, trying to keep him close as soldiers dragged him from the house. Her father had shouted for her to stay back but she'd only held him tighter. Until a soldier had knocked her to the floor.

They hadn't even returned Duncan Ellington's body. King Newlan didn't allow proper burials for traitors. After the raids on the city, piles of bodies had rotted in the city square, feeding the crows for weeks and delivering a strong message. The fact that rebels had only started to crawl out of hiding recently was a testament to the effectiveness of that long-ago warning.

Clare desperately hoped she wasn't about to become another message.

The commander stepped forward and every muscle in Clare's body tensed as she retreated a step, her back hitting the wall.

His voice was low. "Are you a traitor like your father, Miss Ellington?"

Clare pressed her shoulders against the wall to steady herself and, summoning every nerve she had, raised her eyes to meet the commander's. "I am not a traitor."

The commander's intent expression didn't waver, but the cloaked man standing behind him shifted forward and lowered his hood, revealing an angular face with sharp features and a neatly trimmed dark beard. Clare couldn't tell if he wore a uniform beneath the long cloak, but he stood with the straight posture of a soldier.

The commander spoke again, snapping Clare's attention back to him. "You tried to kill the princess tonight."

"No. I saved her."

He ignored that. "You will be executed at dawn."

Cold fear hit her. Then anger flared and she clenched her fists, chains rattling. "I demand a fair trial."

"You're not in a position to demand anything."

"You spoke with Towdy. You must know I'm—"

"He believes you're innocent, but I'm not constrained by his beliefs."

Clare's heart pounded, but she spoke past that. "Let me speak with the princess or her guards." One of them had to have noticed she'd saved the princess. The blue-eyed guard had tried to stop the giant bodyguard from striking her—maybe he had seen the truth behind her actions.

The commander's lips pressed into a severe line. "I've already interviewed them. None of them will speak for you."

It shouldn't have sliced her so deeply, but she struggled to find her voice again. "I . . . I could appeal to the king."

Actual amusement sparked in his eyes. "I doubt King Newlan would grant you an audience." He cocked his head, almost musing as he said, "Most peasants wouldn't dare address a commander in such a way."

The words could have been insulting or threatening, except for the calm way he spoke them. The shift in his behavior unnerved her, making her wary. Her spine stiffened. "You're not giving me a choice."

"No, I suppose not." He glanced at the bearded man, who gave a nod. Clare frowned, but didn't have time to question their silent communication; the commander stepped closer, putting him right in front of her.

Clare tensed. "I've told you, I'm—"

"Innocent. Yes." His mouth curled faintly upward. "I know."

She stared at him, her breath wavering as she tried to make sense of those simple but bewildering words. "You . . . *know*?"

The commander straightened. "The princess spoke for you, corroborating your story. Two of her guards did as well."

"But . . . ?"

He arched a brow. "Why haven't I let you go?"

She chafed against his cruelly mocking tone. He'd threatened her with execution, even though he'd known she was innocent. Why?

The commander smiled slowly. "You're going to make a choice, Miss Ellington. A choice between life and death."

Clare's eyes flew to the bearded man who shifted closer, a silent observer. She bristled when she turned back to the commander. "I'm innocent. You have to let me go."

"I really don't." His chin dipped as he leaned in. She forced herself not to cringe back. "Witnesses may have spoken for you, but that doesn't mean you walk out of here. Who's to say I didn't arrive too late with the knowledge of your innocence? I came to free you, but the guards had already killed you during your interrogation. An unfortunate blow to the head." His eyes drifted to her temple and Clare shivered. The commander leaned back. "If you want to walk out of this cell, you will answer my questions. Do you understand?"

Clare jerked out a nod, even though she didn't understand at all. Sweat gathered on her palms despite the chill that gripped her.

"How old are you?" the commander asked.

She hesitated at the unexpected question. "Eighteen."

"Do you know how to read?"

"Do I . . . ?" The commander's mouth drew tight, so she cleared her throat. "Yes, I can read." Her mother had taught her the basics, anyway.

"Do you know any other languages?"

"I speak the common tongue." Most people learned to speak it, since it was needed in nearly every occupation.

The commander switched to the common tongue. "Who taught you to speak the trade language?"

"My parents," she answered in kind. "My father was a carpenter."

He inclined his head, acknowledging her ability with the language before switching back to Devendran. "Do you know how to ride?"

"No." They'd never been able to afford a horse, even before her father's death.

"Which kingdom is Devendra's greatest enemy?"

Were these questions even related? Tension coiled in Clare's shoulders, but she forced herself to speak. "Mortise. Or perhaps Ryden."

The answer wasn't definitive, but that didn't seem to be an issue for the commander. "What do you know of the royals in Mortise?"

She frowned. "Serjan Saernon is sick. Serjah Desfan is helping to rule in his father's stead. The prince is a sailor, though some say a pirate. They're the only surviving members of the royal family. The rest died years ago. In a shipwreck, I think. There are rumors that Mortise is plotting another war against us." Which made the presence of Mortisian emissaries here at the castle all the more alarming.

The commander didn't comment on anything she said. He simply moved to his next question. "What do you know of Ryden?"

The northern kingdom was reclusive. They traded sparingly with the rest of Eyrinthia and rarely crossed borders. One of their previous kings, long before Clare's birth, had tried to conquer all of Eyrinthia. He'd failed, but the resentment between the four kingdoms lived on. The current king of Ryden was said to foam at the mouth and have red eyes. Stories of his demonic sons were often whispered during stormy nights.

"Miss Ellington?" the commander prompted, tone sharp with impatience.

"King Henri Kaelin is rumored to be a demon," Clare said,

coloring a little as she shared the terror-stories she'd heard since childhood. "He hides in his mountain fortress, destitute after his grandfather's armies were destroyed. He has five sons. It's said they drink the blood of their kills—animal and human alike."

The commander didn't mock her for repeating the over-dramatic stories. "What do you know of Zennor?"

"They're our allies. King Zaire Buhari has ruled the southern kingdom for years. Even the tribes look to him to manage Zennor's borders, though they don't always agree with his laws. King Buhari has many children. His sister was Queen Aren." The Devendran queen had died three years ago, but her kindness was still remembered by everyone in Devendra.

Disappointment crossed the commander's face. "I would have expected you to know more." He scanned her face. "You clearly have some Zennorian blood. A grandparent, perhaps?"

Clare raised her chin and spoke tightly through her growing frustration. "I'm loyal to Devendra."

The commander glanced again at the bearded man, whom Clare had almost forgotten, he was so quiet. "What do you think?" the commander asked.

"Her voice isn't quite right." The cloaked man studied her. "Though as you said, she speaks surprisingly well. Her posture could use correcting, but she doesn't cower. And did you notice how she lifted her chin? That in particular is right." His hooked nose wrinkled. "She's smaller than I wanted. Her skin isn't dark enough, but that can be managed. Her eyes are nearly a perfect match, which I never imagined we'd find—it's so rare. And her hair is almost the same shade. How long is it? Unbraid it, girl."

Her cheeks warmed but her words came out strong. "I'm not some woman for hire."

The bearded man's mouth twitched. "You're right, Commander. In spirit, they're nearly equal." He stroked his short beard and Clare caught the glint of a gold ring on his forefinger. "Miss Ellington, I would like to offer you a unique opportunity."

Clare's eyes darted between the two men. They'd arrested her, threatened her, and now they were offering her something? Suspicion sang through her. "I don't understand."

"What is there to understand?" Apparently the bearded man had taken over the conversation. "I believe the commander laid things out clearly. You will accept my offer, or you will not leave this cell."

She clenched her jaw. "What offer?"

"To become Princess Serene's decoy."

It took a moment for the words to make any sort of sense. "You want me to be the princess's *decoy*?"

"Yes." His eyes sharpened. "The threats against her are mounting, as you witnessed tonight. She needs a double. You resemble her and your deficiencies could be remedied. You could learn to act like her."

"But, my brothers—"

"You'll never see them again if you refuse."

Desperation pinched Clare's throat. "I'll die either way."

He shrugged one broad shoulder. "Probably. But if you become the decoy, I give you my word your brothers will be cared for. Even if you lose your life as a consequence."

Clare's wrists ached with the weight of the chains that bound her. She was trapped in every way. Their threats were real. They would kill her if she refused.

And if she accepted?

Her life wouldn't be her own. She would become the princess's decoy—a target for assassins. She would live in the castle until she died. And while she was apart from her family . . . they would have everything they needed. Thomas and Mark would no longer have to work in the stable at Motley's Tavern. They could have real tutoring—Thomas wouldn't have to become a soldier; he and Mark could be anything they wanted. They could have everything they'd dreamed of—a real future.

But she wouldn't be with them.

An ache pierced her heart, because she knew what she was going to choose. What she *had* to choose. There wasn't a real choice. She could die, or she could provide for her family.

She would do what she'd always done.

Clare cleared her throat, hating how brittle and weak it sounded in the awful silence of the shadowed cell. "I'll do it."

The bearded man lifted his chin. "You'll swear an oath?"

"Yes."

His eyes flashed with triumph. He straightened, his voice deepening. "Do you, Clare Ellington, willingly give your oath to serve King Newlan Demoi until your death and keep his secrets as your own?"

Her mouth had dried, but she forced herself to speak. "I do."

He stretched out his hand, the one with the gold ring she'd noticed before. When the crest caught the flickering light, instinct overcame her and she fell to her knees.

"Seal your oath," King Newlan ordered.

Dizziness stole her breath but Clare leaned forward, pulse pounding in her ears as she kissed the royal crest. The stone beneath her knees was hard and cold. She fought back a shiver. The man who'd ordered her father's death and would have looked on as the commander killed her in this cell now owned her completely.

Newlan's deep voice boomed in the small cell. "Stand."

She pushed up from the floor, avoiding the king's eyes.

"Take those chains off her."

The commander fished a key from his pocket and obeyed

the royal order. But even when the chains fell and Clare fingered her sore wrists, she knew she wasn't free.

The torchlight brushed the king's face as he viewed her. "In the morning you'll go home and tell your family you've been promoted to serve as one of the princess's maids and that you'll live at the castle now."

So many emotions roiled inside her, but the thought of going home—even briefly—was a lifeline and she clung to it.

"The visit will be short," the king continued. "You will need to be prepared to attend a private dinner tomorrow night. I want to show you to those few who will be aware of your role. Not many will be told the truth. You're only useful if our enemies don't know about you." He glanced at the commander. "See she's given whatever she requires—for herself and her family—and keep her secure. I want her in your suite tonight." Without another word, the king lifted his hood and strode from the cell. In the torch-lit corridor, a group of soldiers took up positions around him, following him out of sight.

Clare stood rooted to the floor. Each heartbeat thudded through her entire body and a chill snaked down her spine. She'd had no real choice, but she still wondered if she'd just made the biggest mistake of her life.

The commander held the cell door open and Clare ducked her head as she stepped out. He led her down a long hall, then up a flight of stairs. They kept to side passages, encountering no one as they ghosted through the sleeping castle. Clare's eyes snagged on the fine carpets, oil paintings, and antique side tables all gleamingly polished and holding vases of fresh flowers. The finery of the upper castle was unfamiliar to her, making this night feel even more surreal.

The commander finally stopped and opened the door to a large suite. The sitting room held a long settee, a couple armchairs near a dead fire, and several tidy bookshelves. A short hall led to four closed doors, though the closest one opened and a maid peeked out, irritation tightening her features. She softly closed the door behind her and kept her voice low as she strode toward them. "The lady just drifted off. She needs quiet."

The commander didn't acknowledge the maid's words, though his voice was low as he gestured to Clare. "You will attend this young woman, Millie. She's staying the night."

The woman's eyes dragged over Clare's mussed braid and worn dress, her lip curling. "Who is she?"

"Millie." Warning lived in the commander's voice.

The middle-aged woman huffed. "But where will she sleep?"

"Put her in the spare room."

"The spare—?"

"Don't argue with me," he snapped.

"Sir, the lady will—"

"My wife doesn't need to know she's here." His voice dropped low. "She *won't* know, Millie. Do you understand?"

The unspoken threat hung in the air until finally Millie's head dipped. "As you will, Commander."

The commander turned his razor gaze on Clare. "Go with her."

Clare took a step forward on instinct, but halted and forced her eyes to meet the commander's. "My brothers will need a caretaker."

His flat stare was intimidating, but she forced herself to continue. "I was promised that I could have whatever I needed, and I require a caretaker of my choosing."

A muscle in the commander's cheek jumped and Clare was sure she'd pushed him too far, but his voice was level when he spoke. "I will have candidates selected before dawn."

Surprise and relief rushed through her. It was a small victory after everything she'd lost, but a victory all the same.

Without another word the commander strode from the suite and Clare was left to follow Millie down the hall and to the last room on the right. The maid left her in the doorway, muttering about fetching a nightgown.

Clare stepped into the room, a musty smell itching her nose. There was no window since they were in the depths of the castle, but the lamp from the hall cast enough of a glow to see colorful tapestries of sunny landscapes and rolling mountains on the stone walls. The furniture was made of dark wood and coated with a thin layer of dust; the bed seemed the only exception to the air of disuse, looking freshly made with a light blue quilt laid on top. A trunk sat in the corner and the shelf above it was filled with dusty toys; model ships, a wooden sword, and blocks with chipped and faded paint.

It was the room of a little boy, but one who hadn't lived in it for a long time. Clare didn't know what had happened to him, but she felt a flash of sympathy for the commander. She knew the sharp pain of loss.

She fingered the scarred cloth of a stuffed panther crouched at the end of the bed, wondering about the boy who had clearly once loved it.

"Don't touch that," Millie snapped.

Clare spun, the feel of the panther's worn texture still on her fingertips. "Sorry."

The maid's eyes narrowed and she shoved a balled-up nightgown into Clare's hands before exiting the room.

Tears scalded Clare's eyes the moment the door snapped shut. She blinked, fighting for control, but it was too much. The sacrifices she'd been forced to make tonight hit her hard, and the pervading sadness of the room didn't help; it was a place that whispered of lost things, regrets, and the ultimate cruelty of fate.

Clutching the nightgown to her chest, Clare perched on the edge of the bed and let the tears dash over her cheeks.

CHAPTER 3

GRAYSON

THE STINK OF LENZEN'S SLUMS LAY HEAVY on the afternoon air. Manure, rotten food, and too many unwashed bodies. Despite the stench, Prince Grayson Kaelin's expression was neutral as he dragged his horse to a halt in the center of the street. He gripped the reins in a black-gloved fist, viewing the wood and stone façade of the inn. He noted the sagging shutters, the warped roof, the bursts of laughter coming from inside, and then he jerked his chin.

The squad of soldiers behind him followed the silent command to march on the inn.

Grayson remained where he was, his brown horse snorting and shifting beneath him when startled shouts and alarmed screams rang out, the frantic cries of women rising above the growls of men.

There was no laughter now.

Patrons were shoved into the street and forced to kneel. Mothers clung to their children and fathers struggled to remain between their families and danger. In the chaos, no one had seen Grayson yet. The soldiers commanded all the attention.

For now.

Grayson waited until everyone was kneeling on the ground, surrounded by soldiers with drawn swords, before he swung down from his horse, boots kicking up dust from the unpaved road.

Silence cut through the crowd. Grown men and young children alike paled at the sight of him. Women whimpered.

The Black Hand. Merciless enforcer of the king's laws. The youngest prince of Ryden and the deadliest. Only seventeen years old, yet Grayson had the power to bring them all to a trembling halt. The truth was a familiar weight in his gut.

"Where is Latham Borg?" he asked, his voice deep and clipped.

A heavy beat of silence, then an old man raised a bandaged hand, his wrinkled face pinched. "Please, Your Highness. This isn't necessary."

Grayson tugged the cuffs of his gloves, ensuring the black leather covered his wrists. "You understand the king's tax?"

Latham Borg cringed. "Yes, but business has been slow."

The captain of the squad snorted, coming to stand beside Grayson. "Your customers fill the street, old man."

Captain Reeve was in his early twenties and was constantly trying Grayson's patience. He edged in on his authority and was most likely a spy of King Henri's, who liked to keep an unwavering eye on his sons.

Latham Borg glanced at the ragged crowd. "They're my friends. They can't always pay."

Grayson placed himself just forward of Captain Reeve—a not-so-subtle reminder for the captain. "King Henri has no use for excuses. Do you have the required payment?"

Unspoken pleas shone in the man's gaze. "I sent a letter . . ."

Grayson's hand shifted, his gloved palm now resting only a breath from his sheathed sword. The innkeeper's eyes flew wide, his throat bobbing sharply.

The woman beside him snatched hold of his unbandaged hand. "Please, Your Highness, we can raise the amount. My husband has been unwell since the accident, but—"

Grayson turned on his heel. "Arrest the innkeeper."

"No!" The woman struggled to hold her husband even as he was levered to his feet. The soldiers shoved her aside but she immediately scrambled to her knees and reached past the soldier blocking her path. "Latham!"

The innkeeper's face was tight with fearful resignation as he was hauled away. "Marie, it's all right."

She ignored her husband's empty assurance and continued to cry out, emotion strangling her voice.

Chains clinked as the innkeeper was shackled, injured hand and all, then he was forced to stand before Grayson.

The words Grayson spoke next were so practiced, they were almost worn. "You'll be taken to the castle for your trial. After your trial, you'll be taken to one of the western labor camps. You'll work until your debts are paid." Grayson's eyes moved to the woman, her face streaked with tears. "While your husband works off past debts, you will be charged with the regular tax. If by the end of the month you cannot pay, the inn will be seized and you'll be sent to a labor camp as well."

"No!" Shackles rattled as Latham fell to his knees, soldiers still grasping his shoulders. "Spare my wife. Let me work for the past and present tax. Please!"

The woman protested, but Grayson didn't look at her. He lowered his voice so only the innkeeper would hear his next words. "If I accept your offer, you'll never earn your freedom."

Borg met Grayson's cold gray eyes, something not many men would dare. "No. But I would earn hers."

A muscle ticked along Grayson's jaw. The street was quiet, awaiting the Black Hand's judgement. It made his words seem louder than they actually were—more final. "So be it."

"No!" Marie Borg sobbed.

"Ride out," Grayson ordered, striding to his horse. He was nearly there when a commotion made him spin. The innkeeper's wife had gotten free and thrown herself at her husband. With his wrists shackled, Borg couldn't embrace her, but she clung to him and cried.

Grayson grit his teeth. Why did they always make this more difficult? He barked a command for her to be restrained and two soldiers jumped to obey.

As the woman was dragged past Grayson, she glared at him, her face flushed with grief and rage. "You're a demon! Fates-willing, I'll live to see the day your black heart is cut out of you. You and your entire family!"

Grayson raised his hand and the woman flinched, but he'd only grasped Reeve's wrist, stopping the captain from striking her. Grayson didn't spare Reeve a look as he shoved his hand away and leaned in to the woman, his voice carefully measured. "If you wish to make your husband's sacrifice a worthy one, I suggest you curb your tongue."

"You know nothing of sacrifice!" she spat, her chest rising and falling with each harsh breath.

"If you value your existence," he breathed coldly, "you will be silent."

Her lip curled, nostrils flared. "You'll never be free of your sins. Not even if you silence every one of your accusers."

There would be no reasoning with her. Grayson turned on his heel and swung onto his horse. With a harsh tug of the reins he put the woman behind him. The soldiers also mounted and the squad rode out, Borg stumbling as he was dragged behind a soldier's horse.

After they had left the inn behind, Reeve edged his mount to the prince's side. "You should have killed her for her insolence."

Grayson barely bit back a curse. It was all he could do to keep his voice level. "If I'd killed her, he would have fought. A dead man can't pay his debts."

"Some punishment was in order, Your Highness."

Grayson hardened his jaw. The other soldiers weren't brave enough to speak to him, much less reprimand him. Most people saw the Black Hand and flinched back. He was a legendary fighter with the scars to prove a life devoted wholly to violence. Perhaps being the king's spy had given Reeve a measure of self-importance.

Still, Grayson's continued silence prompted Reeve to let his horse drift away.

"You're a demon."

The memory of the woman's words made his lips twitch dryly, because they were true. King Henri and Queen Iris had five sons, all created expressly to serve the crown, each raised with unique—and usually violent—skills. Defiance was inconceivable. Resistance, pointless. Grayson was his father's puppet. He had to be.

"You know nothing of sacrifice."

He glanced over his shoulder at the innkeeper. The man's head was bowed, arms stretched taut as he was pulled behind the horse.

"No. But I would earn hers."

Latham Borg would die in the labor camp. He wouldn't survive the lumber yards with an injured hand. And even if he lived a week, month, or year, he'd never be free. And when he died, his debts would fall on the woman he loved. Borg hadn't saved her. He'd merely shielded her for the moment.

Eyeing the castle that towered over the city, Grayson knew how that felt. The fatality of it.

Freedom didn't exist. Not when you cared about someone more than you cared about yourself. Not when you would do anything to protect someone else.

Latham Borg knew it.

Grayson knew it.

His father, King Henri Kaelin, knew it, and he wielded the knowledge like a weapon. As long as he had in his power the one person Grayson cared about, he kept an invisible blade at Grayson's throat, ensuring his son's obedience.

And no matter how much Grayson hated what he had become, he could never risk rebellion.

CHAPTER 4

CLARE

CLARE WINCED AT EVERY BOUNCE OF THE carriage as it clattered down the streets of Iden, headed for the lower city she called home. Her head throbbed from the hit she'd taken from the princess's large bodyguard and the fitful sleep and tears of last night hadn't helped. Her neck was bruised and her throat still sore, but she was on her way to see her brothers, and that was all that mattered right now. She was still afraid of her future, but she'd made the only choice she could. She needed to focus on the benefits this would bring her brothers, not the pain it caused her. It was that or drive herself insane with panic and grief.

She wore a borrowed blue dress the commander's maid, Millie, had thrust at her, and she'd braided her brown hair into a crown, the routine task easing some of her tension. She was as prepared as she was going to be to face her brothers.

During the night, the commander had selected three staff from the castle nursery, which was used by the nobles who lived there. Clare had met the women before dawn and choosing Mistress Keller had been easy. The matronly woman had kindness in her eyes and a ready smile, assuring Clare her brothers would be well cared for—even loved.

Still, nerves danced in her belly as the carriage rolled to a stop, making her hands twitch in her lap. The carriage was surrounded by a handful of soldiers on horseback, though Clare hadn't bothered to study them when the commander had herded her to the carriage in dawn's weak light. Mistress Keller had spent the first part of their journey asking eager questions about Mark and Thomas, until at one point she had pursed her lips and studied Clare thoroughly before asking if she was all right.

Clare had jerked out a nod. As far as Mistress Keller knew, Clare had been hired as one of Princess Serene's maids. It was a grand position. And even though the woman could not have missed the moisture trapped in Clare's eyes, Mistress Keller hadn't pressed her.

Through the small window Clare could see people on the street gawking at the fine carriage and uniformed escort. A carriage from the castle never stopped in Lower Iden.

Horses snorted and soldiers dismounted, boots pounding the dirt road as they hit the ground.

Clare's hands twitched in her lap, nerves sparking through her.

Mistress Keller set a hand on Clare's knee. "Would you prefer to go in alone? I can wait in the carriage until the boys are ready to meet me."

Appreciation loosened the knot in Clare's throat. "Thank

you."

The carriage door swung open and one of the uniformed men held out a calloused hand. Clare took it without looking at the soldier and he assisted her to the cobbled street. Her eyes were drawn to the slightly crooked door of her narrow house, smashed between Motley's Tavern and a cobbler's shop. It was suddenly hard to breathe.

The soldier squeezed her hand and Clare glanced up—and stared. Familiar blue eyes met hers and when he offered a thin, almost reassuring smile, she jolted with recognition.

It was the princess's young bodyguard, the one with the sand-colored hair. The one who had tried—and failed—to stop the massive guard from hitting her.

Tension seized her, tightening her shoulders. It was only too easy to guess why he was here. The commander hadn't trusted her. He'd placed a royal guard on her already, to make sure she didn't run.

The bodyguard's face tightened when he caught her hardening expression and his lips parted, but the front door burst open before he could speak.

"Clare!" Mark's shout split the air and Clare dropped the soldier's hand, rushing forward to meet her brothers as they bolted from the house. She threw her arms around them when they crashed into her, their thin arms strangling her in return.

"What happened?" Thomas demanded, all the authority of a thirteen-year-old in his voice. "You didn't come home!"

"I'm sorry." She pulled back enough to brush her hands over their dirt-streaked cheeks, assuring herself they were all right. Their grins flashed and her fingers faltered. The ache of missing them already strained inside her chest.

Thomas and Mark eased back, looking beyond her for the first time to eye the carriage and soldiers.

"Fates," Thomas muttered.

Clare glanced at the blue-eyed soldier watching them and stiffened. "Let's go inside—I'll explain everything." Mark latched onto her hand and she held his smaller one tightly. He was ten years old, but he seemed younger in this moment. But perhaps that was just her own fear rising.

She guided her brothers toward the house and were nearly to the door when Thomas lowered his voice, shooting a nervous look at the soldiers behind them. "I went to Eliot last night. I'm sorry, Clare—I didn't know what else to do. He's hiding inside."

Clare's heart tripped. The soldiers couldn't know he was here. But that wasn't the only reason she didn't want him here. If anyone would question her lie of being hired as the princess's maid, her older brother would. But Thomas looked so pale and worried, Clare reached for his shoulder and squeezed. "It's all right."

Despite her nerves, the moment Clare stepped into the small house she was enfolded in comfort. Everything about the space was familiar. The table their father had crafted. The rug their mother had made from rags. The dusty mantle and scorched fireplace. Dried herbs hung from the ceiling, spicing the air and mingling with the scent of lye soap.

Thomas moved to the back bedroom where the boys slept and pushed the thin portal open, releasing Eliot to stride into the main room.

Eliot was tall and slender, but strength lined his form, hardening his shoulders and arms. Even though he wasn't in uniform, he stood with the bearing of a soldier. His face was clean-shaven, his brown skin smooth over his angular jaw. His dark hair was tousled, like he'd been running his hands through it for hours. Clare barely had time to blink before Eliot clasped her arms, holding her gaze with worried intensity. "What happened? I went to the castle last night, but no one could tell me where you were—I couldn't even find Towdy. I heard something about an attack, and—"

"An attack?" Mark's grip on her hand spasmed.

Clare tightened her hold on him, her words for all of her brothers. "I'm fine, as you can see. I was caught in the attack and detained for questioning. We all were." She swallowed, not able to hold anyone's stare as she continued. "I actually helped save the princess, and, to thank me, I've been promoted. I'm now one of her maids. I'm to live at the castle."

They all began talking at once, but Eliot's firm voice over-rode Thomas and Mark's shocked protests. "You can't take this position."

"I don't have a choice." It sounded horribly like the truth, so she softened it by adding, "*We* don't have a choice. I'll finally make enough to take care of the family. The boys won't have to work anymore—"

"Can we talk about this privately?" Eliot cut in, already moving for the bedroom.

Clare sighed, glancing at Thomas and Mark. "Stay here. I'll be right back."

Once in the closed bedroom, Eliot faced Clare, one hand grasping the back of his neck. "I'll give you more coin," he said lowly. "I'll work another job if I have to, but don't do this."

"I've already given my word."

"You can change your mind. You *need* to change your mind. You don't know what you're getting into. I'm a soldier—I know the danger the royals are always in." His eyes sharpened. "I forbid you from taking this position."

His hard tone sparked the anger and frustration that had been building inside her since everything had fallen apart last night. Anger swelled in her chest. "You *forbid*?"

"Yes," he gritted out. "I'm the head of this family and—"

"You left us!" The words burst free, all her frustration coming out at once. "The moment you were old enough, you took Mother's name so you could go play soldier without the stain of Father's treason. You left me here to raise the boys on my own."

Hurt splashed Eliot's face and regret instantly shot through her.

"I'm sorry," she whispered, eyeing the space between them. She didn't know when she would see him again—she couldn't leave like this. Stepping forward, she wrapped her arms around his waist and rested her cheek against his chest. She could feel every thump of his heart, going too fast. "I know you want me safe, but I've made my choice."

He was stiff against her, his back painfully straight. Beneath her hands she could feel the rough scars hidden by his shirt; two-year-old lash marks from a flogging that had nearly killed him. By the time Clare made it to his barracks, Eliot was wracked with fever, his back a bloody mass of ruined flesh. The captain who'd whipped him near to death and ensured Eliot would never advance from the city guard hadn't even had a good reason; he'd simply wanted to assert his dominance on someone he viewed as lesser. Clare hated him for it.

Gradually, Eliot relaxed and embraced her in return, tucking her head under his chin. "I don't like this," he muttered.

He'd like it even less if he knew the truth.

On the other side of the door, voices flared; Thomas and Mark were talking about the soldiers waiting on the street outside.

Clare sighed and pulled back from her older brother. "You should go. Sneak out the back door. Mistress Keller can meet you later, but it would be best if she doesn't see you avoiding the soldiers." She took a step toward the door, but Eliot gripped her hand.

"Wait." He fumbled with the belt around his waist before holding out a simple dagger, hilt wrapped in leather as it dangled in the sheath.

Her scalp prickled at the sight of the weapon. "Eliot—"

His eyes hardened. "You'll take it, or I'll march out there and tell those soldiers to give your regrets to the princess."

Clare rolled her eyes and Eliot watched as she secured it around her waist. She set her hands on her hips. "Happy?"

His eyebrows drew together. "No."

Warmth spread through her chest; her brother wanted her safe. It was a good feeling, even if there was nothing he could do to protect her. Clare planted a kiss on his smooth cheek before they returned to the main room. Eliot promised the boys he would check in soon and then, with a last look at Clare, he slipped out the back.

When Clare invited Mistress Keller into the house, the caretaker swept inside with a beaming smile and an eagerness to meet Thomas and Mark. The boys were a little wary, but their eyes widened when they saw the two trunks the soldiers carried in. The first trunk held food. The second was filled with clothing, books, and toys.

Thomas and Mark made quick work of unpacking that trunk while Clare and Mistress Keller put the food away. Clare showed the older woman around the house, and when they'd returned to the main room they found the boys had lined up small tin soldiers and were eagerly playing.

Clare had never seen them look so youthful. So happy. Despite the fear, she also felt a measure of peace. Even if she died tomorrow as the decoy, her brothers would still have this.

She smiled as she knelt beside them on the floor. She plucked a blue-uniformed soldier from the pile. "He's my favorite."

Mark frowned. "He's got a dent."

She rolled the figurine in her palm, easily finding the dent in his back. "It'll make him easier to find."

"I suppose." Mark glanced away, a toy soldier clenched in each hand. "I don't need toys," he whispered.

Clare's shoulders dropped and she wrapped an arm around him. "I *want* you to have them, Mark. And I don't want you to work at Motley's anymore. This is a chance for all of us to have a better life."

Thomas watched her closely. "You too?"

"Yes. Me too." The words burned in her throat and she hoped they wouldn't hear the lie. "I'll come visit as often as I can." She doubted the king would ever let her visit, and that made her gut churn.

Clare made a show of looking through the trunk, and when she pulled out a set of wooden blocks they all built a castle for the soldiers to defend. As they played, Mark pressed the dented tin soldier into Clare's hand. His voice was quiet. "You should keep him, since he's your favorite. He can keep you safe."

Pressure sparked behind her eyes and she blinked to clear the haze.

The morning bled into afternoon and Clare wanted to ignore the passage of time. But too soon a knock sounded on the door and it opened before she could speak. The princess's bodyguard ducked in, thrusting a hand through his sand-colored hair. Clare stiffened at the sight of him.

He viewed their game, apology edging his expression. "I'm sorry, but a storm's building. We need to start back."

Mark latched onto her wrist, instantly tensing. "You can't go!"

Clare laid a hand over his small one before looking back at the blue-eyed guard. "I need a moment."

He darted a look at Mark and his features softened. "Of course."

But a moment wasn't long enough to say goodbye. Clare's heart cracked when Mistress Keller had to pry Mark's clawed fingers from her arms. His frantic eyes and panicked cries cut her, and as she strode away, her arms ached to hold him.

Wind tore up the narrow street, dirt stinging her skin and eyes as she moved for the waiting carriage. The air itself felt different. It caught painfully in her lungs and she didn't think the coming storm was to blame. No, everything felt raw because her little brother was screaming her name and she couldn't go to him.

The dented toy soldier bit painfully into her hand, but she only squeezed it tighter.

CHAPTER 5

CLARE

TEARS DASHED DOWN CLARE'S CHEEKS AS the carriage rolled toward the castle. Her teeth grated and her knuckles whitened as she gripped the tin soldier Mark had given her. To watch her. Protect her.

No one could protect her.

The storm broke and rain hammered the city, pelting loudly off the canvas roof of the carriage. It was only late afternoon but the storm cast the city of Iden into premature darkness. Clare thought of the blue-eyed soldier, drenched on his horse. Let him be wet. He'd been sent to ensure she didn't run from the king. He was as bad as the commander. He deserved some misery.

A shout rent the air and the carriage lurched to a stop, nearly throwing Clare from her seat. Screams rose above the drumming rain and the agonized shriek of a horse pierced through the chaos. A chill raced over Clare's skin, lifting the hairs on her arms and neck. The crash of metal striking metal echoed through the street.

The carriage was under attack.

Her heart kicked in her chest and her breathing spiked. She let out a strangled cry when something heavy—a body?—crashed into the side of the carriage, rocking it. The same adrenaline she'd felt when the princess had been ambushed rushed through her, and Clare grasped the door handle with a trembling hand. She wouldn't wait in here to be slaughtered.

Clare crouched behind the opening door, using it as a shield as she dropped to the ground. She was grateful for the braided crown that kept her long hair out of her eyes; the sheeting rain did enough to blur her vision. A tall building rose directly in front of her, the thin opening of an alley only several paces away. The soldiers fought in front and behind the carriage, struggling against men with dark cloths tied around the lower halves of their faces. Even at a glance, Clare could see that the masked attackers horribly outnumbered the uniformed guards.

"Get back inside!"

Clare jolted at the shout, looking to the blue-eyed guard. He stood mere paces away, twisted toward her, expression hard as he gripped his sword. Rain soaked him, darkening his sandy hair and sluicing off his face and shoulders. "Get inside!" he repeated.

A masked man popped up behind him, raising his sword for a deathblow.

Clare's heart seized. "Look out!"

The bodyguard whirled, ducking as he spun. He avoided the attacker's blade and slashed up with his own, the two of them exchanging blows too quickly to track. Rain flew off the swinging blades, but Clare didn't stay to watch. She bolted for the nearby alley, abandoning the carriage and the brutal fighting. She launched herself onto the narrow street, rain stinging her face as she ran. Beggars huddled against the alley walls, a feeble shelter from the storm. They stared as she darted past and one even called after her.

Escape. She needed to escape the danger and—

Escape.

She nearly stumbled. She could actually escape. She could run home and grab her brothers. By the time the king learned of her disappearance, it would be too late. And, thanks to the king, they had enough food and coin to make the journey possible. They could leave Devendra and her oath. Forever. She didn't have to be the princess's double.

It was a split-second decision, but Clare embraced it. She reached the end of the alley and turned left. Away from the castle, back toward home.

The street was crowded with people hurrying to escape the storm and Clare plunged through them, ignoring the bruising elbows and curses flung after her.

A scream shattered the normalcy of the street and Clare twisted a look over her shoulder. Her stomach dropped.

A masked man with a drawn sword shoved through the crowd, heading for her. Air punched out of Clare's lungs and she pushed through the people now scrambling to escape the armed man. Her long dress beat against her legs and she hitched up the sodden skirt as she ran. The cobblestones were uneven and the rain made for slick footing—she stumbled, but caught herself. She threw herself down another alley, shoulder knocking painfully against a stack of wooden crates. Her hands slid over the wet wood, fingers curling to wrench them to the ground behind her.

She was nearly to the end of the alley when her stalker

swore, wood snapping and scraping as he kicked the crates aside.

Clare crossed another street, running hard for the next alley which was narrower than the last. She couldn't resist looking back, praying she'd lost him.

The masked man was getting closer and another man followed him. People on the street cried out when they spotted the two armed men and Clare's fear surged, locking her throat. Her heart beat so wildly she didn't know how it was still inside her chest.

She kept running, not looking back even when she heard a grunt and a body hit the ground. Had one of the attackers shoved someone in the crowd?

Clare flew into the alley, wishing the shadows could swallow her. She could almost feel the whisper of a blade against her back, straining to reach her. Footsteps pounded behind her, cutting through the shrinking space between them.

"Stop!"

Her body jerked but she ignored the furious shout and kept running. She was nearly to the end of the alley when fingers swiped her arm, a failed grasp. She cried out, adrenaline spiking.

The reaching hand snagged her skirt and Clare stumbled as she fell, rearing her head back to protect her face. Her palms scraped against the cobblestones and the breath was knocked from her lungs. Her attacker landed on top of her, his weight crushing her. For a split second, she wasn't aware of anything but the pain. Then terror exploded in her gut.

The man exhaled hotly against her ear before he levered back, knees digging into her sides as he braced himself above her. His fingers bit into her shoulder and he twisted her onto her back.

Clare blinked as rain fell into her eyes, blinding her. She

shoved her hands against his chest, as if that would stop him from killing her. His body was hard as rock beneath her stinging palms, a muscled wall she would never be able to move. His knees gripped her sides, pinning her in place beneath him. Her shuddering breaths made her chest rise and fall sharply, and her eyes flicked to her splayed hands, still pressed against him. Her attention snagged on the material peeking between her spread fingers.

Blue. It was a blue uniform.

Her eyes cut to his face.

The princess's blue-eyed bodyguard stared down at her, his stubbled jaw tight. His breathing was as ragged as her own and his hair swung wetly around his hard face. Tension rolled from him as he hunched over her, a soldier still locked in battle. "I told you to stop," he ground out, the storm in his voice rivaling the elements raging around them. "Why didn't you?"

Fear clogged her throat, snaring her words. His strong hands gripped her shoulders, keeping her trapped against the wet cobbled road. Her dress was already soaked, but the puddled water caused a shiver to rip through her. When lightning flashed and thunder clapped, every hair on her body lifted.

His grip tightened. "Why didn't you stop?" he repeated.

"I didn't know it was you!" she snapped.

His expression hardened, all rigid lines and harsh angles. Her stomach churned, her heart still thumping madly. Caged against the hard alley floor by the man who had ruined her best chance to truly escape, Clare felt a stab of anger.

Not fair, a distant part of her recognized. *He saved your life.*

The rain fell harder, muffling all other sounds and effectively cutting them off from the rest of the world. After the chaos of the fight and the panic of running, this moment felt locked in time. Drawn out. Slow.

Clare was aware of each place their bodies touched. His fingers digging into her shoulders. His knees bracketing her sides. His short breaths against her face.

A raindrop rolled to the tip of his long nose and splashed against her chin.

Clare flinched.

He released her and shifted into a crouch, every muscle in his body coiled. His gaze was wary as he studied her, and his tone came out more evenly as he asked, "Did I hurt you?"

"No." She sat up stiffly, glancing back down the alley. "What happened to the man chasing me?"

"He's not a problem anymore."

Clare blinked at the level response. His face was smooth, revealing nothing, but his meaning was clear. He had killed her pursuer. The same hands that had just touched her body had taken a life. She wasn't sure if that fact rattled her more than the realization that—if he *hadn't*—the assassin would have tackled her instead. She shivered, crossing her arms over her chest so she could finger her aching shoulders.

She cleared her suddenly dry throat. "What happened to the other soldiers?"

"They were losing." He extended a hand. "We need to get you to the castle."

Clare eyed his offered palm before slowly taking it. He squeezed her fingers as he tugged her to her feet. Clare cringed at the spark of pain across her hand, and his sharp eyes caught it.

He instantly flipped her hand over and examined the abrasions on her palm. Blood seeped from the largest cut and he thumbed the edge of it. "I'm sorry. I didn't mean to hurt you."

His soft touch sent a disconcerting shock through her, almost as much as his genuine tone. The glimpse of kindness was at odds with his cold efficiency as a soldier, and certainly didn't match the type of man who knew—and didn't care—that she had been forced to become the princess's decoy.

Clare tugged her hand free. "You didn't hurt me. I'm fine."

He dipped his head in a nod, his long fingers falling as he paced a few steps away and bent to retrieve his sword. He must have thrown it before tackling her. He examined the blade with a critical eye, and while he did, Clare swiped at the wet strands of hair clinging to her face and took inventory of her cuts and bruises. She nearly cursed when she found Eliot's dagger hanging at her waist. In her panic, she hadn't even thought to grab it.

With instincts like hers, it would be a miracle if she survived a week as the decoy.

A painful throb drew attention to her hip and Clare drew the tin soldier out of her pocket with a scowl.

"An interesting choice of weapon."

Clare raised her head. The soldier had sheathed the sword at his waist and now gripped the hilt. Drenched by rain, no one should look as confident and controlled as he did, though there was something reassuring in the strong set of his jaw. His eyes were on the toy in her hand and she curled her fingers around it. "It was a gift from my brother. He thought it might protect me."

The corner of his mouth lifted. "A kind gift, then."

Thrown by the honesty in his response, she made no reply.

He flexed his grip on his belted sword. "We need to get back to the castle. Stay close to me."

Clare pushed the toy into her pocket and kept pace beside him as they made their way down the alley. They paused at the alley's mouth, standing so closely their arms brushed. The soldier cautiously checked the rapidly emptying street as everyone hurried to escape the rain.

Clare cleared her throat. "Those men who attacked us. Who were they?"

He eased into the street, turning right. "I think they were rebels."

Her pulse quickened. That was awfully bold of them, to strike the princess last night and make another attack today. But they couldn't have been targeting her; she'd only just become the decoy. "Why would they attack the carriage?"

"It came from the royal stable. That would have been enough for them." His voice was low as they stepped briskly down the street, dodging clusters of people. The drumming rain kept their conversation between them. "Most likely one of their spies saw the carriage leave this morning. They had hours to plan the ambush."

"Are they loyal to Carrigan?" Even speaking the name of the man her father had followed to his death hollowed her insides.

"Doubtful," the guard said. "Rumors say he fled to some mountaintop in Zennor."

Clare hoped he was right. Ivar Carrigan had destroyed her family; she didn't want to think of him stirring up trouble in Devendra again.

The rain fell more heavily, pooling and running down the street. Tendrils of hair hung loose from her braided crown, sticking to the sides of her face and neck, and her dress was plastered to her body and splattered with mud. As much as she disliked the idea of returning to the castle, it would be nice to be dry.

"It's good you didn't get back in the carriage." The soldier's tone was matter-of-fact as he scanned the street around them. "One of them got past me." He shot her a slanted smile. "You could have obeyed when I asked you to stop running, though. My sword would've appreciated it."

Her mouth twitched despite herself. "Was it damaged?"

"Merely scuffed."

"Then it and my hands have something in common."

He huffed a soft laugh. "I *am* sorry for hurting you, but I didn't think you'd stop."

She wouldn't have.

It wasn't until the conversation halted that Clare realized how much she needed it. His voice was deep, strong, and surprisingly comforting. She cleared her throat. "I didn't get your name."

His eyes stayed trained ahead. "Venn Grannard."

"You must be well-trusted."

Venn glanced at her. "What makes you say that?"

He'd been tasked with watching her, which spoke of the regard the king and commander must have for him; learning about the princess's decoy before even the princess did must make Venn quite trusted. She didn't say that, though. "You must be the youngest royal bodyguard to ever serve in Devendra."

His lips quirked. "You wouldn't believe how many people underestimate me because of it."

It wasn't his age that threw her off-balance, but his unpredictable personality. She wasn't sure if he was going to joke with her, show compassion, or drag her back to the castle like a captive.

Venn touched her arm suddenly, slowing their steps.

She followed his gaze, catching three masked men who'd just emerged from a cross street a dozen yards ahead. Their swords were sheathed, but they peered purposefully around the scattered people still hurrying through the rain.

Clare shrank against Venn's side.

"There's a tavern to the left," he said quietly. "We'll hide there until they pass." He kept his fingers against her arm as he guided her across the street. She was grateful to have his tall body between her and the killers searching for them.

The tavern was larger than Motley's, where Thomas and Mark used to work, and the common room was crowded; people had taken an early day due to the rain, seeking the comforts of a tavern rather than home. The overall mood was jovial, in sharp contrast to the emotions roiling inside Clare.

Venn shouldered his way through the thick crowd and Clare kept close to his back as they shuffled forward. Laughter exploded and conversation blurred around them. Spiced drinks and roasted vegetables scented the air and wooden mugs pounded against tables.

Venn halted, taking Clare's arm and pulling her around so she stood facing him, his body between her and the door. He grinned down at her, rainwater dripping from the curling ends of his hair. "Act as though nothing is wrong. Smile."

Her lips curved obediently, though her mouth was dry.

"I think they saw us," he said, still smiling as if they discussed something amusing.

Clare's heart sped. She didn't realize her hands shook until Venn's warm fingers folded over hers.

"Easy," he murmured. "This will be over soon."

Assurance poured from him, and though Clare appreciated his calm, tension still rode her hard as she peeked around his shoulder, tracing back the way they'd come. She stiffened when she saw one of the rebels in the shifting crowd. The black mask had been tugged down to circle his neck like a kerchief and his narrowed eyes sliced through the thick crowd.

Clare's fingers clamped around Venn's. "I see one."

Venn didn't visibly react; even the pulse thrumming in his

neck remained steady. "Has he seen us?"

"No, he's still searching the crowd."

"Any sign of the others?"

"No." Clare's eyes flew to Venn's. "What do we do?"

His mouth flattened, the first sign of any distress. "Forgive me."

Clare frowned, but he shoved her away before she could open her mouth. She crashed into a man standing behind her and he let out a curse as half his drink sloshed over the rim.

"Oy!" He rounded on Clare as he shook out his drenched arm. "Watch it, fool!"

She stumbled back, bumping against the hard wall of Venn's chest.

The sound of his booming voice made her jump. "You yelling at my girl?" His fist swung and Clare ducked under his moving arm. The punch landed with a fleshy thud against the older man's jaw and the rest of his drink wet the floor as he fell back.

Three men around them tensed—obviously the man's drinking companions, because they now stood shoulder to shoulder in front of Venn.

Clare stiffened as the man on the right hauled back his fist, obviously not caring Venn was in uniform, but Venn easily dodged the blow. The man on the left took a swing next, but Venn grabbed a bystander's arm and flung him into the other man's fist.

A tavern-wide brawl sprang to life, as if all these men had been waiting for the cue to come to blows. Tables were thrown and food littered the floor as shouts filled the room. Clare crouched to avoid a chair being hurled, cringing as she was splashed with ale.

In the chaos, Clare didn't know which way to run. Then

Venn snagged her wrist and drew her close, keeping her smaller body firmly against his. "We'll hold out until the city guard gets here," he called against her ear, the clamor of the brawl nearly swallowing his words. "The rebels won't risk capture."

Someone knocked into them but Venn's strong arms locked around Clare, saving her from the worst of the impact. She gripped his arms and kept her head tucked against his chest, feeling every steady breath he took.

New shouts soon rang out. "The Guard! The city guard is here!"

The fight continued, but those who heard the warning disentangled themselves and bolted.

Venn continued to shield Clare as men rushed past. One skated so close Venn twisted away, pulling her with him.

Her darting eyes caught the assassin pushing against the tide of fleeing men, his dark eyes trained on her.

She gasped. "Venn!"

The corded muscles in his arms pulled taut at her shout. His fingertips brushed her stomach as he grabbed her waist—no, Eliot's dagger.

He pushed her aside and spun, shoving the small blade into the assassin's gut.

Clare tripped on a man lying prone on the floor. She fell, arms swinging, and pain exploded at the back of her head.

CHAPTER 6

GRAYSON

GRAYSON LEFT HIS HORSE WITH THE STABLE hands and tried to shove aside all thoughts of Latham Borg and the innkeeper's condemning wife. It never did any good to remember what filled his long days.

Patrolling soldiers slid back when they recognized him and servants halted mid-step, eyes clinging to the ground as they waited with bated breath for him to pass. With darkness falling, there weren't many members of Ryden's nobility milling about the yard, but they also kept their distance. Some dared peek at him as he passed—the youngest Kaelin Prince, the king's Black Hand.

Grayson tried to ignore all of them. The stares. The whispers.

The fear.

He trudged up the steep yard, the shadow of the hulking castle covering him. In true Rydenic fashion, the castle was sturdy, intimidating, and stark. Thick gray walls made it a fortress and unadorned towers ensured it looked more like a military keep than a palace. It certainly was not a home.

Once inside, Grayson kept to the least travelled passages as he wound his way up to the second floor, which primarily housed the royal family. His hands automatically drifted above his belted weapons as he walked the familiar corridor where all the apartments were located, his fingers ready to draw at the slightest provocation. He was always on alert, but especially when he came closer to his family.

The hall remained empty, though tension still stiffened his body as Grayson unlocked his door and slipped inside. He pressed it closed and bolted it, but even then he didn't relax. He searched every corner and shadow, lit every lamp, checked the latch on the window. Only then did the knots in his back loosen.

One hand rubbed the base of his neck as Grayson gazed out the tall window. The view of the northern mountains, covered in dark pines perpetually tipped with snow, was always impressive. It whispered of freedom, and even if he would never experience such a thing, the mere ghost of it never failed to catch his eye.

But there was a view he craved more than the mountains, and she was waiting.

Grayson peeled off his black and emerald uniform, leaving him in his black breeches. At the wash basin, he tugged off his leather gloves and plunged his hands into the shallow water, seeing the scars he normally hid.

Most of the marks on his body were from Tyrell, the brother just a year older than him; he enjoyed leaving scars, especially in exposed places so he could smirk over them later.

Grayson's hands fisted in the water, tendons rising and corded muscles standing up on his arms. As the youngest, he'd been the whelp of the family. He'd had no choice but to learn to fight. His survival depended on it, though his father had found other ways to motivate him. Now Grayson could beat them all, though Tyrell still provided the greatest challenge.

Grayson unclenched his fists and turned his hands over in the water, the reddish-purple burns on the fingers of his left hand standing out starkly against his pale skin.

Queen Iris was a practical woman. She knew her sons would always have enemies, so she'd taught them to be suspicious of everything. They'd learned the different reactions of every poison, both local and exotic, so they could know the signs and antidotes in case they were ever poisoned. Grayson's first experience with this was at six years old, when she poisoned his dinner. He'd been sick for three days and she'd threatened to poison him again if he didn't name what she'd put in his leek soup.

Garn Root.

He'd gotten better at dodging her tests. The last to slip through his defenses was two years ago, a fine powder left on his quill that caused excruciating burns.

Flame's Breath.

Grayson rubbed his thumb over the old burns, then shoved the memories away. Dwelling on old pain accomplished nothing. He scrubbed water over his neck and arms, rinsing off the city's grime. Shivering at the splash of cold water, he gritted his teeth and washed quickly, snatching up a towel and turning as he dried.

His room was dominated by a large four-post bed, the thick curtains drawn back. He only pulled them closed on the coldest winter nights, since he preferred to keep an unobscured view of the door. The king had once asked Carter to practice the art of an assassin, so he'd snuck in with a dagger and sliced open Grayson's arm while he slept. Carter had been fifteen at the time. Grayson had been ten.

He'd learned his lesson and always slept lightly.

There were no personal touches in the room. The armchairs before the cold fireplace were old relics and there were no tapestries or paintings to decorate the gray stone walls. Queen Iris believed art was a needless distraction and she'd rid the castle of it when she'd married King Henri. The few personal items Grayson cared about were locked in his desk. Near the bottom of the cupboard was a stack of drawings he rarely took out for fear of someone glimpsing them. Though some had been done by his childish hand, most belonged to a far more talented artist.

Tossing the towel aside, Grayson strode for the wardrobe, lifting out a black long-sleeved shirt. The muscles along his back tensed and rolled as he fitted the shirt on and the cloth stuck to a few places of still-slick skin. He tugged the shirt away from the clinging wetness, too impatient to grab the towel again. The moment he ensured his hidden daggers were secure he moved for the door, once again electing to use the narrow servants' passages. The few maids and pages he encountered bowed their heads and pressed against the wall as he passed. One young boy even held his breath, as if the very air around the Black Hand was deadly.

No one dared speak to him, so he made good time to the dungeon.

The prison's upper floor wasn't as miserably cold as the lower cells, but it was still cool year-round. The ends of Grayson's hair had gotten wet during his quick washing and the longer locks curled against his neck. He fought a shiver and followed the dim light offered by the lanterns bracketed to the wall.

There was only one door in the corridor that remained under constant guard. At Grayson's approach, the day guard —a man named Fletcher—came to attention, his gray hair highlighted in the dim light. Without prompting he dug a key from his pocket and unlocked the door, holding it open with a bowed head as Grayson slipped into the room.

There were no bars or chains in this cell. A bed sat along the back wall, a stand with a wash basin nearby. A square wooden table with two worn chairs stood on the right and an old glowing stove rested against the right wall. The stone walls were made up of varying shades of gray, the ones by the stove stained with black soot. A connecting back room housed a man and woman King Henri had assigned as caretakers. But even with all that, there was no doubt this was a prison.

Fletcher closed the door behind Grayson, the lock clicking quietly.

Mia sat on the bed against the wall, alone. Her caretaker, Mama, was probably in the back room sleeping off one of her headaches; the smell of ale hung in the air.

Mia was sixteen, a year younger than him. Her dress looked a little worn; Grayson needed to purchase something new for her, but the faded blue color did not dull her beauty. Rich brown hair fell in thick curls around her shoulders and her olive skin made her look more tanned than he was, even though she never left this room.

Mia bent over her drawing board, pencil moving in soft, careful strokes. Her brow was wrinkled in concentration, though her posture was otherwise relaxed. She was so intent on her drawing she hadn't heard the door, so Grayson hung back, watching her work.

He had discovered Mia eight years ago. He'd entered the dungeon to escape his brothers and when he realized where his feet had taken him, he prepared to go back. That's when he caught a soft voice drifting through the cold stone halls, carrying a haunting melody. He'd stilled, frozen by the unfamiliar sound of a lullaby. Entranced, he'd followed the ethereal sound, the words taking shape as he approached the cell, though he didn't understand the foreign words.

Fletcher had let him peek through the food gate at the base of the door, and the small girl had noticed him spying almost at once. Her eyes flew wide and her song cut off.

Heat slammed into Grayson's face and he would have scrambled back if her expressive brown eyes hadn't pinned him.

In his nine years, he'd never seen anything as beautiful as her round, dirt-streaked face. She was soft and her skin looked warm in the glow of lamplight. Grayson expected revulsion from the small girl, or at the very least alarm—even as a child, people skirted around him in the castle hallways, and his newest scar from Tyrell cut right across his left cheek.

But she didn't cry out. Instead, eight-year-old Mia knelt by the door and asked in broken words if he wanted to play, her tongue clearly uncomfortable with the Rydenic language. When Grayson jerked out a nod, she found a pebble and flicked it through the small gate.

They played for a long time, shooting the pebble back and forth between them. And when Grayson's scarred hand accidentally brushed hers, Mia didn't cringe away. She *smiled* at him, and his entire world changed in an instant. Everything had realigned so this girl was the center of his existence.

Fletcher had soon allowed him inside, and Grayson had been surprised to find a woman there. Mia introduced her as Mama, but confided when they were alone that she wasn't her real mother, just someone who looked after her. A man named Papa also lived there, but he spent his days as a guard working in the lower prison.

Excited at the prospect of having a friend, Grayson visited Mia every day. He brought her treats and toys when he could steal them, and she taught him games and rhymes. He loved it when she sang, even if he didn't always understand her words. He was endlessly fascinated by the beauty of her voice. He'd been mesmerized by *her*.

He still was.

Mia leaned back from her drawing and caught sight of him. She grinned, pushing the drawing desk aside. "Grayson!" She leapt from the bed and flung her arms around his neck.

His arms instinctively came around her and he ducked his head, his cheek pressed against her temple, her soft hair brushing his nose.

He used to shy away from her embraces. The constricting hold had made his stomach roll. All he could feel was the bruising grip of his brothers, pinning him down so they could hurt him. His lungs would freeze and alarm would flash through him, but physical contact seemed necessary for Mia. She didn't seem aware that her small hands could coil his larger body with tension. When she'd held his hand the first time, it had been quite against his will. But she hadn't been deterred by his rigidness.

"I'm glad you're here," she said against his shoulder.

"Me, too." He tugged her closer and filled his lungs with her light scent, a mix of lavender and jasmine. He could only label the smell because she'd claimed the soap he'd brought her was lavender and jasmine. For him, the names didn't matter—it was just Mia. It was what peace smelled like.

Mia pulled back but gripped his gloved hand, tugging him toward the bed. "I need your help. I can't get it right." She settled next to the small drawing desk that fit in her lap, and once he sat beside her, she gestured at the page with her free hand. "What's wrong with it? It's too steep, isn't it?"

Grayson tried not to notice how the glow from the stove highlighted her rounded cheeks and delicate nose. It was hard to ignore her beauty when she was the only thing he wanted to see, but he forced himself to eye the drawing. "The northern mountains are about that steep."

She frowned. "Then what's wrong with them? They don't look right."

"If you want to make them the northern mountains, you'll need to cover them with pines."

"Pines?"

If Mia's brown skin and lilting accent hadn't painted her as a foreigner, comments like those certainly did. Pines covered most of Ryden; how could she not know them? But then, he already knew she wasn't from Ryden. As children, they'd had to communicate almost solely through the common tongue, until she learned to speak his language. Perhaps if he'd traveled beyond Ryden, he might be able to place her accent. All he really knew was she didn't speak in the tight and clipped manner he did. A part of him wondered if her accent was unique to her.

In the beginning, he hadn't been curious about Mia's origins. But as he'd grown older, curiosity needled. He was twelve when he finally asked about her past.

Mia had stiffened. "I can't talk about that."

He frowned at the tightness in her voice. "Why not?"

She avoided his gaze. "When I first came here, I thought about home all the time. I used to ask for my mother. My *real* mother." She cringed. Of course she was holding his hand, so he felt her shudder.

He gripped her fingers, a pang firing in his chest because he knew what she was about to say would be bad.

It was worse than he imagined.

"When I cried for my mother, Papa would hit me with his belt."

Grayson's vision hazed red.

Mia's lower lip trembled, her voice growing softer with each word. "If I talked about my life before, he'd hurt me."

"Does he still hurt you?" Grayson asked darkly, his jaw locked.

"No." Her whisper wavered, and the vulnerability gutted him. "Not unless I upset him."

It took everything in him to keep his voice level. "If he ever hurts you, tell me." Papa might be a grown man, but Grayson was a Kaelin—he'd make the man bleed.

"It's all right," Mia said, though it wasn't. "But I can't talk about before. I don't even think about it." Her breathing turned thready. "Please don't ask."

Her anxiety was palpable, and he'd do anything to ease her fear. So he'd given his word and he'd kept his promise. He'd also started training Mia in self-defense and he'd had a conversation with Papa—and his own father—to ensure Papa never hurt Mia again.

But despite his promise not to pry, curiosity about her past still stabbed him sometimes.

A pencil poked his nose and he jerked.

Mia lowered the pencil with a soft chuckle, her breath caressing his cheek. Her nearness clenched his gut. "You didn't hear me, did you?"

He leaned back. "What?"

"I asked if you could sketch a pine tree for me." She held out the pencil and Grayson took it, unable to deny her anything.

Mia leaned in while he drew a small pine onto the mountain she'd been laboring over. When he finished, he realized she was watching him, not what he was drawing.

Grayson pulled back, swallowing hard as his cheeks warmed. "There." He cleared his throat and held out the pencil. "You try."

A smile played on Mia's lips as she accepted the pencil, pulling back to return to the drawing.

Grayson tried to watch her careful strokes as they coaxed more life onto the page, but he ended up watching her instead. His attention kept getting caught on her lower lip, which she bit in concentration. In quiet moments like these, all Grayson wanted to do was pull her close and set his mouth to hers. Every part of him thrilled at the thought, but he'd never do it. There were a thousand reasons to keep things exactly as they were.

So he remained where he was, seated beside her. In this moment, he wasn't the Black Hand. He wasn't even a Kaelin.

He was only Grayson.

CHAPTER 7

CLARE

"Has she stirred at all?" a deep voice asked.

"A little," a woman answered. Both voices were vaguely familiar, but locked as she was in semi-awareness, Clare couldn't place them.

"We need her ready," the man's voice clipped. "The king will be angry enough over what happened. He'll be furious if he can't present her tonight."

"She'll wake soon, I'm sure."

The man growled. "I want to speak with Bennick. Get him, Grannard."

Grannard. The name meant something.

Venn, she realized a heartbeat later. The angry man was talking to Venn.

The voices faded as she was pulled back into darkness, but

60

she surfaced a little when she heard Venn's unmistakable voice. She could almost feel the rumble of it vibrate through her, like it had when she'd been pressed against him in the tavern. "We were betrayed. Did you tell anyone else?"

"No." It was the same deep voice from earlier, but Clare knew it now—the commander. His presence, along with the musty smell of the room, convinced her she was back in the sad room she'd slept in last night. "The only other person who saw her last night was Millie and she was told nothing."

There was a period of silence. Clare tried to crack her eyes open but the flickering light made her wince.

The commander cleared his throat. "Your first explanation makes the most sense. The rebels simply took advantage of a passing opportunity. It wasn't an attack against the girl specifically. That's what I'll tell the king."

A pause, then Venn asked more quietly than before, "How is she?"

"She'll be fine. Millie says she was stirring a few minutes ago." A slight hesitation. "You protected her well."

"She reacted well." Venn's voice drifted. He was leaving the room.

Clare's fingers twitched under the quilt covering her, but she couldn't summon the energy to call out. The door closed and she knew from the stillness in the room that she was alone. She fell back into a restless sleep.

A hand shook her. "Miss Ellington. Clare."

Clare's head ached, but when she peeled back her eyelids this time, they remained open.

Lamps glowed, lighting the dusty room that had once belonged to a little boy. Millie, the commander's maid, was perched on the edge of the bed. "Hurry, we don't have much time."

Clare fingered the back of her throbbing head. She flinched when she found a raised knot. She didn't fully understand how she was back at the castle. Images of Venn carrying her unconscious body sprang to mind and she felt color bleed into her cheeks. He must think her the most incompetent woman alive, and she didn't know why she cared.

Millie's mouth tugged down. "Due to circumstances, I've been told about your new position. Others are here to help prepare you for dinner with the royal family."

Clare sat up slowly, a wave of dizziness assaulting her. Her braided crown was a tangled mess and her dress was still damp from the rain. Another maid stood in the doorway watching her with a frown. She had vivid red hair and was probably in her thirties.

Millie handled the introductions. "Clare Ellington, meet Bridget Firth. She's the princess's head maid."

"The resemblance is there," Bridget said, brows drawn severely together. "Still, it will take a considerable amount of work to make her look like Serene. I need several hours at least, not one." She sighed sharply. "Vera, Ivonne, come inside. We haven't a moment to waste."

Two maids dressed in white and gray dresses stepped in, carrying a medium-sized trunk between them. They were around Clare's age and both had light blonde hair. They looked so similar, Clare guessed they were sisters.

Bridget urged Clare to stand and then proceeded to size her with a length of measuring rope, issuing orders as she worked. "Vera, pull out the red gown. Ivonne, organize the hair supplies.

It would be best if we could keep a portion of her hair up, to add a bit of height—she's a little shorter than the princess. Luckily their torsos are nearly the same length, that will make fitting dresses easier. Millie, get to work on her hair."

The ache in Clare's head spiked as Millie untangled her braid. Her skin felt too tight having so many people around her.

Bridget seemed wholly unaware of Clare's unease as she stepped back, looping the measuring rope around the back of her neck. "I wish we had time for a bath, but we'll have to make do. And we'll need to darken your skin a bit. We'll have to rely on powders for now, but we'll find a decent stain." Her eyes darted to the left. "Vera, grab a clean shift. We need to get this filthy dress off her."

Clare's skin crawled at the thought of these women seeing her without her dress. "Please, can't I change behind the screen?" It stood in the corner, only steps away.

Bridget's eyebrows drew together. "You'll need assistance with the stays."

"At least let me change into a shift. Please?"

Bridget rolled her eyes and flicked an impatient hand.

Clare ducked around the screen, sighing in relief at being shielded from their critical eyes, even for a moment. She began to undress, freezing when her hands landed on the empty belt around her waist until she remembered Venn had grabbed Eliot's dagger in the tavern. She hadn't lost it.

The maid Vera passed her a clean shift and when Clare took it she couldn't help but caress the fabric. So soft, it felt unreal beneath her calloused fingers. Nothing like the threadbare shift she currently wore.

She gathered up the discarded blue dress, her fingers snagging on the pocket. Her breath caught. The tin soldier. She'd nearly forgotten him. She searched the pocket, her heart thumping when she found nothing.

"Are you done yet?" Bridget snapped.

Clare ignored her, dropping to her knees so hard they cracked against the stone. The pang in her chest hollowed her stomach.

Mark's gift was gone. She'd probably lost it in the tavern brawl, or when she'd been carried to the castle. Her fingers curved against the floor and her shoulders hunched. Everything inside her felt poised to shatter. It felt like losing Mark all over again.

Vera came around the screen and knelt beside her, the two of them shielded from the rest of the room. "Have you lost something?" she asked gently.

Clare's eyes burned. "Everything. I've lost everything."

Vera's lips pressed together, compassion firing in her light green eyes. "I'm sorry, but we need to get you dressed. We don't have long before dinner."

Heart thudding dully, Clare let Vera pull her to her feet and they rejoined the other maids.

Bridget's critiques were constant, but Clare's numbness protected her from any sting and, an hour later, Clare studied the stranger in the mirror. Her dark brown hair no longer fell to her waist but ended below her shoulder blades. The top half of her hair had been twisted up into an elaborate bun. She wore a red velvet dress with a gold chain belted low around her waist. Perfume had been rubbed onto the skin of her wrists so she smelled faintly of lilacs. Cosmetics that itched her skin covered her hands and face, darkening her brown skin a few degrees. Powders of red and gold brushed over her eyelids and a gold pendant with a red gem ringed the base of her neck, choking her.

Her own face was foreign to her. She'd been so embellished, she hardly recognized her reflection.

A knock hit the door and the commander stepped inside, tugging at the cuffs of his sleeves. "Is she ready yet? We're late." His head lifted and he froze.

Bridget grinned at his stare. "I work miracles, don't I?"

"You do." Shock and awe colored the commander's tone, and his study of Clare was intense. His surprise made her grit her teeth; after all, he'd been the one to choose her for this. Should he really be so shocked by the result?

The walk to dinner was a hurried blur. The commander led her through empty corridors and dimly-lit servants' passages until finally they stepped into the private royal dining room.

Clare's palms were slick with sweat as her eyes skirted the large space, noting several guards standing against the walls between hung torches. Dinner had already been set out— steaming meats, roasted potatoes, buttered green beans and fresh white bread. Large candelabras were evenly spaced along the length of the table, candles flickering. Twelve red cushioned chairs sat around the table, though only two were occupied.

The king sat at the head, facing Clare. His eyebrows rose, betraying his surprise at her altered appearance. The chair to the king's right held a young man Clare knew at once, though she'd never seen him before. Crown Prince Grandeur Demoi was seventeen years old and, like his older sister, he had dark hair, brown skin, and blue eyes. He wore a bright blue tunic and a wineglass dangled from his fingers. He rolled his eyes at her. "Finally. I was waylaid by Emissary Havim and still managed to be on time. What's your excuse?"

Clare froze where she stood, her dress feeling far too tight around her chest. She looked to the king, unsure of how to answer.

Newlan merely stared at her, a smile ghosting across his lips.

Grandeur took a sip of wine but frowned when she didn't move. "Fates, Serene, do you intend to stand there all night?"

The main doors pushed inward, and a young woman with beautiful deep brown skin swept inside, wearing a soft pink dress and a pinched frown on her angular face. "This evening has been horrendous," she growled. "Half my maids vanished and I . . ." Her words faltered when she spotted Clare.

In a room so large, there should have been plenty of air to breathe, yet Clare's lungs were empty. Her fingers twitched against her skirt as the princess's sharp blue eyes—nearly a mirror of Clare's own—dragged their way over every part of her. The princess's frown turned into a silent snarl.

The crown prince rose from his chair, gaze darting between Clare and Serene. "What . . . ?"

Clare's heart thudded, every beat exacerbating the pain in her aching head. The silence was terrible. Almost as excruciating as having every eye fastened on her.

A soldier stepped up beside the princess and Venn's familiar face sent an unexpected wave of comfort through Clare. Despite the tension of the moment, she offered a small smile.

Venn eyed her, his expression shuttered. A trickle of ice slid down Clare's spine. The kind soldier was gone, replaced in an instant by the cold soldier—the one who knew she'd been manipulated and didn't care.

Princess Serene rounded on her father. "What is the meaning of this?"

"Take a seat, Serene," the king said. "As you might imagine, we have much to discuss." He looked beyond his daughter, to Venn. Only, that's not the name he used. "Bennick, get the doors."

Clare watched as Venn responded to the command without hesitation, and confusion spiraled through her. It wasn't until the doors thudded closed that realization hit.

His name wasn't Venn.

He returned to the princess's side, his hands clasped behind his back, shoulders pulled back. He stood at perfect attention, and this time when his eyes brushed Clare's, she was the first to look away, her back stiff. Her pulse snapped high and fast.

Princess Serene shoved a finger at Clare. "Who is this imposter? Explain!"

King Newlan exhaled. "I will, once you sit down." He shot a look at Clare. "Sit."

The commander gripped Clare's elbow and pulled her forward. It was probably good he did, or else she might have remained grounded forever. The velvet skirt was heavy against her legs and the hem skimmed the floor as she moved toward the table. And though she kept her eyes trained forward, she could feel a pair of crystal-blue eyes watching her, and she tensed.

Why give her a false name? It was a small lie, compared to the many enveloping her, but that almost made it worse. Why lie about something so simple? It hurt more than it should have. After all, the commander had struck her and the king had threatened her with death unless she agreed to his terms. Those were worse crimes, but Venn—no, *Bennick*—was a part of all that, and he'd manipulated her further with his charming smiles and easy lies. She shouldn't have let her guard down and allowed herself to be fooled. He was not her friend. He was her captor, just as much as the commander was.

She never should have trusted him, not even when her life had depended on it.

Perhaps especially then.

The commander guided her to the foot of the table and Clare sat stiffly on the extreme edge of her chair. He took the place on her left while the king repeated his order for his children to sit. Grandeur sank obediently into his seat and Serene finally came to the table, though she glared alternately at her father and Clare as she moved. There was no sign of recognition; if Serene realized Clare was the same kitchen maid who had saved her life last night, she didn't show it.

The king glanced past his livid daughter. "Join us, Bennick. This concerns you."

From the corner of her eye, Clare saw Bennick sit beside the princess, near the middle of the table.

Newlan cleared his throat. "Let me introduce our guest." He waved toward her. "Clare Ellington."

Every eye found her. Clare resisted the urge to wilt under their scrutiny by straightening her spine.

Princess Serene's long nails tapped against the table, irritation pulling at her features. "Why does she look like me?"

Newlan eyed his daughter. "I've devised a way to offer you more protection."

She arched a sculpted brow. "You intend to replace me?"

The king's mouth thinned "Miss Ellington will be your decoy. She will be the target for any assassins that strike, thus ensuring your safety."

Grandeur glanced at Clare, concern sparking in his eyes. "That will put her in a great deal of danger."

"Miss Ellington knows the risks," Newlan said. "She's been well compensated and she'll have protection."

"This is absurd!" Serene burst out. "I don't need a decoy."

Newlan laced his fingers on the table, clearly striving for calm. "The threats against you are real."

"All royals are at risk," she shot back.

"You were singled out and attacked in the castle."

Her eyes narrowed. "I know. I was there."

Newlan's knuckles bloomed white and his nostrils flared. "I'm doing this for *you*."

"You're doing it for your *treaty*."

His arms tensed. "The threats against you will increase as we move forward with your marriage."

Clare's mouth dropped open. Princess Serene was to be *married*?

Serene glowered at her father. "A marriage I'm not in favor of."

"Serjah Desfan is a needful match for Devendra," Newlan said tightly. "You know what's at stake."

Clare stared. Serene was going to marry Serjah Desfan of *Mortise*? The presence of the Mortisian emissaries suddenly made more sense, but Clare was still reeling. Mortise was Devendra's enemy, despite their uneasy peace over the last few years. A marriage between their kingdoms seemed insane.

"Your engagement will be announced in three days," Newlan continued, unaware of Clare's struggle to process the conversation. "Emissary Havim assures me a similar announcement has already been made in the Mortisian court."

Serene's mouth curled derisively. "So you hired an imposter to ensure your perfect wedding isn't disrupted by something as trivial as my death."

"Miss Ellington's presence could save your life," Newlan snapped. His face smoothed with visible effort as he turned to Bennick. "What do you think?"

Clare could feel Bennick's gaze on her, but she refused to meet it. She tried to ignore the flash of heat stealing over her face as he answered Newlan. "I approve of your choice."

Something about his careful answer bothered her, though

she wasn't sure what. Maybe it was just the sound of his voice that irritated her.

Serene's nails continued to rap against the table. "I assume this girl is the reason my maids were absent tonight. And you probably intend to put her in my rooms to further your ruse."

"I do," Newlan said.

"So I'm to be horribly inconvenienced so you can once again assert your power over me?"

Clare cut a look at the princess. *She* felt inconvenienced?

The candlelight flashed against the temper flaring in Newlan's eyes. "I'm sorry if you find the preservation of your life inconvenient, Serene, but this isn't negotiable."

The princess's brow furrowed. "What does this mean for the trip to Mortise? Is she coming?"

"Of course," the king said.

Panic gripped Clare. A trip to Mortise hadn't been part of their bargain. But did that actually matter? She'd sworn an oath. Her life belonged to Newlan. If he wanted her in Mortise, she had no choice but to go.

Newlan leaned back in his chair. "As the Mortisians insisted, the betrothal agreement must be signed in their court at summer's end. The journey is long and your route will be highly publicized. It will be easy for our enemies to attack. Which is why I intend to leave the public travel to the decoy and have you take a different route."

Serene's eyes narrowed. "But I have appointments at nearly every stop!"

"I've seen your itinerary," Newlan said dryly. "Balls, dress fittings, teas with noble families—these don't demand your presence."

"And the required speeches?" she demanded. "The dedication of your new road? These require a *royal* presence, not some *imposter*!"

Newlan's mouth pressed into a line. "Those rare appointments *do* require your attention. And you'll be there long enough to fulfill your duties before turning your tour back over to the decoy so you can travel in anonymity." The king once again looked over them all. "We have three months to prepare Miss Ellington for this journey. I expect everyone to assist her so she can gain the required skills." His eyes sharpened. "No one can know about our use of a decoy. This secret is to be guarded by each of you. If I'm betrayed, I won't have to look far for the traitor."

Serene marched from the dining room the moment dinner ended. Bennick followed, casting a last look at Clare that she refused to return.

King Newlan rubbed his brow. "Commander, show Miss Ellington to the suite. If Serene resists, send her to me."

"Of course." The commander rose and Clare followed suit. She hadn't eaten much, but the evening's developments had driven away her hunger. She was eager to escape the room and hopefully find a bed. She was exhausted, both physically and emotionally.

The commander led her back through the same servants' passage they'd used before. The silence, apart from their shuffling footsteps, only agitated her further. Desperate for distraction, she said, "I didn't realize our differences were reconciled enough for Mortise to become an ally."

"Not all differences have been settled. But Mortise is a valuable trade partner and they have elite warships." He shot her a glance. "I'm explaining this only so you understand the gravity of your position. You probably grew up on stories of our war with Ryden. They've had time to recover and now pose more of a danger than you could possibly imagine. Mortise is currently the lesser of two evils and this alliance could mean our victory in a future war with Ryden. Or prevent it entirely."

Allies. Enemies. War. It was staggering that Clare was somehow part of such things. Her shoulders tensed against the sudden weight. "Why wasn't I told last night about the trip to Mortise?"

"It wasn't important for you to know."

"It's important to me." Leaving her family to live in the castle had been hard enough, but to leave for another kingdom . . . Her hands fisted at her sides. "I never agreed to leave Devendra."

"You agreed to do whatever the king orders, Miss Ellington." His tone was stern, brooking no argument.

They climbed two flights of stairs and eventually stepped into a wide corridor, abandoning the narrow hallway. As they neared a guarded suite, Clare heard the princess's unmistakable voice ringing against the stone walls. "I won't stand for it! I draw the line here, Bridget! You will hand over my pillows or I will scream until I pass out!"

Bridget's voice rose. "My lady, your father ordered the rooms to remain untouched. Only your most private things should be moved to your new chambers, to keep from raising suspicions. It's for your safety."

"That imposter will *not* sleep with my pillows!"

Bennick stood outside the open door, hands clasped behind his back. He turned at their approach, his stubbled jaw tensing briefly. He dipped his head. "Miss Ellington."

She looked pointedly past him and into the princess's open chamber. The main room was spacious and bustling with maids making final preparations to move the princess. Serene still argued loudly with Bridget.

Behind Clare, the commander grunted. "I don't think the king would appreciate the shout she's using to complain about his great secret."

"No," Bennick said. "I doubt he would."

Princess Serene noticed her audience. She immediately stopped her rant, snatched up a large pillow that had fallen—or more likely been thrown—and marched forward. She stopped in front of Clare, who did her best not to cringe back. "Don't you *dare* go through my things." Without awaiting a reply, Serene swept past and Bridget hurried after her, toting a large bag stuffed to the brim with clothing and anything else the princess had deemed necessary to remove from the room.

Bennick poked his head into the suite, his tone mild. "Cardon, remain with the room. I'll send Wilf to relieve you soon."

Clare was surprised when she recognized the guard he spoke to. He'd been there during the hallway ambush. The long scar on his cheek stretched as he cast her a short smile before nodding to Bennick. "Good luck with the princess, Captain."

Clare startled at the title. Bennick was too young to be the captain of the princess's guard. The scarred guard—Cardon—was probably ten years his senior. How was Bennick his superior?

Nothing about the blue-eyed guard made sense, she decided. Nothing.

Bennick twisted to go, but paused when he noticed Clare watching him. Fates, when had she started staring? He cleared his throat. "How's your head, Miss Ellington?"

She gave him a flat stare, shooting venom into her tone. "Well enough, *Captain.*"

A muscle in his cheek jumped.

"Bennick!" The princess's shout rang down the hall.

Bennick straightened, eyes still fixed on Clare. "I'm relieved to hear that, Miss Ellington. I hope you sleep well." He inclined his head before striding after the princess.

The commander took his leave as well and Clare stepped into the princess's suite. It was similar in design to the commander's apartment, but more elaborate and decidedly feminine. The main area was dominated by a fireplace, a low fire crackling inside the hearth and lanterns glowing along the walls. A settee and some arm chairs gathered around a low table, creating a cozy center for the room. Flower arrangements and small sculptures artfully dotted the space and fine rugs spread over the stone floor in shades of blue and cream. There were five doors that led to other chambers but only one was open, allowing a glimpse into the bedroom.

Clare realized Cardon was watching her. His eyes and hair were deep brown and his smile caused the pale pink scar on his cheek to wrinkle at the corner. "It's good to see you again, Miss Ellington. I wanted to thank you for saving the princess's life last night. It was very brave of you."

It had been the stupidest thing she'd ever done, but she didn't tell him that.

Cardon bid her goodnight, assuring her he'd be in the hall if she needed anything. She knew he was really there to make sure she didn't leave.

Once he was gone, Vera—the kind maid from before—stepped out from the bedroom. She offered Clare a short curtsy. "Miss Ellington."

"Please. Call me Clare."

The girl nodded and clasped her hands in front of her. "Since the princess can't spare another maid, I'm afraid you're left with only me."

It was Clare's first bit of fortune. Out of any of the maids, Vera was the nicest. "I'm relieved to hear it," she admitted.

Vera smiled, color brushing her cheeks. She helped Clare out of the heavy gown and gently removed the cosmetics from her skin before leading her into the princess's bedroom. It was large and decorated in silver, cream, and varying shades of purple. The space was scented with lilacs and undeniably beautiful, but when Clare climbed under the covers she struggled to find sleep.

Every nicety in the castle could never soothe the pang of homesickness in her chest.

CHAPTER 8

CLARE

CLARE UNFOLDED THE SHEET OF PAPER carrying the day's itinerary while Vera twisted her hair into a bun at the nape of her neck. Vera's hands were gentle, but it felt strange having someone else do her hair. Still, the seventeen-year-old maid had looked mildly offended when Clare suggested she do it on her own, so she tried to relax under the girl's ministrations.

They were in the princess's dressing room, one of the five rooms that broke off from the main sitting room. There was the princess's bedroom and a room for the maids, which would only house Vera for the foreseeable future. Another room was a private washroom with a large brass tub and rows upon rows of soaps, lotions, and perfumes. The final room remained closed and locked, and Vera revealed it was the princess's private study. The locked door wasn't exactly welcoming, so it matched the princess perfectly.

Clare lifted her itinerary and bit back a groan. "I have to have breakfast with the princess."

Vera peeked at her in the mirror. "Perhaps it won't be so bad. She can be quite pleasant, sometimes."

Clare grunted. She hadn't known what to expect from the princess, but she had assumed Serene would be at least mildly grateful—if not for Clare saving her life the other night, then at least for sacrificing her safety to be Serene's decoy. Instead, the princess had been hostile.

Clare cleared her throat and continued reading. "After breakfast I have a meeting with the royal librarian to evaluate my studies." The prospect was intimidating, but it would probably be a relief after spending time with Serene.

The next appointment made her stomach drop: *Defense training with Captain Bennick Markam.*

The fates hated her. That was the only explanation for her life.

She must have grimaced, because Vera's fingers gentled in her hair. "Oh no," Vera said suddenly, reading over Clare's shoulder. "Mistress Henley is going to teach you etiquette? She's awful."

If Vera thought the princess could be *quite pleasant* but Mistress Henley was *awful*, Clare hated to think how terrible her etiquette teacher would be.

The rest of the day didn't look much better. After lunch she'd have her first riding lesson, and if she wasn't thrown or trampled, she got to suffer a dress fitting with Bridget. The only part of the agenda that looked appealing was a quiet dinner here in the room.

Vera had just finished pinning Clare's hair when there was a knock on the main apartment door. They left the dressing room together, Vera hurrying ahead to open the suite door. She immediately dipped into a low curtsy. "Your Highness."

Prince Grandeur wore a green tunic and his smile was warm as he faced Clare. "Miss Ellington, I hope I'm not interrupting."

"No," she managed to speak past her surprise. "Not at all."

He waved back two bodyguards who attempted to follow him into the room. "I hoped to catch you before you left," he told her.

"Oh?" Her palms were suddenly sweating. How was she supposed to act around the crown prince? Vera stood near the door with her head bowed respectfully, so Clare lowered her head, but Grandeur immediately lifted a hand. "Please, there's no need for that. You're practically part of the family now." He came to a stop a couple paces away, hands clasped behind his back. "Your resemblance to my sister is truly remarkable. Although I must say you seem far too pleasant to be her."

Clare's mouth twitched, but it didn't seem right to actually agree with him.

The prince glanced around the room. "You're settling in all right?"

She nodded, then dared ask, "Is there something you needed, Your Highness?"

"I merely wanted to wish you luck on your first day of lessons. What's your first appointment?"

"Breakfast with Serene." The words tasted sour.

"Ah." He winced. "I truly wish you luck, then. And every blessing the fates can spare."

She once again found herself fighting a smile. "Thank you."

The prince's expression grew more serious. "Please let me know if she creates any trouble for you."

Clare doubted she'd ever feel comfortable searching out the crown prince of Devendra, especially to complain about his sister. Even so, she inclined her head. At least one royal showed her kindness.

When Grandeur bid her farewell and left, another man entered the suite. He wore the blue uniform of the castle guard and he was young, probably only a year or so older than Clare. His skin was dark brown, similar to Prince Grandeur's, making Clare confident one of his parents was Zennorian. His features were angular, his face smooth and attractive. His long black hair was tied at the nape of his neck and his brown eyes shone brightly. "Good morning, Miss Ellington." His heels clicked together as he came to attention. "Venn Grannard, royal body-guard, at your service."

The familiar name slapped her. No wonder the lying Captain Bennick Markam had been able to find his fake name so easily; it belonged to one of his men.

The real Venn's smile was sincere and charming, and it wasn't his fault his captain was a snake. Clare met Venn's smile with her own. "Sir Grannard, it's a pleasure."

"Please, call me Venn."

"Then I insist you call me Clare."

"Happily, Clare." He clasped his hands behind his back. "I've been assigned to escort you this morning."

"I didn't realize I'd need a guard when going out as a maid." Unless the king was that worried she'd run. Perhaps he didn't realize how effectively he had her trapped. Trying to run yesterday might have been her best chance of escape, but in the light of day she knew it had been foolish to think she could truly leave. Taking her family and running would have upended their lives, and if they'd been caught? The king wouldn't have shown mercy. Clare needed to protect her brothers, no matter what. They were the reason she'd labored in the castle kitchen for more than half her life and she wasn't about to stop sacrificing for them now. Even though being the princess's decoy terrified her, she knew she couldn't turn back on her oath. Not when her family was being provided for.

"I'm more of a guide than a guard," Venn clarified, oblivious to her deep thoughts. "The castle is a bit of a maze. Easy to get lost. And Bennick insisted someone be with you at all times."

"I see." Perhaps Bennick *had* realized she'd tried to escape yesterday and he wanted to make sure she wasn't given another opportunity.

Venn shifted his weight. "I'm on my second shift without rotation, so forgive me if I nod off. Especially during your meeting with the royal librarian. He's extraordinarily boring."

Her mouth twitched despite herself. "I'll forgive your sleeping if you don't tell anyone if I start snoring."

He smiled, but his eyes shone with gentle understanding. "It can be difficult sleeping in a new place. But I'm sure you'll become comfortable here."

"Of course." Unless death caught her first.

Venn turned toward the door. "If you're ready, we—" He straightened when he spotted Vera, who had remained tucked behind the open door. "Miss Smallwood! I didn't notice you before."

The girl blushed and fingered her gray skirt, not meeting his gaze. She hadn't been nearly as flustered in the presence of the prince. "Hello, Sir Grannard." Cheeks flaming, she shot a look at Clare, swallowing so hard it was almost a gulp. "You'd better hurry. Serene won't want to be kept waiting."

Though Clare was curious about Vera's reaction to the handsome soldier, she spared her new friend and said nothing as she and Venn left the room.

They made their way down the hall and into the narrow passage Clare and the commander had used last night. As they walked, Venn pointed out different passages and explained where each hall led.

"How long have you been the princess's bodyguard?" she asked when he paused for breath. He was clearly close to Bennick's age, yet he seemed more youthful.

"About two years. Promoted when I was seventeen." He tossed a grin over his shoulder. "Youngest royal bodyguard in the history of Devendra. Even Bennick, the prodigy, was a year older."

Clare made a quick calculation. Bennick was twenty, then. Definitely young to be the princess's lead bodyguard. "I had no idea young men were given such high positions," she said, ghosting her fingers along the stone wall. In the dim lighting, she liked having the grounding touch.

"Well," Venn said, "as much as I hate to admit it, I only got the promotion because of Bennick's recommendation. My own skills ensured my position, but no one would have looked twice at me without his word."

"You know Captain Markam well, then?"

Venn grinned fondly. "We had our first fistfight when we were eleven. Been friends ever since."

They entered a wide corridor and Clare spotted Cardon at the end of the hall, standing before a closed door. He looked up at their approach, greeting Clare and then focusing on Venn. "You're on a double shift too?"

Venn grunted beside her. "Could be up for a third if Bennick doesn't figure out some decent rotations."

"Well, we've got two princesses to protect now." Cardon said, smiling at Clare. The motion stretched the pale scar on his cheek, but it didn't detract from the kindness in his expression.

After the threats and manipulation that had begun her new life as the decoy, she hadn't expected nearly so much politeness.

It struck her then that these guards might not know anything about the coercion that had been used to get her here. Or perhaps they were simply in her same position—regardless of how the king treated her, they had a job to do. But they did not have to be enemies, even if they trapped her as much as they guarded her.

Cardon was still smiling. "How are you this morning, Miss Ellington?"

"Please, call me Clare. And I'm quite well, thank you."

"Glad to hear it." He glanced at the closed door beside him. "The princess is already inside, if you're ready."

Clare pulled in a breath and jerked out a nod.

Cardon leaned in, his voice low. "Don't let her intimidate you. She's lost a great deal and doesn't always make a good first impression."

Lost a great deal? The princess had lost her bed. Clare had lost everything but her life—and that would be lost, too, if the rebels had their way.

Clare stepped into the room, surprised to find not a dining room but a sitting room. Buttery sunlight slanted through a short but wide window, adding vibrancy to a colorfully patterned Zennorian rug covering the floor. Princess Serene sat on the edge of a velvet settee, picking at a crescent roll with slim fingers. A silver breakfast tray rested on the low table before her, laden with colorful fruit, delicate pastries, and a steaming pot of tea.

The door closed behind Clare, sealing the women alone.

Serene arched a brow. "Are you going to stand there gaping, or join me?"

Clare grit her teeth at the princess's abrasive tone, but she moved to the chair across from Serene, pausing to offer a belated bow.

The princess grimaced. "Sit down." As Clare did, Serene set her pastry aside and brushed her fingers over a linen napkin. "Let's get to the point. I don't like you. I don't like the inconvenience of you, or that you're pretending to be me."

Irritation flared, rolling Clare's hands into fists on her lap. "I'm sorry you feel intruded upon."

"You're stealing my life. How else am I supposed to feel?"

She bristled. "I'm not stealing your life." If anything, the princess had stolen hers. "I saved your life in that ambush, remember?"

Serene arched a dark brow. "Oh, yes. The disheveled kitchen maid. Forgive me, I didn't recognize you before—you looked too much like me last night. I suppose you want a reward?"

"No, I—"

"Or perhaps you think being the decoy *is* your reward? Maybe you think this position gives you power."

There would be no reasoning with her; not when Serene was determined to hate her. Still, Clare tried. "I'm only following the king's orders. The least you—"

"Yes, your orders. Let's talk about them." She leaned back, shoulders bumping against the settee's cushion. "You're my father's puppet, obviously. His spy as well, I assume?"

"Spy?"

The princess's eyes rolled. "Let's dispense with the coyness. My father doesn't trust me to go through with my betrothal to Serjah Desfan, so you're here to sniff out my intentions like a dutiful mutt."

Heat flashed over the back of Clare's neck. "I'm your decoy. That's all."

"You are a thorn. An annoyance at best and an enemy at worst."

"I don't want to be your enemy."

"Of course not. You wish to be my friend. Even as you steal my life. Oh, I don't hate you for it," she added, when Clare's mouth fell open to protest. "If anything, I pity you. I pity anyone foolish enough to be blinded by gold, fine gowns, and pretty promises spoken by a man as brutish as my father." She quirked a smile. "Do use the word *brutish* when you relay this conversation to him. I adore the thought of his scowl."

Clare's fingernails dug into her palms, anger tightening her voice. "I already told you, I'm no spy."

"If you insist. Now, my father ordered me to get acquainted with you and tell you anything I could think of to make your charade easier. I believe I've become as acquainted as I wish to be, so I'll proceed with his second request." She leaned forward, her mouth a thin line. "If you want to succeed, stay out of my way." Serene swept to her feet. "Another piece of advice? If you wish to fool anyone into thinking you're me, you'd better learn to argue better. You're quite horrible at it."

Clare surged to her feet, only the low table between them. Heat pounded in her cheeks, throbbing hotter with each beat of her heart. "You don't know me."

"I know enough. You're easily bought and all too eager to plunge headfirst into matters you have no understanding of. You're either ignorant of the danger or too blinded by greed to care. You've allied with vipers, and they've thrown you into a pit." She smoothed her hands over her already smooth skirt. "Enjoy breakfast. And don't worry, it's already been checked for poisons."

Serene strode from the room and slammed the door shut.

Clare's morning didn't improve at the library. Ramus, the royal librarian, was a wiry old man with a stern frown. His small office was littered with books and papers, maps and scrolls. He puffed on a pipe and asked Clare all manner of questions, gauging her knowledge on everything from kingdom geography to the royal genealogy. Then he started in on foreign languages and politics. Nearly three hours passed in that crowded room filled with dust, books, and pipe smoke, and Clare was utterly drained by the time she was dismissed. She would never learn all she needed to. The hopelessness made her head pound.

She and Venn each carried a stack of books which Ramus had instructed her to read. As they made their way to the princess's suite, Venn loosed a chuckle.

"You find something humorous about this?" Clare asked, still irritated by her abbreviated breakfast with the princess, not to mention the degrading experience of being told by Ramus—repeatedly—that she was appallingly ignorant.

"Just thinking about Ramus. Do you think he's cross-eyed because of the endless reading, or because he has to spend so much time with himself?"

She grunted, shifting the books in her aching arms. "I would think the latter."

"I don't envy you this reading." Venn peeked over his shoulder. "Are you managing all right?"

"Your stack is twice as high as mine."

"But yours is half as tall as you are."

She snorted. "You're not short on wit, are you?"

He grinned, white teeth flashing against his dark skin. "I'm not short on anything."

A laugh burst from her as they stepped into the main hallway, where she saw they were not alone. Her mouth snapped shut.

Captain Bennick Markam stood before the princess's room, his fist lifted to knock. He scanned them and quirked a smile. "Been to the library, I see."

"Took it with us, more like," Venn quipped.

Bennick intercepted them and scooped the books from Clare's arms, his eyes searching her face. "How are you?"

She rubbed a hand over her inner elbow, where a particularly sharp-edged book had dug into her skin. Anything to avoid looking at him. "Fine."

Her shortness didn't dissuade him. "Are you sure? Venn can be irritating."

"Hey," Venn protested.

Just hearing Bennick say the name *Venn* brought all her annoyance back to the surface. She lifted her head, stared right at him, and smiled thinly. "Oh, no," she said, gratified that the sudden sweetness in her tone caused wariness to enter his eyes. "Venn has been an absolute delight. Far better than the last Venn I met."

The barb had the desired effect. The corner of Bennick's mouth pulled down. "Is that so?"

Her eyes narrowed. "Undeniably."

Venn glanced between them, still clutching his stack of books. "I'm missing something, aren't I?"

"Nothing worth recounting," Clare assured him.

Bennick's stubbled jaw flexed. "I'm sorry for any misunderstandings." He darted a look at Venn and Clare realized her jabs hadn't been the reason for his sudden tension.

Venn didn't know Bennick had used his name. Interesting. It made her wonder what else Bennick was keeping from his friend, because he was clearly keeping secrets.

She crossed her arms over her chest as she lifted her chin. "I'm sure you are sorry. You should be."

Bennick's forehead lined.

"Fates." Venn whistled lowly. "Bennick, I think she's upset with you."

A muscle thrummed in his jaw. "Thanks, Venn."

Clare moved around Bennick and yanked open the door, feeling the two men follow her into the princess's suite.

Vera glanced up from her sewing. "How was breakfast?"

"Delightful."

"Good," she said, obviously missing the sarcastic bent of Clare's response. But then, her eyes were on Venn as he and Bennick deposited the books on a low table.

Bennick turned to Clare. "We were never properly introduced." He extended a hand. "I'm Captain Bennick Markam."

She eyed his hand, not bothering to take it.

Bennick's hand wavered, then dropped.

She felt a flash of guilt for her rudeness but shoved it away. He might have been one of the guards who spoke in her defense that first night, telling the commander she hadn't attacked the princess, but he hadn't defended her against the king's machinations. He had let the king use her—fates, he'd helped him by shadowing her on her visit home. And though he might have saved her life yesterday, he'd also brought her back to the king, and he'd lied about something as simple as his name—was he even capable of uttering truth? Did he enjoy manipulating her?

She pursed her lips as she viewed him. "I suppose you've come to fetch me for our lesson?"

His hand fisted at his side. "Yes. We'll be on the training field and I wanted to escort you."

She frowned. "Won't it be strange for a woman to be seen on the training field?"

"Not if she's the princess's maid. Anyone close to the royal family receives basic defense training and instruction on how to work with the royal bodyguards."

She shot a look at Vera, who confirmed this with a nod. Clare sighed, turning back to the young captain. "Venn could have escorted me."

"I know." Bennick didn't expound, but he turned to Venn. "Walk with us."

Venn eyed the tense space between Clare and Bennick. "Is that an order, or are you begging me?"

Bennick shot him a look. "Venn."

His hands flipped up. "All right, all right." He glanced back at Vera. "Will you say a few kind words at my burial if I'm caught in their clash of wills?"

Vera's cheeks pinkened. "Of course."

Venn grinned and led the way out. Bennick held back, waiting for Clare to go next. Her shoulders hardened as she strode after Venn. Bennick exhaled slowly as he closed the suite door and fell into step behind her.

Their footsteps clipped over the stone floor, the only sound between them. They'd gone down two short staircases in the servants' passage when Venn cleared his throat. "I'm going to assume from this horrible silence that your first impressions yesterday weren't pleasant." He shot a look over his shoulder. "I thought you found her in that tavern already unconscious. How could you offend her when she was unconscious?"

"Venn," Bennick warned.

Venn rolled his eyes.

Clare's eyes narrowed. So Venn didn't know Bennick had accompanied her home. She didn't know exactly what that meant, but she marked it.

They reached the end of the corridor and Venn pulled open a thick wooden door, greeting the two guards on the other side as he passed.

Clare blinked at the sharp sunlight as she stepped into the castle yard. She stuck close to Venn as he led her across the grounds. She could see the royal stable in the distance to her right, leaving intricate gardens to fill the space between. The castle yard bustled with activity; servants and nobles alike milled around and barking dogs darted between the crowds.

To the left was a wide expanse of dirt ringed by grass—clearly the training yard. Men were scattered across it, all of them locked in training. Some were sparring with wooden swords, others with real blades. Some threw daggers at wooden targets while others wrestled, knocking each other to the ground as spectators hooted and jeered. Most were not in uniform, and a great many had shed their shirts, revealing bulging muscles and skin slick with sweat.

As Venn led them onto the field, the men took notice of Clare. They scanned her small form and a few smiles stretched —some even called out to her. She sped her step, keeping close to Venn's back.

Bennick drew even with her, scanning the waving men with a frown. "They're harmless, but let me know if they ever bother you."

She bristled. "I can handle myself." She'd been taking care of herself and her brothers for years.

They reached the far corner of the field where trampled tufts of grass poked through the dirt. This corner was also empty, allowing them privacy to talk and train as they needed.

Coming to a stop, Venn twisted to face them. "Do you need me to stay and protect you?"

Bennick scowled. "I'm not going to hurt her."

Venn raised an eyebrow at his captain. "I was talking to *you*."

Clare fought a grin.

Bennick rolled his eyes. "I'll be fine, Venn."

"It's charming you think so." Venn tipped his head at her. "Clare, it was lovely spending the morning with you."

"Likewise, Venn."

With a lazy two-fingered salute, Venn sauntered away, leaving Clare and Bennick alone.

CHAPTER 9

CLARE

SILENCE FOLDED AROUND THEM AS CLARE and Bennick stood staring at each other. The energy of the training ground hummed through Clare, grounding her somehow, even though they were alone in their corner. The men on the field laughed and shouted as they trained, the snap of wooden training weapons and grunts of exertion puncturing the air, the sounds wild yet somehow predictable.

Clare knew all the anger she felt didn't belong solely to Bennick. The king, the princess, the commander, even Ramus, the librarian who thought she knew nothing—she was upset with them all, and her fury was a slow burn that scorched her entire body. The emotional upheaval in her life had caused tears yesterday, but today she clung to her anger like a shield.

When Bennick opened his mouth, she already knew she was

going to cut off whatever explanation he'd prepared. "Miss El-lington—"

"Can we begin the lesson?"

His tense shoulders strained against his uniform, his gaze intent. "Are you sure you don't want to talk about—?"

"Quite sure."

His brows slammed down. It looked like he was going to argue, but then he placed his hands on his narrow hips, his tone carefully measured. "In the event of an attack, your priority is to stay out of the danger as much as possible. You have guards for a reason—we do your fighting. You *never* engage in our fight."

Her jaw firmed. "So if I see someone coming for your back, I let them stab you?"

"Yes."

She could do that. She also recalled how Serene had acted in the hallway ambush, her knife drawn and looking for a place to enter the fight. Clearly, the princess needed this lesson.

Bennick shifted his weight and elaborated. "If you come into the fight, you're only going to distract me, or Venn, or whoever is trying to protect you. Then we all die. Fighting is always your last resort. And your last defense—if running or fighting aren't possible—is to pretend you're dead. Understood?"

The finality in his voice needled ice through her blood, but Clare nodded.

A shout on the field jerked her attention. A soldier had just hit the ground and he was cursing hotly, rubbing his abdomen while his sparring partner laughed and swung his practice blade through the air.

"Clare?"

Her gaze shot back to Bennick. "What?"

He pursed his lips. "The second thing to remember is *focus*. You need to concentrate on the moment you're living. Let everything else go. Third—never freeze. Freeze, and you're dead."

There was no warning.

Clare sucked in a breath when Bennick snatched her wrists and pulled her arms forward, his fists making unbreakable manacles. Her heart thudded and she tried to jerk back, but he anchored her in place, his fingers flexing to hold her. Her extended arms stiffened. "Let go of me."

"No." His head bent, his voice low. "It's time to learn a vital lesson."

His hold was absolute. The powerlessness she felt sliced cold fear through her. "Let go. Now!"

Bennick's eyebrows drew together. "Calm down. I'm not going to hurt you."

"Then let go!"

"No. You need to break free."

"What?"

The corner of his mouth lifted, and for that alone she wanted to hit him. "Break free," he repeated. "It's the only way you're getting loose, because I'm not going to let go."

Her pulse kicked as she stared up at him, her empty hands tingling. With how he held them, elbows bent and palms facing her, she could feel the blood draining from her fingertips. She knew he wasn't lying—he wasn't going to let go.

She yanked her arms.

He barely rocked forward and his hands didn't give. "Pretend I'm attacking you. Break free."

Clare's mouth firmed and she pulled until her wrists strained and a grunt escaped her. Bennick's hold only tensed.

She redoubled her efforts, ignoring the bruises his fingers were surely forming on her skin.

After a silent moment of struggle, Bennick spoke. "You'll

need to actually try."

Heat flared in her cheeks. "I don't think an attacker would be this aggravating."

"Probably not," he allowed. "They'd just kill you. Now come on. Show me what you're capable of."

She ground her teeth and pulled again.

After an unsuccessful moment, he said, "My grip is weakest at my thumbs."

She adjusted, grunting as she twisted against his hold; all she gained was a deeper throbbing around her wrists. She stopped and glared at him. "You're stronger than I am."

"Yes." He was infuriatingly calm.

Her glare sharpened. "Is that what you want to teach me? That I'll be weaker than my attackers? That I can't win?"

"You might be physically weaker, but that doesn't mean you can't win. There's a different lesson here." He dug in his heels, settling back as if getting comfortable. "I'm sure you'll figure it out."

Her face was flushed from anger and exertion. "Why don't you just tell me?"

"This is a lesson you need to teach yourself."

Her lip curled. "I think you're a lazy teacher."

His mouth twitched. "Quit stalling."

A growl rolled up her throat. He claimed the point wasn't to teach her she was powerless, but that was how she felt. It was how she'd felt too often in her life. The pain, humiliation, and hopelessness of all those moments slammed into her, ugly and horrible and raw.

Screaming as her father was hauled from the house by soldiers. Kneeling at her mother's fresh grave, only a child but now a mother herself. Clutching a three-year-old Mark and begging the fates to take away his fever, because she didn't know how to save him. Eliot marching from the house, leaving her behind. Every hour she slaved in the castle kitchen. Her wrongful arrest and the moment she'd been forced to give her oath. Mark, screaming for her as she climbed into the carriage.

Her insides were flayed open. Her breath rattled out of her and when she looked up and saw Bennick watching her, waiting for her to do the impossible, something in her snapped.

Clare dropped, throwing her body down.

Bennick grunted and shoved back his shoulders, centering their weight as he still held her captive. A vein in his forehead stood out and his knuckles were white. He eyed her with approval, but she didn't dwell on that.

She lunged forward, pushing between their arms and invading his space, but he merely stepped back to compensate for her advance. She jerked back, using his grip on her wrists as an anchor so she could shove her foot against his shin without losing balance. He swayed from the planted kick—even hissed out a breath—but when their eyes locked he grinned, his hold remaining fast.

Clare growled and repeated the move, more confidently than before. While she kicked, she wrenched her wrists against his thumbs and his hold slid. Triumph flashed, but his fingers clamped down.

They were both breathing hard and adrenaline shot through her. She didn't care if she hurt him. She *wanted* to hurt him. Clare's knee shot up, going right for the space between Bennick's legs. Her knee slammed into his thigh, because at the last second he'd twisted.

He let go of her.

Clare stumbled back, rubbing her red wrists, her knee throbbing.

Bennick choked on a short laugh and scrubbed a hand over

his thigh. "That would have been entirely effective, Miss El-lington."

Her chest rose and fell as she glared at him. "Too bad you dodged it."

He pushed back hair that had fallen across his forehead. "Did you figure out the lesson?"

"Every man has a well-placed weakness."

He chuckled. "Not the point I was trying to make, but a good thing to keep in mind."

"Then what *was* your point?"

Bennick's expression softened as he searched her face. "You're never helpless, Clare. There's always a way out. You just have to be willing to take it."

Never helpless. Those words sank inside her, pushing against the rage and fear—the powerlessness and shame—that had been overpowering her. Something else took up the space left behind. Strength. She didn't quite know how he'd managed it.

Bennick spoke into the short silence. "When it comes to pro-tecting yourself, there's nothing you cannot and should not do. You can't hesitate to hurt whoever is trying to hurt you. If you have a knife, you stick it inside them. You take advantage of any vulnerability. Bite their fingers, claw their eyes, break their nose, or—" He ducked his head and caught her gaze. Though his face was serious, a smile edged to life. "Put a knee between their legs. It doesn't matter what you do to them. You. Be. Merciless."

She was locked in his stare, still holding her aching wrists, pressure clamped around her thudding heart.

Bennick's forehead creased at her continued silence. His at-tention fell to her red wrists and he winced. "I'm sorry I hurt you. I—"

"Why did you lie about your name?" she asked quietly.

Bennick took a step back and raked a hand through his dark

blond hair, a muscle pulling in his jaw. "I didn't have a choice." A shadow crossed his face. "The commander came to me in the middle of the night. He told me about you—that you were going to be Serene's decoy. By doing so, he went against the king's orders."

"Why did he tell you, then?"

He exhaled hard. "Things in the castle have been . . . tense. The court is unsettled with having emissaries from Mortise here, even though no announcement has been made about Serene's betrothal. Threats have increased and the rebels are growing bolder. All that considered, the commander felt I needed to be told about you so I could begin guarding you immediately. After what happened yesterday, I'm glad I was there."

Clare was, too. And she thought she understand the reason behind Bennick's deception. "When we were attacked, you couldn't risk the king finding out you were there. What the commander did was treason. And you . . ."

He tipped his head. "Also a traitor, by that definition." His expression turned grim. "I shouldn't have used Venn's name. Or maybe I should have told you everything right there in the street."

"There were more pressing concerns at the time."

His mouth twitched. "True." He glanced down as his boot scuffed over the short grass. "I know you're upset with me for lying, and you have every right. But I'd appreciate it if you didn't tell the king. Or my men. It would be safer for them if they didn't know, so they can maintain full deniability."

Clare didn't feel any need to protect the commander, but Venn and Cardon? They'd only been kind to her. And Bennick, well . . . kindness had been his dominant trait, too.

With her anger dissipated, holding a grudge was like fisting sand. Impossible. She lifted her eyes to meet his. "I won't tell the king."

Relief eased out the lines that had bracketed his mouth. "Thank you, Clare."

She nodded once.

"I'm, ah, sorry for pushing you yesterday," he said, a little sheepishly.

It was such a small thing, she actually smiled. "Which time?"

Bennick flashed an apologetic smile. "I was rather pushy, wasn't I?"

"You were. But you did save my life."

He bowed deeply. "All in a day's work." She chuckled, and when he straightened, his hands shifted over his pockets. His eyes sparked. "I nearly forgot. I believe this belongs to you." He reached into his pocket and withdrew a small figurine.

She froze at the sight of the dented tin soldier.

"I found it in the tavern," Bennick said. "It must have come out of your pocket when you fell."

Her fingers shook a little as she took it. Her throat closed and the backs of her eyes burned.

"Clare?" He shifted closer, concern tightening his tone. "Is something wrong?"

"I thought I'd lost it." Her voice rang hoarse. She gripped the soldier so tightly the edges dug into her palm.

Bennick tensed at the tears streaking down her cheeks. "Please don't cry."

As if she could stop. Her breath hitched as she choked, almost a laugh.

"Fates," he muttered. "I'm useless with tears." He stepped closer, angling his body so he blocked her from the rest of the field. He glanced around them, looking anywhere but at her. He didn't say anything. His hands opened and closed at his sides, but she didn't feel impatience from him. He'd probably stand there all day, if that's how long she cried.

It took a few moments for her tears to stop. "I'm sorry." She sniffed sharply, hating the ugliness of the sound. That he'd had to witness any of this made her cheeks burn. She swiped at her wet face. "I . . . didn't expect to see it again. Thank you."

The skin around his eyes tightened. "If I give you something else, will those tears start again?"

She huffed a short laugh. "I hope not."

He grunted in agreement, then tugged a small knife from his belt. Clare's eyes widened—it was Eliot's. "Thank you for letting me borrow this. I'd already thrown my knives before we got to the tavern, so this little blade saved our lives."

Clare's fingers curled around the leather handle as she peeked up at him. "Thank you." She was thanking him for more than the dagger and he seemed to realize it.

He dipped his head. "If you're ready, I can teach you how to use it."

Clare slid the toy soldier into her pocket, then flexed her hold on the dagger. "I'm ready."

CHAPTER 10

GRAYSON

GRAYSON TUGGED AT HIS STIFF COLLAR as he waited for the throne room doors to open. His brother Tyrell stood beside him in the shadowed corridor, using the tip of his dagger to clean beneath his nails. At eighteen, Tyrell was only a year older than Grayson, but he wore that year with great superiority. Whenever he smiled, he always showed the sharp edge of his teeth.

Being around him tensed every muscle in Grayson's body. Even though he'd surpassed his brother in skill, Tyrell was still an exceptional fighter. As the youngest, they'd been forced to be better than their brothers. When Grayson became King Henri's enforcer, Tyrell had been put in charge of training the castle guards. He loved terrorizing new recruits.

"Liam's returned," Tyrell said suddenly, as if they'd been conversing. "I wonder if he brought news and Father wants to share it with us."

Grayson frowned. "When did Liam get back?"

"Last night. You should pay your spies more."

Grayson didn't have spies. Now that he could protect himself, he didn't really care what his brothers did.

Tyrell straightened, sheathing his knife. "My sources tell me Liam looked sun-browned. I assume he's been in Mortise." Grayson made no response and Tyrell switched to another topic; he was such a gossip. "Mother showed me some new additions to her garden yesterday." It sounded deceptively pleasant, much like the term *mother*. But Queen Iris's garden grew only poisons, since bottling death and pain were her life's passion. "Mother asked about you." Tyrell leaned his shoulder against the stone wall so he could face Grayson. "She wanted to know if I thought you enjoyed serving Father."

Grayson kept his mouth shut, focused on a chipped gray stone in the opposite wall.

Tyrell snorted and shook his head. "You're Father's favorite, yet you never act grateful. You don't *enjoy* it."

Grayson's stomach hardened when he thought of the people he'd intimidated, arrested, and executed; the homes and fields he'd burned, the coins he'd pried from a father's bleeding hands while his wife and children sobbed. He thought of Latham Borg, the innkeeper he'd arrested mere days ago, and his hysterical wife who had cursed Grayson.

He was the Black Hand. A fates-cursed monster. Why would he enjoy that?

Before Tyrell could open his mouth again, the doors to the throne room swung outward. Members of court filed out, bowing wordlessly to the two princes as they passed down the long corridor. As the men and women swept into the hall they were careful to keep space between themselves and the princes; the women even held their skirts close, not wanting their hems to graze Kaelin boots. Every eye was lowered in respect or fear—

probably fear.

When the last nobles had slipped past, Tyrell and Grayson were given entrance to the throne room.

The space was designed to make one feel small. The vaulted ceiling had taken generations to build, with stone pillars ringing the open space. Towering windows along the east side revealed the morning light. A black carpet cut across the floor, ending at the royal dais. An emerald banner hung behind the thrones, the Kaelin crest stitched in the center with black thread—two serpents twisted around a longsword, fangs bared over the hilt, mountains outlined behind them. The snakes were poised to strike each other.

It was a fitting symbol for the Kaelin family.

Other than the torches bracketed to the gray stone walls, there were no other adornments. Three thrones rested atop the dais at the head of the room. King Henri sat on the middle throne, fingering his brown beard as he watched his youngest sons approach. Grayson glanced away, despising the flash of pride and possession in his father's eyes.

Carter must have slipped in through the servants' entrance, because he was already kneeling before their father's throne. He was always eager to be first—second only to Peter, of course. It had been that way since his birth. He was twenty-two years old and wore his dark hair long, letting the ends brush his shoulders. He had Father's deceptively warm brown eyes but his chin was pointed sharply, like Mother's. He was missing most of his right forefinger—Peter had cut it off when they were children—and his other fingers were stained from making poisons alongside their mother. He always reeked of herbs, poisons, and the other substances he experimented with. Carter was thinner and weaker than the rest of them, and they all knew it. He posed a threat only because he was so loyal to Peter and their parents; he would do anything for them, even break the only rule the Kaelin family had—Carter wouldn't hesitate to slip a blade between any of their ribs. Or, more likely, poison them.

Liam knelt beside Carter, shoulders back and head tipped up as he stretched his neck. His stiffness was clear; he probably hadn't left this room since returning to Lenzen, having months to report on. Only twenty years old, but he led Ryden's spy network. The middle Kaelin brother had the lightest brown hair of them all and a short brown beard—more stubble than anything. Some foreign fashion, no doubt. His shoulders were broad and led to his tapered waist. He was handsome; probably the best looking of them all, since he'd somehow managed to keep most of his scars off his face. His brown eyes were intelligent, peeking out from a tanned face. A black leather wristband wrapped around his left forearm, the width of a hand. He'd acquired it a couple years ago during his travels, and though Grayson didn't see his brother often, he had yet to see Liam without it.

Peter, the oldest brother, sat on a wooden throne on the king's right. He was twenty-five years old and had brown eyes with gray rims. The crown prince was the shortest brother by a handbreadth, though he still managed to look down on everyone. His elbows were balanced on the arms of his throne, his eyes cutting through Grayson and Tyrell, a fragment of a cool smile twisting the corner of his mouth. His left fingers slowly spun the signet ring on his right hand. Made of heavy metal and intricately designed with the Kaelin family crest, there were four small emeralds placed as glittering snake eyes. Grayson knew the design well, and the weight of the ring—it had been plunged into his face and gut too many times to count.

Queen Iris sat on the last throne, on her husband's left. She wore a sweeping white gown with tight sleeves that sheathed her long arms. Grayson had never seen her in another color, though sometimes she tied a colored sash around her thin waist. Today the sash was black. She didn't tolerate excesses in anyone, including herself. Subtle lines dug into the skin at the corners of her eyes and mouth, but she didn't yet look aged. Her black braid was long and thick, trailing over one shoulder. She caught Grayson's eye and her lips curved a little. That wasn't new; he suspected she tried to cultivate the same level of intimacy with each of her sons, as if they alone shared a special bond. All she and Grayson shared were their eyes; they were the same shade of stormy gray.

Whenever the entire Kaelin family occupied the same room, Grayson had to wonder if they'd all walk out.

Tyrell and Grayson took their places beside Carter and Liam on the floor, Grayson on the end, their heads bowed. The poison master, the spy, the soldier, and the enforcer. King Henri's private army.

Their father's voice rang in the vast room. "Rise." They did, hands behind their backs, feet spread, chins lifted to attention. The king waved at Liam. "Tell them the news from Mortise."

Liam cleared his throat, angling his head so he could view his brothers. "As you probably know, Serjan Saernon Cassian has been ill for some time. Serjah Desfan has taken advantage of his father's illness, and as regent he's arranged a marriage alliance with Princess Serene."

Carter's gaze narrowed. "Devendra and Mortise, allies? That seems unlikely."

"Most of the Mortisian nobles are against it," Liam said. "But Desfan is insistent, as is King Newlan. The betrothal agreement will be signed before summer's end, in Mortise."

Tyrell snorted. "Newlan is a fool. Doesn't he realize Desfan will stab him in the back?"

"Of course he does," Carter said, beady eyes darting to their father; he was always eager to show off. "He'll increase trade between the kingdoms and use Devendra's armies as a shield when we invade. They must know the great war is coming and they fear us."

Peter shot his brother a look. "You forget what Prince Desfan stands to lose. The support of his court, if they truly are against the alliance, and the revenue of a higher tax. Devendra depends on Mortisian ports and the tax is heavy in favor of Mortise. If they become allies, those taxes will be lessened and Desfan will lose coin. So will the nobles and merchants in his kingdom."

"If we decide to attack Mortise by water, we'll take them all by surprise," Tyrell said from beside Grayson. "Then Devendra's army would do Mortise no good."

Liam shrugged. "In the end, both sides gain something with the marriage, despite the losses. I doubt there will be any double-crossing between the royals. The nobles and merchants, however, will probably prove different."

Carter looked to the king. "We need to either challenge the alliance, or condone it. Publically."

"Why get involved in the politics now?" Tyrell asked.

"Because we can play this to our advantage." Peter leaned forward on his throne, arms resting on his spread legs, hands pressed together. "We could send a representative to Mortise to congratulate the union. Perhaps dangle the thought of entering peace talks ourselves. Then we play them against each other. Princess Serene and Prince Desfan are strangers—we estrange them further. Goad the nobles into attacking each other, or better yet, attack their leaders. Let them tear each other apart. Weaken them at the heart so both kingdoms fall more easily to us when the time comes."

Liam frowned, considering his words. "It won't be easy. They'll suspect us and our sudden attempt to play the friend."

The king braced an elbow on the throne's arm. "I'll think on this. You may all go."

Grayson was the first to stand, but he froze when Henri lifted his chin. "Grayson, you stay."

The back of his neck prickled as his brothers walked from the room. His nerves tightened further when even Iris stepped down from the dais. She gave him a thin smile as she drifted past, which Grayson did not return.

Only when the doors closed, leaving only a handful of King Henri's guards as an audience, did Grayson meet his father's eyes.

The king of Ryden struck a powerful figure. Tall, muscular, and with a square jaw, he was handsome in a way Grayson never would be—there were no scars on his face. His thick brown hair, edged with silver, was combed back and his short beard was well-trimmed. His angular face still managed to look strong and his cunning brown eyes had long had the ability to pin Grayson exactly where he was. Though the king rarely lifted a personal hand against his children, he had manipulated them into abusing each other all their lives.

"I've had a troubling report." Henri straightened on his throne, his simple gold crown catching the morning light from the high windows. "While you were arresting an innkeeper, his wife insulted the Kaelin name. And you allowed that slur to go unpunished."

Irritation flared, but Grayson strived to keep it from his voice. "If I'd arrested the woman, the innkeeper would have fought and I would have had to kill him. No one would have been left to pay the tax."

"A street full of peasants saw a prince of Ryden ignore a blatant crime," Henri returned sharply. "Judgment should have been swift. Losing the tax earned by a run-down inn wouldn't damage my coffers. Unchecked defiance, however, damages the heart of our kingdom." He leaned back, gripping the throne's wooden arms. "I've corrected your error. The innkeeper's wife was hung this morning."

Grayson didn't blink, didn't allow any emotion to cross his face, even though his gut wrenched.

Henri released a sigh, closing his eyes briefly as he fingered his temple. "Your behavior is unbefitting a prince of Ryden. No insult can stand against the Kaelin name. The great war is coming and we cannot let ourselves be weakened from the inside. Do you understand?"

He bowed his head, jaw straining. "Yes, Father."

The king continued to eye him. "You will prove your dedication by journeying to the villages in the northern mountains, demanding all tax payments in full. They've been lax in their offerings. Captain Reeve will accompany you. You leave in two days."

Grayson didn't protest, though his lungs squeezed at the thought of being away from Mia. The mountains were steep and the passes narrow, still clogged with snow—it would take a fortnight at least, if not longer. All while being spied on by Reeve.

But he would do it. Because if he didn't, Mia would pay the price.

Grayson found Latham Borg as the old innkeeper was being led from the dungeon, on his way to the remote city of Kavan that housed the king's western labor camp.

Grayson had nearly turned back twice, but he forced himself

to keep walking. Now that Borg was in sight, Grayson's stomach clenched. It was too late to turn back. He waved at the guards surrounding their prisoner. "Wait at the end of the hall."

The two soldiers bowed and retreated, careful not to step too close to the Black Hand. In seconds, Grayson was alone with Borg.

The graying man's arms were chained before him and blood seeped through the bandage on his left hand. Something painfully like hope burned in his eyes.

Grayson firmed his jaw. "Your wife was executed this morning."

Borg stared. His blank expression gradually melted. Shock turned to disbelief, which then crumpled into understanding. His hands trembled, rattling the chains that bound him. He fell to his knees, curving in on himself.

Grayson remained where he stood, stiff and silent as he watched the grown man rock against the floor, gasping cries shaking his narrow shoulders.

I'm sorry, he wanted to say. *I didn't order it. It was my father. I tried to protect her. I'm sorry. I thought you needed to know. I would want to know . . .*

He said nothing. There were no words to take away this man's pain. Grayson had witnessed more executions than he cared to remember and he'd even been the executioner, but he'd never found peace with death.

Latham Borg's sobs finally choked off and he lifted his head. Tears still rolled down his hollow cheeks, but his eyes burned with fire. "I'll find my freedom. And when I do, I'll kill you."

Grayson gripped the man's elbow and dragged him to his feet. His voice came out low and rough with emotion he fiercely bit back. "Embrace your anger. It may keep you alive."

CHAPTER II

CLARE

CLARE'S THROAT TIGHTENED AS SHE AND Cardon crossed the castle yard, heading toward the royal stable. It was late afternoon and the yard was bustling. Chickens strutted and clucked, nobles strolled toward the gardens, and dogs barked and chased soldiers jogging around the training yard. Clare barely noticed any of it as anxiety sliced through her.

After a week at the castle, Clare's riding instructor wanted her to actually ride a horse. Master Lank's sharp eyes had picked up on her fear the moment she'd entered the stable a week ago, and he'd decided to get her comfortable with horses before forcing her to mount one. Her lessons had involved grooming and tending the animals, including feeding them. Clare could still feel the horse's lips pull at the food on her palm, bristled hairs tickling her skin. The memory made her shudder.

Cardon glanced at her, but thankfully he didn't talk about the coming ride. He went for distraction instead. "I caught the end of your lesson with Bennick today. You're doing very well."

Her pulse quickened as memories flooded her. Bennick grabbing her from behind, her back pressed against his chest, his head ducked beside hers, his warm breath fanning her ear. The low timbre of his voice as it vibrated against her spine, giving her instructions. His lessons were rigorous. Challenging. But when she succeeded in the task he put before her, the warmth of Bennick's smile expanded her chest. He had a calming presence overall, and his assurances that she could learn to defend herself built her confidence in ways he probably didn't even realize.

She wished she had that confidence now. The large stable came into view and Clare's steps lagged. The smell of horses and manure assaulted her nose, making it twitch. Cats stretched out in the sun, tails curling lazily, hooded eyes watching their approach with indifference.

The open floor of the stable was tidy with dozens of individual stalls stretching out along the back wall. The other wall was covered in saddles, bridles, and leads—everything one needed to ride, all organized and hung on hooks. The scents of leather, sweat, oats, and straw layered the air, though the stable hands who milled around didn't seem to notice it as they went about their chores. The horses were all well-fed, powerfully muscled, and terrifyingly massive.

Master Lank ran the stable with efficiency and attention to detail. He was probably the commander's age, but he had more gray in his hair and beard. He was an unassuming man with gentle eyes and, despite his unreasonable adoration of horses, Clare liked him.

He stood near the entrance, speaking to a palace guard who

looked to be a few years older than Clare. He was tall with broad shoulders, and even though Clare could only see him in profile, the resemblance between the two men was obvious. Master Lank spied Clare and his eyes brightened. "Clare, this is my son, Gavril. Gavril, Miss Clare Ellington. She's the princess's newest maid," he lied easily.

Like all her tutors, Master Lank knew her true purpose at the castle; it was the only way he could teach her to not only ride the princess's horse, but ride like Serene as well. And, like the other tutors, he was sworn to keep the secret—even from his son.

Gavril turned to face Clare and she tried not to stare. The left side of his face was terribly burned. The red, rippled scarring swept down his neck and disappeared under his uniform collar. He carried himself stiffly, as if the scars still caused him physical pain. He gave her a controlled nod. "Miss Ellington."

She offered a smile. "A pleasure to meet you."

Cardon's boots scraped the hay-strewn floor as he stepped forward and took Gavril's hand, a grin lifting his own scarred cheek. "I didn't know you'd returned to duty."

"It's my first week back." Gavril's throat bobbed and he turned to his father. "I must return to the castle."

"Will you join me for my morning ride tomorrow?" Master Lank asked.

Gavril bowed his head, strands of brown hair falling into his eyes. "As you wish." He bid them a good day before striding away.

Master Lank sighed heavily as he watched his son leave, a large hand scrubbing over his brow.

"He looks good," Cardon said quietly.

"He's a shadow of himself." Worry filtered through Master Lank's gaze as he turned to Cardon. "If you see him in the castle, you'll take a moment to speak with him?"

"Of course." Cardon's brow furrowed. "He isn't being mistreated, is he?"

"You know how soldiers can be," the stable master huffed. "Especially those in fresh uniforms who believe a good soldier is invincible."

Cardon's jaw hardened, his scar jumping. "I'll keep an eye out for him."

"I'd appreciate that." Master Lank shook himself and faced Clare with a small smile. "Well, Clare, I've got Jinn saddled for you."

The words stiffened her spine, but she walked forward with the stable master, leaving Cardon to hang back. The gray gelding stood beside the mounting block, one large black eye trained on them. Clare approached exactly as Master Lank had taught her, holding out her hand and allowing Jinn to come the final distance and settle his nose in her sweating palm. She flinched at the foreign touch but forced herself to rub her hand up between his eyes, watching as his ears flicked in silent greeting.

"May I join you?"

Clare's heart skipped at that familiar deep voice and she twisted to watch Bennick approach, leading a saddled horse from a nearby stall. The animal was noticeably taller than Jinn, with a deep brown coat and black hair. The sight of such a powerful horse unsettled her, but it was the flip in her stomach that distracted her now.

Bennick's throat bobbed as he neared, drawing her gaze to his angular jaw coated with its usual layer of stubble. The longer Clare stared, the harder it was to look away. It didn't matter that she'd spent the morning training with him. No matter how familiar she became with Bennick, something about him inevitably snared her.

He halted before her and Clare realized she hadn't answered. Her cheeks warmed and she cleared her throat. "Of course you can join me."

"What a relief." Mirth crinkled the skin around his eyes. "I worried you might be sick of me after this morning."

She quirked a smile. "Sick of getting stabbed, yes."

"You'll have to get better at disarming me."

"Bennick," Master Lank warned as he stepped forward. "You said you were here to help."

"Of course." Bennick turned to Clare and pressed a hand over his heart. "I promise to chase after you if Jinn gallops off."

It was ridiculous how much that meant to her. How much his presence alone meant. He knew she'd been nervous about her first ride—he'd even asked how she was feeling during their lesson today. He hadn't revealed any intention of coming to support her.

Master Lank gestured to Jinn. "Ready, Clare?"

Swallowing back her anxiety, Clare stepped onto the mounting block while Master Lank held Jinn's bridle. She wasn't allowed to straddle the horse, since apparently fine ladies were to risk their lives by riding sideways, so she lifted herself up onto her unnatural perch and Master Lank handed up the reins.

She gripped them fiercely and the stable master laid a hand over her fists. "Remember, he'll sense your tension. Relax."

Clare sucked in a breath, trying to ease her tight muscles. All that effort seemed wasted a moment later when Master Lank guided the horse forward. Clare strangled the reins as her world rocked. It felt like she was going to pitch off the horse—almost like he was stumbling beneath her. She hated horses.

Bennick had swung up onto his own horse and he kept close beside her as they entered the yard. Master Lank led them to the riding track circling the space outside the stable, and as he walked

Clare around the first circuit he offered praise and advice. He stepped aside for the second rotation and Clare tensed without his steadying presence. She was all the more grateful for Bennick riding gently beside her.

After plodding halfway around the track, Clare finally loosened her jaw enough to speak. "You must be bored with the slow pace."

"I'm not," Bennick assured her, even as his horse snorted and shook his head.

Clare would have laughed if her lungs weren't so tight. "I think your horse disagrees."

Bennick leaned over and patted the long brown neck. "He's fine. We both like a leisurely ride from time to time."

She glanced over at him. "Thank you. You didn't have to come. I know you're busy."

"It was no trouble." Bennick shifted in the saddle, stretching his back. "How are your other studies going?"

"Quite well." She was actually doing better in languages than Ramus had expected, and it was nice to know she had a talent somewhere. Of course, the irritable librarian always found ways to stump her when she gave too many satisfactory answers.

"How did Mistress Henley treat you today?" Bennick asked.

Mistress Henley was her etiquette teacher, and the woman was a tyrant. Clare snorted. "I didn't know there was a wrong way to hold a teacup, but she corrected me for an hour."

He laughed once, shaking his head. "At least now you can mend your ways."

"At least for once it's an easy habit to fix."

"What else does she have you changing?"

"Apparently my laugh is too harsh."

He squinted at her, incredulous. "What?"

"That's what she tells me." She vented a breath. "Nothing

seems to satisfy her."

Bennick shook his head. "From where I stand, you're adjusting perfectly."

A slight hitch in the horse's step had her strangling the reins and set her heart pounding.

Bennick nudged his horse closer. "Easy," he murmured. "Relax."

She tried. She really did. But her knuckles were still white.

"Tell me about your family," Bennick asked.

Clare cut him a look. "What? Why?"

He lowered his voice to a conspiratorial whisper. "I'm trying to distract you."

"Oh." She hesitated, her attention still focused on every shift and clop of the horse beneath her.

Bennick asked the names and ages of her brothers and Clare answered without much thought. But as his questions deepened her tongue loosened, and words began to flow. She hadn't realized how badly she needed to talk about her brothers until the stories poured out, requiring little prompting from Bennick now. She shared amusing arguments Mark and Thomas had gotten into, her fears of Thomas wanting to become a soldier, and memories of raising the two boys. Pride lifted her voice when she shared Mark's thirst for learning and Thomas's excellent memory, and Bennick listened to it all attentively, grinning, laughing, and commenting, sometimes asking her a question which launched her into a new story. The more Clare spoke, the less aware she became of the horse's jerking steps and the knot in her belly gradually loosened.

Her words stopped only when she realized how much time had passed—her shoulders and legs ached and in the distance, back near the stable, Master Lank was signaling for them to finish their final lap. Color touched her cheeks. "I'm sorry. I didn't mean to go on like that."

"Don't apologize. I enjoyed every moment."

Bennick's sincerity was obvious and gratitude warmed her chest. "Thank you."

He smiled. "It's clear you love your family very much."

"My family means everything to me."

The corner of his mouth rose, but he glanced away.

Sudden curiosity about his family burned. He hadn't mentioned siblings, or even his parents. She opened her mouth to ask, but Bennick spoke first. "For the record, I don't agree with Mistress Henley at all. Your laugh is perfect."

The compliment was unexpected and she flushed as she stumbled over her softly spoken thanks.

Master Lank beamed as they reached the stable and he stopped Jinn with a simple gesture. "Well done, Clare!"

Bennick swung down, passing the reins of his horse to a ready stable hand and Clare gripped the saddle horn, trying to build up enough courage to dismount. Before she could move, Bennick stepped forward and wrapped his hands around her waist. Her breath caught and she gripped his arms with sweat-slick palms, tensing as he carefully pulled her down. She didn't let go until her feet were flat on the ground, and Bennick's fingers were slow to lift away. Even after he'd taken a step back, Clare could still feel his hands pressing against her sides.

"Bennick!"

Clare spun with Bennick to watch Venn come toward them at a run. Tension lined his face.

Bennick stiffened. "What's wrong?"

Venn skidded to a stop in front of them. "Wilf."

"Fates." Bennick raked a hand through his hair. "Where?"

"Training yard."

Bennick cursed again and twisted to Clare, his brows slamming down. "Stay with Cardon."

Her pulse raced. "But—"

"Stay with him!" Bennick said, already darting off with Venn.

Clare watched them go, biting her lower lip. Wilf was the pox-scarred bodyguard who had knocked her unconscious after nearly crushing her throat that fateful night in the hallway. His name alone made her skin tighten. She'd been lucky enough not to see him since; he and another guard she hadn't met, Dirk, were usually assigned to Serene.

She glanced at Master Lank. "Do you think Wilf's all right?"

The stable master grunted. "He's not the one I'm worried about."

Clare knew what he meant. That bear of a man would not easily become a victim.

Cardon reached them, a deep frown carving his face as he stared in the direction of the training yard. "Not again," he muttered.

Unease crawled up Clare's spine. "Do you know what's happening?"

Cardon glanced between her and Master Lank. "Wilf can sometimes get . . . out of control."

Master Lank huffed. "Out of control? Last time it took all four of you to stop him."

"Yes," Cardon said, still frowning. "And Dirk is with the princess."

Which meant Venn and Bennick were facing this—whatever it was—alone.

Clare took a breath. Bennick had helped her today; if he needed Cardon's help dealing with Wilf, she would make sure he got it.

She began walking.

"Clare?" Cardon asked tightly.

She tossed a look over her shoulder. "I'm going to the training yard. Since you're supposed to stay with me, you'll have to follow."

CHAPTER 12

CLARE

EVEN THOUGH THE TRAINING YARD WAS filled with soldiers, Wilf stood out. He was every bit as large as Clare remembered. As wide as two men and two heads taller than anyone around him, he was beyond intimidating. His thick limbs bulged with corded muscle and his dark hair and beard were shot with gray. His hair was a tangled mess, his blue uniform rumpled. He wielded a thick wooden staff and was currently using it to beat a man senseless.

Clare approached the field's edge as Bennick and Venn reached Wilf. She sucked in a sharp breath when Wilf rounded on Bennick, swinging his staff with a monstrous roar.

Bennick dove aside and Clare flinched at the near miss. She pushed through the loose ring of spectators, reaching the front of the crowd as Venn lunged at Wilf's legs. He tripped the giant, crashing them both against the dirt.

Bennick kicked the staff away and sat on the thrashing Wilf. Clare's eyes widened when Bennick punched Wilf in the jaw. The man roared anew and tried to slam his head into Bennick's face. Bennick reared back, barely avoiding the blow.

Clare's pulse raced. She was shocked by the ferocity of the fight. They were truly attacking each other. Wilf could have broken Bennick's ribs with that staff.

Cardon shouldered past Clare and jumped into the fray. The spectators remained back, but they weren't hooting and yelling as observers of a fight usually did. The absence of sound chilled her.

While Bennick, Cardon, and Venn wrestled against Wilf, a couple soldiers darted to the man Wilf had been beating and dragged him to safety. Clare edged forward, wincing as she got a closer look at the man pulled from the field. Blood and drool dribbled down his chin and he held his crooked arm carefully, panting jaggedly. From what Clare had witnessed, he was lucky to be alive, let alone conscious.

Her attention cut back to the field, heart in her throat. The three guards had managed to keep Wilf on the ground. Bennick talked in hurried, low tones, his nose only a breath from Wilf's snarling face. But the huge man was no longer bucking against them—that was something. Her view became blocked when the crowd shifted forward, perhaps hoping to get close enough to hear Bennick's words.

Clare was frozen, but her hands shook at her sides. Bennick trusted that raging monster to be one of Serene's *bodyguards*?

"He's insane," a soldier muttered. "Totally mad."

"Why does Markam tolerate him?" another asked.

"It's the commander!"

Clare was elbowed in the side by a soldier who snapped to

attention, and everyone around her stilled.

The commander stepped into view, his bearded face hard. His eyes flicked to her, narrowed, then cut to Wilf, who was still pinned on the field. A muscle ticked along the commander's jaw. He stepped up to the beaten soldier, still lying on the ground.

The man cringed as he tried to get up.

"Stay down," the commander ordered. He eyed the crowd. "Has someone fetched a physician?"

"Yes, sir," a soldier said. "He should be here soon."

The commander focused back on the bleeding man. "How did the fight begin?"

Blood smeared the man's lips and chin. When he spat out a gob of blood, a tooth came, too. "He wanted to spar."

"And you agreed?"

"Yes."

The commander's eyebrow lifted. "Did you think that wise?"

The man's mouth twisted, his face swollen and bruised. "He was insistent and . . . With respect, sir, I wanted to test myself."

"Your behavior was beyond idiotic—it was suicidal. You know his reputation." The commander scanned the gathered crowd. "*No one* is allowed to spar with Wilford Lines. Is that understood?"

Mumbled replies sounded around Clare.

The commander looked back at the soldier. "Was Lines inebriated?"

"Yes, sir."

The commander's mouth thinned.

Clare bit her lip, sending a furtive glance back to the field. Bennick no longer leaned over Wilf, but he still sat on his chest, talking rapidly. Venn rubbed one eye, his other hand braced on Wilf's knee, and Cardon was crouched on his other side.

The physician arrived to tend the soldier and the commander

scanned the faces around him. "I hope you've all learned from this man's stupidity. As for Sir Lines . . . I'll discuss disciplinary actions with Captain Markam."

A soldier near Clare grunted. "Disciplinary actions? Anyone else would be dismissed."

The commander looked over his shoulder. "Do I hear disagreement?"

"No, sir," they all chorused.

"Good." The commander brushed past Clare without a glance, making his way toward Wilf.

Once he was out of earshot, a soldier snorted. "Nothing will happen. Captain Markam won't punish Lines, and the commander won't go against his son. He never does."

Clare stared, the man's words not making any sense. Her eyes cut to Bennick and she studied his profile, denial spiraling through her even as she searched for proof.

As if he could feel her gaze, Bennick glanced at her. And when his blue eyes met hers, she knew the soldier's words were true. Impossible, but true.

Bennick was the commander's son.

Clare and Venn sat in a deserted corner of the royal library. Light filtered through the dusty window that stretched up the wall beside them and bookshelves towered around them, the old wood bearing thousands of leather books. The dark wood table they sat at was solid, worn smooth with years of use. Maps of Devendra and Mortise were spread out, but Clare couldn't focus on them.

"Venn?"

"Hmm?"

The wooden chair creaked when she shifted. "The commander. Is he . . . ?"

Venn glanced up from the book he held—*Zennorian Weaponry and Battle Strategy*. "Is he what?"

"Is the commander Bennick's father?" The question had burned in her chest since yesterday afternoon. She hadn't dared voice it until now. It felt like prying. Which, admittedly, it was.

Venn laid his open book on the table, his gaze suddenly narrowed. "Why do you ask?"

She fingered the edge of the table. "I heard some soldiers on the field yesterday, while you were busy with Wilf."

"I do recall the moment," he said dryly, fingering the purple bruise surrounding his left eye.

She pursed her lips. "Is he Bennick's father?"

Venn sighed. "Yes."

Though expected, the confirmation still hit her hard. She'd seen Bennick and the commander together—watched them exchange words—and nothing in those interactions hinted at a familial relationship. She'd known the commander had a son. That sad room, long abandoned with the fabric panther and the chipped wooden blocks had clearly belonged to someone. But Bennick? It seemed impossible. She couldn't reconcile that the man who had forced her to become the decoy was also Bennick's father.

"Why is it a secret?" she asked.

"It's not."

Her forehead creased. "Then why are you looking at me like that?"

"Like what?"

"Like I'm asking something wrong, or . . ."

Venn lifted a brow. "Private?"

She flushed, but didn't look away. "Yes. Something personal."

Venn nudged the book closed and folded his arms atop it, his elbows resting on the table. "Because for Bennick, it *is* personal." He expelled a breath. "You'll hear rumors, I'm sure. I only ask—as his friend and yours—that you don't pursue them." He hesitated, but then reopened his book, clearly ending the conversation.

Clare turned back to the maps and rested her palm over the pulse in her neck, trying not to focus on the curiosity still beating through her. She tried to concentrate on the task at hand—memorizing the geography of two kingdoms—when Venn suddenly came to his feet.

Clare lifted her head and blinked as she saw Prince Grandeur round a corner, headed straight for them. She lurched to her feet and dipped into a bow along with Venn.

"Good day, Miss Ellington." Prince Grandeur came to a stop beside the table, a bodyguard on either side of him. In his hands was a small leather-bound book so worn Clare couldn't make out the title. He quickly waved Venn and Clare up from their bow, his focus on her. "I must say, I'm grateful our paths crossed. I've been meaning to seek you out."

Surprise flitted through her. "You have?"

He nodded. "I wanted to make sure you're settling in all right."

"That's very kind, Your Highness."

"Please, call me Grandeur. And it's the least I can do, considering the great service you're doing for my family. Fates know we're not the easiest to get along with."

"The king and princess can be a little overwhelming," she admitted.

"That's a delicate way of putting it." He glanced at his men and gestured for them to step back. They did without hesitation. Venn, on the other hand, remained beside the table until the prince eyed him. "I only wish a brief word with Miss Ellington," Grandeur said. Venn glanced at Clare but deferred to the prince and retreated down the row of shelves. He kept in sight, but wasn't close enough to hear the prince's soft snort. "Bodyguards." Grandeur shook his head. "They never give us a moment's peace."

"It *is* their job to remain close," Clare said.

"True. But sometimes I wish for a moment of privacy." Grandeur lowered himself into the chair Venn had vacated and Clare resumed her seat, watching the prince as he looked over the maps. "Enjoying your studies?"

"Sometimes."

"A diplomatic answer." He grimaced. "I could never stand Ramus, or his cluttered, smoke-filled office."

Her mouth quirked. "I'm grateful for the days he lets me study here."

"The library has always been a sanctuary of mine, too." Grandeur set his book on the table and drummed his brown fingers on the leather cover. "How are things going with Serene?"

Clare lifted a shoulder. "I don't see much of her."

"How did that breakfast go?" he asked. She winced and Grandeur's fingers stilled, his expression both uneasy and sympathetic. "I don't know if I dare ask."

Clare shook her head and looked down at Devendra's capitol city—Iden—marked in gold ink on the map. "She was quite vocal about her feelings toward me, and I don't think they're going to change."

Grandeur exhaled slowly. "My sister isn't always rational. When our mother died, Serene became extremely demanding. She spat out orders, and my father acquiesced to every desire. One of her wishes was to go to Zennor and mourn our mother's death with King Buhari—our uncle—and his family." Grandeur's mouth pursed. "She didn't give any thought to the support our father might need, or the help she could be to our people. She just left. For a year."

Clare's voice was a whisper. "She left you." She knew what that felt like. When Eliot had left, it had hurt something deep inside her.

Grandeur's brow furrowed, still looking at the map. "I remained with Father and his rages, and she did fates knows what in Zennor."

"I'm sorry."

He blinked up at her. "Thank you. But I tell this story only so you can understand. Serene doesn't consider the feelings of others. Her rudeness . . . You can't take it personally. It's been her way since our mother's death and I believe she only strengthened the habit in Zennor. She became the darling of my uncle —of Zennor, really. He allowed her to join him in court meetings and she became known for her skills in politics and diplomacy."

Clare snorted.

Grandeur flashed a half-grin. "She *can* be diplomatic, when she wants." He shook his head and straightened in his chair. "Studying for an exam?"

She blew out her breath, looking over the maps as she spread her hands on her lap. "Yes, and I'm going to fail."

"Surely not. Especially if I help you study."

She shot him a look. "Aren't you busy?"

He waved a dismissive hand. "I came to the library to disappear for a while. I'm in need of the distraction. So—what's the focus of the exam, Miss Ellington?"

Grandeur's kindness was at odds with the rest of his family, but she was grateful to have at least one royal on her side. Her mouth curved into a smile. "Call me Clare."

His eyes lightened. "Clare. Where shall we begin?"

CHAPTER 13

GRAYSON

GRAYSON SNATCHED MIA'S WRIST, STOPPING her fist before it could strike his jaw.

Her breath flew out, round cheeks red with exertion. She tugged at his hold, pulling against his gloved thumb and forefinger like he'd taught her.

Grayson locked his fingers and twisted. The sharp but controlled motion flipped her around, slamming her back against his chest. Her dark curls swept under his nose, the soft scent almost as distracting as the fact that her back now pressed against his front.

During their fierce bout of training, his breathing hadn't altered.

Until now.

Lungs hitching, Grayson forced himself to focus on the

mock fight. Not the thudding of his pulse. Not the brush of hair skimming his jaw. Not the feel of her heart thudding against his own chest, or the warmth of her skin he could feel even through his gloves.

Before she could spin away, Grayson clamped his other hand around her free fist. With his arms crossed over her and strangling her wrists, he had succeeded in immobilizing her in a caging embrace.

His pride swelled when she dropped all her weight, a move that had succeeded in throwing him off-balance before. But then, that might have been more due to her nearness than anything else. Today, he forced himself to focus. He grunted, his arms flexing to hold her upright, keeping her locked against him.

She ground her heel into his booted toes and he felt a spark of pride, even though his hold didn't budge.

He had been training her since they were children. They focused on quick, violent ways for Mia to take an attacker by surprise and buy herself enough time for the guard on the other side of the door to reach her. They didn't train with weapons. Not only was Grayson unwilling to risk a weapon being turned against her in a fight, he also knew his father would not approve of Mia having a weapon.

Henri Kaelin didn't approve of her at all.

Grayson would never forget the day his father had learned about Mia. Grayson had only been nine years old, but the memory of that day was sharp.

Mia had been singing to a doll he'd made her out of a meal sack, the inked-on face terribly crooked. Mia had named the doll Tally.

King Henri's large frame had suddenly filled the doorway. Grayson scrambled to his feet, heart pounding against his ribs as he came to attention. Mia lurched to her feet as well, clutching Tally to her chest.

Perhaps Fletcher had told the king that Grayson had befriended a prisoner, or maybe the rumors were true and Henri could read minds. In that moment, Grayson's fear overwhelmed his questions.

Henri had eyed the doll, his lip curling in disgust. "Did you make that for her?"

Grayson's face burned. He wanted to lie, but there was no point. "Yes."

Henri cut a look at Mama, who stood in the corner. "How long has this been going on?"

The woman shifted her weight, hands twisting together. "Several months, Your Majesty. I thought you knew."

A muscle in the king's jaw thrummed. He focused back on his son and his expression was terrible.

Grayson lowered his eyes, his pulse racing. The muscles in his neck jerked when Mia's eyes brushed the side of his face. He felt her fear and it mixed with his own. He could taste it as he swallowed. "Please," he whispered. He didn't know exactly what he was asking for. Mercy. Forgiveness. He just didn't want to lose *her*.

Henri's hard expression didn't change and everything inside Grayson shriveled. "Take the doll," his father ordered.

Grayson's throat constricted, fingers twitching at his sides. Slowly, he turned to Mia.

Her rounded eyes darted over his face and whatever she saw made her breaths come sharper. Her grip on Tally spasmed and she slid back a step.

It hit him as strongly as one of Peter's punches—Mia was frightened of him.

His hand faltered.

His father growled. "I said *take* it."

Grayson grit his teeth and snatched the doll from Mia, trying to ignore her strangled cry.

Henri's tone was clipped as he thrust a finger toward the glowing stove. "Burn it."

"No!" Mia shot forward, her fingers digging into Grayson's arm. He flinched, though her grip didn't really hurt. Not physically. "Please give her back," she begged, voice pitched high and frantic. She tried to grab Tally, but Grayson lifted the doll out of reach. She kept dragging at his arm, but it was useless—he was taller. Stronger. "Grayson, please—"

"Now," his father barked.

Grayson looked at Mia and caught the sheen of tears burning in her eyes. He strangled Tally in his fist. *I'm sorry.* He choked on the words, unable to say them. He tore away from her, lurching toward the stove. A horrible keening broke out behind him and he cringed as he yanked open the small door. The heat scalded his hand, his face.

"Grayson, no!"

He threw the limp doll into the fire.

"*Tally!*" Mia's agonized scream rang in the small stone room and ripped through him. She fell to her knees, her hands slapped over her mouth. Her entire body shook and her shoulders rolled inward as she hunched into a ball.

Grayson's chest burned, as if the flames that ate Tally now devoured him. He staggered toward her. "Mia—"

"Don't," Henri snapped, steel in his voice. "Do *not* go to her."

The space between Grayson and Mia gaped. Her cries tore up his insides and grated on every raw nerve, but he didn't move closer.

"You are a prince of Ryden," Henri said coldly. "You don't show emotion." The king eyed the girl crying on the floor and his lip curled in disgust. "We're done here." He turned sharply, motioning for Fletcher to open the door. When he reached the doorway, he glanced back.

Grayson hadn't moved. His frame vibrated with fear as he faced his father. "Please," he whispered. "Let me stay."

Henri's eyes burned Grayson in a silent study. When the king finally spoke, his tone was level. "You can return when you beat Tyrell in a duel."

Dread knifed him. "But that's impossible! He's better than—"

"You will do it," Henri said. "Or you'll never see this girl again."

Grayson had done it.

It took him nearly two months and countless injuries, but he'd done it. Terror had gripped him the first time he'd stepped back into Mia's cell, covered in sweat and blood from the fight he'd just won. He didn't know if she'd even want to see him after what he'd done to Tally—to *her*.

The moment he'd stepped into her cell she'd thrown her arms around him and hadn't let go.

Henri continued to set new goals for him, but he didn't restrict his visits to Mia. He had learned to follow orders quickly, so it wasn't necessary. There was an unspoken arrangement between them. Grayson would obey, and the king would ignore Mia, as well as keep her existence from the rest of the Kaelin family. So Grayson had become the Black Hand. He had done everything his father ever demanded of him, and he would continue to do so. He would do anything to keep Mia safe.

Even train her to defend herself, though the thought of her in a fight terrified him. It didn't matter that she was quite good; he still couldn't stomach the idea of her being forced to defend herself. But while Grayson could give her precious little, he could teach her the skills that had been beaten into him.

Mia breathed raggedly, her back swelling against his chest.

"Is there a particular reason you're not letting me win?"

Grayson's brows drew together, his crossed arms tightening over her chest. "I never let you win."

She snorted, her chest rising and falling against the cage of his arms. "Because of course it's believable that I can beat you nine times out of ten."

The corner of his mouth twitched. "You are very good."

Even though he was looking at the back of her head, he knew she rolled her eyes.

His smile hiked. "Perhaps in the beginning I let you win." At eleven years old, her beaming smile had been blinding. He'd have done anything to see it. "But not anymore. You're stronger than you think."

She shook her head a little. "Even if you don't *let* me win—and I'm not saying I believe that—you at least make it *possible* for me to win." She glanced over her shoulder at him, color still high on her cheeks. "But something's bothering you, because winning wasn't an option today."

He frowned. "What do you mean?"

"Grayson, you've never held me this hard before."

He instantly released her.

Mia stumbled at the abrupt loss of his support and his hands flashed out to steady her. "Sorry." He cursed himself. "Did I hurt you?"

"No." But she was rubbing her wrists and the skin was red.

His stomach dropped, as did his hands from her shoulders. "Mia—"

"I'm fine. You don't need to apologize. Bruises happen in training, remember?" Her head tilted as she eyed him, her voice losing the humor of before. "What's wrong?"

Everything was wrong. A woman had been executed yesterday, her only crime that she loved her husband and hated the ones responsible for taking him away. Her husband had been crushed by her loss, and yet he was still on his way to a work camp—a slow and brutal death. Grayson had to leave in the morning to ruin more lives, and he would always be his father's weapon. There was no escape. No end.

And then there was Mia. It was horribly wrong that she was here. That she suffered. That she would live under constant threat, just so Grayson remained obedient.

Perhaps he *had* let his emotions influence their training. He needed to make sure that didn't happen again.

Grayson swallowed roughly. "I'm fine."

Mia's brown eyes gentled. "You can tell me the truth."

Never. His sins were not hers to bear. "I'm fine," he repeated. He shifted back a step, feeling her closeness too much. He cleared his throat. "I have to leave again."

Her lips pursed. The only sign of her anxiety was her fingers falling to twist in her skirt. "How long will you be gone?" It was the only question she asked now. The first time he'd left her, she'd pressed for details. He'd hedged, not wanting to show her the darker side of him.

After he'd returned, she must have seen the haunted look in his eyes. She hadn't asked again.

"Two weeks," he told her. "Maybe three."

She glanced away, her throat bobbing. "So long?"

Grayson eased closer and wrapped his gloved hands around her nervous fingers, making them drop the folds of her skirt. "I'll return as soon as I can."

She searched his face. "You'll be careful?"

"Of course." He brushed a stray brown curl from her cheek and hooked it behind her ear. "Is there anything you need before I go?"

Mia gave him a firm look. "You worry too much about me,

Grayson Kaelin."

His mouth quirked. "You'll make me gray before my time," he agreed.

She huffed a short laugh. "I think I see some right here." Her fingertips brushed his temple and pleasant tingles raced over his scalp.

He expected her hand to fall immediately, but it didn't. Her touch drifted down from his temple, the soft pads of her fingers tracing an old scar that crossed his cheek before sliding to wrap around the nape of his neck. With gentle pressure, she laid her palm against his suddenly hot skin and drew his head down so their foreheads rested against each other.

Grayson's heart raced as their breaths mingled, the smell of jasmine swimming around them.

Her thumb slid over the hollow under his ear, the simple stroke raising every hair on his body. "Promise me you'll come back." Vulnerability cracked her soft words.

Every protective instinct he had surged to life. He eased back, lifting his free hand to cradle her face, their gazes holding. "I'll *always* come back to you, Mia."

She held his fervent stare for a moment, then wordlessly folded her arms around him, drawing him in for an embrace.

Grayson's arms tightened around her, an ache rising in his chest. He prayed he'd have the strength to let go.

CHAPTER 14

CLARE

BENNICK'S ARMS BANDED AROUND CLARE, pinning her arms to her sides and hauling her back against his chest. "Break free."

His exhales thrummed warmly against her neck and his hard body expanded against her back as his lungs filled. Even after weeks of training, she still wasn't used to being so close to a man. It made her skin tight and she was hyper-aware of herself. She prayed he hadn't noticed how much she was sweating.

She dropped her weight and Bennick shifted his stance to balance them both. Before he could stabilize, she stomped on his foot and shoved an elbow into his ribs.

His grip loosened and Clare took the opportunity to tear free. She planted a foot on the ground and spun her other foot, aiming for his gut.

Bennick caught her leg and grinned, his blue eyes shining.

"Excellent."

Clare's balance wavered but he released her before she could topple. Breath fanning out, she swiped loose hairs away from her hot face. "I didn't hit hard enough."

"No, but you're getting more confident." He spun a finger. "Turn around, I want to show you something."

Clare pivoted, trying not to tense as Bennick locked his arms around her chest. They'd been training for three weeks now. She should be used to his nearness, the surrounding feel of him pressed up behind her, but she wasn't. If she could feel his every breath, he must feel hers. It only made her breaths come faster.

Bennick took her hand and splayed it against her abdomen, his hand resting atop hers. Her breath caught. He'd been touching her throughout the lesson, but the weight of his fingers stretched along hers felt new. She could feel the calluses on his skin and even though she was overheated, she fought a shiver.

Perhaps it was her imagination, but Bennick's voice seemed deeper than before. "Feel the pull of your muscles here. Twist your shoulder inward as you turn."

Clare swallowed and twisted as he'd instructed, trying to ignore the racing of her heart.

Bennick's mouth dropped to her ear. "Did you feel it?"

His hand was still resting on hers, his breath warming her neck. Her skin prickled and her cheeks heated. "Yes."

"Good. Remember the power there."

Too soon, his hand withdrew. Clare tried to be discreet as she rubbed the sweat from her palm against her skirt before Bennick's arms tightened around her again.

"Break free."

She followed the order, this time pulling her body up in a ball to throw him off balance. She even managed to land her elbow in his ribs as she twisted, and his grunt was genuine. One of these times, she'd manage to actually free her arms like he wanted and he'd get an elbow in his face.

Hard to say if that would make her grin or splutter an apology while blushing furiously.

"Good!" Bennick said. "That was better." He caught sight of her red face and his forehead creased. "You're flushed."

"I'm not." The denial spilled out, only adding to the burn covering her face.

He eyed the sun, which burned at its zenith. "Let's take a break."

Clare took a step back, turning away from him as she fought to regulate her breathing. Training was exhausting. Her body was bruised from the mock fighting and sore from repeatedly taking up the different positions Bennick showed her. Her legs ached from all the lunges and kicks, and new blisters kept finding their way onto her hands. Yet this hour of the day remained her favorite.

"Here."

Clare spun, arm swinging on instinct.

Bennick jerked back with a curse and water sloshed over his hand from the tin cup he held. The cup he'd filled for her.

She slapped a hand over her mouth. "Sorry!"

His lips twitched as he passed the cup to his other hand so he could shake out his wet fingers. "My own fault. I should know better than to sneak up on you now."

There were moments in training when Clare felt attuned to Bennick, able to mirror his movements and act in perfect unison with him. Then there were *these* moments. Clare had never considered herself clumsy, but when he caught her off-guard with his nearness, or a sudden half-grin . . . She'd stumbled into him, tread on his foot, and now she'd almost hit him across the face.

Bennick held out the cup, no longer fighting his smile.

"Would you like what's left?"

She took the cup, grateful for something to do. "Thank you." The water was tepid, but gloriously wet. It soothed the dryness in her mouth and throat.

Bennick looked toward the gray stone castle that towered over the training yard. She took advantage of his distraction. Her eyes swept his face, noting the slightly crooked nose and stubbled jaw. She glimpsed a hint of sweat gathered along his hairline, but his scent hadn't changed—sunshine, leather, and spice. It wasn't fair; her dress was sticking to her back, her breathing was still fighting to slow, and all the lilac oil in Serene's rooms couldn't have helped her. His blue eyes were much more impressive than the commander's, his hair lighter, but she could see the resemblance now that she knew to look. It was still hard to reconcile the fact that he was the commander's son. Her brief conversation with Venn this morning had only whet her curiosity to learn more about their relationship.

Bennick took the empty cup from her and took it back to the water barrel. After gulping down a drink of his own, he returned and waved for her to sit.

She sank gratefully to the ground and braced her arms behind her, the strands of sparse grass at the edge of the field tickling her palms. Soreness radiated from her shoulders, legs, and arms, but it wasn't as painful as the first few days had been. Her body was adapting.

She tilted her head back, relishing the cool spring breeze. She appreciated the braided crown that kept all but several loose tendrils of hair off her neck. She closed her eyes and felt the flush slowly leave her skin.

Bennick sat nearby and when Clare opened her eyes she caught him rubbing his wrist, his focus on the other fights progressing across the field.

"Did I hurt you?" she asked.

He glanced at her. "Is that pride I hear?"

Her lips curved. "Maybe a little."

Bennick chuckled. "It's well-deserved."

A dozen paces away, a soldier knocked his opponent to the ground with a cheer.

When Clare looked back at Bennick, he was examining his wrist.

She straightened sharply. "You're bleeding!"

"Your nails are sharp."

She grabbed his hand, eyeing the crescent-shaped incisions and the crimson blood smearing his skin. "I'm so sorry!" She balanced the back of his hand on her palm while her free fingers tugged a handkerchief from her pocket.

"Don't—ruin it," he sighed the last part, since she'd already pressed the cloth against his bleeding wrist.

"I didn't realize I'd hurt you."

"I can claim worse injuries, you know. Wilf nearly broke a rib yesterday."

She peeked up at him. "Wilf is quite . . ." *Terrifying* was the word, but she didn't want to say it.

Bennick seemed to hear what she hadn't voiced. He winced. "Wilf isn't always like that."

Clare propped his arm against her leg, still holding the cloth to his skin. "I heard some of the soldiers talking."

He scowled. "Soldiers gossip more than old women." His fingers flexed and a muscle in his cheek jumped. "Wilf has served as a royal bodyguard for almost thirty years. He's saved my life and the lives of each member of the royal family multiple times. He trained me when I was just a boy. I wouldn't be who I am today without him."

Holding Bennick's hand and sitting close to him under the

warm sun made her bold. "He sounds almost like a father to you."

His jaw firmed, but her words didn't coax out any answers about the commander. "He was, in many ways." He used his free hand to rub his forehead, effectively blocking her view of his face. "Wilf caught the pox five years ago. All the physicians agreed he was a dead man but his wife, Rachel, took care of him for days with barely any rest. Sometimes I think her determination alone saved him." He lowered his hand and his voice. "Lady Rachel wasn't so blessed when the illness claimed her. Wilf was inconsolable when she died."

Pity swelled in Clare's chest. Even if the man frightened her, she knew the pain of losing a loved one. It wasn't an agony she'd wish on anyone.

"He drank and gambled away his earnings. He never endangered the royal family, but he became less dependable. He was Prince Grandeur's lead bodyguard at the time, and the men who served under him grew impatient with his grief; they demanded his replacement. This was two years ago; I'd just been appointed to the position I have now, and I was looking for a fifth man I could trust. I asked for Wilf, and the king consented." He shook his head. "Yesterday was a bad relapse, but he's coming around."

"What do you think caused it?"

Bennick stretched his legs to a more comfortable position, his hand still in hers. "He's been on edge since the Mortisian emissaries arrived. Wilf fought on the front lines during the old war and lost good friends."

"So he doesn't want the alliance?"

His forehead creased. "I wouldn't say that. Experiences have made him distrustful, but he's not against peace. I put him in a holding cell until he was sober enough to calm down." He glanced at her. "Wilf never gave up on me, even when I was a blasted pain, so I refuse to give up on him."

A small smile caught her lips. "You're a good man, Captain Markam."

Bennick huffed out a laugh. "I have my flaws, same as anyone." He tilted his head and viewed her with suddenly narrowed eyes. "Venn told me something troubling, Miss Ellington."

Her mind flashed to the library and her prying questions. Her mouth ran dry. "Oh?"

Bennick's lips twitched. "He says you've always called him *Venn*. I've known you a day longer, yet I'm still *Captain Markam*."

She grinned. "To be fair, I knew you as *Venn* for that first day."

"True. It still seems wrong, though."

"Perhaps I'm more at ease with Venn," she teased.

"Are you?" His hand hadn't moved, but the rest of him seemed suddenly closer.

Clare's eyes dipped to his slightly parted lips, striving to keep her light tone. She didn't quite manage. "Venn doesn't mock assassinate me every time I see him."

Bennick eased closer and she leaned back, chin lifting. His hand twisted in hers and roughened fingertips brushed against her calluses. His arm was warm where it rested against her leg. "I'm not *always* fighting with you," he said softly.

Clare's heart skipped a beat. "True."

His thumb stroked the center of her palm and she sucked in a breath, her hand flinching away in surprise.

Bennick drew back, a thin smile on his face. "Whenever you feel at ease with me, you're free to use my given name."

If her thudding heart was any indication, she doubted she'd ever feel at ease around him.

CHAPTER 15

CLARE

CLARE TOOK THE PRINCESS'S SEAT AT THE formal dining table
and tried to keep her breaths even. It was her first public dinner
as Serene and she was dressed in all the princess's finery, all of
her exposed skin stained a shade darker. The adjustments to her
complexion were slight, but powerful. Breathing was a battle;
nerves made her chest tight and her hands twitch, and the fitted
bodice of her green gown didn't help. Knowing she must fool a
crowd of people tonight—and please King Newlan with her act
—she barely dared open her mouth. Even after four weeks of
training, she didn't feel ready.

Stringed instruments created a soft backdrop for the laughter and conversation filling the vaulted room. Roasted pig and
stewed vegetables spiced the air and Clare's stomach tugged with
a mix of hunger and nerves. Too bad all of Mistress Henley's

cautions about proper etiquette made her dread the moment she had to lift her fork.

The sight of Bennick and Venn watching from a few paces away calmed her frayed breathing a little. She caught Bennick's eye and his familiar half-grin infused her with warmth. She sent a small smile back at him.

"Princess Serene."

Clare twisted to find a stranger standing near her chair. He was clearly Mortisian. His clothing was a different style, more loose and flowing, and a wide sash of crimson crossed over his shoulder and chest. He looked to be in his early twenties with brown-tinted skin and dark hair that fell to his shoulders. A well-trimmed beard framed his lower face.

"You look beautiful as always," he said, bowing low.

"Thank you," she managed.

There weren't many Mortisians in the castle, and when the young man took the seat beside her, her guess was confirmed —thank the fates she'd memorized the seating chart—the handsome young man was Ser Amil Havim, son of emissary Ser Bahri Havim.

Ser was the equivalent of *lord*, she'd learned from Ramus. Mortisians used the titles interchangeably, since the Garvins Treaty had been signed two hundred years ago, establishing fair trade among the four kingdoms of Eyrinthia. The same treaty had also accepted the common tongue, which assigned titles for the nobility throughout the kingdoms. "As a show of respect," Ramus had explained, "we use their traditional titles. King Saernon is the *serjan*, Prince Desfan is the *serjah*. Lords and ladies of the nobility are *sers* and *serais*, respectively."

Now facing the son of the Mortisian emissary, panic flooded Clare. Too much to remember—she'd surely make a mistake.

Ser Amil smiled, his brown eyes soft. "You seem distracted.

Have I interrupted the great Princess Serene in the middle of some deep thought?"

She choked on a weak laugh. "No. I'm afraid I'm simply distracted."

"I haven't seen you since the betrothal was announced. How has the news been taken by your people?"

"Relatively well." It was what Newlan had told her to say, if anyone asked.

Ser Amil's dark eyebrow arched. "I heard there was a skirmish in Iden's market yesterday."

"Was there?" Clare hadn't heard about that, but she imagined many people were unhappy about the prospect of peace with their long-time enemies.

"My father grumbled about it for quite some time. You know how he is."

She didn't. But Serene might, so Clare nodded. "Where is your father?"

"He said he might be delayed."

Clare was saved from having to make more conversation when King Newlan stood at the table's head. Silence fell among the gathered nobility and they listened raptly as Newlan gave a speech about peace, hope, and a stronger future. When he finished, the lords and ladies clapped politely, Clare with them.

As everyone began to eat, Ser Amil leaned toward her. "Have you picked a favorite yet?"

"A favorite?" It felt like she'd missed something, because his question didn't make sense.

"It would be hard to decide," Amil said, "but I must know."

"I . . . I'm not sure . . ."

Seeing her confusion, he frowned. "During our conversation about Zennor the other day—I asked what your favorite part of living abroad was."

"Oh! Yes. Of course. Forgive me." Clare scrambled to think. "It's difficult to say, but, I think it was the culture." She'd been learning all about Zennor's rich culture from Ramus and it was the first thing to spring to mind.

Amil smiled. "I trust you'll find Mortise to your liking, then. We have many traditions and our culture isn't as divided as Zennor's." He took a sip of wine, then asked, "Have you begun preparations?"

Fates, she hated feeling like she was missing half the conversation. "Preparations?"

"For your journey to Mortise."

"Oh. Yes." Her cheeks warmed. Serene wouldn't be flustered. Clare needed to regain control.

The dancing candlelight from the table's candelabra caught the flash of his teeth as he smiled. "Duvan is beautiful. The palms, the architecture, the beaches . . . You won't be disappointed, Princess." His gaze dipped to her lips, pressed against her glass. "Though, as beautiful as Duvan is, it pales beside you."

Clare set down her wine. Why hadn't anyone prepared her for Amil's flirtations? She wasn't sure how to react, but surely Serene wouldn't respond—not when she was engaged to marry the Mortisian prince. Clare cleared her throat. "Do you know Desfan well?"

Amil leaned back. "A little. The serjah didn't spend much time at the palace, until the serjan's recent illness."

"Rumors say he's a pirate."

Amil chuckled. "If anything, he *hunted* pirates. He would spend months away at sea."

"His father never complained about his long absences?"

"No. The serjan didn't seem to worry about Desfan's lack of influence in court."

"But others did?"

He tipped his head in acknowledgement, then lowered his voice. "Between us, I think there are many in court who feel Desfan is not, perhaps, the best choice for regent. Some say he's not trained enough in politics to lead us until the serjan's health returns."

"I suppose these same people think his first mistake was to insist on this betrothal?"

"Only because they have not met you, Princess. You are a gift to Mortise."

Across the table from them, an empty chair was suddenly filled by Amil's father. Two Mortisian guards took up positions behind the emissary, their curved swords and shielded expressions sending a tendril of unease down Clare's spine.

Ser Bahri's beard was as dark as his son's, but fuller. There were lines at the corners of his eyes, but that was the only sign of his age. The emissary greeted her curtly and reached for his wine.

Amil sighed beside her. "Please excuse him. He's quite preoccupied these days."

"I assumed his duties would relax after the betrothal was decided."

"There's still much to coordinate. He writes letters almost constantly. I've tried to help, but he insists on doing most of it alone."

The dinner continued, and though Amil was pleasant and chatted passionately about the wonder of Duvan's coastal markets, Clare couldn't shake the nervousness bunching her shoulders. She cast a look around the table and caught the old emissary scowling at her, his gaze sharp. Her scalp prickled, a shiver rippling through her.

Ser Bahri glanced away and the meal continued. Amil talked beside her, silverware clinked against plates and laughter rang out in the room. Ser Bahri never looked at her again, but Clare didn't relax.

An odd chill remained with her throughout the remainder of dinner, making her all the more eager to retire. When Bennick and Venn finally escorted her to the princess's suite, she hurried to climb into bed. It had been a tiring day, and stretching out on the soft mattress felt wonderful. She pulled in long and deep breaths and felt her muscles relax.

The lilac scent was strong—the maids must have just freshened the room with new flowers—but Clare was growing used to the sweet fragrance.

She shifted, settling in more deeply as she inhaled. Another scent was mixed with the lilacs, but she couldn't place it. A yawn cracked her jaw and she rubbed her closed eyes, sleep claiming her quickly.

Her last thought was that the scent was overpowering, making it hard to breathe.

CHAPTER 16

BENNICK

BENNICK CLACKED HIS WOODEN MUG against Cardon's, Venn's and Gavril's. Venn hooted when ale sloshed against the scuffed table and then he threw back his drink, gulping it down without pausing for breath.

Cardon shook his head, a grin pulling at his mouth. "It must be the Zennorian in your blood."

"Are they better drinkers?" Venn asked, swiping the back of his hand over his mouth as he lowered the empty mug.

Cardon rolled his eyes. "Once again, I know more about your mother's kingdom than you do."

Venn blinked. "You want me to ask my mother about her ability to drink?"

Cardon shook his head, keeping his mug firmly on the table. Bennick had never seen Cardon drunk; he shared the occasional drink with them, but he came for the company. Bennick wasn't one to overindulge either, so he never asked Cardon's reasons. Perhaps they were similar to his own; losing his ability to think and react quickly wasn't something he cared to experience. And he feared the drink might loosen his tongue. He trusted the men at this table with his life, but that didn't mean he wanted them to know every thought in his head. Especially when it came to Clare, who was on his mind almost constantly these days.

She'd done well tonight, posing as Serene at the dinner. Bennick had been close enough to hear most of her conversation with Amil Havim, and though he hadn't appreciated the Mortisian's less-than-subtle flirtations, Clare had handled the man excellently. Pride had filled Bennick as he'd watched her adapt yet again to her situation. Whether she was an unassuming kitchen maid diving into danger to save the princess's life or squaring off against him on the training field, Clare was amazing. He was fascinated by her—something he could admit to himself but didn't want spoken aloud.

Venn was loud enough for all of them, anyway. He'd tried pulling Gavril into the conversation, but had soon given up. It was a victory alone that Gavril had accepted their invitation to join them at The Arrow tonight. The tavern sat near the castle's outer walls and was frequented by soldiers who didn't want to trudge all the way to Lower Iden to escape the barracks for a while. Other patrons filled the square tables as well, but soldiers —both in and out of uniform—were the majority. Card games, drinking competitions, and bellowing voices filled the room, along with lively flute music.

None of the merriment seemed to touch Gavril. He occasionally quirked a partial smile at something Venn said, but he sat with shoulders hunched as he nursed his mug. The burns on his face and neck garnered more stares in the common room than Bennick had expected, and if he noticed the stares, Gavril certainly must.

When they'd been younger, Gavril had often acted in the role of an older brother to Bennick. He'd ridden with him, sparred with him; even though four years separated them, Gavril had gone out of his way at the academy to make sure Bennick settled in. Gavril had always been soft-spoken, but quick to laugh. Now the laughter, the softness—it was gone. Stripped away in a horrible instant that had taken everything from him.

"You know something I *do* know about Zennorians?" Venn asked, breaking into Bennick's thoughts.

Cardon sighed. "I think you're about to tell me."

Venn snatched up his long black ponytail and dragged it above his head so they could all see it. "Did you know a Zennorian warrior wears his hair long in times of peace and shaves his head for war?"

"I did not," Cardon said carefully, mouth twitching.

"It's true!" Venn threw his ponytail down. "My sisters wanted me to shave my head when I entered the academy."

"Why didn't you?" Bennick asked.

Venn had two sisters, one older and one younger, both married and living in Iden near their mother, Zoya, one of the kindest people Bennick had ever met. Venn's father, a Devendran soldier, had died in battle when Venn was only two years old. But even though Venn's life hadn't been perfect, Bennick couldn't help but think him lucky; Bennick's family was far more fractured, even though his parents were still living.

Venn snorted. "My mother said if I entered the academy with the intent to make war, I couldn't go. So I kept my hair long, and I always will, even though she rolls her eyes at me."

"You mean *because* she rolls her eyes at you," Gavril said

dryly.

Venn laughed and Bennick and Cardon chuckled.

Gavril's thin smile flashed, disappearing too quickly. But it had been there.

Bennick leaned back, the wooden chair creaking under his weight. "Maybe I'll slip up in practice and rid you of your long locks."

Venn gasped. "You wouldn't!"

"I can't have my men care too much about their hair."

"You're just jealous." Venn straightened suddenly. "Let's talk about Clare."

Bennick shot a pointed look at Gavril, who was taking another sip from his mug.

Venn rolled his eyes, silent communication that clearly said, *I won't tell him she's the decoy—I'm not* that *drunk!* While Gavril was trusted, the king didn't want any of the palace guardsmen to know about the decoy. Venn cleared his throat. "You certainly watch her closely, Bennick."

Cardon cracked a smile. "You *do* stare at her."

Bennick's jaw tightened. "I don't know what you're—"

"Please," Venn thrust out a hand and looked to the other men at the table. "He's never paid so much attention to one of the princess's maids. You've all seen it. Personally, I'm quite interested."

Bennick frowned. "Venn—"

"He has a point," Cardon said, lifting his mug toward his lips.

"Thank you!" Venn's hands thumped the table, drawing looks from surrounding patrons. "What do you intend to do about it, Bennick?"

His hands fisted below the table. "Nothing. Our positions make it impossible." The stare he sent Cardon and Venn communicated what he couldn't say in front of Gavril: Clare was the decoy. There could never be anything between them. The king would not allow it.

Gavril thumbed the handle of his mug, his voice low. "When you have feelings for a woman, they don't go away." His words quieted them all, even Venn.

The muscles in Bennick's neck tightened. Gavril never talked of Bonnai, his dead wife. It was a subject none of them broached.

Gavril's shoulders rolled inward as he peered at Bennick, the lamplight catching the purple-red burn marring his face. "If you care for Clare, you need to tell her. If she feels the same, you'll make things work. But don't wait. Life is not as lasting as it seems."

The night was half gone by the time they returned to the castle. Gavril walked toward his barracks and Venn, Cardon, and Bennick entered the castle through a side door, their boots echoing in the empty corridor.

"I think the night was good for Gavril," Cardon said.

Bennick nodded. "We should do it again."

Murmurs of agreement went up. The castle was quiet at this late hour. Guards nodded to them as they passed, but even the servants were mostly abed. When the corridor split, Bennick took a left toward the royal wing.

"Where are you going?" Venn asked. He and Cardon halted, studying him in the dim light.

"Just checking in with Wilf," Bennick said. It was a captain's duty. It had nothing to do with the fact that Wilf was guarding

Clare.

Venn and Cardon exchanged a knowing look.

Bennick rolled his eyes and turned away, but he heard them trail after him. A few moments later they reached the top of the staircase and entered the long corridor outside the princess's rooms. Wilf stood at the door with two palace guards, and all three of them looked up as Bennick and the others approached.

Wilf grunted, his thick arms folded over his broad chest. "I figured you'd all be passed out drunk by now."

"No," Venn answered smoothly. "We're not you."

Wilf growled.

Bennick glanced at the closed door. He caught the faint glow of light spilling from the crack underneath and his brow furrowed. "Has the princess not gone to bed?"

Wilf glanced at the palace guardsmen beside them—they thought they were guarding the real princess, and it needed to remain that way. "She retired hours ago." Wilf's gaze was also drawn to the light under the door and he frowned. "I hadn't noticed . . . Perhaps the maid forgot to blow out the lamp."

"Vera?" Venn's voice was steadier, joking gone. "She wouldn't forget that."

Bennick's heart drummed faster. He grasped the door's handle and pushed into the room.

Every lamp was lit, the flames burning brightly behind their glass shields. The scent of lilacs was heavy on the air—the vases must have been recently refilled. Vera was curled in a cushioned chair in the corner, her head tipped to the side, stretching her slender neck. Soft blond hair fell around her shoulders and her face was pale and still, her eyes closed. A dress lay on her lap, as if she'd fallen asleep mending. A spool of thread had rolled across the floor, leaving a thin trail of bright crimson.

Bennick might have relaxed—after all, it appeared as if Vera had simply drifted off—but there was something horribly wrong about the scene.

Vera wasn't breathing.

Venn cursed and shoved past Bennick. He grasped Vera's pale face with both of his dark hands, his shoulders bunched with tension. "Vera? Vera!" He threw a hard look over his shoulder, his focus beyond Bennick. "Get a physician—now!"

One of the guards darted away, but Bennick barely heard him. Because only now could he make out the strange scent buried in the overwhelming lilacs—it was too sweet. Too cool.

His stomach dropped.

Night Sigh.

With a strangled curse, Bennick darted for the closed bedroom door, praying to the fates he wasn't about to find Clare dead. He rushed into the room and bent over the bed, struggling to ignore the chill that raced over his skin and raised every hair on his body. The room was saturated with the heavy smell of lilacs and poison, and Clare had been breathing it for hours.

She was on her side, turned toward him and the door. The light from the sitting room filtered weakly inside, just revealing the pale cast of her usually brown skin. She was unmoving under the blankets. Night Sigh lulled victims into a deep sleep when inhaled, swelling their throat and filling their nose until they no longer breathed.

Bennick gritted his teeth and ripped the blankets off her, scooping her into his arms and dragging her against his chest. "Clare? Can you hear me?"

No response. No flutter of breath or flicker of movement.

Wilf darted into the room and shoved open the window, allowing fresh air to sweep into the room. He began hurling vases of lilacs out the window, anything to get the Night Sigh out of the room. It was still too thick in the air, though. Bennick carried Clare back into the sitting room and saw that Wilf must have already disposed of the lilacs that had been in here. With the doors open, it was easier to breathe in here now.

Across the room, Venn knelt in front of Vera. The girl was doubled over, fully awake and wheezing as she struggled to fill her lungs. Venn's hands still framed her face as he urged her to breathe, his thumbs stroking her cheekbones. She clung to his wrists, her wild eyes locked on his.

Cardon was the only guard still in the hall. "I sent them for a physician," he explained shortly. His shoulders tensed as he gripped the doorframe, his gaze intent on Clare. "Force her to stand, shake her—whatever it takes to wake her."

Bennick was already dropping Clare's legs, supporting her weight when her knees buckled. He shook her, demanded she open her eyes, but she sagged against him, her head bumping against his chest.

Panic knifed him. He shook her again, harder than before, and this time when her head snapped back, her eyes dragged open.

Relief hit him so hard, his legs nearly gave out. "Clare!"

She squinted at him, weary and confused. She tried to suck in a breath and when she failed, her body locked. Terror flared in her eyes and she tried to jerk away from him, as if space would help her breathe. He clung to her—he wouldn't let her fall. Not even when her fingers scrabbled weakly over his arms, frantic for him to release her.

Bennick ducked his head so their eyes were level. "You're fine," he said, his voice too rough to be comforting. "I promise. Just breathe. Slowly. You're going to be all right."

Clare trembled, her fingers curling into his sleeves as she inhaled thinly. Rich brown hair fell over her shoulders, her face still pale. Moisture blurred her deep blue eyes and when the first tear slipped over her cheek, it cut him. He cupped the side of her face with one hand and thumbed the wet trail away. She opened her mouth, but no words scratched out and her tears fell faster.

Bennick didn't think. He pulled her in, his hand at the back of her head as he pressed her cheek to his chest, his other arm banding around her waist. "It's all right," he breathed into her hair. "A physician is coming. He'll be here soon. You're going to be fine. I promise." He kept repeating the words as he embraced her, throwing in any useless things that leapt to mind.

Several long minutes passed before the physician arrived, but he soon had Clare and Vera breathing salts to clear the Night Sigh from their lungs.

Bennick had retreated a little so the physician could tend Clare, but he stood rigidly nearby and observed each shallow breath she took—they were becoming more measured, and yet his tension only grew.

Cardon eased up beside him, his voice low. "We need to report this to the king."

Bennick jerked a nod, but it took a while before he could pull his gaze from Clare. He'd almost lost her tonight. The knowledge rang in his head, pushing out nearly every other thought. But Cardon was right. King Newlan needed to be told.

A quarter hour later, once Clare and Vera were settled back into bed and guarded by Wilf, Cardon, and Venn, Bennick finally faced the king.

Newlan was livid. "How did this happen?" he hissed.

Bennick stood rigidly, head bowed. Not many were allowed in the king's personal suite, and Bennick had never been at the center of attention in this room. His skin prickled with the awareness that his position—even his life—was currently under scrutiny. "Sire, I take full responsibility."

King Newlan towered over him, wearing a green robe. His hair was rumpled from interrupted sleep, his face red and twisted with rage. Commander Markam stood beside the king, still in uniform even at this late hour. Prince Grandeur stood on the king's other side. Serene wasn't present. Bennick assumed it was the king's attempt to protect the princess. Bennick had no doubt she'd learn about the attack soon enough, and she'd probably be furious about being left in the dark.

Newlan's hands curled at his sides. "How did the poison get into her room?"

"The Night Sigh was dusted on the lilacs," Bennick said. "The maids didn't notice, nor did my men."

"Inexcusable! Such an obvious poison should have never slipped past you!"

Bennick swallowed, shoulders rigid, head still ducked. "I will make a full investigation. We'll increase security on the princess's suite."

"Which maid placed the flowers in the room?" the king demanded.

Bennick swallowed tightly. "Vera Smallwood, but she's not to blame. Not only is she a trusted maid that almost succumbed to the poison herself, she also knew Serene wasn't sleeping there. This attack must have come from someone who doesn't know about the decoy."

"Where did the flowers come from?" the commander asked, speaking for the first time.

Bennick grit his teeth as he always did when he heard his father's voice. "The market in Iden. Serene's head maid, Bridget, has used the same supplier for years."

King Newlan eyed Commander Markam. "You will open an investigation of this merchant. And I want to know everyone who had access to the flowers."

The commander bowed.

"Night Sigh is native to Mortise," Grandeur said quietly.

The king shot a look at his son. "You think a Mortisian was behind this?"

"Anyone could have purchased Night Sigh, but I think the connection bears thinking about." The prince hesitated, then added, "Emissary Havim was overheard the other day venting his frustration with some of the betrothal terms."

Commander Markam's brows drew together. "He's an emissary of peace. He wouldn't be behind something like this. It doesn't make sense."

"We can't make accusations against the emissary," Newlan said firmly. "This could have easily been the rebels."

"Poison isn't their usual method," Commander Markam mused. "With the betrothal now public, it could be anyone. An upset noble or merchant could have hired an assassin." He glanced at the king. "The danger was anticipated—thus, the decoy."

"Anticipated, yes," the king allowed. "But I didn't expect an assassin to make it into her room." His eyes cut back to Bennick. "You failed me tonight."

Commander Markam cleared his throat. "Your Majesty, I think the captain's successes should be taken into account. He and his men have avoided several attempts since the decoy—"

"It only takes one failure," Newlan cut in.

Bennick avoided his father's gaze, keeping his eyes trained on the king. He should probably be grateful for the commander's defense of him. Instead, he just felt an irritated prickle at the back of his neck.

Newlan's jaw flexed as he pinned Bennick with a dark stare. "Your laxity could have cost me the decoy. Our time is too short —we wouldn't be able to prepare another one in time." His eyes narrowed. "If you can't protect her in a fortified castle, how will you do so on the journey to Mortise?"

The question churned Bennick's gut, because he'd been wondering the same thing.

CHAPTER 17

GRAYSON

GRAYSON PUSHED INTO THE EMPTY BUTCHER shop, dragging mud across the dusty floor. None of the streets in the mountain villages were paved and many had been washed-out with the melting snows. Gevell was no different. This remote village was just as desolate and cold as the others, and his boots were three times their weight due to the clinging mud. Grayson's feet were wet. Mountain air had stung his face raw and his lips were cracked. No cloak was thick enough to protect against the constant time spent outdoors.

For over a week, Grayson had entered village after village, and every time it was the same. People saw the band of soldiers coming, the Black Hand riding at the head, and they fled into their homes. They were terrified, but they couldn't hide. Grayson approached every door, demanding the king's tax. Their faces blurred, as did the villages. All the buildings were constructed of logs and stone, with the spice of pine and the stench of poverty clinging to everything.

Captain Reeve's boots thumped behind him, stomping off bits of snow and mud. "This shop was raided a long time ago."

Grayson eyed the space, forced to agree. A butcher's counter, stained with old blood, stood bare near the side wall. Broken crates and tools had been left strewn about the shop and some floorboards had rotted through, proving the shop hadn't been in good repair even when operational. Dust covered every surface and cobwebs dangled from the rafters. Anything of value had been stripped.

"The butcher is long gone," Grayson said. "There's nothing here to collect."

Reeve ignored him, moving toward a corner stacked with empty crates. He crouched, and when he rose, he held a child's ball in his hand. "There's no dust on this. Someone was here recently."

Grayson plucked a cobweb that swung near his face and let it flutter to the ground. He glanced pointedly at Reeve. "The shop is deserted."

Reeve looked to a soldier near the open door. "Find someone from the village. I want to question them."

The soldier hesitated, glancing at Grayson.

Grayson barely bit back a sigh, but he knew by now Reeve would not be diverted. He flicked a hand and the soldier darted to follow Reeve's order. "You're wasting time," Grayson told the captain. "A child probably came in to play and left it."

Reeve fingered the ball. "This belongs to a small child. One who couldn't be left unsupervised. An adult was with them here. Recently."

"And you think the child belongs to the butcher?" Grayson

snorted. "The man's long gone."

Reeve's features pinched. "There are times, Prince Grayson, when you don't seem wholly committed to our task."

That he dared suggest such a thing to Grayson's face proved Reeve was Henri's spy, and thus had his protection. That knowledge kept Grayson from snapping. "I grow tired of the mountains." He tried to sound bored instead of desperate. They'd been gone from Lenzen for over a week. He missed Mia and he was sick of taking coin from hands that had nothing to give.

Reeve lightly bounced the ball in his hand. "Word has spread to the other villages. People are fleeing from us. We should divide our forces. I'll finish here and you could take a group of men to the next village before they can hide."

As much as he'd like to put distance between himself and Reeve, he feared the damage Reeve would inflict without supervision. "No."

Reeve frowned, but the soldier who had left returned with a gray-haired man. The man's misty eyes darted from Grayson to Reeve and back again. He bowed his head, wiping a shaking hand over his mouth. "Your Highness."

Grayson locked his knees, arms crossed over his chest. "Tell me what you know of the butcher named Hogan."

The old man's throat bobbed. "Branton Hogan died six months ago."

"What happened to his business?"

He shrugged, glancing around. "Fell apart, didn't it?"

"Who inherited this shop?" Grayson asked.

"He had a brother, but I don't know where he lives."

Captain Reeve stepped forward. "Did he have a wife? Children?"

The neighbor eyed the ball in Reeve's hand. "He did. They left Gevell just after the burial."

"Where did they go?" Reeve pressed.

"I don't know."

Grayson's gaze wandered to the shop's back room. The door sagged on its hinges, unable to close completely. Through the narrow opening he caught a shadow of movement and his heart thudded faster. Someone was back there, watching them. Hiding.

Whoever it was would be punished for evasion—or squatting —if they were discovered. Grayson made an impulsive decision as he focused back on the nervous old man. "Thank you for your help. You may—"

"Do you know who this might belong to?" Reeve asked, rolling the ball in his palm. "Are there any young boys in the village?"

The man fiddled with the tattered hem of his shirt. "A few."

"Did Hogan have a son?"

"I—yes, two. But Mistress Hogan took the boys and left. As I said."

"Yes, I heard you." Reeve bared his teeth in a smile and fisted the ball. "I want the names of all the young boys in the village."

Grayson heaved an irritated sigh, shifting so he casually blocked the back room from Reeve's view. "Forget it, Captain. It's a waste of time."

"I see no harm in pursuing the matter."

Grayson could order Reeve to stop, but that would be reported to the king, and Henri would question him. So he forced himself to shrug. "Engage in this foolishness if you wish, but it will only earn you a lack of sleep."

"Thank you for indulging me, Your Highness." Reeve bounced the ball in his hand as he nodded to the soldiers, who escorted the old man outside.

Reeve continued to bounce the ball as his eyes drifted over the shop, his gaze moving toward the back room.

Grayson snatched the ball from the air.

Reeve actually flinched.

Grayson smiled narrowly, his tone carefully measured. "Watch yourself, Captain. You try my patience." He strode out the front door, not allowing himself to look over his shoulder. The back of his neck prickled, knowing he'd left Reeve in the shop that was not, after all, empty.

Come on, Reeve. Follow me . . .

Grayson stepped onto the muddy street and Reeve exited the run-down shop behind him. His voice lowered so only Grayson would hear him. "I mean no disrespect, Prince Grayson. I only wish to serve our king, as you must."

Grayson turned on his heel and leaned in, their faces only a breath apart. They were the same height, even though Reeve was three years older. "Your place is not to question me, Reeve. You overrode me in front of the men. Do so again and it will be your last act."

Fear crossed Reeve's face and he shifted back on instinct. But then anger flashed in his eyes and his mouth drew tight. "I *will* find out who's been in that shop. And if I can't do so by morning, I'll burn it to prove no one is above the king's law." He eyed Grayson meaningfully. *"No one."*

Grayson watched the man stride away. The ball was in his fist and a muscle throbbed along his jaw. He glanced back at the shop, his expression carefully blank as his thoughts raced.

Grayson waited until full dark before he slipped from camp. No one saw him go. Reeve would never discover what he was about to do, which meant his father would never know. It was an exhilarating thought.

The night air in the northern mountains was frigid. Grayson kept his cloak pulled tight around him as he followed a deer trail that tracked back to the village of Gevell. Sticking to the shadows and unconventional paths, he arrived with no witnesses.

Grayson sighted the butcher's shop from the tree line and spent a quarter hour watching it. He saw no sign of Reeve, but he still used the back entrance.

Once inside the hollowed-out shop, he strained his ears. Pinched breathing and a rustle of fabric came from the back room. He eased forward, carefully navigating the rotting floor. He didn't enter the back room, just stood near the door, his voice pitched low. "I mean no harm. I've come to warn you. You can't stay here."

The thin breathing halted. Then, "Please," a woman begged weakly. "Please help us."

Grayson placed a gloved hand on the door and nudged it open. The room was small, merely a storage space. A woman sat in the corner, two children curled in her arms, the three of them wrapped in frayed blankets that could not have actually warded off the cold night. The smallest child couldn't have been more than three years old, the other maybe seven or eight.

Grayson's jaw tensed. "The soldiers will find you if you stay. They're going to burn the shop at dawn. You must go."

The woman's face was dirt-streaked, and pale brown hair trailed in a thin braid over her shoulder. She obviously didn't recognize the Black Hand. Otherwise, she wouldn't have looked at him with such desperate hope burning in her eyes. "I have nowhere to go and Garyn is sick." Breath rattled out of her, shaking her fragile body. Clearly, the boy wasn't the only one who was sick. Her eyes watered as she peered up at him. "Please help us."

He hadn't expected this. He'd thought the squatters might be Hogan's family, but he only intended to warn them; they would flee and he'd return to camp. But this woman looked too frail to move herself, let alone two children.

The smallest boy moaned and the woman clutched him to her chest, stroking his grimacing face. The older boy was thin and small. Grayson didn't have much of a childhood to draw on, but he knew no child should have such terror in their eyes. Fates, he knew that better than most.

His hands curled into fists. "I can carry the boy. I'll take you to the Julne river. From there you can make your way to Kevid." He'd already led the soldiers through there. And if they hurried, the Hogans could reach the river and he could run back to camp before sunrise.

The woman's tearful words of gratitude slurred together, another sign of her illness. Grayson lifted the youngest child and shifted him to one arm, cringing as the hot forehead pressed against the side of his neck.

The mother scrambled to grab their blankets and the older boy shouldered a bag of their sparse belongings.

The shop's front door creaked open.

Grayson lifted a finger to his lips, a silent order for the mother and older boy, inwardly cursing when he heard Reeve's low voice. "... every corner of this place. We'll find that thief and her brats. No one steals from the king."

Grayson counted the footsteps; there were four men, including Reeve. They would discover them within a minute.

The toddler in his arms groaned. Grayson thrust him at his mother and reached for his sword, but before he could draw it the other boy crouched on the floor and silently pried a couple planks from the floor. He went into the hole he'd made and wordlessly took his brother into his arms before disappearing. The mother waved for Grayson to follow as she slipped into the dark cellar.

Grayson slid in behind her, scanning the cramped space below the shop. By the time he got his bearings, moonlight sliced inside from the outer cellar door the mother had pushed open. He didn't take the time to try and replace the floorboards. He rushed after the small family as they exited the cellar and darted into the night. The mother was in the lead, cradling her sick child, with Grayson and the older boy following right behind.

Reeve's muted shout tore through the shop. The hole in the floor had been spotted.

Grayson snagged the boy's thin arm and hauled him toward the tree line, running across the frozen ground. When the child stumbled, Grayson swung him into his arms. If they didn't make the trees before Reeve got outside . . .

The shouting increased. Grayson bolted behind the first thick tree in the woods and halted, gripping the boy to keep him from squirming.

Torches flared but didn't come closer. Reeve shouted orders in the yard, organizing a search of the nearby shops and houses. He didn't know they were in the woods, but he'd figure it out.

Grayson spotted the woman, also huddled against a nearby tree. He kept his voice low. "We need to run."

Her chin trembled and sweat covered her brow, but she jerked out a nod. Grayson shifted the older boy to his back, ordering the child to hold on. Thin legs locked around Grayson's waist and thinner arms looped his neck. He took the sick child from the mother, knowing she couldn't have any extra weight if she was going to keep up.

They'd only been running a couple of minutes when footsteps pounded behind them, tearing through the dead leaves.

"I see them!" Reeve yelled. "To me! To me!"

Grayson shoved the small boy into his mother's arms. "Keep going," he ordered, already shrugging the older boy off his back. He itched to pull out his sword, but Reeve had seen him draw it too many times. He might recognize the long blade, even in the dark. He plucked out two knives instead, and when he glanced up he found the older boy peering at him, something like awe in his blue eyes.

"Brant!" the mother snapped, fear coating her voice.

Brant darted after his mother and Grayson lifted the cowl of his cloak to shield his face. Hopefully the night's darkness would do the rest.

Reeve barreled through the trees, apparently alone. The other soldiers hadn't caught up yet. Grayson ran to intercept him. For a split second, he considered killing Reeve. No one would know he'd done it, and he'd be free of the spy.

But Henri would grow suspicious, and Grayson was not a murderer. A killer, yes. But if he took Reeve's life tonight, it would be murder.

Still several paces away, Grayson threw the first dagger. It grazed Reeve's arm, drawing a pained hiss. Reeve's eyes flashed and his nostrils flared as he drew his sword.

Grayson swerved and ducked. Reeve swung his sword, but it whistled harmlessly through the air. No doubt Reeve had spent hours a day on a training field.

Grayson had been raised on one.

With one dagger he delivered a few painful cuts. Nothing fatal. Just enough to frustrate Reeve. Distract him. Draw other soldiers to the sound of the fight so the Hogans had a little more time to escape.

When he'd taken as much time as he dared, Grayson kicked

Reeve's knee so the man staggered. The hilt of Grayson's dagger found the captain's temple and Reeve crumpled to the icy ground.

Grayson took a step back, breathing deep. Air misted in front of him and his eyes raked the snow-crusted ground, stopping when he spotted his thrown dagger. Sheathing both knives, he strained his senses, but the woods were silent. Reeve must have entered the woods alone and the soldiers had been too deep in the village to respond to his call.

No reinforcements were coming.

Grayson glanced back at Reeve's still form, his grip on his knives flexing. He should return to camp now, before Reeve woke and could discover him missing. He'd done his job—he'd helped the family escape. No more was required.

He took a step forward, back toward camp, but instead of continuing on that path he found himself tracking the family.

It took a few minutes to locate them.

The woman startled at his approach, her hold on her youngest child cinching tight, but when recognition flashed in her eyes, her shoulders sagged in relief. "It's you. Thank the fates."

Not the response he usually got.

The older boy's eyes brightened. "You came back!"

"We should keep moving," Grayson said, probably too gruffly. He tried to even his tone. "I'll escort you to the river." He reached out and the woman was quick to lay her young son in his arms—her own visibly trembled from the strain of carrying the small boy.

Grayson wished he could slow their pace, but the family needed distance and he needed time to slip back into camp before Reeve made it back.

Several long minutes passed before they reached the Julne river and Grayson passed the sleeping child to the mother. His shoulders tensed at the loss of the weight. "You know the way from here?"

"Yes." Her chin quivered as she fought tears. "I don't know how to repay you. I don't even know your name . . ."

Grayson grabbed the pouch at his belt and dropped it in her hand. The weight of the coins stunned her; she nearly dropped it. "Find a physician," he told her. "Then get as far from here as you can. Don't linger in Kevid." It was too close, if Reeve insisted on continuing the search for her.

Tears still brimmed, but the woman smiled. "Fates bless you."

Brant stepped up to Grayson, a grin splitting his tired face. "I'm going to be like you one day. I'll even carry a sword."

"Pray you don't have to." Grayson hesitated, then pulled the small ball from his pocket. "Does this belong to you?"

"It's Garyn's." Brant took the ball. "He loves it."

Something in Grayson's chest tightened. "You'll take care of him?"

Brant's eyebrows drew together, confusion coloring his tone. "Of course. He's my brother." As if there could be no other answer.

A wry smile twisted Grayson's lips. "Good." He took a step back. "You need to go now."

"Thank you," the mother said again, before the family slipped into the night.

Grayson watched them disappear, a small smile still on his face.

CHAPTER 18

CLARE

"I THOUGHT TEA WAS NORMALLY SOMETHING ladies shared?"
Clare asked, taking a sip from her cup.

Prince Grandeur's lips curved smoothly. "Yes, well, I enjoy
a good cup of tea, and the list of people you can invite to practice
with is quite limited—you being a secret and all."

They were in a small sitting room near the royal apartments,
sharing a late morning tea. Clare fingered the fine porcelain cup
in her hands. It was delicate and hand-painted with small blue
daisies. It felt fragile in her hands—almost as fragile as she felt.

It had been two days since the Night Sigh incident. A shiver
skated down her spine every time the memories came. The jolt
of surprise she'd felt when she'd shaken awake in Bennick's
arms. The rush of confusion at finding herself in the sitting
room with Bennick talking sharply at her, his expression etched

in alarm. The bite of panic she'd felt when she tried to take a breath and couldn't.

In that terrorized moment, reality had hit her hard. She was a decoy. Her whole purpose was to be in danger—to face death —so Serene could live. She'd known it from the beginning and she'd thought she understood. But she'd gotten caught up in the day-to-day activities of her new life. Her lessons. Her new friends. But as she'd stood there, staring up at Bennick's pale face, she hadn't been able to stop the tears from falling.

Fear was cold and unshakable. She'd nearly died. Would have, if Bennick hadn't checked the room. She and Vera would have lost their lives. Thomas, Mark, Eliot—she never would have seen them again. She might still be killed and lose them forever, and they would never know the truth about her death. That gut-wrenching loss had pierced through everything, and when Bennick had seen her tears, his fingertips brushed her cheek before he pulled her into a firm embrace. She had leaned into him, let him support her as the tears fell. There was no point in regret, yet she wished she'd never gotten caught in the ambush that fateful night. She wished she hadn't been arrested and forced to make an impossible choice.

The good and bad were tangled together. Her family was cared for, yet she'd lost them. She was learning more than she'd ever dreamed, but she was treading the edge of a cliff—the slightest mistake would cause her to fall. She was building a new family with her friends here, yet she might lose them, too.

As if that wasn't enough to have on her mind, she also had the King's Ball to worry about. It was still nearly two weeks away, but the castle staff talked of little else and preparations had brought a bustling chaos to the castle. It would also be the first big event since Princess Serene's betrothal had been an-nounced, and Clare knew everyone was anxious to see how the nobility would act toward the princess.

Clare had learned last night that the king intended Clare to be the princess for the first half of the ball. If there was an attack or demonstration, he thought it would take place near the beginning, possibly even during his speech. He also wanted to see if Clare and Serene could seamlessly exchange places and fool Devendra's noble court. Clare knew the king was very aware the ball marked six weeks since Clare had become the decoy, which meant half her time to train was gone. He was eager to put her to the test.

Mistress Henley had been teaching Clare several dances, including the traditional round dance. Dancing lessons were better than her usual etiquette lessons, though Mistress Henley still drove her insane. At least Vera and her sister Ivonne, along with a few other maids, joined in the dance lessons. Clare didn't like being alone these days.

Prince Grandeur sighed. "You're drifting."

"Sorry." Clare straightened in her chair, tightening her hold on her teacup. "You're trying to cheer me up."

"Yes, and you're not doing your part. I need you cheered." The corner of his mouth rose, but she couldn't quite manage to copy the expression. His lips pursed. "Nothing more has been learned about the Night Sigh?"

Clare shook her head. "I don't think we'll get any answers." Which meant the would-be assassin would surely strike again.

Grandeur took another sip of tea. "Captain Markam is an exceptional bodyguard. I'm sure he's increased your security."

Yes, but would it be enough?

The prince leaned forward on his cushioned chair and set his cup on the saucer, which rested on the low table between them. The small clink of porcelain seemed loud in the otherwise empty room. "How did your Zennorian exam go?" he asked, in Zennorian.

She answered nearly at once—in Zennorian. "Very well, thanks to your help." He'd been finding her in the library again every couple of days to help her with whatever she was studying.

Grandeur grinned. "Amazing," he said in Devendran. "You truly have a gift for languages."

Heat bloomed in her cheeks, but she smiled. "It's the one thing I have some talent for. Ramus has me studying the High Families of Zennor, and memorizing their names and histories is exhausting."

"And utterly boring," Grandeur added.

"Well, since you and Serene are related to many of them—and Serene lived among them for a year—I don't have much choice but to learn about them."

"True." Balancing his forearms on his knees, he threaded his fingers together. "Your warmth and enthusiasm reminds me of how Serene used to be." He glanced away, shoving a hand through his short dark hair. "Is it wrong of me to sometimes wish she'd stayed in Zennor?" Before Clare could reply, he shook his head. "Forgive me. You don't need to be privy to every thought in my head. I just worry her temper will do more harm than good. If she does something to ruin this alliance with Mortise . . ."

"She seems willing to marry Serjah Desfan." *Willing* might be too strong a word.

He grunted. "Is she?" He shook his head. "Her attitude alone could jeopardize the peace we've all been working so hard to make, but what if she doesn't go to Mortise?"

Clare frowned. "Why wouldn't she?"

Grandeur hesitated, and when he spoke his words came slowly. "This can't be repeated, Clare."

Her belly tightened, though with nerves or anticipation she wasn't sure. "Of course," she whispered.

His expression remained guarded. "My father fears Serene intends to run away. Violating the treaty would spark a war."

Clare's eyebrows pulled together. "But, surely she wouldn't do that." Serene had her flaws, but the princess wouldn't betray Devendra.

Grandeur's eyes raised to Clare's. "It wouldn't be the first time she put her needs above Devendra's. She left for Zennor when she could have made such a difference here in Devendra." He exhaled, shaking his head. "I pray my father is wrong. We need an alliance with Mortise—Devendra's future depends on it. If Ryden strikes us alone, we would be doomed. Knowing King Henri and his evil spawn, it's only a matter of time before war comes." His brow wrinkled. "We have no choice but to ally with Mortise. And yet . . ."

A prickle of unease caught the back of her neck. "What?"

Grandeur swallowed. "There are things Serene has said. Things she's done since returning from Zennor. I'm afraid she picked up ideas. In my uncle's kingdom, the firstborn rules, regardless of gender."

Clare stared. "You think she wants to steal the throne?"

Grandeur's throat bobbed. "It sounds far-fetched when you say it, but I don't know her anymore. I haven't for years. I don't know what she's capable of. What if she *does* marry into the Mortisian line and she stirs them up against us? Or what if my father's right and she runs, starting a war?" He scrubbed a hand over his angular jaw and exhaled roughly. "I'm sorry. I don't mean to burden you."

Clare set aside her teacup. "Have you talked to Serene about this?"

He shot her a look. "Oh, yes, we chat all the time." He shook his head. "If there's a shred of truth to my fears, she'd only deny it."

Clare supposed that was true. But as much as she personally disliked Serene, she couldn't imagine the princess would turn against her own kingdom.

Grandeur eyed her. "May I beg a favor?"

"Of course."

The skin around his eyes tightened. "Would you be willing to keep an eye on my sister?" Clare blinked, but before she could speak he rushed ahead. "I know you don't see her often, but it would ease my mind to know you'd tell me if you heard or saw something—anything—that might prove dangerous for Devendra."

"You . . . want me to spy on Serene?" She had no real loyalty to the princess, yet the thought made the back of her scalp prickle with sudden unease.

Grandeur blew out his breath. "I didn't mean to make it sound so dramatic. I only hope you'd feel comfortable coming to me if you were to learn anything distressing."

Clare wet her lips as she leaned back. "Of course."

His expression tightened. "I don't mean to make you uncomfortable."

"You didn't," she said at once. Maybe too quickly.

But Grandeur smiled, and when she saw his tension ease, she felt a little better.

Clare stepped out of the princess's bedroom and paused when she saw the door to her private study cracked open. Clare had never seen anyone inside the locked room, and alertness sharpened her nerves. She could hear soft movement inside, and since the muted voices of Vera and her sister, Ivonne, came from the dressing room, Clare knew it wasn't one of the maids.

Thoughts of assassins and rebels flashed through her head, quickening her breath. Clare cut a look across the sitting room, toward the suite's main door. Should she call the guards?

Before she could, the study door dragged open and Clare came face-to-face with Serene.

The princess seemed just as shocked to see her standing there, though her features pinched almost at once. "Spying?" she asked crisply.

Clare flushed, her mind darting back to the conversation she'd had with Grandeur yesterday. "No."

Serene arched a dark brow and stepped closer, tugging the door shut behind her. "You have another reason for lurking outside my door?"

Something about the princess's tone broke through Clare's nerves. She straightened her spine. "I just stepped out of the bedroom. I wasn't spying on you."

The princess rolled her eyes and pulled a key from her pocket. She fit it into the lock and twisted, once again sealing her study. Curiosity pricked Clare; what was she hiding in there?

"I trust you've recovered from your first poisoning?" Serene asked.

Clare pulled her eyes from the door. "What?"

The princess turned and pocketed the slim key. "Well, at least your wits don't seem any more dulled than before. That must be a relief."

Clare's eyes narrowed. "There's no need to be cruel."

Serene shifted away from the closed door. "Perhaps you're right. I should throw myself at your feet and sob my thanks continually to you for stealing my life."

Clare bristled, but kept her voice smooth. "The Night Sigh

was actually quite relaxing. Maybe you should order some for yourself."

Serene snorted. "The kitchen maid has found a backbone. Fates help us all." She picked her way across the sitting room, halting near the suite's main door. She glanced over her shoulder. "I suppose I should thank you."

Clare's mouth tightened, her fingernails cutting into her palms. "Oh?"

The princess's eyes narrowed. "I'm trying to be sincere."

Clare huffed a short laugh. "Really?"

"Yes." A muscle thrummed along her jaw. "That night in the hallway, before you became my decoy, you did save my life—even if you threw me into the wall."

Clare stared at her. "What are you saying?"

Serene exhaled, irritation lining the sound. "I'm thanking you."

Surprise flared. "You are?"

The princess folded her arms. "Yes. But of course that same night you were blinded by my father's promises and conspired with him to be my imposter, so that mars your record."

Clare kept her tone mild. "You haven't actually said thank you."

Serene rolled her eyes, arms dropping as she pulled open the door and stepped into the hall.

Vera and Ivonne exited the dressing room, carrying dresses to mend. They seemed oblivious to Serene's visit to the suite and continued chatting with each other as they settled on the settee and began their work.

Clare would have preferred to join them in their simple task, especially since irritation still pricked her after her interaction with Serene, but a thick book on Mortisian culture waited on an end table. All she'd really learned was they had a celebration for everything—even funerals held traditions of feasting, dancing, music, and brightly colored clothes. She didn't really want to read it, but Ramus would be testing her tomorrow.

Clare plucked up the book and sat in an armchair, grateful for the background noise of the sisters' easy conversation. It was much better than studying in silence. It reminded her of home.

A quarter hour passed before there was a knock on the suite door. Clare rose before either of the maids could; she needed an excuse to stretch her legs. She pulled open the door and came face to face with Gavril Lank, the stable master's son. The burns trailing over the side of his face and down his neck caught her eye first, but she lifted her gaze to meet his and offered a smile. Gavril was often stationed outside the princess's room, especially since Bennick had increased the guard after the Night Sigh attack.

He tipped his head. "Miss Ellington."

"Please, call me Clare." She'd asked him before, but he seemed determined to be formal.

Gavril lifted a hand, brandishing a small stack of letters. "These arrived for you."

Clare knew they were from home—no one else would have written to her. Her hand trembled as she reached for the letters and when she flipped them over and saw Thomas's familiar handwriting, warmth spread through her chest. "I didn't know I could receive letters," she whispered.

Gavril frowned. "Why wouldn't you be able to?"

Clare swallowed, unable to answer. She tightened her hold on the letters and tears stung her eyes as she met Gavril's gaze. "Thank you."

The fervency in her voice seemed to take him off-guard. He shuffled his feet, eyebrows pulling downward. "I didn't do anything."

"You brought me news from home." She reached out her free hand and caught his fingers, squeezing gently. "Thank you, Gavril."

He tensed, a muscle in his jaw flexing. But he didn't pull away. "I hope it's good news."

Clare grinned and released his hand, closing the door when Gavril retreated. Twisting back toward the sitting room, she rifled through the letters. There were three—one each from Thomas, Mark, and Mistress Keller.

Vera's voice was low and confidential as she spoke to her sister. "Millie said she's getting worse. The physicians don't know what else to do."

Ivonne tugged her needle through the dress she was mending. "There's no cure for madness. Everyone knows that, and the commander's abuse drove her insane."

The commander. The words pierced through Clare's distraction and her head jerked up from her letters. "What did you say?"

Ivonne and Vera shot her a look, hands freezing in their work. Vera wet her lips. "Nothing."

Clare's eyes narrowed. "Are you talking about Commander Markam?"

The sisters eyed each other, and it was Ivonne who finally straightened in her seat. "Yes."

"Ivonne," Vera warned lowly.

"Oh, it's hardly a secret," Ivonne said, dropping her mending to her lap as she focused on Clare. "The commander used to beat his wife. And Bennick."

Ice shot through Clare's veins and her grip on the letters clenched. "What?"

Vera frowned at her sister, her small nose scrunching. "It's not our affair."

Ivonne ignored her, focused solely on Clare. "You met Millie—she's Lady Markam's maid and has been for years. She knows the family better than anyone. She says the commander used to abuse Bennick and the lady—and now Lady Markam is insane."

"She isn't insane." Vera glanced uneasily about the room, as if she expected the woman to suddenly appear. "She's just ill."

Ivonne's mouth thinned. "That's what the commander says. He doesn't want any stains on his name."

Clare's stomach rolled. The images that sparked to mind of a young Bennick—only Mark's age—being hit by the commander . . . everything inside her screamed. Having felt the commander's heavy hand, Clare shuddered to think of what he'd done to his wife and child. Fates, was Lady Markam still being abused? She couldn't believe Bennick would allow that. Even if he'd been helpless against his father once, he certainly wasn't now. But his hatred of his father made more sense. Clare felt her fury rising.

Vera picked up her sewing, her mouth a thin line. "This isn't our affair," she repeated. She turned to Clare. "You should read your letters. We don't have long before your dance lesson."

She was right. And while Clare could stand here reeling from the revelations about Bennick's past, she knew there would be no answers. Not right now, anyway. But she could have news from home, and she craved that.

She sank onto the settee and unfolded the thick parchment of the first letter, written in Thomas's deliberate script.

Dear Clare,

I hope you're well. We miss you every day, but things are good. We got even more toys and books and Mistress Keller is teaching us a lot. When will you come visit? I hope soon.

Eliot came by the other night. Don't worry, Mistress Keller didn't see him. He wanted to know if we had heard from you and he was worried when we hadn't. He said you're in danger, and now I'm worried for you. Please write and let me know you're safe.

Love, Thomas

Clare frowned as she re-read the lines about Eliot. Why couldn't he keep his fears to himself? With a sigh, she set the letter aside and opened Mark's letter. His handwriting was hurried; ink splotched the page and the words were a punch to her gut.

Clare,

I miss you. Thomas says you'll never come back. Please come back.

Mark

"Clare?" Vera asked, brow furrowed in concern.

She flashed a weak smile. "I'm missed, that's all."

Compassion lit Vera's eyes. "Would you like to write replies?"

Clare nodded, still overcome with her rioting emotions.

Vera left the room to fetch writing materials and Clare opened Mistress Keller's letter. It was a kindly written update on the boys, though she also expressed her worry for them. She encouraged Clare to write and to visit as soon as she was able.

Though Clare wanted to run home and see them now, she knew that wasn't an option. So she took the supplies Vera brought her and composed letters, including one for Eliot, reusing the same assurances that she was well and pleading for them to be happy. She prayed they'd listen. She couldn't find the words to tell them she would be accompanying the princess to Mortise. She didn't know if the king would let her visit them before the journey, but she would prefer to tell them in person if at all possible.

She addressed the four letters, but someone rapped on the door before she could seal them. Wilf in all his terrifying intensity was on the other side, ready to escort them to Mistress Henley for the dance lesson.

Clare wasn't about to argue with him. She left the unsealed letters on the table and followed Vera and Ivonne out.

CHAPTER 19

BENNICK

BENNICK'S MEETING WITH KING NEWLAN was not pleasant. The king was still livid about the Night Sigh incident and that nothing more had been learned about the would-be assassin. The king had also learned about Wilf's outburst on the training field and he made it clear that one more misstep from Wilf would mark the end of the man's career.

Bennick had been the princess's lead bodyguard for two years, but as the king reprimanded him and second-guessed every decision he'd made in the last couple weeks, Bennick had felt like a novice. With Newlan glaring down at him, it didn't matter that Bennick had worked hard to win his place. It didn't matter that he'd proven to the king, the princess, himself, and his men that he could manage this position.

When Bennick was finally dismissed he left the spacious

throne room and hurried through the halls, trying to shake the dark mood away as he quickened his step. What he needed was to see Clare. He might even reach her in time to escort her to her dance lesson.

Bennick was always eager to see her. Their time in training wasn't enough, though he relished every moment. It was a good thing Clare was a diligent student; he didn't think she'd noticed how much he studied her during their sessions. He tried to focus, and the discipline he'd learned in the academy saved him—until he caught her sweet scent as she spun away from him, or her back pressed against his chest. Sometimes all it took was seeing her flushed face, a grin twisting her features as she stared up at him in triumph, the sunlight catching in her hair. Her eyes danced, and he couldn't breathe.

Clare was beautiful. Bennick had known that the first moment he saw her, even with her stained apron and loose braid. She was soft and kind, strong and resilient. The love she had for her family burned in her eyes and her dedication to them staggered him. She remained undaunted despite the long days and challenging lessons, withstanding even the danger with a quiet confidence that astounded him. The more time he spent with her, the more fascinated he became, and what he felt for her . . . that was growing, too, becoming more than mere attraction and treading deeper than friendship.

Gavril stood outside the princess's open door and Bennick tried to bury the rush of regret. Clare was already gone, or else Wilf would have been at the door.

He greeted Gavril and glanced into the open room. A page stood at a low table in the sitting room, his back to the door.

"Clare received letters from home," Gavril explained. "When they left, Clare mentioned she'd finished her replies, so I sent for a page."

"Sir?" The young boy edged forward, holding the folded letters. "They're not sealed, but the wax is out, like she just forgot. The one I opened looks finished."

"You read her letter?" Bennick asked, arching a brow.

The boy's ears reddened. "Not really. I just saw it was signed. Should I seal them?"

"And have you manage to read the rest?" Bennick shook his head and stretched out a hand.

The page passed the letters over and Bennick entered the room. He perched on the edge of the settee and lifted the stick of wax, holding it over a flickering flame to warm it. He sealed the letters, and while the wax finished drying he flipped one over. Clare's handwriting was small and precise. Not the artistic curls the ladies at court practiced, but elegant in its simplicity. It suited her. His mouth tugged into a smile. Then he noticed the name those careful letters formed and his smile fell.

Eliot Slaton

Tension coiled his shoulders as he scanned the address. The barracks was correct, and the rank. Fates. How did Clare know Eliot Slaton?

"Sir?" Bennick's eyes cut to the page, who shuffled his feet impatiently. "It's probably dry now."

Bennick's fingers pinched the stiff paper. For a brief moment, he thought he wouldn't give it up. Then he handed the letters to the page. The boy turned to leave, but before he could reach the door, the question leapt free. "Which letter did you read?"

The page twisted around. "I didn't read it, Captain. Honest."

Bennick forced his expression to loosen. "You're not in any

trouble, but do you remember which one?"

Obviously fearing a reprimand, the boy moved slowly as he lifted Slaton's letter.

Bennick's heart thumped a little faster. "Did you see how she began the letter?"

"Just the man's name. Eliot."

She called him Eliot. They were familiar, then.

Bennick swallowed, though his voice remained a little too tight. "Did you see how her signature went? You mentioned she signed it."

"She did, sir. Just with her name." He paused. "Well, she said, 'Much love, Clare'."

Bennick dug in his pocket and tossed a coin to the boy, and as he dashed off, Bennick raked a hand through his hair. The image of Slaton's name written in Clare's hand was seared into his mind. Why would she be corresponding with him?

Much love, Clare.

The obvious reason soured his stomach.

CHAPTER 20

GRAYSON

GRAYSON STEERED HIS HORSE UP THE narrow mountain path, soldiers riding in front and behind him. Steep inclines were edged with drifts of crusted snow and dead leaves sprang up on both sides of the trail. Tree branches hung over the road, a mix of skeletal oaks and heavy pine boughs. White, gray, and dark green were the prominent colors in the winter-locked mountains, but the weeds along the ice-edged river bled with muted red, dull gold, and brittle brown. Breath misted in the sharp morning air from both man and beast. Hooves clopped, leather creaked, and soldiers talked and laughed with each other.

They should reach the next village by nightfall, where Grayson would once again enforce his father's tax. It was a never-ending cycle and he was beyond ready to return to Lenzen—to Mia.

During these long rides his thoughts drifted to the small family he'd saved in Gevell. He remembered the tears of gratitude welling in the mother's tired eyes. The eight-year-old boy's quirk of a smile, his insistence that he would be like Grayson someday. Fates willing, they'd made it to Kevid and the mother had found a physician for herself and the littlest boy.

Sometimes when Grayson squeezed his fist, he could still feel the small ball in his hand. It made the corner of his mouth lift. What he'd done didn't make up for all the wrongs he committed in his father's name, but it was a piece of rebellion he could always hold.

Reeve nudged his horse beside Grayson's. "I'd hoped we'd turn a higher profit for His Majesty." Reeve had grown more hot-tempered since losing the Hogan family in Gevell. He was quick to snap at the soldiers and Grayson had felt the man's glare more than once when he thought Grayson wasn't looking. "I pray the king will be understanding," the captain continued. "I won't have this held against me."

Grayson sighed. "I'm sure the promotion you crave will be yours soon." His father had a habit of rewarding evil.

"It can't come soon enough." Reeve shifted on his horse, the sunlight coming through the pine boughs catching the emerald in his uniform. "The great war is coming. I intend to be in a position of importance when it does."

The war. Soldiers whispered about the anticipated conflict like it was a prayer. As if the battle was a holy rite, a chance for Ryden to correct all the generational wrongs done by Devendra and Mortise. Grayson hoped the war remained unrealized. He didn't think his blackening soul would survive it.

"My grandfather was a general," Reeve continued. "A hero in the Battle of Sine. He raised me to live up to his legend, and I intend to."

Tension climbed up Grayson's back, as much from Reeve's tone as his topic. The Battle of Sine had been a horrific massacre of innocents. It wasn't anything to be proud of. The city's only crime was unknowingly harboring Mortisian spies. And Grayson's grandfather had ordered the deaths of nearly every man, woman, and child in the city.

"Serving with the Black Hand will elevate my status," Reeve said. "But only if we're successful." His eyes drifted to the daggers on Grayson's belt. "Those are fine weapons. They'd do well in a close fight."

The hairs on Grayson's arms rose. Reeve couldn't know about his involvement in the Hogans' escape. If he had identified Grayson, he would have accused him days ago.

Grayson forced his voice to remain level. "They've proven effective many times."

Reeve opened his mouth, but he didn't have a chance to reply. A startling roar ripped through the air and men poured down the steep slopes by the road, an array of weapons in their hands. Hunting bows. Rusted swords. Hoes. Rocks.

Peasants were attacking the patrol.

Grayson fisted the reins, jerking his horse to a stop. He barked orders, heart slamming as he twisted his mount around. The soldiers were well-trained; swords were drawn, bows were raised. When the peasants reached them, soldiers swung weapons from atop their mounts. The horses were just as trained as the men —they didn't flee, even as they tossed their heads and pawed the ground while the battle raged around them.

The violent frenzy chilled Grayson's blood even as his body flashed with heat. He fought alongside the soldiers, though the patrol was horribly outnumbered. Grayson was soon surrounded, and though he spun his sword and hacked at the men trying to kill him, his cloak was snatched from behind and he was dragged off his horse.

He crashed onto his back on the muddy road, the breath knocked out of his lungs. He blinked, vision hazing, then sharpening. A savage face hung over him. It was a middle-aged man with long red hair tangled around his face. The peasant reared back, a bloody axe clutched in his hands. With a roar, the man plunged the axe down, toward Grayson's chest.

Grayson rolled. He felt the swipe of the axe as it blurred past him and slammed into the earth. The attacker jerked the axe free, dead leaves fluttering in the air, but Grayson lunged before he could swing again. He buried a knife in the man's side, all the way to the hilt. He watched as the man crumpled—a threat, then nothing. The axe thumped harmlessly to the ground.

Grayson's chest rose and fell sharply and his nostrils flared. Crouched low on the road, he clutched the bloody knife. Howls and screams cut through the crisp mountain air. Swords slashed and struck, the familiar crash of weapons and bodies locked in furious struggle. Horses snorted, keened, and pounded their hooves.

A twig snapped.

Grayson whirled, thrusting his dagger into a peasant's abdomen before the man could run him through with a rusted blade. When the man fell, Grayson saw a young soldier fumbling to draw his sword, two peasants cornering him against a pine.

Grayson darted forward. He swung his sword and his dagger flashed. Two more men fell, dead.

The soldier stared at him with rounded eyes and a sweaty forehead. He clutched his sword, still half in the sheath, and gulped. He couldn't have been more than fifteen years old.

Grayson ground his teeth. Weakness would get them both killed. "Draw your sword," he snarled. "Kill them or die."

The soldier jerked a nod, using both hands to yank out his blade.

Grayson spun, cutting through the next attacker and the next. He used every skill his family had ever beat into him. This is what he'd been trained to do and any other thought had no place here. He focused on his actions—the balance in his stance, the flex and release of his muscles as he swung his sword, stabbed with his dagger, bent away from an enemy's blow only to swing back around and end them.

Time blurred, but he knew it passed. The fight was waning. Even though the peasants outnumbered them, they were no match against trained soldiers. Against him.

As the battle eased, Grayson's eyes swept the scene. He tracked the last skirmishes, noted the fallen horses, the bodies of soldiers and peasants strewn across the road.

He watched as Reeve was kicked to the ground. His sword flew from his hand, bouncing out of reach. The captain blinked, clearly dazed from the fall. The peasant stood over him, pitchfork raised, ready to shove it into Reeve's unprotected gut.

There was a moment of hesitation. A split second of pause before Grayson lunged, driving his long sword through the peasant's back.

The man seized, muscles locking before he fell, sliding off the blade.

Reeve inhaled raggedly. He gaped up at Grayson, lip bloody, fists pressed into the ground. His eyes were still flooded with terror but shock edged in, lined with relief.

Grayson tightened his hold on his bloody weapons, knuckles flaring with pain. He stared down at Reeve, his expression hard, but he didn't respond to the silent question in Reeve's gaze. He turned on his heel and walked away, leaving the captain staring after him.

CHAPTER 21

CLARE

CLARE'S FINGERS DANCED OVER HER loose braid, feet dragging a little as she made her way to Serene's large bed. The scent of lilacs pervaded the room, reminding her of the Night Sigh that had been masked by the heavy perfume. Several days had passed, but fear still stabbed whenever she thought of that night.

Vera always offered to assist Clare into bed, but even after a month at the castle, Clare preferred to do it herself. She pulled the quilt down and slid into the soft bed, yawning before she blew out the bedside lamp. The afterglow of the flame remained in her vision as she blinked and laid against the many pillows, letting the darkness pool around her. She pushed most of the pillows away and curled on her side, her arms stretched out with one hand resting beneath a satin pillow.

Something brushed her curled fingertips.

A chill tracked down her spine. She jerked her hand out from under the pillow, fingers dancing over her prickling skin, but she found nothing.

Rubbing out the uncomfortable feeling, Clare slowly pushed up in the bed. A chill lifted the hairs on her arms. She half-expected to see a deeper shadow in the darkness—an assassin standing over her, dagger raised. Her pulse kicked, instincts screaming. Her palms were braced against the mattress, senses straining against the heavy darkness and oppressive silence.

A gentle tap hit against the smallest finger on her left hand.

Clare snatched her hand away and slid to the edge of the bed, fumbling for the bedside lamp. With shaking hands she managed to light the wick and light flooded the room.

Clare froze when she saw the spider curled beside her pillow.

It was huge. Easily the size of her spread hand and nearly as thick. The brown spider sat so still, yet somehow Clare knew it could move lightning fast. Lungs locked, she slid slowly back, only shifting one muscle at a time. Panic keened inside her. A whimper stuck in her sealed throat—she didn't dare scream.

Then she felt a horrible brush against her ankle, and she stopped breathing. Terror choked her, because she could feel the long, hairy legs scrape over her skin, moving up her leg.

There was a second spider.

Instinct begged her to kick, scream, shake free of the blankets, but a deeper instinct held her immobile. Fear, yes, but also a whisper of reason that told her one false move could kill her. These spiders weren't from Devendra, and if they were in her bed—the princess's bed—she could only imagine the terrible venom they carried.

Trembling, Clare bit her lip until she tasted blood. Her white-knuckled fists were pressed into the bed beside her and her eyes darted between the spider still waiting beside her pillow to her sheet-covered leg, and finally the closed door that sealed her in the room.

"Help." It was a croak, but even that slight noise made the spider next to her skitter, legs grasping the rumpled sheet.

Tears burned Clare's eyes and slipped down her cheeks, but she didn't brush them away. Everything in her world focused on the feel of that large spider slowly dragging up her bare leg. When it reached the slight curve of her knee, it hesitated. The spider's weight wasn't much, but it was everything. The spider brushed tentatively at the twisted hem of her nightgown. Clare could actually see the thin sheet rustle as the spider tried to navigate the best way to continue its climb.

From the corner of her eye, the other spider moved. Her heart crashed in her chest and her lungs strained. It was crawling for her fist. She had to move. She couldn't have two of those monsters touching her.

At the same time the spider's first leg brushed her knuckles, the spider on her knee slid, dropping off her. It thumped against the mattress, but that was lost in the sound of Clare's scream. She tore from the bed, ripping away from the sheet and the spiders. Her shoulder slammed into the wall and her bare feet burned against the cold stone floor.

She was still screaming, shoving her hands over her arms, her legs, her hair—she had to scrub the tingling sensations away. Phantom spiders were crawling all over her, and no matter how hard she rubbed her skin, the prickling remained. Breath shuddered out of her, hitching her sobs.

"Clare!" The bedroom door banged open and Bennick's gaze sliced over the room, snagging on her. Two strides and he was in front of her, grasping her shoulders. "What happened? What's wrong?"

Her hands knotted in his shirt, gripping him so tightly her

fingertips were already going numb. Her cry had pinched off, but she couldn't speak.

Wilf and Venn barreled into the room. Clare knew when they saw the danger, because they both drew up short.

"Holy fates!" Venn cursed.

Bennick jerked his head around, following Venn's eyes to the bed. His hold on her spasmed and he swore as he twisted back on Clare. "Were you bitten?"

She wrenched her eyes away from the bed and stared into Bennick's panicked eyes. She managed to shake her head, but words were still beyond her.

His fingers flexed around her arms. "Kill it," he snapped at Venn.

"*You* kill it!" he spluttered.

"Venn—"

Wilf shoved around Venn and slammed his dagger straight through the spider's middle. The many legs jerked, but the spider couldn't bolt—it was pinned to the bed.

"Ogai," he grunted. "One bite will kill a grown man."

Venn's eyes bugged. "And you just killed it like it was nothing? Are you *insane*?"

A shiver ripped through Clare and Bennick's hold tightened, one arm banding around her waist. She couldn't stop shaking. "Another," she gasped.

Bennick tensed. "What?"

"There's another," she said, speaking past the bile that burned her throat.

Wilf snagged the blankets and ripped them off the bed. As the linen fluttered, his dagger flashed again, slamming down.

Clare shuddered and Bennick cupped her face. "Clare, look at me." Her eyes slid to his dark gaze. She'd never seen his jaw so rigid. "Are you sure you weren't bitten?"

"I'm fine." She sucked in a breath and tightened her hold on his uniform.

Bennick's hands dropped, but didn't leave her. They brushed over her shoulders, her arms, her back, checking to make sure nothing clung to her. His perusal was quick and sure, ending only after he'd stroked a hand through her loose hair. "You're safe," he whispered.

Her body shook and she planted her forehead against his chest, sagging against him. His hand wrapped around the back of her head, holding her there against his drumming heart.

Bennick lifted his chin. "I've never heard of an Ogai spider. How did you know it, Wilf?"

The bedding stopped flying as Wilf finished his search. "I saw my share while fighting in Mortise," he said, his voice a low rumble that filled the room. "It was long ago, but the Ogai is hard to forget."

Clare shuddered. Fates, how would she ever sleep in this bed again?

"Someone tried to kill Serene with demon spiders from Mortise." Venn's swallow was audible. "Where would one even find them in Devendra?"

"The shadow markets," Wilf said at once. "You can buy anything in Lower Iden if you know who to ask."

Bennick eased back from Clare, fingers brushing her wet cheek, prompting her to look up. "Go with Vera. We'll search the entire room."

Clare finally noticed Vera standing inside the room, her blonde braid resting over her shoulder. The maid's eyes were locked on Wilf, who stood beside the bed, dagger lifted, the second spider still skewered on his blade. Clare's belly lurched, but it wasn't the dead spider that chilled her blood. It was the feral gleam in Wilf's eyes.

"Clare?"

Her gaze flew to Bennick. Concern bled from him but she managed to pull away from his comforting hold. "I'm fine," she whispered, though fates knew she wasn't.

His eyebrows drew together but he didn't question her. She slid past him, grateful to reach Vera, who wrapped an arm around her back and helped draw her from the bedroom.

They sat on the settee in the sitting room, a single lamp glowing in the dark. Clare pulled her feet up, knees pressed against her chest. Her toes curled into the cushion, safe off the floor, and a tremor shook her. Her thoughts—which had been consumed by the terror of the spiders—were now racing. Tripping.

Bennick, Wilf, and Venn spoke in low tones in the other room, their words an indistinguishable murmur.

Vera's face was pale in the semi-darkness. "First the Night Sigh, now this—how is someone getting so close?"

Clare's fingernails bit into her palms. "Wilf said the spiders are from Mortise."

"Night Sigh is, too," Vera murmured. "Do you think that's a coincidence?"

Clare's lips pursed. "Wilf knew about the spiders and he wasn't afraid to kill them."

"Wilf isn't afraid of anything," the maid snorted.

Clare's expression didn't change. Her thoughts were no longer jumbled, but perfectly clear.

Vera saw the steadiness in Clare's eyes and read the thoughts there. Her features pinched. "You think *Wilf* had something to do with this?"

Clare swallowed past the dryness in her throat. "As a guard he has access to the room. He was on duty when the Night Sigh was brought in. And he seemed to know where to purchase those spiders."

"That doesn't make any sense," she protested softly. "Wilf is a trusted bodyguard!"

"Doesn't he make you uneasy?"

"Of course! He's terrifying. But he's no traitor."

Ice needled through Clare's veins. "He doesn't want the alliance."

"He's not alone in that," Vera pointed out. "People are fighting in the streets about it."

"But he's unstable—volatile. I watched him attack Bennick, Venn, and Cardon on the training field." Not to mention she still clearly remembered the fury in his gaze as he'd strangled her the night she'd saved Serene's life.

What if Wilf's anger hadn't been because he thought Clare was one of the assassins, but because she'd saved Serene's life? What if Wilf had been allied with the assassins? Would he go that far to stop the peace? Did his hatred run that deep?

Vera shook her head. "It doesn't make sense. Wilf can't be trying to kill Serene—he knows you were the one in that bed."

She nodded slowly. "You're right. But if I die and he can frame Mortise, then the peace is ruined. And he wouldn't even have to sacrifice Serene to do it. Just me."

"You're forgetting something," Vera said.

"What?"

Vera eyed her. "Bennick trusts Wilf. Don't you trust Bennick?"

"Of *course* I trust Bennick. But I know what Wilf means to him. He may not see things clearly."

"And you do?" she asked.

Clare had no answer. Adrenaline still spiked through her and she wasn't sure if it sharpened her thoughts or made her jump at shadows.

But when Bennick and the others stepped out of the bedroom, declaring it safe, Clare couldn't ignore the prickle that rushed over her skin when her stare connected with Wilf's. Something dark lived in his eyes, and it stared back at her.

CHAPTER 22

ELIOT

THE THORN WAS PACKED TONIGHT. People swarmed the common room, voices booming, and music poured from the musicians in the corner. There were no empty tables, so Eliot stood against the back wall. With the King's Ball set for tomorrow night, the whole city was in a festive mood.

Eliot couldn't fight his scowl as Michael, his best friend, went to grab them drinks at the crowded bar. He'd been scowling since he'd received the letter from Clare, each word pounding inside his skull. Snatches of it repeated constantly. *I'm doing well. The princess's bodyguards have my confidence.*

Eliot didn't trust anyone to keep Clare safe in that den of vipers—certainly not the princess's lead bodyguard, Markam.

Don't worry. I'm safe.

She wasn't safe. Eliot knew the danger anyone close to the

princess faced. Fates, the same day Clare had left to live at the castle, Eliot had learned about an attack on a royal carriage. He'd known it was the carriage that had taken her away. He'd quizzed his captain in the city guard until he'd learned that a castle maid had been involved in the attack, but that she had escaped with her life.

Eliot hadn't had a good night's sleep since.

"Are you going to tell me what's bothering you?" Michael asked, his voice rising over the din.

Eliot straightened and accepted the offered tankard. He'd been so distracted by his thoughts he hadn't noticed Michael's return. "Nothing. I'm fine."

Michael was a head taller than Eliot and his accent was slightly rounded from growing up near Mortise. He had a thicker build and lighter skin, but they were brothers in all but blood. His brown hair curled over his brow, nearly shielding his green eyes. He usually wore a grin, but at the moment his square face was pulled into a frown. Eliot hated lying to him, but he didn't want Michael to know about Clare's new position in the castle.

When Michael continued to eye him, Eliot snorted. "It's nothing. One of my moods. You know me."

"I do, which is why I'm worried." Michael shifted, thumbing the mug's worn handle. "You've been moody for weeks. If the concern is more coin for your family, I've always said you can take some of my wages."

Eliot took a sip of the biting drink. Temptation licked at him, but he knew Clare wouldn't reconsider, even if he could give her more coin. She was too stubborn. "No, thank you."

Michael's brow furrowed, but he didn't press. Eliot took another swallow and the ale warmed through him, bringing him muted peace like a good drink always did.

Men shifted around them, laughing and bellowing at each

other, elbows and shoulders knocking. Eliot shielded his drink from a red-faced man who staggered close, and by the time he passed, Geflin and Paven were standing before them, gripping drinks of their own.

Eliot straightened. The ale he'd drunk settled in his empty stomach and exacerbated the hollowness that had been there since he'd read Clare's letter, but he needed to put that from his mind and focus on the issue at hand—because certainly, there was an issue. Paven and Geflin wouldn't have arranged this meeting otherwise.

Geflin was middle-aged with ample muscle covering his body. He was a blacksmith who did occasional work in the castle prison. He smelled like his smithy—smoke, metal, and leather. His wild red hair and thick beard drew as much attention as his size, but the glances were passing. He made people nervous, even when he edged out a smile.

Paven was older, his gray hair gathered at the nape of his neck in a short ponytail, and wrinkles framed his eyes. He'd been a soldier before losing his arm during a bout of border violence with Mortise. The stump ended just below his shoulder. His captain had given him a handful of coins, courtesy of the king, and he was required to turn in his uniform. A soldier without a sword arm was useless. He hadn't been able to find decent work since.

"You weren't followed?" Geflin asked, his voice barely heard over the crowd's roar. There was a reason they met here; any private conversation was lost in the roaring noise of the tavern.

"No," Michael assured him.

Paven darted a look around, but no one paid them any attention. They were a rugged group of men like any other collected in the room. "As you know, our last attempt against the princess failed."

"It should have worked," Geflin muttered. "The keys I made

were good. The princess must have had an increased guard, even for walking down the fates-blasted hallway."

Eliot threw back another drink, wincing as it burned his throat. He'd known the rebels had been planning a strike, but he hadn't known his sister would stumble into it. It was a fates-blessing she hadn't been hurt, but it had gotten her into a mess, hadn't it? Now she was the princess's blasted maid. Guilt soured on his tongue.

Paven ignored Geflin's muttering. "We've been blessed with a new opportunity."

Michael perked up, anticipation lending a rasp to his voice. "You have a mission for us?"

"Nothing concrete," Paven said, shooting another look around—he was always wary. "We can't risk using you too soon." Because Eliot and Michael were soldiers. Valuable. Their time would come. "For the first time in two years, we have an opportunity to recruit someone close to the princess."

Geflin took a pull from his tankard, then spoke just over the swarm of noise. "She has a new maid."

Every part of Eliot locked. His body. His breath. His thoughts. The common room rippled with bodies and laughter, but it was muted to his ears.

The rebels knew about Clare.

Eliot wanted to curse the fates, or Clare—or, better still, himself. He should have realized the rebels would find out. They were always looking for any change around the princess.

The others seemed oblivious to his stiffening. "What do we know about her?" Michael asked, his green eyes nearly glowing in the lamplight.

"Not much," Paven said. "That's where you come in."

"Use your palace connections to ask some basic questions," Geflin said. "We want to know who she is, who her family is, where her sympathies lie. If she can be turned or bought—" He grinned a little. "Or threatened."

Eliot's jaw hardened, but Michael nodded beside him. "I'll play dice with Bevins tomorrow and ask what he knows about her."

Bevins wasn't a rebel, but he was an idiot. The palace guardsman didn't know it, but he was one of their best informants.

"Don't rush this," Paven said. "We want results, but we want good ones. Ever since the princess's marriage was announced, we've been plotting the best options. This girl could play into our plans nicely."

A war rioted inside Eliot. He wanted to go to Clare now and demand she go home. But he'd already tried every persuasion he could—what else could he do to convince her, short of telling her about his involvement with the rebels? He couldn't do that. It would put her in danger, and he couldn't betray the rebellion.

He could tell the rebels that Clare was his sister. If he did, they might feel more confident that she would join the cause. They wouldn't hurt her. Or would they? The rebels could be ruthless—they had to be, to fight a ruthless king. But if Eliot kept silent, Clare would surely get hurt. The rebels would try to recruit her, and if that failed . . .

His eyes drifted to Geflin and Paven, his body tightening. There was no easy answer. And whatever he did right now would carry serious consequences. Silence, or confession? Neither one felt right.

"Eliot?" Michael frowned at him, finally picking up on his tension.

He forced his teeth to unclench. "I'm fine."

Geflin's eyes narrowed. "You don't look fine."

Paven's mouth also tugged into a frown. "I can see your thoughts spinning, boy. Let's hear them."

Eliot lowered his mug, fingers clenched around the worn handle. The danger surrounding Clare was growing. He had to protect her, at least from the rebels. "The new maid is my sister."

Shock splashed their faces, but the emotions that crossed afterward varied. Hurt flashed in Michael's eyes; Paven began to smile, and Geflin eyed him with suspicion. "Why didn't you come to us about this?" the blacksmith asked roughly.

"I only just found out," Eliot lied, his throat dry despite all he'd drunk.

"Do you think she would join our cause?" Paven asked.

"Yes." Another lie. Clare wouldn't be able to stomach the grittiness of the rebellion, and Eliot would never put her in that position. But they didn't need to know that. "I can sway her to our side, but I need time." Time to convince her to return home.

Geflin scowled, but Paven nodded. "We can offer whatever assistance you need."

"Thank you," Eliot said.

It wasn't long before Paven wandered away. A few minutes later, it was Geflin's turn. Before leaving, he pinned Eliot with a look. "I eagerly await your report, Slaton." Warning edged his words, but Eliot ignored that.

Once they were alone, Michael turned on him. "You just lied through your teeth!"

"I don't know what you're—"

He choked on a hoarse laugh. "You'll *recruit* her? We both know you won't." He shook his head. "You're walking the edge of treason."

Eliot snorted. "That's sort of expected in a rebel."

"This isn't a joke."

"No," he agreed. "This is my sister's life."

A man hooted across the room and bursts of laughter rose.

Michael hesitated, dropping his voice even lower. "We've

never had anyone that close to the princess. She wouldn't have to do anything dangerous. Just leave a door unlocked, or pass us information."

"No. I'm going to convince her to go back home."

Michael stiffened. "You've known for weeks. That's why you've been so irritable. You tried to convince her to leave, but she wouldn't listen."

"That holds no bearing—"

"Of course it does! She isn't going home. Don't you want to make her as safe as possible?"

"You think recruiting her will keep her safe?"

"If she knows about the attacks, she'll know what to avoid."

"My sister isn't a traitor. She doesn't have what it takes to make those decisions. To sacrifice people. Recruiting her would be a mistake."

Michael exhaled sharply, reluctant acceptance in the sound. "Paven and Geflin will expect a report."

"I'll stall for time until I can convince her to leave."

Michael used his free hand to rub his temple. "This is going to bite you faster than a rabid dog."

"Better me than her."

Michael's hand dropped suddenly. He blinked. "Oh, fates."

Eliot's defenses rose, tension flooding him. "What?"

He glanced at Eliot, mouth pursed.

Unease danced up Eliot's spine. "What?"

"Trust me, it won't improve your mood."

"Michael . . ."

He exhaled slowly. "I think I saw your sister today, on the training field. I thought maybe it was just another castle maid, but now I think on it, she resembled you."

Eliot's blood chilled. His sister was on the training field, squaring off against a soldier who was probably double her size? But then, he should have realized she'd be trained; every direct servant to the royals learned to fight, in case they were required as a last line of defense.

Eliot pinched the bridge of his nose. "Perhaps it's a good thing. Maybe this will convince her of the danger."

Michael sipped at his drink, gaze wandering.

Eliot's scalp prickled. "What aren't you telling me?"

His friend eyed him. "I saw who she was training with. It . . . it was Markam."

The name hit Eliot with all the power of a boulder. He was a little surprised he didn't stumble back. Sparks of anger and protectiveness leapt over his skin, tightening every nerve in his body. His tone darkened. "Did he hurt her?"

Michael searched Eliot's hard face, caution sparking in his eyes. "Not that I saw."

That didn't reassure him. The image of Markam coming at his sister, even with a practice blade, infuriated him. Markam had already hurt Clare, Eliot was sure of it.

His vision hazed red and he shoved his free hand through his hair, cursing. He needed to get her out of there. Away from the princess and the rebels—and from Markam.

CHAPTER 23

GRAYSON

EVERY MUSCLE IN GRAYSON'S BODY ACHED, but as he made his way down into the castle dungeon, his stiff movements came faster. It was late, but he was home. He'd made a rapid report to his father before leaving Reeve to make his private report to the king. He prayed Reeve wouldn't mention his suspicions about Grayson saving the Hogan family. After saving Reeve's life, he hoped the captain would keep that between them—a lie for a life.

Whatever happened, he'd deal with it later. Right now, he needed to see Mia.

Fletcher said nothing as he unlocked the cell door and Grayson stepped inside the dimly lit room. His eyes hadn't even adjusted before he was hit with Mia's body. Her arms swung around his neck and he latched onto her, holding them both steady. His throat was tight; no words could squeeze out. He buried his head in her shoulder, inhaling her lavender and jasmine scent and warming his bristled jaw against her smooth cheek. His hand slid up and down her spine, bringing her even closer.

She squeezed him so hard her slender arms trembled. "I missed you so much," she said, voice cracking.

A muscle feathered along his jaw. He pressed his forehead into the curve of her neck and shoulder. Her skin was soft and hot against his chilled body. "I missed you, too."

Mia continued to crush herself against him, arms locked around his neck, a frantic edge spiking her words. "I had so many nightmares. I saw you die." Her breathing hitched. "You could have died and I'd never know. No one would tell me. I—I can't lose you. I'll go mad, I know I will. What if you never came back?"

The panic fraying her voice forced him to pull back. He held her face in his hands and thumbed away the tears that leaked from her wild brown eyes. "Mia, I'm fine. I'm here. I'll always come back to you."

"I can't go back to a life without you," she whispered, blinking rapidly. "I can't." A shudder wracked her body.

A bolt of unease shot down Grayson's spine. He slid his hand up to her brow, and even through his leather glove, heat warmed his palm. His heartbeat stuttered. He tore his glove off with his teeth and pressed the back of his bare hand to her forehead.

She was hot with fever.

He swore. He should have realized it sooner. Would have, if not for the chill still in his bones and his cursed gloves. Grayson swept her into his arms, cradling her against his chest. Her grip around his neck didn't loosen and her tears fell against his shirt as she continued to cry.

"Fletcher!" he roared.

The lock fumbled before the door swung open. The old guard's eyes rounded at the sight of them.

Grayson strode forward. "Out of my way," he barked.

The old guard's throat bobbed, but he held his ground in blocking the doorway. Grayson might have been impressed, if he wasn't ready to snap the guard's neck.

"What's wrong with her?" Fletcher asked.

Grayson grit his teeth. "She has a fever."

The old man's eyes darted over Mia, frowning. "That can be treated here, by her caretaker. Those are the king's orders."

Grayson's nostrils flared. His rage was only partially for the man in front of him. Years ago, Grayson had once begged Henri for a physician to tend Mia—she'd been throwing up, unable to eat anything. His father had made it clear no resources were to be wasted on Mia unless she was on her deathbed. Henri had also kept Grayson so busy with extra training he couldn't be with her while she struggled to recover with Mama's sporadic care.

He'd learned his lesson; he wouldn't draw his father's eye toward Mia unless absolutely necessary.

Grayson twisted away from Fletcher with another curse. Mia whimpered as he lowered her onto the bed, and that small sound of pain cut him. He needed to cool her down.

He was aware of Fletcher leaving the room, closing the door and locking it, but his focus was on helping Mia. He killed the fire in the stove before removing his second glove and rolling Mia's sleeves up her arms, letting the slight chill in the air brush her heated skin. He used the tepid water in the washbasin to wet a rag and then sat on the edge of the bed beside her.

Grayson had barely touched the wet rag to her temple when she grabbed his wrist, fingers digging into his skin. Her face twisted as she wept, shuddering with a pain he didn't know how to soothe. "I'm sorry," she cried. "I'm sorry I let go."

His heart spasmed. She was delirious. She probably didn't even see him. Not really. He strangled the cloth in his fist. "You're going to be fine," he said, forcing his voice to remain even.

Tears rolled down her cheeks and her mouth trembled. "It's my fault," she gasped. A rapid spill of words followed, but Grayson couldn't understand her. Zennorian, Mortisian, Devendran, Rydenic—the languages twisted together, garbled and nonsensical. But her agitation was building, her sobs shaking her body.

He grasped her wrist, squeezing hard as he leaned over. "Mia, stop. You're here with me. You're safe." Promise throbbed in his words, but she wasn't comforted.

Her nails dug into his skin, her eyes clinging to his. "I killed you," she gasped.

"You didn't kill me, Mia. I'm right here."

She shook her head, choking on her tears. "I deserve to die."

"No." Grayson's stomach rolled at the self-loathing and agony in her pained words. His hold on her tightened. "Mia, what—?"

"I killed her!" Her brown eyes were blurry with tears and fever, but her fervency hit him hard. "They all died. Everyone died." A spill of incoherent words followed and she thrashed her head away from him.

Grayson's heart thudded. She wouldn't release his wrist, so he grabbed the cloth with his other hand and began to bathe her face and neck, desperate to soothe her. But he couldn't stop the torment in her mind. She continued to cry and often broke into muttering. Not everything was a confession; some of her words were softer, and even though he couldn't understand most of it, he knew she was lost in the past. The details she shared were disjointed, giving him a glimpse into her life that he didn't have enough context to actually understand. He only knew she was hurting and he couldn't stop it. When she cried out for her mother, Grayson grit his teeth and thumbed her tears away, pleading with the fates to give her rest. Anything to take away her pain.

Perhaps a half hour later the cell door opened and Fletcher strode in, lifting a pouch. "I told the physician my wife had a fever," he said, moving to the square table to prepare the medicine.

Before Grayson could decide to thank him, the door to the back room opened and Mama stumbled out. Her eyes snapped to him and she whitened. "Wha—what's going on?"

Mia flinched at Mama's voice.

Grayson fisted the wet rag, his jaw cracking as he faced the older woman. "Get out of my sight. Tell your husband neither of you are welcome here tonight."

"But—we have orders from the king!" she protested.

"Your orders were to care for Mia," he said darkly. "You failed. Tell the king if you wish. Pray that I do not."

Mama paled further. She snatched a few belongings and fled the cell, shutting the door behind her.

Grayson returned his attention to Mia while Fletcher resumed his work with the medicine.

After a moment of silence, Fletcher whispered, "I didn't know."

Grayson didn't look away from Mia. Her cries had quieted to low moans, though tears still leaked from her eyes. "Didn't know what?" he asked distractedly, his voice gruff.

"I didn't know she was ill." The softness of Fletcher's tone didn't hide the man's emotions. Regret was there, as well as concern.

Surprise filtered through Grayson and he glanced up. Was it possible the impassive guard cared for Mia? He wasn't sure what to think of that.

He'd waited too long to respond, so he cleared his throat. "Thank you for the medicine." Fates knew it wasn't something the physicians would have given him. For being a prince, he had little power in the castle.

Fletcher grunted, avoiding the thanks. "You should get the hair off her neck. And take off her shoes and stockings."

Grayson took the man's suggestions, and by the time he'd finished baring her feet, Fletcher arrived with the cup of medicine. Once she'd taken it—albeit reluctantly—Grayson pressed a kiss to her hot temple, his lips throbbing with the scorching heat of her fever.

"She needs rest," Fletcher said. "If the fever still rages in an hour, give her more tea." The guard eyed him, his hand on the door handle. "The night guard will be here in an hour. I'll be outside until then, if you need anything."

Mia drifted in and out of sleep, but even when awake she wasn't fully conscious. She relaxed marginally when Grayson kept the cool cloth pressed against her skin, so he continued the motions even though his muscles strained. He held her close, kissed the top of her head and her hot cheek. His throat ached from whispering to her, an endless spill of soothing words that probably meant nothing to her. The fever continued unbroken into the night, and though time was difficult to gauge in the cell, Grayson thought it could only be a handful of hours until dawn when Mia finally settled into a deep sleep, her brow no longer radiating a feverish heat.

Grayson didn't realize he'd fallen asleep until a feather-light touch brushed his jaw. He pried his eyes open. He'd slipped onto his side at some point, so they lay facing each other. His right arm was stretched out and Mia's head rested on it. The whole limb was numb, even his fingers, but he didn't care—Mia was awake. The lamp burning on the table across the room cast imperfect light, but Grayson easily met her unclouded gaze.

"You're back," she whispered, her words rasping a little. Her hand cupped his cheek, the other resting on the bed between them.

"How do you feel?" he asked, his voice roughened from sleep.

"Tired." Her throat bobbed. "How long have you been here?"

"I don't know. Several hours." He studied her shadowed face, his chest squeezing when he realized their noses were only a breath apart. They'd never laid together like this. One of his hands curled over her waist, his thumb resting against her belly. The intimacy of this moment stunned him. For all the times he'd embraced her, she'd never seemed this close. His focus dropped to her lips. They were pressed together, soft, pink, and so near his own.

Grayson had learned years ago to breathe through the pang of desire. He knew how to look away, to curl his fingers instead of stretch to reach her. And yet the need to kiss her pulled on every part of him and he didn't shift away.

She was perfect. Beautiful.

Which was why he could never do this.

He didn't deserve her friendship, let alone anything more. His scars were not just skin deep. The wrongs he'd committed in his father's name stained him. He was the Black Hand. He'd killed. He wasn't worthy of her. And he was afraid. What if he told her his feelings and she rejected him? Terror kept his mouth shut.

That didn't mean the temptation wasn't there, riding him so hard right now he couldn't breathe.

Mia's lips parted.

His eyes flashed to hers and he knew she'd caught him staring. Heat spread over his face and he lowered his gaze.

"May I have some water?" she asked softly.

It meant moving away, but that was probably for the best; it was hard to concentrate when he was hyper-aware of every breath she took. He lifted his fingers from the curve of her waist and eased his dead arm out from under her head. She resettled against the pillow while he rolled to his feet, shaking out his hand that sparked with needles of pain as sensation rushed back.

When she finished drinking, he set the cup aside and sat on the edge of the bed. She caught his free hand and twined their fingers, pressing their palms together. It was the first time in years their hands had touched like this, skin to skin. He almost always wore gloves.

"I'm glad you're back," she whispered, thumbing his hand.

His throat clenched. He didn't want to ruin this moment, but they needed to talk. Normally he could curb his curiosity about her past, but after what she'd said in the throes of fever, he couldn't remain silent. "You asked for your mother," he said quietly.

Mia stiffened. "What?"

"During the worst of your fever, you cried for your mother."

Mia dropped his hand. Her chest rose and fell too quickly as she stared at him.

Grayson swallowed, forcing himself to continue despite the sudden chill between them. "You spoke other languages. I didn't understand most of it, but you talked about your mother. A sister. Learning to swim. Playing with a dog. A painting you gave your father—"

"Stop." Tears sparked in her eyes, wavering in the lamplight.

He couldn't stop. The need to know burned inside him. "You had a life before this. A good one. What happened? How did you get here?"

Mia shuddered, drawing her knees up to her chest. "I don't want to talk about this."

Grayson leaned in, every protective instinct he had roaring to life. "I need to know what happened to you." It was killing him not to know.

"It doesn't matter."

He grit his teeth. "It matters, Mia. You said you deserved to die."

She cut him a look—panic, grief, guilt, and shame swam in her eyes. When she spoke, emotion strained her words. "Please, Grayson. Don't ask me about this."

He refused to let his gaze drop. "You know other languages. Your accent is foreign, but I can't place it. Your skin isn't like mine. Are you from Zennor? Mortise? Devendra?"

Her tongue darted over her cracked lips, pleading in her eyes.

Grayson laid a hand on her raised knee, feeling the tremble that ran through her body. He softened his voice. "You were seven years old when you came here. Did my father take you away from your family? Did he kill them?"

Her breath caught.

He forced himself to continue, despite the moisture building in her brown eyes and his rising nausea. "You said everyone was dead. My father killed them, didn't he? And he brought you here. Why?"

Mia still wasn't breathing. Her body shook, her expression frantic.

Grayson tightened his hold on her bent knee, steadying his voice. "Whatever happened, you don't deserve this. You don't deserve to be here."

"You don't know that."

"Yes, I do." He hesitated, and his voice lowered. "You said you killed someone."

Mia paled, but said nothing.

"You said you killed me, and then you said you killed *her*." Pain flared in her eyes and Grayson's brows slammed down. "You're not a killer, Mia. Whatever happened wasn't your fault."

"You don't know that." They were the same words she'd spoken a moment ago, but they were so much weaker this time.

He ducked his head, catching her wet eyes. "I know *you*. You would never kill anyone."

Mia's shoulders tensed and she glanced away, her voice pinched. "You don't know anything about me."

The words punched him in the gut, because they were true. Grayson ground his jaw so tightly, his teeth ached. "Then tell me. I can help."

"No. You can't help me."

He wanted to argue, but how could he? What had he ever done for her, really? He stole moments with her, gave her gifts when he could, but what did it matter? He couldn't free her. Couldn't protect her from the evil his father had already wrought. He couldn't take Mia home, wherever that was. And she was right; he didn't know anything real about her. He didn't know where she came from, why she was here, or what tortured her. He didn't know what she dreamed about or hoped for. And he couldn't fault her for not confiding in him, because fates knew there were things he hadn't shared with her—things he'd never share.

Grayson's hand fell from her knee and he turned so his back

was to her. He remained sitting on the edge of the bed, his head bowed, arms slung over his knees. Tension coiled in his shoulders and the silence burned his ears.

Mia exhaled softly and he felt the bed dip as she shifted closer. "I'm sorry," she whispered.

"It's fine." His voice was carefully even.

Mia moved to sit beside him, her arm threading slowly through his. She leaned against him, her temple pressing against his hunched shoulder. "I didn't mean that."

His eyes remained trained ahead, his words low. "It's the truth. I can't do anything for you."

"No." She twisted until her free hand cradled his jaw and she forced him to meet her steady gaze. "You've saved me a thousand times and in a thousand ways. Without you, I would never have survived these years."

Truth rang in every word, her conviction palpable. Her thin fingers felt delicate against his skin and her touch warmed every part of him. When he could no longer take the sweet torture he eased away, throat bobbing hard. "I brought you something."

Her brow furrowed as he reached for his nearby satchel. He drew out the brown egg-shaped object and Mia took it carefully, examining the prongs and ridges with squinted eyes and curious fingers.

"It's a pinecone," Grayson said. "They're everywhere in the mountains. They fall from the pine trees."

She lifted it to her nose, inhaling the earthy scent. "It's beautiful. Thank you." She picked up his hand and kissed the back of it. With his gloves off, he could truly feel her lips against his skin. The satin touch seared all the way to his thudding heart.

She didn't share anything more about her past, and Grayson didn't ask. When she drifted back to sleep, Grayson remained wholly alert. His pulse still kicked from her impulsive kiss and he didn't know if the back of his hand would ever stop tingling. There were things he didn't know about her, but he knew enough. She was good. Pure.

And she had given him every good moment in his life.

Slowly, he bent his stiff neck and pressed his lips against her warm temple. "I love you," he whispered, saying the words for the first time.

Mia's breaths remained even, her chest rising and falling gently as she continued to sleep.

Grayson knew he should move to one of the wooden chairs across the room, give her space, but that didn't stop him from stretching out on the bed beside her. He wrapped an arm around her waist and tipped his forehead to rest against her shoulder, the tension in his body finally fading.

CHAPTER 24
CLARE

NERVES FLUTTERED THROUGH CLARE, knotting her stomach and tightening her lungs. She wore an exquisite gown of deep blue with silver accents sewn on, sparkling like a swirling trail of stars against the night sky. Draping outer sleeves gathered at her elbows and brushed against the full skirt, leaving tight inner sleeves to reach her wrists. Matching blue gloves covered her hands and the bodice of the dress was fitted. Powders and the now-familiar stain once again darkened her exposed skin so she could pass for the half-Zennorian princess. With her dark brown hair meticulously curled and piled on her head, Clare felt every bit the imposter.

Ivonne helped Bridget pin the dress's hem. Rather than make two identical gowns, Clare would change dresses with the princess when her part was done and the skirt could then be unpinned and fall the extra length Serene needed. Serene would also take the silver and diamond necklace currently pressed around the base of Clare's throat. The expensive piece was a gift from Emissary Havim and his son, Amil, and it was decidedly uncomfortable—heavy, cold, and constricting.

A moment later the temporary hem was in place and she was declared ready. As Bridget left to arrange the princess's hair, Bennick strode into the suite.

Clare stood in the doorway of the changing room and a flush bloomed in her cheeks as Bennick drew to a stop. His gaze tracked over her, taking in every detail of her appearance—the hair, the dress. And while he studied her, she couldn't look away from him.

Bennick always looked perfectly suited for his uniform, but the dark blue dress uniform lined in gold thread looked especially good on him. The clean cut of the fabric outlined his wide shoulders and narrow hips, his long legs and strong arms. His dark-blond hair was a little untidy, as if he'd run his fingers through it recently, and the stubble lining his jaw lent a rugged edge to his overall appearance. His sword was at his waist, as well as a dagger, but it didn't drag at him. He wore the weapons like they were a part of him.

What she felt for him was growing beyond friendship. She could recognize that, even if she didn't entirely know what to do with it.

Bennick's crystal-blue eyes met hers and she struggled to pull in a full breath. She fingered the heavy diamond necklace encircling her neck, needing something to do with her suddenly trembling hands. "I feel a little ridiculous."

He took one of her gloved hands and kissed it as if she were truly one of the nobility. He peered up through his lashes. "You look beautiful, Clare."

Heat pooled in her abdomen. "Thank you."

Bennick smiled and extended an arm. She took it and together they made their way to the ballroom, Venn and Dirk trailing behind them. Dirk was the bodyguard Clare had interacted with the least, but the middle-aged man was soft-spoken and had a calming presence. Clare was grateful for his quiet peace tonight.

Flutes and violins weaved music just loud enough to be heard over the murmuring voices, swishing skirts, and tittering laughter. Colors swam before Clare as she entered the large ballroom and a wave of heat slammed into her from so many bodies pressed together. The ceiling towered above them, torches and candles spread throughout the room. Heels clacked as the nobility wandered the floor, greeting each other and laughing too loudly. Pine boughs and long ribbons had been used to decorate the walls and tables and the smells of cakes, cheeses, and sliced fruit drifted in between the perfumes saturating every man and lady in the crush.

For a terrified moment, Clare froze. But she'd trained for this. For weeks, she'd studied to walk like Serene, talk like her. She couldn't let fear cripple her now. She set her chin forward and swallowed back panic as they stepped into the ballroom.

Many nobles waved to her, offering their congratulations on her upcoming marriage or trying to engage her in conversation, but Bennick steered her through them, leading her to the dais where the king waited on his throne. Grandeur sat on a slightly shorter throne on the king's right, his guards around him. The throne on the king's left was empty. Seeing it made Clare's heart stumble.

Bennick paused at the base of the dais and bowed to the royals already seated. Clare dipped into a slight curtsy, just as Mistress Henley had taught her, and the king nodded for them to rise. Clare didn't ease her grip on Bennick's arm as he helped her up the few short steps. She lowered herself onto the princess's throne, shifting uncomfortably in it. Bennick slid into position behind her and she saw Venn and Dirk at the front corner of the dais, scanning the colorful assemblage, mirroring the other royal bodyguards.

Clare caught sight of Ser Havim and Amil near the dais. The emissary's son shot her a grin, raising his wineglass in a wordless salute. She gave him a tight nod, trying to force her smile into a relaxed curve.

King Newlan stood. The musicians cut off and talking ceased. Newlan spread his hands. "Noblest of Devendra, I welcome you tonight. I won't bore you with long speeches. Many of you were in court today and have no doubt heard enough from me." Polite chuckles and headshakes rippled through the crowd. Newlan smiled, the torchlight catching his white teeth. "Tonight's celebration is, from the outside, a celebration of my birth. But that's an unfair reason to celebrate in such spectacular style. No, I think of this day as a celebration of Devendra. Our nation is strong and will become stronger still when Princess Serene becomes Princess of Mortise. As royals, our lives are dedicated to you and the service of our kingdom. That's why tonight isn't about me, but about us all."

The crowd cheered, and as Clare glanced over their faces, she wondered how many smiles were fake.

Newlan raised his hand, calming the room. "This historic alliance with Mortise will benefit us all, and bring new prosperity to our kingdom. My daughter will pave the way to a glorious future for Devendra. Those who were once enemies will become family. We will be stronger than before. Devendra will never fall!"

Applause rang sharply in Clare's ears and her stomach pitched as she thought of the dangerous journey ahead of her. She wondered if the alarm she felt was an echo of what Serene felt at the thought of marrying Serjah Desfan. A stranger. An enemy.

"A round!" Newlan called.

Grandeur came to his feet and took Clare's hand, pulling her up. His rich brown skin gleamed in the torchlight as they descended to the dancefloor, the entire room watching them.

Grandeur squeezed her hand and his white teeth flashed with his smile. She returned the gesture a little shakily and took her place in the traditional circle across from him.

The musicians began to play and Clare watched from the corner of her eye for the lady beside her to sweep into a curtsy. She followed at once, and then stepped back as Grandeur stepped forward, sliding into the practiced dance.

As they moved together, Grandeur leaned in and whispered. "You're doing well."

"Thank you."

He smiled, watching her as they circled each other. When the dance brought them back together, he tipped his mouth toward her ear. "Captain Markam can't take his eyes off you."

Heat infused her cheeks but she darted a look toward Bennick. Their eyes collided and her heartbeat quickened. She glanced back at the prince. "He's my bodyguard. He's supposed to watch me."

Grandeur's mouth twitched. "Ah."

Her brow furrowed. "What?"

He took her hand as the dance dictated and spun her, first away from his body and then back to his side. He leaned in, his words lower than before. "When you admit it to yourself, please feel free to tell me."

She lifted her chin. "I don't know what you're talking about."

He rolled his eyes and Clare fought a smile. The more time

that passed since their conversation over tea, the more Clare thought less about her flash of unease when he'd asked her to spy on Serene. Grandeur was her friend among the royals, and he was only worried about Devendra. She couldn't fault him for that, even if the thought of spying on Serene made her uncomfortable.

Grandeur was a graceful dancer, his hands strong as he guided her through the practiced steps. When it was time to switch partners, he spun her smoothly into the next man's arms and the round continued unbroken.

The heat in the room increased as the night dragged on. The music was loud and a drum pounded incessantly in the corner. The spinning of the dancing didn't help Clare's growing headache. She was pulled from one circle to another, the dancing never-ending. Occasionally she spotted Venn, Dirk, or Bennick watching from the sidelines, only to lose them in the next turn.

Clare managed to beg her way out of the next dance and she drifted to the crowd's edge for a brief reprieve. She caught sight of Bennick and some of the tightness in her chest loosened. He mirrored her steps, keeping close without actually joining her.

She wished he'd join her. If he were to dance with her, she would happily ignore her aching feet. She wondered what it would be like to have his hands around her on a dancefloor instead of a training field. Imagination sparked, quickening her pulse.

Behind her, sliding in between the music, laughter, and boom of conversation, Clare heard a low voice, thickly accented and speaking the rounded Mortisian language. The heat in his voice made her angle her head, straining to make out the conversation without drawing attention to herself.

"... doubt his logic," Ser Havim growled.

"You should hold off on the wine," Amil said, his voice stiff.

"Bah! You've been pulled in by her beauty, but she's *Devendran.*"

"Father," Amil hissed. "You forget yourself."

"No. But Desfan does. The Cassian line has been pure for hundreds of years. Mortisian, through and through. If I hadn't been manipulated into brokering this peace, I wouldn't have come."

"Enough!" A glass slammed against a side table. "Father, you should retire for the night."

Emissary Havim let out a growl. "Fine. I'll go. Only because it wounds me to have my son disrespect me."

Clare tensed as the emissary marched past, his guards following. She glanced toward Bennick, but she knew he'd been too far away to hear the heated exchange. He eyed her, though, one eyebrow lifted in question.

She sensed someone draw up behind her and she turned. Amil stood close, wearing a red tunic that complimented his olive skin. He was undeniably handsome, but when he smiled, she couldn't help but feel a lack of sincerity. "Princess, could I trouble you for a dance?"

Clare swallowed. "Of course." They took their places across from each other, their palms pressed together in a newer Devendran dance, not as complicated as the round.

Amil's voice was soft. "You overheard."

There was no point denying it, if she wanted to learn more. "I didn't realize your father thought so little of me."

Amil grimaced. "He's traditionally-minded."

"He's quite vocal about his opinions."

"He's overworked and indulged in too much wine tonight. Please, forgive him."

She didn't think she could.

Ever since the Ogai spider incident, Wilf had been her primary suspect. She hadn't shared her thoughts with anyone outside of Vera, but after the conversation she'd just overheard, she knew she couldn't dismiss Amil's father as a suspect. If Ser Havim hated the idea of Serene entering the Cassian family, it was possible he could be the one trying to kill her. The emissary had access in the castle that many did not and he had loyal bodyguards to do his bidding. True, he'd been working to build the alliance, but it was clear he didn't want peace, and now that the alliance was falling into place, he might want to sabotage it.

"The necklace suits you," Amil said, breaking into her thoughts. "Breathtaking, just as you are."

The weight of the necklace—knowing it had come from the emissary who despised Devendrans—nearly strangled her. "Thank you. It's lovely."

His fingertips pressed more firmly against hers. "I sent for it after our first meeting. I knew it would be perfect for you."

Her chest tightened uncomfortably. "Ser Amil—"

"Serene!" Venn barely acknowledged Amil as he stepped up to Clare. "Princess, your attention is needed."

Amil shot an irritated look at Venn, but the expression tamed by the time he inclined his head toward her. "Thank you for the pleasure of your company, Princess. I hope we can share another dance before the night is over."

Clare offered a vague response and took Venn's offered arm, allowing him to lead her off the floor.

Once they were away from Amil, she murmured, "Thank you."

He shrugged. "You looked uncomfortable. As your bodyguard, it's my job to keep you from discomfort."

Her mouth twitched. "Somehow I don't think saving me from social distress really fits."

"Oh, it does. There's a whole training segment that covers tea parties."

Clare grinned. "You're even more qualified than I realized."

Venn winked. When they reached one of the many refreshment tables lining the vast room, he lifted a glass for her. While she sipped the red wine, she glanced around. "Where's Bennick?"

"The king wanted a word."

Uneasiness skittered down her spine and she lowered her glass. "He's not in trouble?"

Venn sighed, tugging her away from the table and walking slowly toward the shadowed side of the room where empty chairs waited for tired dancers. "The king is still upset about the Ogai spiders."

"So am I," Clare muttered.

Venn's mouth twitched. "Yes, well, the king's been angry with Bennick since the Night Sigh. Concerns about his competency have been raised."

She sucked in a breath. "That's unfair."

Venn's jaw tightened. "We're all blaming ourselves, but . . . well, the king isn't impressed with Bennick right now." His eyes narrowed suddenly, fixed on a point behind her. "Fates," he cursed.

Clare twisted to follow his gaze.

A thin woman sagged in a chair nearby, though out of earshot—especially with the music and laughter filling the room. The woman gripped a glass in skeletal hands, staring into the sea of dancers and swirling colors, but clearly not seeing anything. Her hair was dark blonde and worn in a loose braid that disappeared down her back. No one was seated beside her—not even near her.

"Who is that?" Clare asked.

A muscle ticked in Venn's jaw. "Lady Markam. Bennick's

mother."

Those words pressed against Clare's chest, and other words echoed in her mind. *Insane. Ill. Abused.*

"The commander shouldn't have made her come," Venn muttered. "She's been ill. Bennick's going to be furious."

Clare tightened her hold on the wineglass. "Would Serene sit with Lady Markam?"

Venn arched a brow. "Serene does whatever she wants."

Clare almost smiled as she stepped forward. Venn hung back, offering privacy, though she could feel his eyes trailing her. She stopped in front of Lady Markam and the woman slowly lifted her head, blinking light green eyes that appeared glassy in the torchlight. She had silver hair at her temples and her cheeks were hollow. Her neck was so slender, Clare wasn't sure how it held up her head. "Your Highness," Lady Markam murmured, her voice as soft and thin as a thread of silk. "I'm sorry, I'm quite tired and don't think I can rise."

"Please don't." Clare settled in the wooden chair beside her. "It's good to see you out of bed, Lady Markam. Are you sure you're well enough, though?"

"I'll manage." She took a sip from her goblet.

Clare could smell the bitterness of medicine mixed in with the wine, and she inwardly cringed.

"I'm afraid I'm poor company," Lady Markam said.

"I disagree."

A fleeting smile lifted the older woman's pale lips. "You're the only one. Dennith left me as soon as we arrived."

Dennith. Clare assumed that was the commander. "I'll gladly sit with you."

There was a slight pause, with Lady Markam viewing the dance floor and Clare fingering her temple. The ache there was building.

"You should enjoy the dancing," Lady Markam said.

Clare's lips curved up. "I've enjoyed it so much I fear my feet will fall off."

Lady Markam chuckled, then fought against an ensuing cough. It was deep and guttural, shaking her frail body. She grabbed for a handkerchief and tried to smother the choking fit. Clare set a hand on the woman's back, but was useless to help.

Finally, the coughing eased and Lady Markam gave her a watery smile. "It always passes."

"Would you like to return to your room?"

"That would upset Dennith." She rocked a little in her chair, her expression shifting into something softer, almost lost. "Is Ben here? I miss him." Her eyes teared up and her fingers curled around her handkerchief. "He blames me, I think. For all that happened. Everything his father did."

Catching a glimpse into Bennick's past without him there brought Clare a stirring of discomfort, but she couldn't leave the poor woman alone.

Lady Markam dabbed the corners of her eyes with her wrinkled handkerchief. "He doesn't care for me like he used to. He doesn't love me. A woman's heart should only be able to break once. But we're never beyond more breaking; each shattered piece can break again."

"Bennick loves you," Clare assured her softly. "I know it."

Lady Markam blinked, confusion pulling at her gaunt features. "Yes. Of course. But Dennith doesn't.' Her chin dropped, lower lip trembling. Sweat slicked her forehead. "Perhaps he never did."

Clare touched her arm. "Lady Markam, I think you should be in bed. I can ask one of my guards to escort you."

Lady Markam seemed oblivious to the offer. Tears slipped

down her pale cheeks. "I'll be dead before the year is done. I feel it." Her heavy exhale rattled out. "It will be a blessed relief, though I hate to leave Ben."

Clare glanced around her shoulder, finding Venn. He must have caught her worry, because in an instant he knelt before Bennick's mother. "Lady Markam?"

Her watery gaze lifted and recognition swept her face. "Venn."

Venn gripped her hand. "Let me help you to your room."

Lady Markam stared at him, mouth quavering for a moment. When she nodded, Clare took her glass and set it aside along with her own. Venn pulled Lady Markam to her feet, and when she swayed, Clare set a steadying hand on the woman's back.

"Gweneth."

Lady Markam froze, every muscle tensing as her face went white.

Clare twisted to see the commander standing over them, anger flashing in his blue eyes.

CHAPTER 25

CLARE

COMMANDER MARKAM'S SMILE WAS TIGHT, his jaw hard and his teeth clenched to hold the false expression. The tenseness strained his words, but steel still lived in them. "Sit down, Gwen-eth."

Lady Markam shuddered and Clare's hand tightened against the woman's back. "Can't you see she's ill?" Clare all but snapped.

The commander's intense gaze centered on her, but she wouldn't be intimidated. Defending this fragile woman gave her all the backbone she needed, but being the princess in the public's eye was an advantage; she knew the commander couldn't hurt her in this crowded room, dressed as she was.

"She's always ill," the commander said, voice low and clipped. "That can't excuse her from the most important ball of the year." He eyed Venn. "Help her to her seat, Grannard."

Venn's eyes narrowed, but before he could speak Clare stepped forward, clearly shifting into a more defensive position in front of Lady Markam. Her expression hardened as she glared at the man towering over her. "I've given her my permission to leave."

The commander's nostrils flared. His tone lowered dangerously as he grit out, "She's my wife."

"Please," Lady Markam shuddered, clinging to Venn. "Don't fight. I can't stand it."

Venn wrapped a supporting arm around her thin back, his tone sharp. "Sir, I think we should do as the princess suggests." His eyes flared with meaning as he spoke Clare's false title, a reminder that they were in a public setting.

The commander's expression tightened. "Set her down, Grannard." His eyes darted around them. "We don't want a scene."

"Then I suggest you give up," Clare said, not bothering to keep her voice as low as his.

The commander's lip curled. His words were barely audible. "You have no right."

"Neither do you. She's ill and needs rest."

His face darkened. "You self-important, manipulative—"

"What's going on?" Bennick slid beside Clare and the commander retreated a step as if on instinct. Bennick shot a glance to his mother and his jaw firmed. The look he cut to his father burned with undeniable hatred.

"Ben," Lady Markam gasped. "I don't think I can stay."

He reached for her hand, everything about him softening when he faced her. "You don't have to, Mother. I'll check on you after the ball." He glanced at Venn. "Will you take her?"

His friend nodded and slowly led the trembling lady away.

The commander's eyes narrowed. "Ben—"

"If you'll excuse us, *sir*," he snapped, taking Clare's arm. "The princess is needed elsewhere." He guided her away, skirting the crowded dancefloor.

Clare's pulse pounded and she wasn't sure if it was the adrenaline or not, but her body vibrated and it felt like she'd been spinning in the round dance all over again. Her headache flared and she felt a little disoriented, but blinking seemed to drive that away. Mostly.

After they'd taken several steps from the commander, Bennick lowered his voice. "What happened?"

"She was ill." Irritation tightened her throat. "I asked Venn to take her to her room, and then *he* came. He would have forced her to stay all night!"

Bennick cut her a look. "So you defied him? Publicly?" She couldn't find an ounce of remorse, and it must have shown on her expression. He looked mildly exasperated, but his mouth twitched. "Thank you," he said, before eyeing her. "Are you all right?"

Perhaps he'd felt her hand shaking against his arm. Or maybe it was her flushed cheeks. "Fine. I just wish I'd hit him."

Bennick barked a surprised laugh. "As much as I'd love to see that, I don't think the king would approve."

It was hard to focus on his words. A buzzing filled her ears. "The king . . . he's angry with you."

Bennick's expression smoothed. "You don't need to worry about that."

"It's not fair, though." From the corner of her eye, Clare caught Amil watching her and she tensed. Bennick followed her gaze, his eyes narrowing.

"I overheard Amil talking with his father," she explained quietly. She swallowed past her dry throat and told him briefly what she'd heard—Havim's angry comments about Serene and how he'd stormed out. "Amil danced with me afterward. He tried to reassure me, but I think his father could be a threat."

Bennick's brow furrowed. "I'll speak with the king."

She nodded, fanning herself with one hand. The room had felt hot for a while, but she was suddenly burning. She was grateful when they left the stuffy ballroom and entered the cooler corridor.

She stumbled a little and Bennick's hand clenched over her arm. "Clare?"

"I'm fine," she repeated. "Are there any other suspects for the assassination attempts?"

"Nothing concrete." She sensed more than saw him look backward, to monitor Dirk, who trailed behind them.

"What about Wilf?"

Bennick glanced at her. "What about him?"

She frowned. She hadn't meant to bring that up. It was a suspicion she knew Bennick wouldn't appreciate. But since she'd spoken . . . "Do you think he could be the assassin?"

Bennick pulled them both to a stop. The corridor glowed softly from the torches spaced on the wall, catching the bewilderment in his stare. "You think Wilf is trying to kill you?"

Her throat tightened, making her words sound defensive. "He has access to the room. And the Night Sigh and Ogai attacks happened after he lost his temper on the training field. He doesn't want the peace—isn't it possible he wants to end it by killing me and blaming the Mortisians?"

Bennick's forehead creased. "You've given this some thought."

"It makes sense. And he never had to put Serene in danger, because he could just target me."

He pursed his lips. "Wilf isn't trying to kill you."

Denials filled her, but she couldn't grasp the right words. She wet her lips, giving herself a mental shake before forcing the words out. "He knew about the Ogai. He fought against the

Mortisians and lost friends in the skirmishes."

"True, but he's not the assassin. You're safe with him. I swear it." His eyes narrowed. "Look at me, Clare."

"I am."

His hands were cool as they cupped her face, forcing her head to tilt up. Her eyelids were suddenly heavy and she couldn't quite hold his anxious gaze.

He cursed and she winced at the sharp sound. "I think you've been poisoned. Can you tell me what you've eaten? Drunk? What are you feeling?"

She snorted and shoved his hands down, taking a step back. "Just because I think Wilf is trying to kill me doesn't mean I'm poisoned."

His shoulders visibly tensed. "No, but you're flushed and your speech is slurring. Your pulse is racing and your eyes are unfocused." He looked beyond her. "Dirk, get a physician to Serene's room. We'll meet you there."

Footsteps pounded away and Clare winced, pressing a shaking hand to her brow. Her vision fuzzed. Narrowed. "Bennick?"

He stood before her, hands outstretched. "You're going to be fine."

His face blurred and she stumbled back. Breathing was difficult. Fates, how long since she'd been able to take a full breath? The wall spun to meet her and Clare lurched away.

Bennick shouted. Clare felt his fingers grasp for her arm, but she was already falling.

The side of her face smacked against stone and everything went dark.

When Clare opened her eyes she was in the princess's bedroom. A lamp glowed, throwing light into the shadows.

Princess Serene sat in a chair beside the bed, one sculpted eyebrow arched. "How are you feeling?"

Clare swallowed drily. "What happened?"

"You were poisoned."

She ground her teeth at the princess's grating tone, but immediately regretted it—the whole right side of her face throbbed. She remembered hitting the stone wall when she fell in the corridor.

"It was the necklace," Serene said, leaning back in her chair. "The diamonds were covered in Vaerue, a poison extracted from snake venom—snakes found in Mortise, as the trend seems to be going. The poison was sealed with a coating that kept it undetected, until sweat wore it away. That's why it took a while for you to feel the effects. Quite ingenious." Her head listed to the side. "My father questioned the Havims personally but they denied all knowledge. They insist anyone could have poisoned the necklace, since it passed through so many hands."

Clare's hands fisted under the blankets. "I heard them talking at the ball. Ser Havim doesn't want a Devendran queen."

Serene grunted. "Bennick told us what you overheard. My father still doesn't see Bahri Havim as a threat; prejudiced, sure, but not about to ruin the peace." She sighed. "Unfortunately, their reasoning is legitimate—the necklace passed through many hands. It could have been compromised anywhere. Although it's a little insulting that they blamed the palace guards who searched the necklace when it arrived."

Clare pushed into a sitting position, holding her aching head as she frowned at the princess. "Why are you here?"

"It *is* my room."

"I didn't expect you to be here." Checking on her. Because

that's what Serene was doing, Clare realized.

A furrow grew between the princess's eyebrows and something almost sheepish ghosted in her eyes. "I recently learned the truth of how you came to be here." She pursed her lips. "You saved my life, and in return you were arrested and forced into becoming my decoy. It wasn't a choice you made for riches or prestige. I misjudged you."

Clare stared. "Is this an apology?"

"No." Serene sniffed, somehow managing to look regal as she did it. "Merely a statement."

A small smile tugged into place. "Thank you," Clare whispered.

A pause. "You're welcome."

Clare startled awake, blinking at the dim glow in the room. After Serene had left—informing her Venn and Dirk stood guard outside—Clare had fallen back asleep, the lamp still glowing faintly. She was still tired, but something had woken her.

Twisting her head on the pillow, she froze at the sight of Bennick seated on the chair beside her. His head was bowed, fingers lost in his hair, his broad shoulders sagged with impossible weight. His elbows were balanced on his knees and he breathed slowly. He still wore his dress uniform, though it was wrinkled now. It was probably the middle of the night.

She thought he was asleep, but his head lifted and bloodshot eyes caught hers. He straightened. "I'm sorry," he whispered. "I thought I could slip in without waking you."

"What are you doing here?"

He avoided her question, dropping his focus to her abused

cheek. His jaw flexed, guilt flashing in his eyes. "How are you feeling?"

She set a hand on his knee and he stilled. Warmth flooded her cheeks at her boldness, but she wanted his attention.

She had it. His blue eyes clung to her.

"It's not your fault I was poisoned, Bennick. You saved my life by recognizing it."

He studied her, saying nothing. She could feel the sting and throb of the bruise forming on her face, but that became muted as she watched him. There was a war in his eyes; Clare didn't know what he fought, but a thrill shot through her when the battle abruptly ended.

His fingers lifted, warm and gentle as he traced the edge of her bruise. Then he bent, the pulse in his neck visibly jumping. His stubbled jaw grazed her smooth skin and his warm lips brushed her cheekbone, where the bruising began. Clare held her breath the entire time he kissed her cheek, and when he eased back, his throat bobbed and her pulse tripped.

Their eyes locked and Bennick swallowed—hard. "I should let you sleep."

As if her pounding heart would let her sleep now. But she didn't protest when he left, even though her throat tightened with words to call him back.

After the door closed gently behind him, Clare fingered her cheek, a slow smile curving her lips.

CHAPTER 26

GRAYSON

GRAYSON RECEIVED HIS MOTHER'S SUMMONS an hour after breakfast. Unfortunately, the invitation to tea wasn't something he could ignore.

Queen Iris's garden was deceptively beautiful. The green hedges were meticulously trimmed and there were flowers in every vibrant color imaginable. The pebbled paths almost looked inviting, but everything in this garden killed, including the woman who tended it. The garden was stocked with all manner of poisonous plants, herbs, trees, and berries. The queen even had deadly mushrooms, slugs, frogs, and fish. Every corner of the world was represented inside this walled courtyard, accessible only through a door inside the castle, located near the dungeon entrance. Her father had made it his life's work to find every poison—both exotic and commonplace—in all of Eyrinthia.

One of Iris's first official acts as queen had been to move her late father's poison garden, piece by transplanted piece, to the castle in Lenzen. This garden was her sanctuary, rivaled only by her tower study where she blended and bottled the poisons.

Grayson took the left path, holding his breath as he passed the olaris bush. The violet flowers were in bloom, which meant their perfume was at its deadliest.

One didn't stop to smell flowers in this garden.

Queen Iris knelt on the path in the back corner of the garden. She glanced up from her work, eyes lighting at the sight of him. "Grayson!" She nodded to the small white berries dangling in front of her. "Do you recognize these?"

"Vellerberries," he said at once, tone even. The abdominal pain they evoked was excruciating; his stomach cramped at the mere memory.

Iris smiled proudly and took up a towel to wipe the dirt from her hands, taking care to clean each finger. She came to her feet and straightened the black sash at her waist, gesturing to the round iron table set off the path. "The tea arrived just before you did."

Beside the table was a long glass cage, filled with dirt, rocks, and other foliage. Somewhere in there, Grayson knew, a snake hid. With summer approaching, Iris would have servants carrying out her menagerie of venomous reptiles. She liked them to have a change of scene.

Iris took her seat, leaving Grayson to sit across from her, his back to the snake's cage. The spot between his shoulder blades itched.

Iris poured tea from the steaming pot. "Honey?"

"No." *Never add anything to your drink,* she'd taught him. It was often how poison slipped past lazy tasters.

Iris passed him a cup and he eyed the dark brown tea rippling inside before sniffing deeply.

She chuckled, pouring her own cup. "You needn't be so obvious. Some hosts would be insulted."

Grayson watched her sip her tea. It could still be poisoned —her cup could be lined with an antidote, or his could have been lined with poison. But he couldn't see or smell anything wrong, so he took an experimental sip. Bitter, but no poison he could detect. Taking a chance, he swallowed, then nodded to her cup. "You didn't add honey."

"No." She peered at him over the rim. "But Tyrell did yesterday."

Grayson stole a look at the innocuous pot, studying the amber honey inside.

"It's quite undetectable," Iris told him brightly. "It was an idea of my father's, which I've finally perfected. I cultivated blossoms toxic enough that, when the bees take the pollen, they *literally* make poisonous honey. Amazing, isn't it?"

Grayson set the teacup aside, his shoulders tight. "What is it you wanted to discuss?"

She shifted the teacup in her hands, amusement playing in her gray eyes. "How was your trip to the northern mountains? Did you enjoy yourself?"

"I don't enjoy anything." At least, that was what people said of the Black Hand.

His mother raised an eyebrow. "Captain Reeve is a spy for your father."

"I know."

"He's been spying on you for months."

"Yes."

"Aren't you curious about the private report he made to your father?"

Yes. "No."

Iris took a sip of tea. "I think you should be."

Grayson leaned back in his chair, portraying a calm he didn't feel. "I did my duty to Ryden. There was nothing else for him to report."

"Reeve told your father you saved his life during the peasant ambush." She frowned. "It was an easy chance for you to be rid of an annoyance. Why save him?"

Because life had worth.

That answer would mean nothing to her. Grayson sighed. "Reeve's death would have been suspicious. The mission was a test—I didn't want Father to think I had anything to hide."

"Hmm." Iris blew a little on her steaming tea. "The captain shared another interesting story with your father."

Unease rolled up his spine. "Oh?"

"He said he battled a skilled fighter on the outskirts of Gevell while perusing fugitives. The fighter was cloaked and hooded, but was an expert with two daggers."

Sweat gathered on his palms, making his gloves feel too tight. "He mentioned the incident to me," Grayson said slowly.

"Why weren't you with him?"

"If you know Reeve's report, you know I found no evidence the widow or her children were anywhere in the village. I ordered Reeve back to camp but he refused to come. I didn't think it worth the fight, so I left him to his own devices."

"Did you?"

Grayson's pulse snapped high and fast, pinned by his mother's stare.

Iris's next words were soft. "Not many men can best a captain in Ryden's army, let alone with only daggers. Reeve had a long sword and still lost."

His face remained a stiff mask, even though panic spiked. "It sounds like he's lucky to be alive."

"You know what I find curious? Reeve was rendered unconscious, not killed. That doesn't sound like most expert warriors. In fact, I can only think of one."

Grayson held her stare, his hard face betraying nothing. Or had it betrayed everything?

Slowly, her mouth curved. "Relax. I don't intend to share this with anyone. Truthfully, I'm surprised your father didn't figure it out. But then, he has a great deal on his mind and Captain Reeve didn't air any suspicions. He glazed over the incident, really. Perhaps as a way of thanking you for saving his life—not once, but twice?"

Grayson didn't respond.

Iris set her cup down and laced her fingers under her chin, elbows propped on the table. "You don't have to tell me the truth. I can see it. Your face reveals little—you've mastered your mask —but your eyes are gateways. I see into your heart. You fought Reeve. You won. You helped that criminal and her brats escape. You undermined your father. You, Grayson, are a traitor."

His lungs were frozen. He didn't blink.

Iris reached out a hand, palm up, and her fingers bent, a silent order.

Grayson slowly set his hand in hers, his heart throbbing.

She squeezed his gloved fingers, a slow and constricting grip. "You're my favorite son. My scarred prince. You have my word; your treason will remain between us."

As long as he did whatever she wanted. Loyalty for loyalty. That was her price. And he had no choice but to agree. Grayson didn't know what his father would do to him if he learned the truth about helping the Hogans escape, but that didn't really concern him. It was the thought of what Henri would do to Mia that made him bow his head, silently accepting his mother's terms.

With his head down, he caught sight of the black viper stretched out inside the glass cage behind him. Her forked tongue flicked out and her black scales glinted in the sun. Her slitted eyes found him, trapped him. Whatever kind of snake she was, Grayson knew one bite would kill.

He didn't expect any less from his mother.

CHAPTER 27

CLARE

CLARE WALKED BESIDE VERA AND IVONNE, unable to stop scanning the faces that lined the streets of Lower Iden. Each step brought Clare closer to home, and even though that wasn't today's destination, she still hoped for a glimpse of her younger brothers in the waving crowd.

Men, women, and children called out greetings to Serene as she rode at the head of the procession, towering and beautiful atop her horse, Fury. She waved to the people of Iden, smiling with an ease and sincerity Clare hadn't realized the sarcastic princess possessed.

It had been two days since the king's ball and Clare was mostly recovered from the Vaerue poisoning, though she was still quick to tire, and a bruise still marred her cheek from when she'd fallen. During training this morning, Bennick had suggested she remain at the castle to rest, instead of going to the orphanage. She'd snatched the wooden practice knife out of his hand and stabbed him with it. She refused to miss this trip into Iden. Even if she didn't see her family, she longed for a momentary escape from the castle.

Serene had planned to visit Lower Iden's orphanage weeks ago, and she was adamant about doing the charitable visit as planned—without a decoy. King Newlan was eventually persuaded to agree, though he'd insisted on a larger guard. All of Serene's bodyguards were present as well as a host of palace and city guards. The maids had been invited to help unload the wagon of supplies, but nothing about this felt like work to Clare. Seeing children laugh and dart through the crowded streets, smelling the fry bread and spices in the market, hearing the regular shouts and haggling—it assured her that life continued. Ordinary people lived ordinary lives, unaffected by the danger that stalked the castle.

Vera had told Clare that Serene's mother established the orphanage years ago, modeling it after the successful orphan homes in Zennor. Out of all the charitable work Serene did, she had a special place in her heart for the orphanage.

When they reached the large building that housed Iden's orphans, Clare did a final scan of the crowd. Soldiers were gently pushing the crowds back so Serene could dismount and Cardon, Bennick, and Wilf remained close as orphans swarmed the princess, carrying handmade gifts and begging for attention. Serene laughed and tried to greet them all individually at once, and it surprised Clare how well she managed. She even knew some of the children by name.

The sight warmed Clare, but she was still distracted as she craned her neck, searching for Thomas or Mark on the edge of the crowd. They didn't know she was with the princess, but the hope that they might still show up burned in her chest.

Vera nudged Clare's side with her elbow. "Are they here?" she asked.

"I don't think so." But she continued to look.

The children moved inside with the princess, leaving the maids, soldiers, and some of the orphanage staff to unload the wagon. Clare helped carry food, toys, and other supplies into the orphanage, and each time she returned to the wagon she searched the crowd lining the street.

Clare was lifting down a couple loaves of bread wrapped in linen when she turned from the wagon and nearly slammed into Gavril.

He snatched her arms, steadying her. "Sorry!"

An embarrassed flush warmed her cheeks. "Sorry, I was distracted."

A snigger burst beside them and Clare turned to see two city guards shooting her and Gavril looks, harsh smiles on their faces as they strode past.

Gavril tensed and released Clare, eyes dropping as he slid back a step. "Apologies if I frightened you."

"You didn't." Clare's fingers tightened on the bread. "Gavril—"

"It doesn't matter," he interrupted quietly.

Her chest squeezed. She didn't know Gavril well, but he was often stationed outside the princess's suite and had always been polite to her. And Clare knew his father—Master Lank—worried about him. Compassion rose inside her and she stepped closer, forcing him to meet her gaze. She kept her voice low but even. "You're not your scars, Gavril."

He eyed her, the lines on his face deepening. "Sometimes that's all I think I am." He turned before she could form a response, lifted down a crate of food, and disappeared into the orphanage.

Clare followed more slowly, and when she'd deposited the bread and ducked back outside, she caught sight of Gavril stalking past the wagon to join the soldiers securing the perimeter. Clearly, he didn't want conversation right now. She sighed and stepped up to the wagon, dragging a wooden crate of books toward her.

Bennick leaned suddenly around her, snagging the crate before she could pull it down.

Her heart tripped at his sudden nearness. He'd been busy settling the princess inside, but apparently he trusted the other bodyguards to keep an eye on her now. "I can carry a crate of books," Clare told him.

"So can I." He tossed her a grin and shifted the crate in his arms. He ducked his head, voice dropping conspiratorially. "Besides, you need your hands free."

She frowned, forehead creasing. "What?"

His attention shifted behind her and she twisted to follow his gaze.

Her heart stopped. Everything in the world stopped.

Thomas and Mark stood in the cleared street, only a few paces away. They grinned at her and Clare couldn't breathe. Couldn't speak.

Mark broke the stillness when he threw himself at Clare. She grabbed him, his ten-year-old arms nearly crushing her as he squeezed her middle.

She held him just as tightly, a laugh and a sob tangling in her throat. Thomas grabbed her, too, the three of them embracing, crying, and laughing. "I didn't know if I'd see you," Clare managed to say through her tears. "I didn't know if you'd come."

Thomas gripped her harder. "Captain Markam came to the house this morning, telling us you'd be here. A soldier even escorted us!"

Bennick met her quick look with a half-grin. He'd set the crate back on the wagon. "I thought you'd appreciate the surprise."

She kept her arms wrapped around her brothers, emotion tightening her voice. "Thank you." The words were inadequate, but Bennick seemed to feel the fullness behind them.

"What happened to your face?" Mark demanded.

Clare's hand fluttered to the bruise on her cheek. "Nothing, just a small accident. I'm fine."

Mark frowned, and Thomas looked like he might question her further, but Bennick stepped in. "We didn't get a chance to really meet this morning." He held out a hand. "You must be Thomas."

Her thirteen-year-old brother shot a last look at Clare's bruise before he shook Bennick's hand. "Yes, sir."

Bennick stooped a little, putting himself more on Mark's level as he extended his hand again. "And you must be Mark."

Mark continued to lean against Clare, but he took the offered hand. "How did you know?"

Bennick's mouth twitched. "Clare told me all about you."

"She did?" Mark twisted to look at her and she nodded.

Bennick straightened. "Why don't you all come inside? I'm sure there's a quiet corner where you can visit."

Clare's heart was so full, she thought it might burst as she guided her brothers toward the orphanage. Fates. Bennick had brought her family to her. He'd gone to them that morning, which meant all through training he'd known she would see them in mere hours. He had kept his secret—even teased her about remaining at the castle.

She didn't want to stab him again with that wooden blade. She wanted to kiss him—a real kiss. And that thought burned her cheeks.

They stepped into the orphanage and her brothers were momentarily distracted by the sight of Princess Serene seated on the floor surrounded by children. She was weaving an old Devendran folk tale, her low voice hypnotic. Her skirt pooled around her and some of the younger children even leaned against her sides. Cardon and Dirk had taken up positions directly behind Serene, but even they seemed swept up in her storytelling. Serene looked up at the Ellingtons and gave them a small smile, though she didn't break from her story. Thomas blushed and grinned, but Mark just squeezed Clare's hand.

Clare led them to the back corner of the room, and she could have sat on the hard floor with her brothers tucked beside her forever. They talked quietly with each other, and though Clare shared some details of living at the castle, she questioned the boys constantly about their new lives. When conversation finally ebbed, they listened to Serene's latest story. Clare rubbed a hand up and down Mark's back, an arm around Thomas's shoulders. Clare glanced across the room and saw Bennick, Venn, and the matron of the orphanage standing off to the side, speaking in low tones. Bennick caught Clare watching and he cast her a small smile, but the alertness in his eyes sent a needle of unease through her.

Thomas spoke lowly beside her, his eyes on the princess. "It's too bad we have to lose her to Mortise."

Mark straightened beside Clare. "No, it's not. When she goes, Clare can come home." His blue eyes turned to her. "Right?"

Clare hesitated, casting a look at each of them. "I'm actually going with the princess."

There was a short silence in their corner, Serene's story continuing to enthrall the rest of the room. Thomas blinked. "You can't go to Mortise. It's dangerous, and too far away."

"I know, but—"

Mark shoved away from Clare, coming to his feet with a jerk. He glared down at her, hands fisted at his sides. "You can't go."

Sharp pain cut into her chest. "I have to, Mark."

Fury bled into his eyes, tightening his face. "No," he snapped.

Clare shifted to her knees in front of him. "I don't want to leave," she said softly, pleading for him to understand. "But I don't have a choice."

"You keep leaving us," Mark ground out. "You don't love us anymore."

"That's not true—"

"I hate you!"

Clare flinched.

Thomas tried to grab Mark, but he shook free of his brother. He turned as if to bolt, but Venn stepped into his path, a steadying hand on his shoulder. "Easy there," he murmured to the boy, before locking eyes with Clare. Tension lined his dark face. "We need to leave. Now."

Instinct and training converged, pulling Clare to her feet. "What's going on?"

Venn glanced toward Bennick, who still stood near the pale matron. Bennick wasn't looking at her, but speaking hurriedly to Wilf, their eyes roving the room. Clare's gaze swept the crowded space as well, but she wasn't trained enough to pick up what they were seeing.

Venn grasped Clare's arm. "There's going to be an ambush," he whispered. "Men came last night; the matron had no choice but to hide them, or they'd kill the children. Bennick figured it out and he told me to get you—"

Bennick bellowed a warning, snapping Cardon and Dirk into full attention a second before crossbow bolts flew from the sides of the room. Serene's story cut off as Cardon dragged her to her feet, he and Dirk shifting into position around her. Children shot up from the floor, screaming, and orphanage staff tried to herd them toward the door as soldiers pulled out their weapons and made a path for Serene's exit.

Clare shoved her brothers toward Venn. "Move!" she shouted, guarding their backs as they pushed to reach the front door. When Mark stumbled, she grabbed his arm. Horror washed through her as bodies fell, screams of death piercing the air. People were everywhere, shoving and hitting in their efforts to find safety outside. In the frantic press of bodies, Clare lost sight of Thomas, though she prayed he was with Venn. She clung to Mark, refusing to let go as they forced their way to the exit.

She couldn't find Bennick in the chaos, though she spotted Cardon and Dirk as they shoved Serene through the open door, Cardon in front and Dirk shielding her back.

Clare wrapped her arms around Mark, shielding him too as they pushed through the narrow doorway and spilled onto the street. She tugged him aside, away from the worst of the rushing crowd, taking a second to gain her bearings. Her heart was hammering, but training kicked in, keeping her muscles loose and her thoughts firing.

Serene was nearly to Fury's side. Cardon shouted orders at the soldiers in the street and, in his momentary distraction, Serene ducked around him.

Dirk shouted, but Serene didn't stop.

A young boy, no more than three or four years old, was running right at Fury in his haste to escape the danger. Clare's breath caught—the anxious horse would trample him.

Serene snatched him up a split second before Fury reared. The same moment she bent to grab him, a crossbow bolt shot into the ground behind her.

Cardon threw himself at Serene—little boy and all—and hauled them behind the nearby wagon, covering them with his body.

If the princess hadn't bent to grab the boy, the bolt would have struck her chest.

New screams sliced through the air and bodies hit the ground as the hail of bolts continued. There were shooters on the surrounding roofs, even atop the orphanage. Clare tightened her hold on Mark as she screamed for Thomas, but she didn't hear anything. She couldn't see him, and she'd already been immobile for too long. She had to trust Venn was with him, protecting him. She tugged Mark with her as she darted for the alley beside the orphanage; it was the only shelter she could see.

When they were shielded around the corner, Clare pressed Mark against the building's wall. His eyes were wild, his face pale and terrified.

"It's going to be all right," she said, squeezing his narrow shoulders. "I promise."

He stared at her, chest heaving for breath. The sight of his fear cut her, but her determination to keep him safe kept her head level. She peeked around the corner, trying to assess the danger, and her gut rolled. The street was a scene from a nightmare. Horses had bolted. Soldiers were lying on the ground, twitching and crying out with bolts sticking out of their bodies. Some were horribly still. Children screamed, and some of them were on the ground, too. Tears stung Clare's eyes and a trapped scream burned her throat.

Mark cried out and Clare spun. Fear blasted through her at the sight of a hooded man at the end of the alley. He must have come from behind the orphanage.

Clare slid in front of Mark and tugged free the knife strapped to her leg. Her mind blanked when the man lifted a loaded crossbow and aimed it at her chest.

She froze. She couldn't reach him before he killed her and

if she moved, even to dodge the bolt, she'd expose Mark.

The attacker's voice was gruff and muffled behind the cloth mask. "Move, and I won't—"

A form dropped from the roof and slammed into the masked man. He wore a blue uniform, and Clare recognized his dark-blond hair even as he fell.

Bennick and the masked man crashed to the ground. The crossbow bolt released and fire ripped through Clare's arm before the bolt pinged against the bricks behind her. She slapped a hand over her bicep with a gasp. Blood oozed between her fingers and a tremble shook her body even though she knew it was only a flesh wound. Mark screamed her name, the shout ringing in her ears.

Bennick and the man rolled, fighting hand-to-hand, but it became clear the attacker was losing. He seemed to notice at the same time Clare did, because a knife suddenly flashed in his hand. The sight of it made Clare's heart lodge in her throat. She cried out, but too late. Bennick hissed as the blade sliced over his chest. He twisted away—right into the fist swinging toward his temple.

Bennick crumpled and the masked man bolted, disappearing behind the orphanage.

Clare shouted for Mark to stay back as she ran to Bennick and dropped beside him, still gripping her wounded arm with one hand. Her free hand swept under the cut on his chest—it wasn't deep, but there was blood. Blood also trickled from his temple, and he was unconscious.

"Clare!" She jerked around at the shout. Venn was at the head of the alley, his sword drawn and bloody, his chest heaving. Thomas was behind him and Clare let out a shaking breath— they were both safe.

Venn's eyes fell to Bennick and he stumbled. "Fates, no."

"He's alive," Clare said. "The princess?"

Venn hurried forward, kneeling beside Bennick to inspect the growing lump on his temple. "Cardon and Dirk got her out. They're probably halfway to the castle by now. The fight's over—the city guard rallied." Venn noticed her bleeding arm and swore.

"It's just a graze," she assured him. Her eyes darted to her brothers. "Thank you, Venn, for keeping him safe."

He nodded once, his eyes still on her arm.

Bennick groaned and Clare's attention snapped to him. "Bennick?" She called his name again and he blinked. His eyes rolled from Venn to Clare and he stiffened. "You're hurt," he slurred. He pushed up, one hand reaching for her.

Venn caught his shoulders when he swayed. "Easy."

Bennick's focus narrowed on Clare's bleeding arm. His fingers curled around hers, peeling them back so he could see the wound. His jaw worked, but after a moment of intense study, he glanced at Venn. "Serene?"

"Secure," Venn assured him.

"Fates," Mark breathed. They all turned to look at him, but Mark stared right at Bennick. "You jumped off the roof to save us."

"I did." Bennick swallowed, shifting on his knees. "Are you all right?"

Mark nodded, still looking a little awed.

Gavril burst into the alley. He was limping a little and his eyes were frantic. "Clare? Bennick?"

"They're fine," Venn said, coming to his feet. "So am I, in case you were worried."

Gavril paled at the sight of Clare's bloody arm.

"It's nothing," she assured him. "The attacker missed."

"Mostly," Venn said.

Bennick shot him a glare. "Not amusing." He focused back on Gavril. "Coordinate with the city guard. I want any surviving attackers rounded up immediately."

Gavril bobbed his head and hurried away.

Mark's eyes were still on Bennick as he eased forward. "You're going to Mortise too, aren't you?"

Bennick half-nodded, wincing as his head must have flared with pain. Still, his voice was kind as he answered Mark. "I am."

Mark pursed his lips, but that couldn't hide the slight tremble. "Will you keep Clare safe?" It was a plea, and Clare's heart burned.

Bennick's focus was entirely on the small boy as he sank to his knees and took Mark's hand in his. Promise throbbed in his serious voice. "I give you my word—I'll protect her and bring her back to you."

Mark's chin wavered and he jerked out a nod. Then he turned and wrapped his arms around Clare, his voice muffled against her middle as he said, "I love you."

Clare swallowed hard and held him tightly, her eyes finding Bennick's, brimming with wordless thanks. "I love you too, Mark," she whispered.

CHAPTER 28

CLARE

"No, like this." Bennick stepped closer, making Clare feel like they were alone in the far corner of the training field. It was an overcast day, but that hadn't kept soldiers from training. Still, they seemed far away—especially when Bennick touched her.

He curled his hand over hers, helping her form a fist. He tapped the first two knuckles. "These are the ones you need to lead with, then make sure you give the punch the full power of your body." His fingers went up her arm, past the slight bump around her upper arm, where she still wore a bandage after the attack at the orphanage two days ago. His hand went all the way to her shoulder. "Right now you're pushing from here, but that's not enough." His hand glanced down her side, tapping against her stomach. "The power needs to come from here."

It was hard to concentrate on Bennick's words—his light

touches stole all her attention.

"Let me show you." He stepped behind her, his hand cupping her waist. Her body sparked and heat spread through her veins when his hard chest brushed her back. He set his hands against her hips, his palms heating through her dress. "Throw the punch again, but slowly. Feel what happens with the muscles in your body."

She complied, careful not to overextend her arm. As she moved her fist forward, Bennick twisted her hips to follow her movement. The muscles over her abdomen rolled, adding a strength that hadn't been in her punch before.

His warm breath fanned her temple and she could feel the hardness of his body against her softness. She'd seen enough shirtless men on the training field to know what shape those hard lines beneath his uniform made, and her cheeks heated. She could feel his heart pounding hard and fast against her back. Fates, was he as affected by this as she was?

Something had shifted between them. Perhaps it was the gentle kiss he'd brushed against her cheek the night of the ball. Maybe it had something to do with what had happened at the orphanage; him bringing her family to her, or how he'd knelt before Mark with all the seriousness of a soldier swearing fealty to a king and promised to keep her safe. But even if Clare couldn't verbalize what it was, she relished the thrill that shot through her.

Bennick released her and stepped away.

Clare shook out her arms, wincing as she pulled the tender wound.

He caught her flash of pain and frowned. "Did I hurt you?"

"No." The graze from the crossbow bolt was a muted throb unless she stretched her arm too far.

Bennick's frown remained, though it was slight. "I think that's enough for today. We should get in some extra riding so you can be ready for Fury."

Clare cringed. She was barely comfortable riding Jinn; facing Serene's spirited mare shot anxiety through her. But Bennick was right. They had just under five weeks before they'd leave on the tour to Mortise and Clare would be expected to ride Fury several times throughout the journey.

She fell into step beside Bennick as they crossed the field, heading toward the stable. "How's your mother?" she asked. She'd paid the lady a brief visit as Serene the other day, just to check on her after the ball.

"A little better."

Something edged Bennick's tone, and she studied his guarded profile. "Is something wrong?"

His eyebrows drew together. "No." She gave him a look and he seemed to realize he was frowning. The corners of his lips pulled deeper. "Sorry. It's nothing."

"Bennick . . ."

He swallowed, his throat bobbing as he glanced away. "I never got the chance to ask . . . While you sat with her at the ball, did she talk about my father?" Wariness sharpened his question and Clare's heartbeat quickened.

"She did, a little."

When Clare said no more, Bennick looked at her. "You can ask me anything."

There was a strange mix of resignation and openness in his low voice. It caused an ache inside her and her words came out muted. "Did your father hurt you when you were young?"

Bennick's jaw locked, a muscle thrumming in his hard cheek. But he didn't seem surprised by the question. She wanted him to deny it—a flat denial that could drive away the images that had been haunting her.

When he spoke, his words were hedged. "Not in the way you're thinking."

Clare wanted to feel a measure of relief, but the tension pouring from him pressed a weight against her chest. "Did he hurt your mother?"

"Not physically." They drifted to a stop. Bennick turned to her, his voice dropping even though no one was near them. "My mother was the youngest daughter of a respected commander in the king's army. My father was one of his soldiers, and when he proposed marriage to my mother, she and her father accepted the match. Immediately after, my father was made a captain." The implication that Dennith Markam had married Lady Gweneth for a promotion was strong in Bennick's hard words.

The sounds of the training field swam around them; grunts, yells, the clacking of wooden swords—they were distant, nearly nonexistent, as Bennick rubbed the back of his neck and continued. "She was sixteen when they married. He was nineteen. A year into their marriage, he received a transfer to Iden's city guard. They moved here, but he thought to further his career by accepting another position at an outpost in Sarvin, near Ryden's border. It was too far for my mother to go." He hesitated. "She'd miscarried and wasn't well. For years, she stayed in Iden and he lived on the northern border. He returned every several months, never gone more than a year at a time, but it was hard on my mother. Her health declined. A few years after their marriage, I was born. My mother begged my father to take a position at the castle so he could be with us permanently, but he was close to another promotion and didn't want to risk losing it.

"He didn't become the city guard commander until I was eight. I saw him before then, of course, when he was on leave. I always tried to impress him. I craved his attention and praise."

Bennick released a long exhale. "When I was fourteen, I returned home unexpectedly from the military academy, on special leave. My mother was away, visiting her family. I came to my father's office in the prison and found him with a woman."

Clare's stomach dropped.

Bennick's body coiled; even his voice tensed. "I yelled at him, demanded answers—like any explanation would help. He admitted she wasn't his first mistress. He said he missed my mother while stationed away all those years." A muscle in his jaw popped as he shifted his stance. "I lost all respect for him. He'd been my hero, and in that moment, I hated him. I *still* hate him." He shook his head, snorting a rough laugh. "I hit him. Hard. When I tried to leave, he begged me not to tell my mother about his mistress."

Clare blanched. "How could he expect you to keep such a secret?"

"Sometimes I wish I had." Bennick rubbed his brow with spread fingers. "When my mother returned home, I told her about the woman in the prison and the others he'd mentioned." A tendon in his neck pulled taut. "She attacked my father as soon as he came into the room. She screamed at him and clawed his face, and he just stood there." He swallowed, gaze falling. "She was never the same after that."

"You were only trying to protect her."

"But telling her wasn't a mercy. She wasn't just heartbroken. The truth *destroyed* her. She always had delicate health, but now she's nearly bedridden and any confrontation reminds her of that day, so she avoids every fight. She's scared to be around my father because her instincts scream to fight him, but she freezes at the thought. She rearranged my old room and set out all my old toys—like that makes everything go back to how it was before."

Clare touched his arm, hoping to ease the pain that tightened his features. "You can't blame yourself for what your father did."

"I know." He shoved a hand through his hair and gripped the back of his neck. "Sometimes the guilt sinks back in, though. I shattered her world."

"No," she said firmly. "Your father did."

His jaw remained hard but gratitude flickered in his eyes. He cleared his throat, shaking his head. "Now that you know every sordid detail about my family, do you think we can still go forward as friends?"

Clare smiled gently. "Of course." It was a chance to end the conversation, but they didn't resume walking. Their hands had found each other, calloused fingertips pressed together, her skin brown and his light. "You're nothing like your father," she told him softly.

He tipped his head, like he agreed but couldn't bring himself to say it.

She pursed her lips, scuffing her foot lightly against the grass. "Soldiers have always frightened me," she admitted softly. "My father followed Ivar Carrigan in the civil war."

Understanding swept over Bennick's face. He squeezed her hand. "I'm sorry. I didn't know."

She swallowed. "Watching the soldiers drag him out . . . that will never leave me. Every time I see a uniform, that moment comes back. But when I saw you for the first time and you smiled at me . . . You were different from the very beginning."

The corner of his mouth twitched. "You didn't always like me."

"No." A smile tugged her lips. "I was angry with you. But I didn't understand the truth—that you're a good man." Her cheeks warmed and she ducked her head. She hesitated, even though she knew Bennick wouldn't judge her for her admission.

"When the carriage was attacked, you stopped me from running. And I'm grateful you did. Escape wasn't really possible. Newlan would never have let me go. You saved me again in that moment, and I didn't even know it." Her grip tightened on his hand and she peeked up at him. "I'm right where I want to be."

He stared at her. She wasn't sure what he'd say—if she'd been too bold. She didn't expect his eyes to sharpen, and she certainly didn't expect him to latch onto the most trivial part of her confession. "What do you mean, *escape*?"

Clare blinked. "What?"

Bennick's gaze was both grim and intent. "Why would you want to escape? My father said—" He froze, then the lines on his forehead creased deeper. "Fates, I'm so stupid." He pulled his hand free and took a step back. His throat constricted as he studied her, looking sick. "He threatened you. He made you become the decoy."

Her breath caught. "You didn't know."

Revulsion cut across his tense face. "No. I knew you'd been carried to the prison for questioning, and when I found my father and told him you were innocent, he assured me he'd free you."

Clare reeled. Bennick hadn't known about the threats that had bound her to the king. She'd hated him for taking part in the ruination of her life, and he hadn't known anything about it.

Fury flashed in Bennick's eyes, his hands balling to fists at his sides. "What happened after you were arrested?"

Slowly, Clare told him. He said nothing, just listened, his jaw working. His anger wasn't directed at her, but his intensity was unsettling and the story left a foul taste on Clare's tongue; she rushed to finish.

Bennick's eyes darted away and he scanned the empty area around them, as if checking to make sure no one had gotten close enough to overhear. "I should have known. Should have realized something was wrong, only . . ."

"You saw my house and family," she finished softly. "It was obvious we needed the coin. It made sense that I would have been desperate for the position, no matter the danger."

His eyes pinched shut. "I should have known," he repeated. "This changes everything. You didn't choose this."

Clare stepped up to him, closing the distance he'd claimed. Her fingers itched to take his hand, but she knotted them in her skirt instead. "I was forced into becoming the decoy," she agreed. "But every day, I've made the choice to stay. I've experienced more than I ever thought my life could hold, and even though I miss my family, I know they're being taken care of. They have all they need and that makes everything worth it."

Her words settled between them and Bennick's shoulders gradually loosened. His tone was milder—more controlled— when he spoke. "What was done to you is unforgivable. I'm sorry." He peeked at her, and the heated emotion swimming in his eyes tightened her belly. "I'm just selfish enough to be grateful you're here."

When Clare finished her riding lesson, Bennick had already returned to the castle for a meeting to discuss security for Serene's farewell banquet. She knew Cardon was on his way to fetch her, but she didn't want to stand in the busy stable waiting for him, so she stepped outside and began a slow walk toward the castle. It was really the first time she'd been alone in weeks and she enjoyed the slight freedom.

As she passed one of the sheds near the edge of the training yard, someone snatched her elbow, jerking her behind the shed. Her heart thudded and she twisted hard, tearing free and spinning to face—"Eliot?"

Her older brother stood in the shadow of the shed, his eyes wide. "You're fast," he blurted.

Clare threw her arms around his neck and squeezed so tightly her own lungs burned. His arms came around her waist, crushing her to him. But Eliot couldn't risk being seen with her. Even though the shed hid them from the training yard, anyone could turn the corner and see them. She pulled back and froze when she realized they *weren't* alone.

Eliot still gripped her arms when he followed her gaze to the young man watching them. The stranger was taller than Eliot, his frame more obviously muscled than her brother's leaner form. He had green eyes and light brown hair that curled a little against his tanned neck. Eliot cleared his throat. "Clare, this is Michael. He's my friend."

"A pleasure," Michael said, giving her a smile as he tipped his head, a curl falling over his brow. He glanced at Eliot. "I'll see you back at the barracks." He offered a quick goodbye to Clare before he disappeared.

Clare stared at her brother, confusion swirling through her. "What are you doing here?"

Eliot's expression tensed. He looked worn, as if he hadn't slept well in weeks. Stubble coated his usually smooth face and strain bunched his shoulders. His dark blue eyes darted around, almost nervous as he spoke. "I needed to make sure you were all right. After the attack on the orphanage, I've been sick with worry."

"I'm fine, Eliot. Really." She glanced toward the corner of the shed. "You shouldn't take this risk—"

Eliot stiffened. "What happened?" he snapped.

Clare realized belatedly that turning had shown him the

multicolored bruise on her cheek—the one that hadn't completely healed from the night of the ball. She tensed. "Nothing."

His jaw flexed. "That's too old to be from the attack. Who did this to you?"

She couldn't tell him the truth—that she'd fallen because of a poisoned necklace she'd worn as the princess's decoy. "It doesn't matter. You shouldn't be here."

"*You* shouldn't be here."

She shook her head. "Eliot, please. Let's not argue."

"I know what happened at the orphanage," he said, anger thrumming in his tone. "I know the boys were there. They came to see you, and you all nearly died. You could have gotten them killed!"

Anger flashed through her, heating her body. "I was terrified for them, but they're safe. And so am I."

He scowled. "You're not. You need to go home."

Clare took a step back, hands shaking at her sides. "*You* left home."

His eyes narrowed. "I had to. You know that."

"You left us," she ground out. "You didn't have to clean Thomas's cuts or tend his blisters after he'd worked a full day in the stable. You didn't have to settle Mark into bed, hearing the sounds of his starving belly." She choked, but she needed him to hear this. "You didn't have to dry their tears when they were sick. You left us. You left *me*! I raised Thomas and Mark on my own and I still had to work every day in the blasted castle kitchen. And you never even thought about how hard that was for me. You sent coin, but you never really *cared*. You just wanted to be free."

Eliot stared, jaw rigid. He wasn't in uniform but he held himself with a soldier's controlled posture. His profile was hard as stone.

Once, she would have apologized. But not now. Not when those words had been burning inside her for so long, and for the first time she felt able to speak them. She could not—would not—take them back.

Eliot's voice was a low growl. "I know my leaving hurt you. I'm sorry for that. But I didn't have a choice. Maybe I could have visited more, or—"

"Or found a different occupation," Clare snapped. "One that didn't make you change your name and run away from us."

"You can't throw that at me, Clare. Not now. Not when you abandoned the boys, too."

His words slapped her and she fell back a step. "I did not abandon—"

"Of course you did! The first chance you got for a better position, you took it, regardless of the danger to you or the cost to the boys."

Clare's eyes narrowed, breath seething out between her teeth. "I didn't have a choice."

"Neither did I!"

Silence stretched between them after his shout.

When Eliot found his voice, it was hoarse. "I'm sorry. I didn't . . . I didn't come here to do this. I just . . . I'm sorry I left you. I'm sorry you and the boys suffered." Their gazes locked. "You mean everything to me. You and the boys. Everything I've done —everything I do—it's for you."

Clare tugged in a wavering breath, tears pooling in her eyes.

"I'm sorry, Clare. I know you're still upset with me, and that's all right. But you can't stay here. It's too dangerous."

Tension lined her shoulders. "You don't have a right to tell me how to live my life."

"Then think of the boys."

"I am."

"They can't lose you."

"I'm protected."

He huffed a hard laugh. "I don't trust them to keep you safe. The princess's bodyguards. Markam."

Clare jerked at the loathing in his voice—as if Bennick's name were a curse. "You don't know—"

"I know him." The animosity pouring from him was so potent it rolled in waves against her.

"How?" Clare's voice was suddenly weak, because her mind had already linked the reason. She'd seen this anger in her brother before, and only one man had ever inspired it.

Eliot stared down at her. Though she knew the words before he spoke them, they still stabbed her. "Markam is the one who flogged me."

Her stomach rolled and her heart thudded in her chest, her ears, her temples—every part of her throbbed. "No."

Eliot ground his teeth. "You don't believe me?"

"Bennick wouldn't have done that." He couldn't have.

Her brother's face flushed. "You think I'm lying?"

Denial screamed inside her. "He wouldn't hurt anyone who . . ."

"Who what?" Eliot's face darkened. "Didn't *deserve* it? You think I deserved that?"

"No!"

He shoved closer, nostrils flaring. "He nearly killed me!"

Clare had pictured the one who'd tortured her brother. She'd imagined the monster as she'd tended Eliot's wounds and fought to save him from the ensuing fever. She'd seen the evil eyes and twisted sneer as she'd worked over Eliot's torn back, his howls of pain piercing her to the core.

That monster wasn't Bennick—couldn't be Bennick. He'd saved her life. Comforted her. Made her heart trip with only a look.

"Is he the one who hit you?" Eliot asked tightly. "A training accident, maybe?"

"What?" She touched her bruised cheek, flushing as she remembered the kiss Bennick had placed there. "No!"

Eliot grabbed her wrist, tugging her close. She clutched his shirt to steady herself. His voice blistered with warning. "I saw you walking with him today. If I see him near you again, I won't stand by." He tightened his hold on her wrist and it strained her injured arm; she gasped at the shock of pain that flared beneath the bandage.

"What's going on?" a deep voice demanded.

Clare wrenched away from Eliot, wrist stinging as she whirled to face Cardon. His scarred cheek was drawn tight and his shoulders were tense, a strong hand wrapped around the hilt of his sheathed sword. A vein in his temple throbbed when he saw her rubbing her reddened wrist. Darkness fell over his hard expression and he took a threatening step toward Eliot. "Who are you?"

Her brother stiffened, lifting his pointed chin in something almost like challenge. "Slaton."

Cardon's eyes narrowed. "You're a soldier?"

"Yes, sir."

Clare touched Cardon's tense arm. "I'm all right."

He glanced at her, his eyes still hard. "Did he hurt you?"

"I'm fine," Clare insisted, throat aching with unshed tears. "Please, Cardon. Let him go."

His jaw flexed, but he focused back on Eliot. "You won't approach her again."

Eliot swallowed hard, flint in his eyes. "Yes, sir."

"Leave."

Clare's eyes burned. She nearly said it then—admitted Eliot was her brother. But she couldn't betray him. His career would be totally ruined if anyone learned he was the son of a traitor.

Eliot spun on his heel, his back stiff as he strode away.

Cardon slid in front of Clare, blocking her view of Eliot's retreat. His voice was flat. "What happened?"

"Nothing." Her chest ached. Everything ached. "Please. I don't feel well."

His features tightened, but he took her arm and guided her toward the castle. "Did he hurt you?" Cardon asked again, tension thrumming through the words.

"No," she whispered.

It was a lie.

Eliot had carved out her heart.

CHAPTER 29

CLARE

CLARE WALKED SILENTLY BESIDE VENN through the servants' passage, headed to her lesson with Ramus. Venn had sensed her mood and wasn't bantering as he usually did. Clare hadn't spoken much to anyone since yesterday afternoon. She couldn't believe she'd stood with Bennick on the training field yesterday, holding his hand and feeling *happy*. It seemed impossible now, after her argument with Eliot. It wasn't just what he'd told her that made her body ache, but the words he'd hurled at her. *You abandoned them.*

When Cardon had escorted her back to the castle yesterday, Clare had begged Vera to cancel her lessons before she closed herself in the princess's room. Every limb felt heavy, each breath too fast and thin. Tears that had been stinging her eyes since her conversation with Eliot finally burst free.

She'd cried for everything. She cried for herself. For Mark and Thomas. For Eliot and the pain he'd suffered—and inflicted. She'd cried about the horrible truth she'd learned about Bennick. She'd cried about the unfairness that had brought her to be the decoy; the terror of being hunted by killers. And through it all, the homesickness gaped inside her, swallowing her whole.

Bennick had come by the room several times, but Clare asked Vera to keep sending him away—to tell him she didn't feel well. She couldn't see him. Didn't *want* to see him. And that cracked something inside her chest. Because Bennick had become her comfort at the castle, and Eliot's admission had taken even that from her.

After Vera had left, Clare had pulled the tin soldier from her pocket. She always tried to keep it close; it was important because Mark had given it to her, a symbol of love and protection. She hadn't pulled it out in a while because a different soldier, one with blue eyes and a ready smile, had taken a vital place in her life.

But now she realized both soldiers were dented. Neither one was perfect. She'd been a fool to think otherwise.

She pushed away her memories when Venn held the door to a narrow passage. She couldn't think too much or she'd begin crying again.

They were still inside the thin hallway when Bennick found them.

"Clare!" His voice rang on the close walls, his boots clipping rapidly against stone as he hurried to catch up.

Venn halted, and though Clare could have kept walking, she didn't. She kept her spine straight as she turned to face Bennick.

Bennick drew to a stop in front of her, eyeing her with a frown. "Vera said you were unwell."

"Yes," she said flatly.

His forehead creased, worry in his gaze. "You seemed fine when I left you at the stable."

"It came on suddenly."

"Are you still feeling ill?"

She thought of what Eliot accused her of and what he'd told her about Bennick. Her stomach clenched. "Yes."

Bennick shot a glance at Venn, but focused back on her. "Is something wrong?"

Clare said nothing, her gaze finding a spot on the gray wall behind him.

Tension thickened the air and Venn shifted uneasily. "I think I'll leave you two alone." He slipped away, but Bennick didn't watch him go. He was staring at Clare.

The moment they were alone, Bennick broke the short silence. "Cardon told me you met with Slaton yesterday."

She froze. The hint of disapproval in his voice was enough to confirm he knew her brother. The small hope that this was a horrible misunderstanding vanished. Fury threaded through her veins, warming her blood.

She could feel Bennick reacting to the coiled tightness inside her. His body hardened. "Did he hurt you?"

She kept her eyes fixed on the black button shining at the collar of his uniform. If she looked directly at him, she knew she'd snap. "No."

His throat visibly clenched. Muscles rippled and bunched as he ground his teeth. "You wrote him a letter."

"How—?"

"You left it on the table. I sealed it."

Anger flashed, thinning her mouth. "Did you read it?"

"No." His hands fisted. "How do you know him?"

"That doesn't matter."

"Yes, it does." He leaned in but she turned away before their eyes could meet. Bennick made a sound of frustration in the back of his throat. "Why won't you look at me?"

She folded her arms, a feeble shield. "I don't think I can."

He flinched.

She crushed the guilt that tried to rise.

Silence stretched between them, turning brittle. "You didn't know," Bennick finally whispered. "Before yesterday, you didn't know. And he told you."

"It's true, then? You were the one who . . ." She couldn't finish.

His words were tight. "I punished a soldier. I was his captain. It was my responsibility."

"How *could* you?" Tears choked her. She hated that she was crying, but she couldn't stop. Just like she couldn't order back the rush of anger or the spike of painful betrayal. This soldier who had befriended her, protected her—he had tortured her brother. "How could you do that to him? To *anyone*?"

His voice was clipped. "It was necessary."

Now she looked at him, their gazes colliding painfully. "You nearly killed him!"

Bennick winced. "Clare—"

"How could that have been necessary? He couldn't move without shattering pain for weeks! The resulting fever nearly killed him, and his back—" She threw a hand over her mouth, bile rising. She didn't have to describe it to him. He'd seen it.

He'd *caused* it.

Clare slumped against the wall and caught her bowed head in her hands. Her voice cracked. "You ruined his back. You tore his dreams from him—made sure he'd never advance from the city guard. How could you be so cruel?"

Bennick was silent, but she could hear his hard breaths. He shifted away and she stole a look at him. Both of his hands were braced against the opposite wall, his head ducked and back rigid.

Clare watched him as she whispered again, "How could you?"

His head dropped further. His arms trembled and his broad shoulders hunched, straining his uniform. His voice was hoarse. "Who is he to you?"

"Will that change anything?"

He said nothing.

Clare's throat burned. "He's my brother."

A shudder ripped through Bennick. His voice was thin. "I was only doing my job."

His words were empty and her insides felt just as hollow. She shook her head. "I thought you might deny it." She swatted at her tears, bitterness swelling inside her. "You're not who I thought you were."

He pushed from the wall and faced her, his cheeks flushed. Frustration tightened his words. "You don't know what he did, do you?"

"I know what *you* did. I saw it! I tended his wounds, and nothing you say will change his pain!"

Bennick shoved a hand in his hair, his face haunted. Seeing his sudden grief didn't make her feel any better. "I'm sorry." The words throbbed with remorse. "I'm sorry for what you went through. What he went through. But—"

"It was your *job*," she flung at him.

He cringed and she spun away, disgust ripping through her. She made it all of two steps before he snagged her wrist.

Clare reacted exactly as he'd taught her. She slammed back into his chest, taking him off-guard. She elbowed him in the ribs and jerked her captured wrist against the weak point of his thumb and suddenly she was free.

Before she could dart away he threw his arms around her chest, locking her arms down.

But he'd trained her for this position, too. She dropped her weight, and when he stumbled she stomped his booted foot. He grunted, but wasn't knocked off-balance. She pushed up on her toes and reared her head back, willing to knock her skull against his jaw despite the pain it promised her, but he jerked to the side.

He knew every move she'd make—he'd taught her everything she knew.

But he wasn't in a position to stop every attack. Even with her arms pinned, she wasn't helpless. She sank her fingernails into his thighs and he hissed into her hair. "Stop before you hurt yourself."

That only enraged her more. She dug her nails deeper, pinching his skin through his uniform, dragging a harsh breath out of him. His hold on her flexed, clamping around her elbows. He pulled at her, but her clawed grip didn't break. "Clare," he grunted. "You—"

"Let go of me!"

"You need to listen," he ground out.

"I've heard enough—"

"He killed a man!" His shout cut through everything—the air, the struggle—her heart.

Clare stopped thrashing. Blood drained from her face, making her dizzy. She panted for breath, nails still embedded in his legs. "You're lying."

Bennick's mouth was at her ear, quieter now. "I could have had him executed, but I didn't."

Her fingers cramped, but she didn't loosen her grip. "Eliot wouldn't hurt anybody."

"He didn't mean to. It was an accident. He showed up for duty fates-blasted drunk. His partner, a soldier named Ferrell, didn't want him to get in trouble, so they still went on patrol. Slaton wandered away only an hour into the shift and Farrell alerted another patrol. They searched everywhere, thinking Slaton might have been attacked. They found him in an alleyway, crouched down like he might be hurt. Farrell rushed forward and Slaton whipped around, striking out blindly."

Clare's insides churned. *No . . .*

Pain frayed Bennick's words. "Farrell had a wife. Two young children. I had to look in their faces and tell them he'd never come home."

Clare's eyes pinched closed and she sagged against his chest. Her fingers curled away from his legs, the sharp nails now digging into her palms. "Fates, no."

Bennick's arms no longer crushed her—they supported her. "I had no choice. He killed his partner. He didn't mean to, but he did." Bennick twisted her in his arms until she faced him, her tears splashing between them. Every muscle in his body was tense as he looked down at her. "Soldiers were demanding his life, but I could see his regret. I couldn't order his death and I didn't want to imprison him for life." His voice roughened. "I swear, I showed the most leniency I could."

Clare's breath hitched and she buried her face in his chest. She cried and he held her, one hand cupping the back of her head, his chin brushing her hair. He murmured apologies as his palm rubbed up and down her spine, and every soothing word he spoke stung. Bennick wasn't the monster she'd imagined from Eliot's accounting. There never had been a monster. Bennick had saved Eliot's life. Why hadn't Eliot told her the truth? Or had his pain, guilt, and regret become so twisted it warped every detail of what had happened?

Eventually, her crying eased. Her fingers knotted in Bennick's uniform and she pressed her forehead more firmly against his chest. "He never told me."

Bennick's chin shifted against the top of her head. "I'm

sorry."

Clare pushed gently away and he let his arms fall. "I'm sorry for hurting you."

"Don't apologize. You were defending your brother."

Her vision blurred with tears. "I wish he would have told me the truth."

Bennick's fingertips grazed her unbruised cheek, deftly wiping the tears away. He didn't say anything for a long moment, just searched her face. "What can I do? What do you need?"

She needed the world to stop spinning. Everything she'd known had been flipped once again. The hate toward Bennick was gone, leaving a pang of regret and a cloud of pain. She needed space and time to process what he'd told her. Ramus would be waiting for her in the library, but she couldn't imagine facing a lesson now. "I want to go to my room," she finally said.

Bennick didn't offer his arm, but he escorted her up to the princess's rooms. They didn't speak until after he'd opened the door for her. Only then did he face her. "I'll cancel your lessons today."

She shook her head. "I can't afford to lose a whole day. At least not riding."

"I'll cancel everything else, then." His throat bobbed. "May I ride with you?"

Clare's stomach knotted. "I . . ."

Hurt flashed in Bennick's eyes before he lowered his head with a nod. "I'll have Venn escort you." He pivoted on his heel and walked away.

Her voice wouldn't work to call him back.

CHAPTER 30

GRAYSON

DRENCHED IN SWEAT, GRAYSON SWUNG his sword at his attacker. The soldier knocked the blade aside with his own but cursed as he stumbled back, arms shaking from the staggering weight of Grayson's continuous blows.

A week had passed since having tea with Iris in her poison garden, but the tension in his body lingered. Between her threats and the constant danger Henri posed to Mia, Grayson felt strangled. He'd spent the last two hours on the training grounds, heedless of the sun beating down on him as he'd vented his anger on nameless soldiers because he couldn't attack his parents. He needed a place for his volatile energy to go so it wouldn't consume him.

These days, Grayson seldom trained this hard or long. His dark hair hung over his sweaty brow and clung to his neck. He'd actually removed his shirt and gloves, something he rarely did because it exposed his scars. He'd lost himself in the fighting, because he needed the feeling of control that inevitably came in the familiar chaos.

Grayson nicked the man's hand and the soldier hissed, jumping back and kicking up dirt. Grayson continued to hammer blows on his opponent's sword, but the man was weakening and it was time to end this.

In a few focused seconds the soldier's sword was knocked to the ground. His hands twitched up in surrender and Grayson lowered his sword, both of them breathing hard.

As the beaten soldier grabbed his weapon and stalked away, Grayson shoved a hand through his sweaty hair, pushing it off his heated face. Spectators formed a loose ring around the field, soldiers who gazed at Grayson with awe-tinged fear.

From behind, slow applause rose, and the calculated sound grated against Grayson's spine. He tensed and twisted at the waist.

Tyrell stood at the edge of the crowd, eyes glinting as he clapped. "Well done." He smiled as he strode forward. "How about we go a round?"

Grayson's right hand flexed, his left still gripping his dangling sword. "I'm done for the day." He angled away from his brother, trying to show his dismissal without giving away the fact that he monitored Tyrell from the corner of his eye. He stooped and grabbed his shirt off the ground, but Tyrell snatched it from his hand and tossed it to the dirt.

His brother's voice was level. "Father insisted we train together."

Grayson grit his teeth, eyes darting toward the castle that loomed over them. For all he knew, Henri watched from one of the narrow windows glinting with sunlight.

Tyrell shed his shirt, powerful muscles rippling over his chest as he tossed it aside. He nodded to Grayson's sword. "You can put that down. We'll be using some of Mother's daggers."

Blades dipped in poison, no doubt.

Grayson sheathed his sword and set it aside. When he faced Tyrell, his brother gripped two long daggers with blue hilts.

The last two hours of intense fighting had taken their toll. Grayson's heart raced and the muscles in his body spasmed, screaming at the abuse. He had to order himself to think past the pain so he could win this fight quickly. He extended a hand for one of the knives.

The dagger flashed and Grayson jerked back, spitting a curse as the knife's tip barely missed his palm.

Tyrell smirked, twirling the blades in his hands. "I never said you got one."

A growl vibrated up Grayson's throat and muscles tensed in his arms as he balled his hands. "Let's get this over with," he said, voice thrumming with anger.

Tyrell grinned. "I think I'd prefer to draw it out." He dove forward and Grayson drew back; the daggers sliced only air, but Tyrell kept coming.

They weren't allowed to kill each other. That was the only rule in the Kaelin family.

Grayson skirted around his brother, spinning from the knives. He kicked at Tyrell's legs, but never made contact. The blows and parries came rapidly, too fast for the eye to track. Instinct and years of training guided Grayson's movements, keeping the expertly wielded knives away from his flesh.

Beyond them, the spectators muttered and cursed at the ferocity of the fight.

Tyrell spun and threw out his leg, heel aimed for Grayson's abdomen. Grayson pivoted and caught his brother's ankle. He yanked and Tyrell swore as he stumbled.

Grayson resisted the urge to twist his brother's foot completely—snapping the ankle was excessive, and whenever he thought of using more violence than necessary, Mia's face came to mind.

Grayson didn't break any bones, but he did twist until Tyrell was forced to fall. His back slammed to the dirt-packed ground, knocking the air from his lungs. He still clutched both daggers.

Grayson stomped on Tyrell's wrist and his brother sucked in a sharp breath, but he still didn't drop the knife. Grayson grabbed for the dagger locked in Tyrell's left hand—his weaker one—prying at firmer fingers than he'd expected.

He realized his mistake and cursed as the other dagger stabbed toward him. He really was tired, to have missed Tyrell's obvious ploy—his brother had pretended to be more dazed by the fall than he was.

Grayson lurched back, barely dodging the knife.

Tyrell growled, drew up his legs and kicked out, leaping to his feet without using his hands. They squared their shoulders as they faced each other. The ring of soldiers had grown; Tyrell would be even more desperate to win. He wouldn't want to be defeated in front of the men he trained.

Tyrell launched himself at Grayson, who danced to avoid the slashing blades. The knives continued to arc through the air, coming at him from every angle. His brother was angry, frustrated—those daggers were coming in a lethal way, nothing held back. In the heat of this battle, Tyrell *would* kill him.

Grayson's body throbbed from all the blows he'd received today, and for the first time in this fight he tasted the metallic tang of fear. As a child, that would have crippled him. Now, it motivated him.

Ducking under Tyrell's arm, Grayson sprang up behind him,

grasped his arm, and twisted as he simultaneously slammed his free fist into Tyrell's shoulder. A sickening *pop* dislocated the joint and his brother howled. The knife dropped. Grayson snatched the blade before it hit the ground, the leather hilt slipping a little in his sweaty palm before his fingers locked. He spun away, low and guarded, weapon ready.

Tyrell's face was flushed. His arm hung oddly at his side and his nostrils flared. He gripped the matching knife in his other hand and glared at Grayson, pain mingling in his brown eyes as sweat beaded his forehead. "I'll kill you," he seethed. "I'm going to squeeze every last breath out of you."

Grayson nodded to the arm that hung lower than the other. "You might need that."

His brother snarled. He brought his dagger to his mouth, holding the hilt between his teeth. He then grasped his limp arm with his good hand and, in a practiced motion, snapped his shoulder back into place.

Murmuring broke out among the soldiers surrounding them. Yes, the Kaelins really did dislocate each other's shoulders, and yes, they knew how to fix themselves. Physicians had been ordered to stop tending that particular injury after the first few times, and, honestly, it got easier to pop back in place. But Tyrell's shoulder would still be tender and weak; Grayson knew that from personal experience.

Chest rising and falling, Tyrell pulled the dagger out of his mouth before launching at Grayson again.

Grayson parried the blow with his dagger, the two blades meeting in a jarring crash. He delivered a punch to Tyrell's side and his brother hit back. The fight became grittier, and Grayson knew it couldn't last much longer. One of them was going to make a mistake.

He prayed it wouldn't be him.

Grayson took a glancing blow to his jaw but he slipped past Tyrell's guard and slammed the dagger's hilt into Tyrell's gut.

His older brother choked, doubling over, and Grayson's knee came up to Tyrell's chin. He flew back, crashing to the ground. Grayson crouched over him, both daggers now in his grip and poised over Tyrell's bobbing throat.

"You're dead," Grayson hissed, lungs straining against his ribs, the adrenaline of the fight rattling through him.

Tyrell glared, a vein popping in his forehead. His face was red and his body shook with pain or rage—or both.

"Yield," Grayson demanded.

When Tyrell didn't reply, Grayson pressed both knifepoints to his neck. "Yield," he repeated. "Or you'll find out what poison Mother used to coat these blades."

The crowd of soldiers had gone silent. The only sound was the distant barking of dogs somewhere in the castle yard.

Tyrell's breath huffed hotly in Grayson's face. "I yield," he gritted out.

Grayson straightened. He tossed the daggers to the dirt on either side of Tyrell and turned, stalking back toward his things. The gathered soldiers shied back, even though he wasn't close to them yet. He tried to ignore the pang of loathing he suddenly felt—for Tyrell, for Henri, and for himself.

He was nearly to his sword when one of the spectators sucked in a breath. Instinct flared and Grayson whirled, but too late. Tyrell was already there, throwing dirt into his eyes.

Grayson closed his eyes reflexively, but the damage was done. The gritty dirt burned, and though he managed to peel open his watering eyes, he couldn't see Tyrell as his brother kicked him in the gut. His back hit the ground and his head slammed twice. The back of his skull pulsed with pain and he jerked in a breath a second before Tyrell's boot stomped onto his bare chest.

Grayson gasped at the shattering impact and grabbed Tyrell's ankle, but before he could break it, a blade sliced into his forearm. He hissed at the familiar burn—a knife slicing flesh wasn't new—but he tensed when the pain turned sharper. Hotter.

Syalla.

A non-fatal poison, but the pain was immediate and debilitating once it touched blood.

Grayson's back arched and he tried to scream past the crushing weight on his chest. He grabbed for his cut arm but Tyrell used his other foot to pin his wrist to the ground. With his brother standing completely on him, breathing was nearly impossible and his ribs creaked.

Tyrell bent low, his voice throbbing with promise. "One day, I *will* kill you."

Grayson's body shook so badly he didn't know how Tyrell didn't lose his balance. The scorching Syalla spread through him, burning up his arm, his chest—his entire body. His heart seized, but he wasn't able to do anything as Tyrell's other blade flashed over Grayson's cheek.

Agony ripped across his face and this time he did find the air to scream, though the ragged sound shredded his throat.

Tyrell stepped off him, clutching the bloody daggers as he walked away. The soldiers melted from the field, leaving Grayson to bleed in the dirt as the poison consumed him.

CHAPTER 31

CLARE

CLARE WANDERED THE ROSE GARDEN, keeping to the narrow pebbled paths that wound through the well-groomed hedges and blooms. The nobles preferred the more fashionable king's garden, making this a perfect place to disappear for an hour or so in the afternoon. Clare had been making regular use of it over the past few days.

It had been four days since she'd seen Bennick. Four days since she'd learned the truth about her brother's flogging. She didn't blame Bennick for what he'd done; all she felt was gratitude that Bennick hadn't executed her brother for his mistakes. His horrible, tragic mistakes.

She'd started a letter to Eliot, but words wouldn't come. Frustration and hurt blotted out everything. He'd been cruel, and he hadn't told her the truth. He'd been drinking while on duty and he'd killed his partner; she couldn't imagine his guilt. But instead of facing the truth, he'd evaded it. Twisted it, so Clare believed he'd been punished for no reason—that his captain had tortured Eliot simply because he could. Maybe that's what he believed now, too.

Her slippers scuffed against the pebbles beneath her feet, the lonely sound standing out against a backdrop of birdsong and the gentle rustling of the leaves. She craved the steadiness and comfort of Bennick's presence, but couldn't bring herself to seek him out. Her emotions were too chaotic and she was nervous of how much damage she'd done by attacking him in the corridor.

For the last four days, *he* had been avoiding *her*.

Clare neared a bend in the path and instinct slowed her steps. In the silence of the garden, whispered voices carried from around the hedge.

". . . running out of time."

"Has it ever been on my side?" Grandeur muttered.

"No," the first voice said, deep and cool. "But the plan you conceived is good."

"I can't force her," Grandeur said defensively. "This isn't a light thing I'm asking."

"You said Miss Ellington would help of her own free will."

Clare's body locked, her ears straining to pick up every word.

"I still believe she will," Grandeur said.

"What makes you confident this maid isn't like the others?" the stranger asked.

"She's not a friend to Serene. And her father was killed by my father's order, which can't sit well with her."

"But—"

"I don't have to explain myself to you," Grandeur cut in, a cool edge entering his tone.

Clare shivered, despite the sun warming her back. She didn't dare move, not even to shift her feet. Grandeur and the stranger weren't moving, but they were just around the bend. She should try to slip away, but the fear of being heard—along with a burning sense of curiosity—kept her in place.

"Fair enough, Your Highness," the man said. "But you understand my concern—*our* concern. You approached Clare Ellington weeks ago and she all but rejected you. Perhaps your sister has already won the girl's allegiance."

"No."

"Then why did she resist your request to spy on the princess?"

"It was too soon," Grandeur said, voice tightening. "I overwhelmed her."

"There are other ways to secure allegiance. Perhaps a well-placed threat against her family. She has two young brothers living in the city."

Clare's breath hitched, her mouth running dry.

"No," Grandeur said at once, finality ringing in his tone.

The stranger's voice was thin. "If they were threatened, she would be yours completely."

Clare's hands fisted at her sides, blood roaring in her ears, nearly drowning out Grandeur's sharp reply. "No. Threats never work as well as conviction. She will *choose* to help me because she'll believe in me. I won't use her family against her."

"Unless there's no other choice."

A short silence stretched. Clare rolled back on her heels, prepared to bolt if their footsteps moved toward her. Finally, Grandeur spoke, and his voice was firm. "Yes."

Clare's stomach dropped.

The stranger spoke. "What is necessary is not always easy. Are you prepared for the choice you may have to make?"

Grandeur's voice was soft, shooting ice through Clare's veins and chilling her despite the afternoon sun. "Sacrifices are made in the name of peace every day. If my sister rises against me, she will become one of them."

Clare spread her damp palms over her skirt, her heart jumping in her chest. She paced because she couldn't sit, couldn't focus on anything but what she was about to do.

The door to the sitting room opened Princess Serene swept inside, her dusky pink skirt brushing over the cheery carpet. It was the same room they'd shared that awful breakfast in, two months ago now.

The door closed, Cardon and Dirk remaining in the hall.

Serene eyed the low table as she stepped closer. "As surprised as I was to receive your invitation, I admit I did expect there to actually be tea."

Clare shifted her slippered feet, her hands clenched before her. "I'm sorry. It was the only excuse I could think of."

The princess's eyes narrowed, catching the edge in Clare's voice. "What's happened?"

Stumbling a little over the words, Clare related all she'd overheard in the garden. Serene said nothing, only watched her.

"I don't know if Grandeur is a true threat to my family," she finished, a cramp tightening her belly. "But I can't take that risk. He sounded so . . . cold. And the man he was with . . . I'm not sure who Grandeur has allied with, but that man is evil. I don't know if Grandeur even realizes how dangerous he is."

Serene hadn't moved during the entire account. She stood still—poised, shoulders back, expression expertly smooth. "You're worried about my brother."

Clare's forehead creased. Despite everything, Grandeur had

been her friend, and that man he'd allied with was dangerous. Of course, Grandeur's friendship could have been a lie. A manipulation.

She rubbed her brow. "Yes, I suppose I am worried about him."

Serene lowered her chin. "You're worried about him, yet you don't trust him. Which is why you're here."

"I can't risk my family," Clare said again. She met the princess's stare. "And I can't let him plot your death."

Serene lifted one eyebrow. "How kind of you."

Clare nearly rolled her eyes. "Your brother is paranoid. He's spoken to me about his fears that you are plotting to take the throne, or betray Devendra by running from your marriage to Desfan. If you could speak with him, assure him that—"

"If you truly thought he could be reasoned with," Serene cut in, "you wouldn't be here talking to me."

Clare glanced away, but Serene was right. She didn't trust Grandeur. She couldn't. Not now.

And that hurt.

Serene sighed. "You don't even like me, Clare. Why did you come to me?"

Clare eyed the princess, who was watching her closely. "Being at the castle, I've learned that everyone wears a mask. You pretend to be sharp, cold, and uncaring, but I saw the real you at the orphanage. When the bolts started flying, you grabbed a little boy and shielded him with your own body. It was your gut reaction, not something you did for show—not like the rest of that day could have been. Anyone can pretend to be something they're not. I'm proof of that. But it's who you are when you think no one is watching that reveals your true character."

Serene said nothing for a moment. Then, "That was surprisingly profound for a kitchen maid."

Clare huffed a short laugh and shook her head. "I knew the moment I overheard Grandeur that I would have to make a choice between him and you." Even if it caused a pang in her chest.

Serene began to pace slowly over the bright rug, her voice carefully low. "There are things you don't know about my brother or my father. If I wear a mask, it's because of them." She exhaled heavily. "You know I went to Zennor after my mother died. While there, I learned the truth about my mother's death." Her voice tightened. "My father murdered her."

Clare stared. The princess's hard expression didn't alter as she waited for Clare to process the words.

They were impossible to process.

"But, the queen was ill—"

"He poisoned her," Serene bit out, fury flashing in her fierce blue eyes. "It took months, and when Grandeur learned what was happening he didn't stand up to our father. He didn't do anything to save our mother's life. He watched her die."

Denials swam up Clare's throat, but nothing came out. She couldn't imagine Grandeur being capable of such a thing. But then, she had heard him threaten to kill his own sister.

Clare finally managed to speak past the dryness in her mouth. "Why would Newlan kill the queen?"

"Their match wasn't made for love," Serene said. "It was purely political. Devendra needed the trade routes and Zennor needed financial security. My parents didn't even meet until their wedding." The corner of her lip curled sardonically. "I used to think it was romantic. Now, as I face something similar, I know the fear she must have felt." Vulnerability leaked through the words and Serene seemed to notice. She moved to the settee and sat on the edge, her hands smoothing over her lap with almost nervous energy. Her spine was painfully straight and she didn't meet

Clare's eye as she spoke. "My father was supposed to go to Zennor and claim her hand, but he sent his cousin to fetch her instead: Ivar Carrigan."

The familiar name made her scalp prickle; the man had incited a civil war and ultimately stolen Clare's father from her.

"Ivar journeyed to Zennor and met my mother. They fell in love, but my mother refused to give into her feelings. She insisted they remain friends only, even though it hurt them both. Ivar escorted her safely to Iden and into my father's arms." Serene's eyes skipped to Clare. "Ivar and my father never saw eye-to-eye after that. Their fall-out was public and bloody, and when my father crushed the resistance, my mother helped Ivar flee Devendra. Somehow, my father found out. He could have spared her. Banished her. Executed her with dignity, even. Instead, he poisoned her. She probably never even knew it wasn't sickness that killed her, but her cruel and vindictive husband." Serene's hands shook; she rolled her fingers to fists. Moisture clouded her eyes. "I've known the truth for two years and I haven't been able to confront him."

Clare moved forward, coming to sit beside Serene so she could wrap an arm around her shoulders. Serene stiffened, then relaxed against Clare's side, allowing the embrace. "I'm sorry," she whispered. "I don't know what else to say."

"Now you understand," Serene whispered. "You understand why I can't trust him or Grandeur."

"Are you sure Grandeur knew about the poison?"

"Yes. I've seen proof. And though Grandeur might mourn our mother, there is guilt there, too."

"How did you learn about this?"

Serene hesitated. "Some things I'm not ready to share, but trust me—my father is a danger to everyone in Devendra."

Clare's lips thinned. That was a truth she knew. "He needs

to be punished for the queen's murder."

"Believe me, I've considered every course," Serene said. "Killing him myself, going to the court, telling my uncle." She shook her head. "My father would either kill me, evade the public accusation, or there would be war with Zennor."

"But he can't go unpunished."

"He won't." There was promise in Serene's dark eyes. A chilling, final kind of promise. "I can't act now, but soon." She stood suddenly, and the look she sent Clare was almost embarrassed. "I'm sorry that I thought the worst of you. I truly thought you were in league with my father. That you were taking the risks of becoming the decoy in the hopes that my father would kill me and make you my replacement."

Clare pursed her lips. "You don't really think your father would do such a thing?" But after what Serene had just told her, Clare didn't know if she believed her own words.

She let out a tight breath. "He will try to kill me someday. I know it. I only pray I can kill him first."

Clare shook her head. "Your family will be the death of me."

Serene's mouth twitched, though her eyes were sober. "Probably. But you could help me. I want to avenge my mother, but even more than that I want to protect Devendra. If you help me, I swear I can help you and protect your family."

Clare eyed her. "Do you have a plan?"

Serene edged out a smile. "Always."

CHAPTER 32
CLARE

CLARE WAS BACK IN THE QUEEN'S ROSE garden, pacing in a small circle to vent her rising anxiety. The sunlight warmed her dark hair and skin, and birdsong trilled nearby. An idyllic scene, but her heart pounded a rapid tempo, each thud echoing harshly in her ears. Yesterday she'd stood in this garden and overheard Grandeur and the man with the deep voice, and now she waited for the prince to appear.

Tension pulled in her gut, and she prayed this would work —that Serene's plan was the right one.

Grandeur strode into view. Concern traced lines over his dark, handsome face, but she didn't trust the sincerity in his eyes.

His guards hung back without prompting, giving them privacy. "Are you all right?" he asked. "Your note sounded distressed."

She forced her teeth to unclench. "I didn't know who else to turn to."

He frowned. "You can tell me anything, Clare."

He sounded sincere. Perhaps he was sincere, and she was making a mistake by calling him here.

But she could not ignore what Serene had told her, or what she'd overheard with her own ears.

Her hands fisted at her sides. "I found a note addressed to Serene. It was on the floor of her suite." She drew out the small square card. "I didn't know what else to do but share it with you."

Intrigue sparked in his eyes as he took the paper, his long, warm fingers brushing hers. He flipped open the note and scanned the words.

Patience. your time will come.

Be careful.

The scrawled message had been written in Serene's left hand, giving it an unrefined look. A messy nobleman's scrawl, or a peasant's untried hand—it truly was anonymous. "My cousin Imara taught me that," Serene had said, true affection in her voice. "She's a master at this sort of thing."

Grandeur's eyes narrowed on the written words and Clare swallowed. "It could mean anything," she said, pouring out the practiced phrases. "It's vague, and yet . . . I keep thinking of your fears about Serene, and what she might plan for Devendra. I can't let harm come to my family." An edge she couldn't control entered her voice. "I would do anything for them."

"You did the right thing," Grander took her hand with his free one. His fingers flexed around hers, dark and strong. When he peered at her, she almost believed his words. "I can protect you and your family, Clare. I can protect all of Devendra. But I need your help."

Though it wasn't part of the plan, she couldn't stop herself from whispering, "Maybe Serene is innocent. Perhaps you should talk with her—tell her your fears."

She wanted him to agree. To prove that he could still be considered a friend, despite the evidence stacked against him.

Grandeur shook his head. "I can't tip our hand. Besides, she'd only deny her treasonous intentions."

"But surely this note isn't a sign of treason—"

"As you said, it could mean anything. We must treat it as the threat it could be." He dropped her hand and tucked the note into his pocket.

Clare straightened. "What are you going to do?"

"This isn't enough evidence to place before my father. We need to watch Serene. Catch her if—when—she truly turns treasonous." He rested a hand on her shoulder, head ducked so their gazes were level. "I need you to watch her."

Clare shook her head slowly, her eyes still locked with his as she gave the response Serene had laid out. "But we leave for Mortise soon. You won't be around to help me."

"You won't be cut off." Grandeur pulled back his hand, only to twist off one of his many rings. It was heavy and thick with a crest on top: a bird with wings outstretched. "This was my mother's. Use it to seal any letter and any city guardsman within Devendran borders will see it safely to me. Convey anything that could be useful in bringing Serene's plans to light, and I swear you and your family will remain safe."

She hoped he didn't notice the sweat on her palm when she took the offered ring. He'd believed her so quickly. Almost like he trusted her.

A waver of doubt, lined with guilt, thickened her throat.

What if Grandeur truly was a friend, and she had somehow misread the conversation in the garden? What if he'd been playing the spy, too?

But what if he was an enemy?

Grandeur looked at her full on. "There's no turning back from this, Clare. Are you sure?"

Her pulse drummed and her heart clenched.

He was right. There was no turning back.

"Yes," she breathed. "I'm sure."

Clare walked briskly toward the garden's exit, hands still trembling over what she'd done. Grandeur had left in the other direction so they could take separate exits in case anyone watched.

The desire to talk to Bennick was strong, reaching past the strain between them. But Clare had promised Serene she wouldn't share any of this. Besides, Bennick could do nothing against Grandeur or Newlan and Clare didn't want to put him in danger. For now, she would follow Serene's lead. Despite their rough history, she trusted the princess.

Clare quickened her step, anxious to shrug off this encounter and focus on her normal routine—as both Grandeur and Serene had urged her to do. She had defense training with Dirk; Bennick had turned the task over to the older guard, after the truth about Eliot had come out. In many ways, training with Dirk was harder because his style was different. She was grateful for the added challenge. It kept her focused on the moment, and she needed that more than ever.

Rounding one of the final corners, Clare hit into a hard chest.

Steel hands grabbed her arms, steadying her. She opened her mouth to apologize, but when she looked up the words caught in her throat.

The commander stared down at her, a frown twisting his face. "Miss Ellington." His hold tightened. "Just the person I hoped to find."

Fear lanced through her chest and her breath came out too harshly. "Release me."

Slowly—deliberately—he lifted a finger at a time and peeled his hands away.

Clare took a step back and gripped her gray skirt in her fists. "Let me pass."

The commander didn't move. "We never had a chance to discuss what happened at the ball."

Anger tightened her skin and she gritted her teeth. "I was trying to help your wife."

A muscle in his jaw ticked. "My wife's well-being isn't your concern."

"Nor does it seem to be yours."

His blue eyes—like Bennick's, but far too cold—narrowed. "Just because you look like Serene doesn't make you the princess. You have no authority. And I think we both know the king wouldn't take well to you parading around as his daughter, issuing orders in her name."

Clare matched his glare. She had no words for this man—this monster. She stepped around him, but his hand snagged her wrist and jerked her close.

Her pulse tripped as his fingers squeezed. He leaned in, his voice low and dark. "If you interfere in my affairs again, I'll tell the king you abused your illusion of power. You'll be at his mercy, and I don't think he'll have much to offer."

"Do you think he'd show *you* mercy?" Clare shot back.

His brows slammed down. "What?"

"You disobeyed the king's orders. You told Bennick about me. I wonder if the king would forgive you?"

His grip on her wrist turned strangling. "You dare threaten me?" The coldness in his voice caused a flash of alarm inside her. They were alone, and while she'd learned defensive skills from Bennick, the commander towered over her.

She tugged her arm against his hold. "Let me go."

Beside them, pebbles shifted underfoot. They both turned to see Bennick round the hedge, Dirk at his side.

Seeing Bennick after four days was an exhilarating kind of shock. Clare's breathing halted. Her eyes latched onto him, scanning him. He looked tired. His blue uniform was well-maintained, but his stubble was thicker and the skin beneath his eyes was shadowed.

His gaze sliced over her, narrowing on her wrist, where the commander grasped her with a white-knuckled grip.

Bennick's nostrils flared. "Release her."

The commander's jaw worked, but he unwrapped his fingers. Clare snatched her arm back and retreated a step, rubbing her wrist.

Bennick was still focused on the commander when he asked her, "Are you all right?"

"Yes."

Bennick's face remained hard as he eyed his father. "Dirk," he ordered curtly.

The older bodyguard moved forward, gesturing for Clare to follow him.

She hesitated, looking at Bennick. "Aren't you coming?"

"No." His voice was pure ice as he glared at his father. "The commander and I need to talk."

CHAPTER 33

BENNICK

TENSION RODE BENNICK HARD AS HE viewed his father. Commander Markam was tall and broad-shouldered. Age had touched him lightly. His features were strong and square and his booming voice carried authority with ease. When Bennick was young—back when he idolized his father—he'd always wanted to look more like the commander. Now he wished nothing tied them together.

He'd been watching his father since the ball, instinct warning that the commander would make a point to corner Clare and intimidate her. Bennick had also been watching Clare, and he knew she'd made a habit of wandering the queen's garden. Apparently, the commander had noticed, too.

He heard Clare follow Dirk's prompting and he was grateful his friend led her away. He couldn't focus on his father when she was there, watching him. He longed to be the one taking her arm, but he knew he'd lost that privilege, and the pain of that loss only flared his anger.

A vein in the commander's temple throbbed, his eyes trained on his son. "It looks like you have something you want to say."

Fury rippled under Bennick's skin and his hands fisted. "You will not approach Miss Ellington again."

The commander scowled, the corners of his eyes creasing. "You have no authority over me."

"In this I do. Miss Ellington was placed under my protection."

"And you deem me a threat?"

"Yes."

The commander huffed. "You truly think I would harm her?"

"You're no fates-blasted saint." Bennick pulled in a breath, fighting for calm. "You won't threaten her, touch her, or even make her uncomfortable, or I'll report you to the king."

Commander Markam stepped closer, voice dropping low. "You fool. You've lost the king's regard. Every attack made against the princess or decoy brings you closer to losing your career." He shook his head. "You never should have thrown away your future in the city guard. Bodyguards fall out of favor too easily."

It was an old argument and it made the muscles in Bennick's neck tighten. Best to ignore it. "I can't be any clearer. If you threaten Miss Ellington again, you and I will exchange more than words."

The commander's lip curled. "You will treat me with respect."

"Respect is earned. You told me that, back when your words meant something." Bennick grit his teeth, cutting himself off. The smell of roses was thick on the warm air, almost smothering him. He retreated a step, hands spread. "I'm done."

"No." His father glared. "This needs to end. You ignore my advice in public and in private. You make rash decisions just to defy me. I offered you more men for the princess's tour to Mortise and you all but spat in my face. Do you truly think you won't need them?"

"I don't need anything from you."

Commander Markam's teeth bared. "Fates curse you, boy, I'm only trying to help!"

"You always act like it's my fault," Bennick snapped. "Like I'm the one in the wrong because I can't forgive you for a simple mistake. But it's never one mistake with you. It's a thousand mistakes, made repeatedly and with no remorse."

"Ben—"

"You threatened her."

The commander stilled. "What?"

"Clare. You threatened her life and forced her to become the decoy. She told me everything." Bennick pushed a hand through his hair, disgust pulling at his insides. "You have no honor."

"The king tasked me with finding a decoy, and once I was assured she hadn't taken part in the attack, I knew she would be an excellent choice. You can't deny she's been the perfect decoy!"

Bennick shook his head. "I should have guessed the truth. I learned a long time ago you don't care who you hurt."

Something like regret ghosted across his father's face, but Bennick dismissed it. Regret, from the man who hadn't seemed the least bit ashamed when his son had found him in the arms of a mistress? Impossible.

Bennick had so much he wanted to say, but he knew his father would meet him with excuses, as he always did. He turned on his heel.

"Don't walk away from me," the commander ordered. "Ben!"

Bennick's footsteps didn't slow, and he didn't look back.

Cardon's hand snapped up in surrender. "I yield," he gasped, chest hiking and dropping roughly as he stepped back.

Bennick ground his teeth and disengaged from the fight. He'd discarded his shirt a half hour ago and sweat slicked his front and back. His hands throbbed, blisters forming as he swung the wooden staff; it had been too long since he'd sparred with it.

He and Cardon stood in the castle orchard. Sometimes Bennick came to train here when he wanted to avoid the other soldiers on the training field. The solitude was comforting, as was the fluttering of green leaves blown in a gentle breeze. The calm surroundings were a contrast to the storm raging inside him.

Cardon breathed deeply, feet spread wide. "Are you going to tell me what war is happening in your head?"

Bennick swiped a hand over his brow, knocking back damp strands of hair. "I'm fine."

The older man snorted. "You're just strangling that staff for no reason. I'm sure you also had no reason to spar here, rather than the training yard where Clare is."

Bennick's head snapped up, chest rising. "Clare has nothing to do with this."

Cardon leveled a look at him.

Bennick's face heated and he looked away. Apple trees lined either side of them, shielding them from view. When he was a child, he'd often lost himself among these trees, playing the long afternoons away. He was lost now, but in a different way.

"You've been avoiding her for days," Cardon said.

Bennick ground the end of his staff deeper into the dirt and looked down the straight row of trees. When he spoke, his voice was quiet. "Have you ever done something, and—even though you had no other choice—you still regret what you did?"

Cardon met the convoluted question easily. "Yes."

Bennick's fingers tightened on the smooth wooden staff. "How did you come to peace with it?"

Cardon's forehead creased. "I haven't. But I know I made the only choice I could have." His cocked his head. "This isn't just about Clare, is it?"

Bennick glanced away from his friend's gaze.

Cardon's voice was quiet. "I know you have regrets about your father. And fates can see he has regrets about you. But you're not him, Bennick. His flaws aren't your flaws."

The words hit Bennick hard, pinching his throat. All he could do was offer a short nod of thanks.

Cardon planted the end of his staff on the ground. "One thing I've learned is that the worst regrets don't come from what we said or did. They come from what we didn't say or do." He shook his head. "I don't know what happened between you and Clare, but she misses you. I catch her searching every room she enters and she's always looking over her shoulder—looking for you."

Bennick wanted Cardon's words to be true, but his stomach clenched. "I did something to someone she loves. Something I can never reverse." He swallowed, throat bobbing hard. "I don't know if she'll be able to forgive me."

Cardon shifted his stance on the uneven ground, gripping his staff. "Don't walk away leaving things unsaid. A man can never make a graver mistake."

Bennick huffed a laugh. "You sound as wise as Dirk."

"It was bound to happen after all the years we've served together." Cardon hefted his staff, spinning it so it whistled through the air. He stopped the motion almost at once and winced, shaking out his arm. "Promise me you'll talk to her.

I'm getting too old for this level of sparring."

Bennick cracked a smile, then clasped Cardon's free hand. "Thank you."

Cardon's grip flexed and his eyes were intent as he met Bennick's gaze. "You're not alone, Bennick. Never forget that."

A knot swelled in his chest and he tightened his hold on Cardon's hand. Despite everything wrong with his father, Bennick had found good men he could look up to.

He would always thank the fates for that.

CHAPTER 34

CLARE

CLARE DIDN'T DARE ADVANCE BEYOND A trot with Fury. The powerful horse snorted and tossed her head often and each step was sharp. Clare's skin was stained darker and she wore Serene's riding dress, but Fury still knew she wasn't the princess. Thank the fates the horse hadn't decided to throw her.

By the end of the ride, Master Lank was grinning. He helped her dismount, pride shining in his eyes. "A lovely job, Princess."

"Thank you."

He took Fury's reins and they walked into the stable, moving away from the stable hands. "May I ask you something, Clare?" Master Lank asked softly. When she nodded, his question took her off-guard. "What happened between you and Ben?"

Her stomach tightened. "What do you mean?"

They entered the shadowed stable and Master Lank shrugged. "You've both been out of sorts and he doesn't escort you to the stable anymore. Have you argued?"

Clare scuffed her foot against the straw-strewn ground. "There was a misunderstanding. That's all."

Master Lank sighed. "I know it's not my place, but I can't watch you both suffer without saying something. I've seen too much sadness. My son . . ." Grief swelled in his voice and he glanced away. "I don't know if Gavril told you, but he used to be stationed along the Mortisian border, near Stills. During some border violence, Mortisians attacked the outpost. His wife, Bonnai, was killed in front of him. His daughter, just three months old, was killed by a fire the Mortisians set. Gavril nearly lost his life trying to save her from the flames. And still he lost her, too."

Clare pressed a hand over her mouth, her chest squeezing. "I didn't know. How terrible. I'm so sorry."

Master Lank cleared his throat, eyes shining with unshed tears. "I tell you so you can understand the advice I've given him: life isn't predictable. Tragedies happen, and there are consequences beyond our control. But we choose the people we want close to us. We choose to be lonely, or embraced. Don't choose loneliness, my dear." He handed her the reins and bowed before walking out of the stable, disappearing into the sunlight.

Clare pursed her lips and tugged Fury forward, leading them deeper inside the stable. She found Fury's stall and set about tending her, as Serene was known to do. She was brushing the animal's shiny brown coat when a boot scuffed against the floor behind her. She twisted, freezing when she saw Bennick.

He stood with one hand braced against the frame of the open stall, his throat bobbing once. "I'm sorry I missed watching you ride. Master Lank said you did well."

The brush stung her palm, she gripped it so tightly. Seeing him loosened the ache in her chest she'd almost grown accustomed too, even though his presence also made her stomach roll. "How did things go with the commander?"

Bennick's jaw tightened. "He won't bother you again."

She wanted details, but it didn't feel right to ask. The tense set of Bennick's shoulders assured her she hadn't been the only topic to rise between father and son. Besides, her breaths were getting shorter the longer they stood together. The air between them was strained, yet also charged, lifting the fine hairs on her body.

"May I join you?" Bennick asked, an undercurrent running beneath the question.

"Yes."

He eased into the stall and stroked Fury's nose. The horse nudged his palm, obviously comfortable with him. "How is defense training going?" he asked, moving around Fury to search for another brush.

I miss you.

"Quite well," she said instead.

Bennick nodded once. "Good." He didn't look at her as he lifted a brush and set to work, the large animal standing between them.

Having him so near, being alone in the closed space of the stall, wreaked havoc on her thoughts, feelings, and body. Her skin felt too tight, her pulse thrummed, and all she could think was how much she wished she hadn't pushed him away. Perhaps she'd needed time, but now she needed him. She just wasn't sure what to say—where to start.

Resting a steadying hand on Fury's warm back, she pulled the brush down with the other.

Soft fingers glanced over hers and her eyes shot to Bennick. His hand slid back, held a breath away from her fingertips against the horse's back. "I've missed you, Clare."

The softly spoken words warmed her. "I've missed you, too."

A thin smile crept into place. "You have?"

Clare nodded, then bit her lower lip. The words began to spill from her. "I'm sorry for how I reacted."

He grimaced. "Please don't apologize. You did nothing wrong."

"Yes, I did. I was angry about a lot of things. Angry with my-self. And I took it out on you." She shook her head. "Avoiding you was wrong, I just . . ."

"I understand," he said gently. "And if you need space, I can give you that."

"I don't want space from you." The words were out before she realized their boldness. And though warmth touched her cheeks, she wouldn't take them back.

Bennick's blue eyes sparked and he dipped his head, strands of sandy blond hair brushing his forehead. "I can tell Dirk not to worry about training you tomorrow."

"I'd like that."

He smiled, and an answering grin tugged her lips. Ducking her head, she pulled back her hand and renewed her efforts to brush Fury.

"Serene!"

Clare and Bennick twisted to face Ser Amil Havim, who stood at the stall entrance. The Mortisian's smile spread wide, though an edge lurked in his dark brown eyes.

"Ser Havim." Clare inclined her head politely, but kept a grounding hand on Fury's back. She hadn't seen the emissary's son since the ball and she'd rather enjoyed the reprieve.

"I'm sorry I missed your ride—I would have liked to join you. Would you indulge me with a walk around the garden instead?"

"No, thank you."

His eyebrows lowered. "I only want to talk."

"I don't think there's anything for us to discuss."

Bennick took the brush from Clare's hand. "I'll escort you to the castle." He didn't look at Amil, but his words were clearly for his benefit.

"Wait. Please." Amil took a step forward and Bennick shifted so he was slightly in front of Clare, clearly defensive. Amil glanced at him, but focused on Clare. "I know you must feel wary—"

"You gave me a poisoned necklace," she interrupted, tone thin.

He winced. "I assure you, my father and I had nothing to do with that."

"It came from your treasury."

Anger flashed in his eyes. "Yes, but it passed through many hands!"

Bennick spoke firmly. "Step back."

The Mortisian darted a look to Clare. "Serene, please—"

"Now," Bennick ordered.

Amil grit his teeth, eyes cutting to Bennick. "You dare address me like that?"

Bennick didn't blink. "Yes."

Amil's eyes narrowed, but Clare stepped forward, her fingers brushing Bennick's arm in a silent request to stay back. He remained an impressive force beside her; she could actually feel the threat of him, ready to spring if Amil even twitched in her direction. She faced Amil, her chin lifting imperiously. "Please leave, Ser Havim. I don't wish to speak with you."

His mouth thinned. "I hope you'll reconsider our friendship, Serene."

"I won't."

Amil's expression locked. "I see." He bowed his head, shoulders tight. "Good day, Princess." He stalked away, a Mortisian guard peeling from the shadows to follow him, his hand on the hilt of his curved sword.

The muscles in Clare's neck tightened as she watched Amil leave. She was beginning to wonder if Amil posed an even greater threat than his father.

CHAPTER 35

GRAYSON

MIA PLACED ANOTHER UCEA BERRY IN her mouth. "Thank you for these."

"They're growing everywhere now." Grayson plucked a red berry from the bowl sitting on the wooden table between them. They had the cell to themselves this morning, since Mama was out. The room was still cool, but the stove wasn't needed. With summer finally touching Ryden, the dungeon wouldn't be such an uncomfortable place.

The back of Grayson's jaw ached from the tartness of the ucea berries, but Mia kept popping them into her mouth, clearly savoring the tang as she chewed. "Do you know what I miss?" she asked suddenly.

"What?"

She folded her arms on the solid square table and leaned

forward, drawing Grayson's full attention. "I miss the days you came back to me *not* bleeding. Those were good days. Rare, but good."

He frowned. "I'm not bleeding."

"You were." Her gaze shifted pointedly to his left cheek.

The knife wound from Tyrell still ached, even though it was days old. The cut in his arm had been deeper, but both ached with the familiar pain of a knife-wound. The Syalla had burned through his blood for about fifteen eternal minutes, but had faded eventually. "I'm fine," he assured her.

"Forgive me if I don't always believe you." Her fingers drummed against her bent elbows, her full pink lips pressed together. "Are you still taking something for the pain?" When he didn't answer, her features pinched. "You didn't go to a physician, did you?"

"There wasn't a need."

"Grayson . . ."

He lowered his voice. "You know how my father is."

Mia's mouth set and she looked away, eyeing the locked door. Her voice was so quiet, he nearly missed her words. "Sometimes I wish I could hurt him as much as he's hurt you."

The muscles in the back of Grayson's neck jerked. "I never want you near him." He'd only seen them together once, in this very room, the day Tally had burned.

"I don't want to be near him, either," Mia said. "But I hate how he treats you. How they *all* treat you." Her throat constricted in a hard swallow, her eyes drifting back to his newest wound. "I hate *that*."

The loathing in her voice stung him. He ducked his head but she reached across the table and cupped his strained face with both hands. A rich brown curl had escaped the knot at her nape and brushed against her perfect, rounded cheek.

They were opposite in every way. The realization wasn't new, but it still hit him like a punch in the gut.

Mia thumbed his high cheekbones until their gazes locked —cold stone and warm earth. "You know I didn't mean it like that. I just hate to see you hurt."

His jaw flexed beneath her hands. "I know how I look."

"You're the most beautiful part of my world."

The words shouldn't mean anything, but Grayson's heart tripped. He tensed when her knees bumped his beneath the small table. He shifted in his chair, drawing his legs back, but he couldn't make himself pull free of her touch.

"Do you remember the stories I used to tell you about fate-sent guardians?" she asked. "Immortals destined to protect a chosen mortal? I used to think that's who you were—my guardian. I wasn't even sure you were real at first, you were that perfect to me."

His pulse sped, thudding heavily in his ears.

Mia hesitated, then her eyes softened. "You're still perfect, Grayson. You'll always be perfect to me." She leaned over the table, the ucea berries forgotten as she used her hands to ease him closer.

Grayson didn't breathe. He didn't think. He did nothing as her lips touched his. Her mouth was soft and hot, gentle but real. She tasted like ucea berries and everything he'd ever wanted. Her satin lips pressed against his mouth and heat shot through his veins.

Mia was kissing him.

Shock froze him for a moment, but then reality hit. This was the line he'd sworn to never cross. The one temptation he'd always resisted, because giving in was wrong. Horribly wrong.

He yanked back, losing her kiss and touch. Thrusting his head aside, he could feel his face burning. His fists clenched uselessly in his lap.

Mia fell back in her chair, her hands dropping to her lap. "I . . . I'm sorry." The words rang hoarse.

Pain swelled his throat. "Don't." He couldn't hear that she regretted the kiss.

Silence smothered the air between them. A muscle in his temple ticked, exacerbating the ache that throbbed there.

"It's all right," Mia finally whispered.

It wasn't. He grit his teeth, having no idea how to apologize to her.

She swallowed, head ducking as her shoulders rolled in. "I should have realized by now that you don't . . . care for me that way."

Grayson's eyes cut to her, his stomach clenching. "You—" His tight throat trapped his voice.

She cringed, her chin still tucked. "I promise I won't do it again."

The words tugged at his core when they came out, too rough and low. "Mia, I love you."

She stilled. Her eyes tracked up and he tensed when he saw the moisture veiling her stare. "What?" The single word cracked out of her.

"I love you," he repeated.

Mia's chest rose sharply and her wavering lips pushed to-gether. "Then why . . . ?"

"Because I *can't* love you."

She flinched, and it broke him.

Grayson pushed out of his chair and rounded the table. She followed his every movement, turning in her chair so she faced him when he crouched before her. Her fingers were knotted in her pale blue skirt, her knuckles bleached of their brown tone. He folded his gloved hands over hers and raised his head, meeting her gaze. "My father is the one who locked you in here."

Her small nose scrunched. "That doesn't matter."

"It matters to me."

"Why?"

His lungs caught. "You were only a child when he stole your life. How can I take advantage of that?"

Her chin jutted stubbornly. "You better have a stronger excuse than that, Grayson Kaelin, or I might hit you."

His mouth twitched, but the weak smile died almost at once. "I'm not good, Mia."

Her hands twisted beneath his, suddenly gripping his fingers. "You're worthy of love."

"I'm not worthy of you."

"Is that what you think?" She shook her head, glancing away. "I'm not perfect." She swallowed hard and her next words came out scratchy—torn. "There are things I've done I can never be forgiven for."

His hands tightened on hers. His mind flashed back to the confessions she'd cried while under the influence of fever. *I'm a killer.* He still didn't believe it, but clearly she did. "You were a child," he argued quietly. "There's nothing you could have done—"

"Stop." She blinked through her growing emotion, shaking her head. "That doesn't matter. *You're* what matters. Every time you chose to follow your father's orders, you chose life. I can never think less of you for that, no matter what you had to do. You've survived, and that's all I've ever wanted." Her voice caught. "I can't live in a world without you."

Her words shot a thrill through him, but doubts still shadowed his thoughts. "If you weren't stuck in this cell . . . Fates, I'm the last person you'd ever choose."

Mia's eyes flashed with steel. "You don't know who I'd choose.

After everything that's been taken from me, how I feel still belongs to me. I won't let anyone take that away—not even you. I love you, Grayson. I always have."

He watched her, not breathing. Slowly, he slid one hand free from her grip. Hurt swept her face, but then he cupped the back of her neck, pulling her closer.

The fates may condemn him for this, but he couldn't bear her tears.

Grayson lifted his chin and brushed his lips against hers. The brief contact sparked every nerve in his body. Heat swelled in his chest and his heart kicked. Everything in his world narrowed to her. The feel of her soft mouth on his, the heat of her neck seeping through his leather glove—the way she melted toward him, as if the fates themselves were pulling her closer.

When he drew back from the gentle kiss he held his forehead against hers, eyes squeezed shut. "I love you, Mia," he whispered. "Always."

She held her forehead to his for another heartbeat before easing back, lifting the hand from her lap.

Confusion filtered through him, until her fingers reached the edge of his glove. He tensed, fingers clenching on instinct. "Mia . . ."

When their gazes locked, he couldn't breathe. Her soft brown eyes were full of warmth, acceptance, and love. "You don't need to hide from me," she whispered. "I love you. Every part of you."

He didn't stop her this time as she tugged his gloves away. His pale hands were riddled with scores of old scars and the burns on his fingers were an ugly smear of purple and red, but Mia wrapped her fingers around his without hesitation. The feel of her skin on his sent a jolt through his entire body.

She lifted his hands to her face, his calloused fingertips brushing her cheeks before she pressed his palms against her smooth skin. He could feel her smile against his bare hands and her soft breaths were caught by his thumbs resting on her lips.

Mia leaned in for another kiss and Grayson grinned. He'd never felt so freed as he did now, locked in this prison with her.

CHAPTER 36
CLARE

CLARE STEPPED INTO THE PRINCESS'S bedroom and stopped short. Wilf stood with his enormous back to her, head bent as he fiddled with the room's only window. Silver moonlight outlined him sharply and the dim lamplight played over his heavily muscled back. At her surprised intake of breath, he shot a look over his shoulder, his usual scowl in place.

Clare tensed and cinched the neck of her robe around her throat. "What are you doing?"

His thick brows dragged down. "Bennick ordered nightly sweeps of the room."

She frowned. "I know. I thought Venn did it before he left."

Wilf shrugged one shoulder and turned back to the window. The double-paned glass rattled a little as he tugged on the lock. Clearly, he wasn't going to say anything more.

Clare remained in the doorway, watching him as he finally left the window and strode to the bed. Vera had already turned down the blankets, but Wilf flipped them completely, gaze cutting over the sheets. He knelt, bracing one hand on the bed as he scanned the space beneath. She should probably be grateful for his thoroughness, and if it had been anyone else, she would have been. But despite Bennick's assurances that Wilf was trustworthy, standing in the room alone with him caused the hairs on the back of her neck to rise.

Finally, Wilf pushed to his feet. "Clear."

She continued to clutch the folds of her robe together as she cleared her throat. "Thank you."

The skin around his eyes tightened; maybe he sensed the doubt in her words. He grunted and strode for the door. Clare sidestepped to let him pass and the moment he was gone she closed the door, her palm pressed against the smooth wood as her attention dropped to the lock. She hesitated only a moment before twisting it, the tension in her shoulders easing a little at the comforting click. It would make sleep easier, since Wilf was the one standing guard all night.

Clare took a moment to make her own inspection of the room, lingering at the window. She checked the lock, but it was engaged. She let out a breath she hadn't realized she'd been holding. She was paranoid—she knew that. But Serene's enemies were becoming bolder. The attack on the orphanage had revealed a carelessness for life that sickened her. Whether it had been the assassin or the rebels, it showed desperation. People wanted to kill Serene before she left for Mortise, and they only had three weeks left to do it.

Clare moved to the bed, quickly righting the tousled covers before she tossed her robe aside and eased between the sheets. Silence covered the suite, and though she was tired, she didn't lie down. She kept the lamp on, casting the room in a soft light. Drawing her knees up to her chest, she surveyed the room. It had been a stranger's room two months ago, but now it felt like hers. Her journey to Mortise was becoming increasingly real, and there was a pang in her chest when she thought about the possibility of not making it back. She was grateful Bennick had arranged the meeting at the orphanage so she could see her brothers again, but she hated to think that would be the last time she held them.

She needed to survive. She *would* survive.

Exhaling, Clare leaned over and extinguished the lamp. The light blinked away and darkness pooled.

The window exploded as a dark form hurtled through it, shattering the glass and spraying shards everywhere.

Clare scrambled back across the bed, horror seizing her lungs and stopping her breath as she watched the dark form straighten and become a man. His clothes were black and a dark hood covered his face. He lunged for her, a dagger flashing in his hand.

Clare rolled away from the plunging blade, kicking blankets aside as she dropped over the side of the bed. She landed hard on her feet and bolted for the door. She jerked the handle, but it didn't open. Fates, she'd locked the door after Wilf had left.

The attacker sprang for her—she sensed more than she saw it—and there wasn't time to twist the lock. Clare shoved away from the door and the thud of his knife embedding in the wood sent a shudder through her.

That would have been her. A second more at the door, and that blade would have been in her spine.

Ice shot through her veins and Clare ran for the side table, where Eliot's dagger rested in its sheath. She was nearly there when she was snagged from behind, a rough hand strangling her arm. She pivoted and slammed her balled fist into his sternum, right where Bennick had taught her.

He grunted, hot breath searing her ear, but he managed to haul her back with a steel arm banded around her middle, pinning her arms to her sides. With his free hand he reached for Eliot's dagger and terror flashed through Clare.

Break free. It was Bennick's voice in her head and it cut through her fear. She grasped her training like a lifeline and bucked against the assassin's hold, clawing his legs and arms —any part of him she could reach. He hissed, breath seething against her skin, abandoning Eliot's knife to wrap both arms around her. He crushed her back to his heaving chest and Clare's ribs groaned, but she remained focused. She dropped her weight as Bennick had taught her, making the assassin stagger. He overcorrected and Clare took advantage of his unsteadiness by throwing herself to the side. They fell, bouncing away from each other.

Clare gasped as pieces of glass from the broken window pierced through her nightgown and tears scalded her eyes. Slices tore up her arms and crimson blood caught in the moonlight, streaking the shards of glass embedded in her skin. She choked on a scream, aware that the assassin was also hissing in pain. He scrambled back, his clothing offering a little more protection than her thin nightgown—he even had gloves.

The door shuddered as a huge weight rammed into it.

Wilf.

Clare hitched in a breath and forced herself to move, even though the broken glass found new, harsher ways to bite her. She had no doubt Wilf would manage to bring the door down, but even with his bulk it would take a moment.

Clare scrambled to her feet, glass crunching under her slippered feet as she sprung up a second before the assassin did. She kicked his knee from the side and he staggered. She darted for Eliot's knife, but the assassin hadn't fallen—he grabbed her arm and threw her back to the floor.

She hit hard, the broken window shards cutting into her body once more. But she couldn't let the pain slow her. She tried to ignore the blood slicking her fingers and the bits of glass that clung to her skin as she snatched up a jagged piece of glass. She could feel the assassin coming for her, crouching over her. She rolled, swinging the glass shard. The sharp edge cut into his reaching arm and he growled.

Clare tightened her hold on the piece of glass, ignoring the bite of pain as the edges cut into her palm. Her makeshift weapon was slick with her blood and his, but she didn't drop it. She cut toward his face but the assassin dodged the swipe and caught her wrist, forcing her shaking arm down until it ground painfully against the glass-strewn floor.

Clare's breath escaped in sharp pants, adrenaline shooting through her, making her body tremble and her pulse roar. The assassin bent over her and she squirmed, kicking out at him, but his knees dug into her sides as he straddled her and he somehow got both of her wrists snared in one hand above her head.

Horror washed through her when his free hand brushed the floor, snagging a curved piece of glass. The point was sharp and wicked—a glass dagger that could easily slit her throat.

Another crash against the door, the boom of impact reverberating throughout the room. Shouting rose, but the pounding of Clare's heart drowned it out.

The assassin snarled beneath his hood and pure evil shone in his eyes, the only part of him Clare could really see. His grip flexed on the shard of glass, a growl in his throat as he brought it toward her face.

Clare screamed in frustration and fear, bucking against his

crippling hold. But he didn't go for her vulnerable throat. At the last second he shifted his hold on the thick piece of glass, aiming for her heart.

When the tip pierced her chest, Clare's back arched off the floor, her shriek ringing off the stone walls. An inhuman roar came from the other side of the door, but Clare's pulse was louder in her ears as the assassin forced the glass deeper, the curved tip tearing toward her heart.

Help would come too late. Realization flashed a second before the assassin grunted, making a final shove.

Clare's eyes snapped wide and her breath hitched—faltered —then guttered out. The tension in her body eased and she slumped against the floor, tears leaking slowly from the corners of her eyes.

Wilf threw himself at the door again and wood cracked.

The assassin jerked to his feet, leaving the glass shard in her chest as he bolted for the window. A rope dangled, tied off somewhere above. He planted his feet on the window ledge, glass snapping underfoot as he swung out on the rope and scaled the castle wall.

This time when Wilf threw himself at the door it splintered and gave way. The giant man staggered through the opening, his mouth set into a grim line as he caught the darkened room with a sharp look, his eyes skipping past Clare's inert body to fasten on the swinging rope. He lurched for the broken window, more focused on catching the assassin than helping Clare. Maybe because he'd seen the glass sticking out of her chest and knew she couldn't be helped.

But Wilf wasn't alone.

Bennick ran into the room, drawing up short at the sight of her. Clare could only imagine what he thought, seeing her stretched out on the floor, surrounded by glittering shards of glass. Her nightgown was torn and streaked with blood, and moonlight caught the glass shard buried in her chest.

Bennick stumbled. It looked as though the air had been punched from his lungs. "Clare." Her name was a strangled gasp, and though she wanted to say something—anything—she couldn't.

Vera came in behind Bennick, and her hands clapped over her mouth.

Bennick dropped to his knees beside Clare, ignoring the glass that crunched beneath him. His hands trembled as he touched her face, his fingertips brushing her tears. He was pale, and not just from the white cast of the moon. It seemed like all his blood had drained. "Clare?" Desperation and despair warred in his ragged voice, and somehow Clare knew he'd been the one roaring on the other side of the door. She didn't know why he was here, but her stomach fluttered as he bent over her, fingers laid against the side of her neck, seeking a pulse.

"She's dead," Vera gasped, her hands still pressed over her mouth. Her shoulders shook with her tears. "Fates, no!"

Bennick's fingers were hot against her skin. He held them there for a silent moment before stiffening. "She's alive." He threw a look over his shoulder. "Go for help. Now!"

Vera spun away and Bennick leaned back over Clare. His blue eyes swam with fear, grief, and anger. "Don't you die," he growled. "Stay with me, Clare."

Practiced fingers explored the wound, fingering the edges of the glass. His jaw hardened and blood now coated his skin. He snatched one of the small blankets folded on the end of the bed and pressed it carefully around the glass, trying to stop the flow of blood.

A shudder wracked Clare and something about that involuntary movement broke through her stiffness and shock. She found her voice, though it cracked. "Take it out."

"I can't." Bennick wasn't looking at her—he was focused on the wound. "Don't move."

"It hurts," she gasped.

His shoulders tensed. "I know. But I can't take it out. It could cause more damage. The physician will be here soon."

Tears dripped from her eyes, rolling into her ears. "I tried to fight, but I couldn't stop him." The haze of pain was making her words slur. "I—I did what you said, in our first lesson. I pretended I was dead." She shifted her weight and pain flared all over her body. She fought a whimper.

A muscle in Bennick's cheek jerked. "Easy," he murmured, the gentleness in his voice at odds with the fire in his eyes. He tracked her tears and moved one bloody hand to cup the side of her face. "Don't try to talk," he whispered. "You're going to be fine. I've got you."

He continued to soothe her with gentle touches and quiet words until the physician arrived, with Vera and Venn at his heels. They were all pale and the physician trembled as he knelt beside Bennick. He thought Clare was Serene, and he knew what Newlan might do to him if she died under his care.

Time blurred. The physician spoke to Bennick more than Clare, and the only time she really focused was when pain sharpened. When the older man began to pull on the shard of glass, Clare's body lifted too, and Bennick and Venn both pinned her down as the shard was gingerly extracted. Sweat slicked her body and beaded on her forehead and she couldn't stop from crying out. Her breaths shuddered when the physician cleaned the wound and then meticulously stitched it. Vera held the lamp, the flame shaking in her hands.

Bennick and Venn helped to pluck the smaller pieces of glass from Clare's arms and hands, and Bennick took one of the physician's bandages and wrapped it around her bleeding palm—the one she'd hurt while wielding her own shard of glass.

When the physician was done, he asked Bennick and Venn to lift her onto the bed. Bennick scooped her up before Venn could even shift his weight, and he cradled her against his chest. Clare could feel his heartbeat, thumping madly against her cheek. The medicine the physician had given her dulled everything, but she was aware of how tense Bennick was. His jaw was locked as he laid her on the bed, every muscle pulled taut while he listened to the physician's instructions for her care. She needed rest—no rough activity for a week. "Thank the fates she survived," the physician concluded, patting a handkerchief over his sweating brow.

While Vera walked the physician out and went in search of a new nightgown for Clare, Venn turned to Bennick, his voice low. "Wilf went after him?"

"Yes." Darkness lived in Bennick's tone. Tension bled from him and his fists were tight at his sides.

Venn swallowed. He caught Clare watching him and eased out a wan smile. "You did well, Clare. Good job staying alive."

"Thank you." Her voice was soft, her eyes stuck on Bennick. Something was wrong. He was avoiding her gaze. Or maybe she was still in shock? Regardless, her heart tripped when he stalked away from the bed, moving for the window. He was nearly there when Wilf swung inside.

His large form dropped to the floor, his dark eyes narrowed on Clare. "She's alive." No inflection, no real emotion.

"Did you find him?" Bennick demanded.

Wilf straightened. "No. Lost him on the rooftops. He was fast. Covered himself well; he was average build and height, but I couldn't tell anything beyond that."

Clare watched Wilf. Her jumbled thoughts couldn't help but

wonder if the assassin had really escaped, or if Wilf had let him go.

Bennick's nostrils flared and he grit his teeth, his focus on Wilf. "I already ordered the gates locked, but I want you to organize a search of the castle and grounds."

Wilf tipped his head and strode from the room, not sparing Clare another glance.

Venn took Clare's hand gently, drawing her attention. "Did you see him, Clare?"

"No, he . . . wore a hood." She wet her dry lips, her eyelids growing weighted. "His eyes . . . there was nothing but hate in his eyes."

Venn's mouth drew into a line. "Did you notice anything else? Did he have an accent? A weapon?"

"This," Bennick said stiffly. Clare and Venn both watched as he jerked the knife out of the door. He examined it, his voice hard. "There's nothing unique about it. Just a plain dagger. You could buy one like this on any corner in Iden."

"Not Mortisian?" Venn asked, surprise lifting his tone. "That's new. Could this have been rebels?"

"They attack in groups," Bennick said, still examining the knife, though clearly it wouldn't reveal any secrets.

"Not always. But if this was the assassin, it's the first time he's come to do the job himself, rather than rely on poison." Venn frowned at Bennick. "Are you all right?"

"Fine." He cut a glance at Clare. The skin around his eyes tightened. "I need to report this to the king."

"I could go—"

"No," Bennick overrode Venn. "Stay with her."

Though her mind was truly fuzzing now, Clare flinched at Bennick's tone. "Please stay," she whispered.

His body remained hard, his face unreadable. "I'll return

soon."

She wanted to beg him, but he was already striding out the door.

Venn sighed and busied himself with hanging a blanket over the window to ward off the chill in the air.

Clare drifted, only partially aware of Vera returning and helping to strip off her ruined nightgown. The blood was bathed away and then she had a new gown and Vera tucked her into bed, mindful of her bandages.

Sleep claimed her, but Clare came in and out of wakefulness. At one point she saw Vera curled at the foot of the bed, asleep, and Venn draped a blanket over her, his eyes softening as he did. But each time Clare peeked at the room through slitted eyes, the one person she desperately wanted to see remained absent.

Bennick didn't come back.

CHAPTER 37
CLARE

THE WOODEN TRAINING DAGGER STABBED into Clare's ribs. She shoved away from Bennick, her side burning and her breaths sharp as she whirled on him.

He matched her glare with coolness. "You're dead."

Clare's hands balled at her sides, her lungs heaving for air. The mostly-healed wound over her heart twinged with pain. "At least give me a chance to fight back."

Nothing in Bennick's hard expression changed. "An assassin won't go easy on you, Clare."

She grit her teeth. It had been over a week since the assassin had attacked her in the princess's room, and although she'd only resumed training with Bennick three days ago, something had changed. It was Bennick squaring off before her, but an insufferable mask of detachment covered his face and never slipped.

Their training had intensified. They worked on the field for three hours now, since Bennick was insistent that they make up for the time she'd lost while recovering from her stabbing. Clare dreaded this time a little more each day, and that hurt went deeper than the throbbing bruises that covered her. Irritation tightened her skin. Impatience had been building for days, but today it flared, nearly swallowing her.

Bennick spun the mock knife, flipping it over his fingers, his gaze level. "Again."

Clare swiped a wrist across her sweaty forehead, her breathing still ragged. "I want a break."

He shook his head. "We're not resting today. We only have a week left."

She ground her teeth. "I need to rest."

Bennick bent, scooping up the wooden knife he'd twisted from her hand a moment ago. He tossed it at her face and she caught it on instinct, before it hit her nose.

She scowled, fingers clenching over the wooden weapon. "I'm not fighting you."

"That will make it easy for me to win." His wooden knife shot out.

Clare stumbled as she dodged his attack. A growl vibrated her throat. "Stop!"

"No." Bennick advanced again and she was forced to retreat.

She knew the men on the field were probably watching them, but she was sick of being stabbed and she knew Bennick wasn't going to allow her a chance at winning. What was the point of losing again and again?

She didn't debate. She turned on her heel and marched away, toward the stable that sat on the other side of the field.

"Clare!"

She ignored his shout. She wouldn't let him give her another bruise or make her feel like a weak fool.

When she heard his footsteps pounding after her, she instinctively lifted the hem of her skirt and slipped into a run, still strangling the practice knife.

His footsteps pounded after her and she knew she couldn't outrun him. She was already winded from training, each sharp breath tugging at the tender flesh over her heart, and though Bennick was also breathing hard, he gained quickly.

Clare had just cleared the training yard when he grabbed her elbow, hauling them both to a stop. "What was that?" he demanded.

She shoved against his chest, but his grip remained tight on her arm. "My first defense is to escape danger, remember?"

Bennick's eyes narrowed, the heat from his body pressing against the small space between them. "You think I'm a danger to you?"

"You hurt me."

"I'm trying to help."

"No, you're not!" Clare jerked her arm again and this time she broke free. More likely he'd let her go, but she ignored that as she stepped back. "I *know* an assassin could kill me in a second. You don't have to beat it into me." He cringed, but she wasn't done. "A week ago I was lying on the floor, bleeding, an assassin on top of me. I know how terrifying that moment is. I could see my death in his eyes, and it didn't matter how hard I fought him—he still stabbed me." Her voice cracked, and she hated that.

Bennick thrust a hand through his hair, throat bobbing. "Clare—"

"No." She made her voice hard, forcing back the break that threatened. "You're not training me, Bennick. You're humiliating me. And I've had enough." She turned and stalked away, spine straight. She still held the blasted wooden knife; she threw it aside.

Bennick followed. Of course he did. They were nearly to the stable when he finally spoke, his voice low and tense. "I'm sorry I've been hard on you, but I need to do my job. I *am* training you."

She laughed, the sound brittle. "Training me how to lose? I don't need that."

He grabbed her arm, jerking her to a stop.

She ground her teeth. "Let go of me, or I'll break your wrist."

"Try," he challenged.

Clare searched his face for a shred of warmth, any glimpse of the man she'd come to know, but there was none. He was gone. The man who joined her for her first ride because he knew she was terrified, the man who had shared quiet smiles with her, kissed her bruised cheek, reunited her with her family, and held her in a way that almost made her believe . . .

Whatever she'd thought was growing between them, she was wrong, and something inside her cracked.

Bennick's eyebrows slammed down as he peered at her. "You're crying."

"I'm not." But her eyes burned and she knew she couldn't blink the moisture away. If she blinked, those tears would fall.

"Clare—"

"I'm the decoy," she said lowly. No one was around them, giving her the freedom to speak. "My job is to *die* for Serene." Bennick stiffened, but she wasn't done. "No matter how hard you train me, I'm going to die. You seem to be the only one who doesn't understand that." She pulled free and walked away.

Clare reached the corner of the stable when Bennick caught her arm. He towered over her as they stood toe to toe, overwhelming her space and her senses. His body blocked some of the sunlight, but his face wasn't hidden in shadow. His searing eyes snatched her gaze and stole her breath.

His jaw firmed, his eyes so intent they nearly blazed. The coldness was gone, replaced by raw emotion and heat. "You're not going to die, Clare. I won't allow that to happen. I'll defy the fates if I have to, but I will keep you alive."

Promise throbbed in every word, making Clare's heart trip. Tension lined Bennick's shoulders, and when his focus dropped to her lips, her lungs froze.

He moved slowly, giving her every opportunity to stop him as he cupped her face with both hands. His thumbs brushed the corners of her mouth as he drew her in. His mouth caught hers and Clare's lips melted against his, absorbing the foreign warmth and feel of him. His lips were a fascinating mix of hard and soft as they slanted over hers. His hands tightened, drawing her closer. Her pulse roared in her ears and she could feel every thump of her heart.

It was over too soon.

Bennick pulled back, both of them breathing thickly, his eyes wide.

Clare's lips parted, but words were impossible. So she gripped his uniform and dragged him back, her mouth falling across his. He smelled of sun, sweat, and spicy soap.

Bennick's hands sank into her hair. One hand cupped her nape and the other spread the length of her face, his fingertips brushing her temple, and his thumb tilting her head up. She didn't realize they were moving until her shoulders bumped against the stable wall—Bennick had guided them around the corner, hiding them from the stable entrance and the training grounds.

Clare held him, kissed him, drank him in until she thought her heart would jump out of her chest. She'd barely dared to dream this could happen—she could hardly fathom it was happening now.

She was kissing Bennick Markam. *He* was kissing *her*.

His lips dragged over hers, the ball of his thumb tracing the curve of her cheek. Every part of her was warm, but where they touched, she burned. Her palms caught the heat radiating from his chest as her fingers slid over the ridges of his shoulders. He shivered when her fingertips touched the skin of his neck, and a groan came from deep in his throat.

Her mouth curved against his in an unstoppable smile. His lips settled against the raised corner of her mouth, their chests rising and falling furiously together.

"Fates," she breathed.

His eyes flashed to hers, lit with an intensity that made her stomach twist pleasantly. "Clare."

Her body thrummed. No one had ever said her name that way, that deeply. She lifted her hands to his face and stroked his stubbled cheeks with her fingertips, watching with fascination as he responded to her touch. Bennick's eyes fell closed as her thumb slipped over his mouth, the pad lingering on his full bottom lip. "I think we might be in trouble," he murmured.

He was right. In so many ways, he was right. "No one can know," she agreed. "If the king found out, there's no telling what he'd do."

"There is that," he allowed. "But I meant the kind of trouble that comes from me not being able to think of anything but kissing you."

She really needed to stop smiling. The situation was quite serious.

Bennick set his lips against her forehead, a kiss so gentle her knees shook. His mouth glided to her temple, pressing another kiss at her hairline. He exhaled slowly, his breath shooting tingles over her skin. "You're the worst kind of distraction."

A grin stretched her lips. "Really?"

He nodded, his bristled cheek brushing hers. "From the very beginning." He pressed one last kiss against the underside of her jaw before levering back. "I'm sorry for intensifying your training, I just . . ." He looked skyward, neck stretching as his throat bobbed. His hands were braced on either side of her against the stable, tension pulling his muscles taut. "I hate that you're a target. I can't stop thinking about every attack, every time I've failed to keep you safe." His voice was strained. "I thought you were dead. You were lying on the floor, covered in blood, with that piece of glass in your chest, and you weren't moving. And I wouldn't have even known you were fighting for your life unless I'd come to check on Wilf. You could have died, and I wouldn't have known."

She touched his hard jaw, bringing his eyes back to her. "It's all right, Bennick. I'm all right."

His head turned, his lips brushing the center of her palm. "I shouldn't have pushed you so hard," he whispered against her hand. "It was wrong of me to take my fears out on you. I'm sorry."

"You're forgiven." Standing with him like this, it was hard to remember her anger. She cleared her throat and tapped a finger off his jaw. "You should probably step back. Anyone could see us."

He lifted a rebellious brow. "I don't think I care."

"Bennick . . ."

He sighed and retreated, his hands sliding off the wall as he moved back.

Clare swallowed at the loss of his nearness. She remained against the stable wall, her flushed skin still humming from his touch. Her lips felt swollen, and when she pressed them together, Bennick watched her with a look so deep it made her toes curl.

He shoved a hand through his hair, swearing softly. "I am really, *really* in trouble."

Chapter 38

Eliot

Eliot finished another drink. Blood pounded in his ears as he slammed the empty tankard on the table and roared for another. It was his fourth, and still he couldn't get the taste of betrayal out of his mouth.

The images were burned into his mind. Clare and Markam, *kissing*.

Eliot had been watching over his sister, trying to be a decent brother even though she hadn't listened to him. And what did he see when he came to check on her? Markam pressing his sister against the stable wall, his hands all over her.

Eliot bit out a curse, scrubbing a hand over a bristled jaw that needed a shave. Fates, he still couldn't believe what he'd seen. Clare's betrayal was crushing and enraging all at once. She knew those hands that ran over her body and made her shiver had tortured him, yet still she'd kissed him. Eliot had told her the truth, and she'd turned away from him—embraced Markam instead.

Not the full truth . . .

Eliot smashed the whisper of guilt before it could swallow him. He hadn't tried to kill Farrell. The drinking had been excessive—he would admit that. But why did Farrell have to spring on him? And why had Markam even spared his life? It would have been more merciful to kill him. Instead he lived on, scarred back, ruined reputation, riddled with guilt that would never leave. The only thing that dulled the guilt was anger. Anger at himself, but mostly at Markam.

He didn't want to focus on Farrell. And he didn't want to think about his last conversation with Clare, either. He'd yelled at her. Tried to make her feel guilty for leaving the boys. He hated that he'd thrown her words back at her, tried to make her hurt. But what else could he have done? She was in danger at the castle. She needed to be home, where it was safe.

His fresh drink arrived. He tried to empty his mind as he tugged the mug to his lips with shaking hands. He'd just finished it when Michael slid into the chair across from him. His friend cocked a thick eyebrow. "You got an early start."

"Leave me," Eliot rasped. How could his throat be dry after all he'd drunk?

Michael caught the attention of a passing maid. "Two ales, please." The maid left with a nod and Michael turned to Eliot. "Are you drunk enough to tell me what's wrong?"

Sometimes Eliot hated his best friend. "No."

Michael leaned back in his chair. Behind them, a man crowed as he won at cards. "Does it have to do with your sister?"

A muscle in Eliot's jaw ticked.

"You're angry she didn't leave, even after you told her what

Markam did."

A growl shredded up his throat. "Apparently I don't have to tell you anything. You've guessed it all."

Michael's mouth drew into a line. He rested his large forearms on the table, hunching over as he leaned in. "Paven reached me earlier this morning. He wanted to know if you've managed to convince Clare to join us."

"Clearly I can't convince her to do anything."

Hesitation crinkled the corners of Michael's eyes. "The danger she's in will only increase when she travels to Mortise. As a rebel, she'd have protection."

"No."

"Eliot—"

The ugly tangle of emotions in his gut exploded. "She betrayed me," he hissed. "Her own brother meant nothing, but Markam? She was *kissing* him. I saw them. That's why she hasn't left the castle. It's his fault. It's always his fates-blasted fault!" He shoved his empty tankard across the table and scrubbed his hands over his face.

Their drinks arrived. Michael thanked the serving maid quietly, then gripped his mug with both hands. "I'm sorry, Eliot."

His head dropped, one hand shoved into his hair. "If she betrayed me for him, she's not going to betray him for the rebels. Her feelings were clear." The hated images sparked in his mind, their bodies pressed together, Markam's hand plunging into Clare's hair. Eliot's stomach churned and he nearly heaved up the drinks he'd downed. "I don't understand why she ever accepted the position. I know their lives weren't perfect," he whispered brokenly. "But doesn't she realize what I sacrificed for them?"

Michael looked away, giving Eliot a bit of privacy.

It helped. He swallowed back the knot in his throat, blinked away the burn in his eyes, and lifted the fresh cup to his lips.

When Michael's eyes found his, they were grim. "I know it hurts. But she wants to be the princess's maid. Nothing you can do will change that."

Eliot snorted a harsh laugh and rubbed his aching head. "That's why I'm here."

"You can't drink this away."

His knuckles were white as he gripped his mug. "My sister shouldn't have to serve her. *Them.* Fates-blasted royals. The king wants Mortisian ships and ports more than he wants vengeance for his people. And the princess! She's a traitor to us, too. She'll run right to Desfan's arms like a hired woman, not caring that he's responsible for spilling innocent Devendran blood. I don't know how Clare can stomach being around them."

Michael leaned in. "I know you don't want her to become a rebel. And maybe you're right, she wouldn't choose it. But what if she could be convinced she's helping the princess, not endangering her?"

"You want to trick her into becoming a traitor?" He shook his head. "She's my sister, no matter what she's done—I won't put her in danger."

Michael fingered the edge of his tankard. "What if she thought she was protecting *you*?"

Eliot stared. The thump of his heart was suddenly loud, pounding in his buzzing head.

"The rebels could deliver a message," his friend said slowly. "It could be written in your hand. Make it clear if she doesn't help us, you'll be tortured. Killed. Would she help then?"

For the first time today, Eliot worried he'd drunk too much. Because even though something inside him protested the thought of putting Clare in any sort of contact with the rebels, a larger part of him thrilled at this idea. Would she betray the princess—Markam—if it meant saving Eliot?

He shouldn't be tempted, but it was hard to think with ale swimming in his blood.

Michael leaned in. "I'll only take this plan to Paven if you're willing, Eliot."

He stared at the stained table, scraping his forehead with the heel of one hand. He stared a long, long time before he gave his answer.

CHAPTER 39

GRAYSON

"THAT'S NEW," LIAM SAID.

"What?"

"You. Smiling."

Grayson forced his mouth into a line. "I'm not." But he had been. He'd been smiling every time he got lost in his thoughts and remembered Mia's kisses.

The corner of Liam's mouth curved. "Very well. Keep your secrets." He leaned back against the stone wall, his slumped posture at odds with the rigidness the other Kaelin princes stood with. Grayson knew Liam was no less dangerous, however.

Grayson and Liam had been summoned by their father and they stood across from each other in the corridor outside the king's study. Henri loved to keep people waiting.

"That's new, too." Liam lifted his chin to the red slice on Grayson's face. "Tyrell?"

Grayson only grunted.

Liam shook his head and twisted the armband on his wrist. Designs were pressed into the dark leather. Grayson couldn't see well in the flickering light, but he thought they were twisting vines.

"Tyrell sees you as a threat." Liam eyed Grayson, his bearded face suddenly serious. "Enemies are all around you. Never forget that."

The door opened. Liam pushed from the wall and strode into the king's study, leaving Grayson to trail him.

Henri's study was a wide room with a large dark blue carpet. Bookshelves were cradled in one corner, leaving the rest of the walls bare. Lamps hung on the walls and sat on the desk. There were no windows, since they were in the heart of the castle, but there were three exits, each guarded night and day against any intruders foolish enough to strike at the king. Maps of Ryden, Mortise, Zennor, and Devendra were strewn on a side table. The one on top was a heavily marked map showing the southern mountains in great detail, with villages, passes, and Devendran outposts all noted. The room was musty and smelled of leather, wood, and melted wax—his father had just sealed several letters.

Grayson hated the trapped feel of the space. Without the vaulted ceiling of the throne room, King Henri loomed larger as he sat behind his enormous wooden desk.

When Henri's heavy gaze landed on Grayson, he was stabbed with the sudden fear that Iris had betrayed him—that Henri knew Grayson had aided the escape of Hogan's wife and children. But if his father were going to punish him, surely Liam wouldn't have been invited.

Whatever Henri wanted, it concerned both his spymaster and his enforcer.

Grayson and Liam paused before the desk and bowed before sitting in the empty chairs across from Henri.

The king's attention shifted to Liam. "I received a royal invitation this morning from Prince Desfan. He believes we're considering peace talks and has invited our presence in his court. I'm sending you as my emissary."

Liam dipped his head. "When do I leave?"

"One week." Henri's gaze slid to Grayson. "You will accompany your brother."

His body flashed hot. "What?"

"You will serve as Liam's bodyguard in Mortise and do anything he asks."

Grayson's muscles locked, a thousand protests on his tongue that he couldn't speak. "How long will we be gone?"

"I don't expect it will be more than a year," Henri said.

His stomach dropped. "A year?"

"Circumstances will dictate your mission's timeframe." Henri spread his hands on his desk, looking at both of his sons now. "Learn all you can in Mortise, influencing the court where you're able. Create animosity between Mortise and Devendra without tipping your hand. When the time is right, Grayson will assassinate Princess Serene and frame Mortise for her death."

The order stole Grayson's breath.

Henri continued easily, as if he hadn't just ordered a woman's murder. "A war will ignite between the two kingdoms. They will weaken each other until they're ripe for picking."

"It will work," Liam murmured, fingers steepled against his mouth. "The distrust is there. We only need to fan the flames."

Henri glanced at Grayson. "Well?"

It was a struggle to find his voice. "I don't know if I'm ready for this."

The king's eyebrows drew together. "You're the Black Hand." As if that answered everything.

"I've never left Ryden," Grayson said, his voice tight. "I don't know enough about Mortise to help Liam."

"I'll train you in the ways of the Mortisian court," Liam said. "It will take us a month to travel to Duvan—two weeks by horse to the coast, then two more weeks by sea. You'll be ready."

Henri leaned back in his cushioned chair. "Liam, I wish a private word with Grayson."

Liam cast a quick look at Grayson before rising, and the moment the door clicked shut behind him, Henri spoke. "You don't want to leave the girl."

Tension bunched Grayson's shoulders. His father rarely referenced Mia. When he did, every battle instinct Grayson had flared to life.

Henri thumbed the desk's edge. "You'll go to Mortise," he said levelly. "You'll do what's expected, or I'll kill her."

"You wouldn't." The words snapped out, desperation and panic fissuring his chest.

Henri's eyebrows lifted. "I wouldn't?"

"You've kept her all these years for a reason," he said. "She means something to you. You won't kill her."

"You think I have some hidden purpose in keeping her?" Henri's lips slowly bent in an edged smile. "Why do you think I brought her here?"

The question caught him off-guard. "I don't know."

"You must have wondered."

He had. But he couldn't say anything, not with his father staring at him. He shook his head.

Henri's eyes narrowed. "Figure it out."

Grayson ground his teeth. "There's no reason for her to be

here."

Henri chuckled. The sound was so dark it raised every hair on Grayson's body. "You're the Black Hand. The Scourge of Ryden. You're feared across all of Eyrinthia, and yet you're ruled by your own fear. Your fear for *her*."

Grayson said nothing but a charge thinned the air, making it hard to breathe. He was on the edge of learning something and he knew it was going to be bad.

King Henri leaned forward, eyes sharp as a falcon's, long fingers splayed against the dark desk. "I knew who you were going to be before you left your mother's womb. I *made* you. I know your thoughts. I know each of you better than you know yourselves. Peter follows every command without hesitation because he knows he'll inherit the domain he's helping to build. Carter's only goal is to be in the shadow of greatness—to stand beside the one who will always take care of him. Liam serves me because he thrills at the challenge and Tyrell is addicted to the power he wields. Then there's you. You serve me because I hold the one thing you care about—the girl." Henri tilted his head. "Did you really think it was fated?"

Grayson's pulse kicked. He clutched the arms of his chair, knuckles screaming. Denials ripped through him, but he couldn't find his voice.

"You were struggling, Grayson," Henri said quietly. "You weren't trying to reach your potential and every motivator I tried failed. Praise, pain—none of it meant anything. You needed something to fight for. Some*one*."

"No." His body vibrated with tension. "You didn't plan this." The brightest and most real part of Grayson's life couldn't be the product of his father's manipulation.

"Why would I arrest a child near your own age? Why give her a cell close to the dungeon entrance? Why encourage your brothers to turn against you so you would be forced to find sanctuary where I wanted you to?"

Grayson's chest rose in a sharp inhale. "No."

"She was small. Weak. Helpless. In need of protection." Henri grinned. "I knew you wouldn't be able to resist her."

Everything inside Grayson roared, refusing to believe Mia was part of his father's twisted design. That Henri had brought her here solely for the purpose of controlling him—to force him to become evil. It was impossible. It meant Mia's life had been ruined because of him. He couldn't believe it. "You didn't know I found her," he said, gritting the words out. "You were angry when you found out I'd befriended her. You made me burn her doll. You kept me from visiting her!"

"The doll was a test. You must know that by now. Everything with that girl has always been a test. And I kept you from visiting her only so you would be motivated to fight for me."

Grayson's ears rang. His grip on the chair was so tight, his fingers were numb.

Mia's imprisonment had never made sense. She'd been imprisoned at seven years old, for fates-sake. There was no crime she could have committed to merit that.

As a child he'd feared her friendship, thought every kindness was some trick. But Mia would never trick him. No. She *was* the trick. His father had stolen a little girl from her life, her family—all to manipulate Grayson. He'd dropped Mia in hell, certain Grayson would fight to shield her from the flames.

And he had.

Every part of him rebelled. This was too calculated. Too elaborate and heartless. But hadn't his father proved his cruelty knew no bounds?

All his life Grayson had been controlled. Tortured. Forced to become the monster his parents wanted him to be. Of every pain he'd suffered, this manipulation cut the deepest. He'd kissed Mia and she was here because of him. She'd lost everything, and it was his fault. His stomach rolled.

"I control you, Grayson, because I control *her*," Henri said. "So when I threaten to end her life, I mean it. Her purpose begins and ends with you. If you don't work as intended, she's useless to me."

Fury snapped inside him; he could feel the storm raging in his gray eyes. "I'll do as you ask. I always have. There's no need for threats."

"You'll do whatever I demand?"

"Yes."

Henri stood, fingers grazing the desk as he rounded it. There had been no knock on the door, but he barked for someone to enter.

Grayson sprang to his feet, dread knifing his gut.

A guard entered the room, hauling a man inside. The prisoner's clothes were in tatters, his long gray hair thin and oily. His foul stench snared the room in seconds.

The guard tossed the old man to the floor and the dirty prisoner coughed blood against the carpet, whimpering. "Please," he rasped. "I beg mercy."

"Kill him," Henri said.

Ice bolted down Grayson's spine.

The king's eyes narrowed at his hesitation. "Kill him, Grayson."

It was the doll all over again. It was Mia's tear-stained face, begging him not to take Tally.

Henri's lip curled. "I won't kill the girl this time, but if you hesitate even one more moment, I'll cut off her hands."

Bile scorched Grayson's throat. He knew his father's words were a promise. His fingers wrapped around the hilt at his waist and he tugged the dagger free.

The old man keened. He tried to scramble away but the guard planted a boot on his back, pinning him to the floor. The man sobbed, tears dripping down his pale, dirt-streaked face. "Please! I beg mercy!"

Grayson grabbed a fistful of the prisoner's stringy hair and jerked the man's head back until his bulging neck stretched. Blue eyes swollen with moisture looked right at him.

Murder. That's what this was. Not killing in self-defense or even an execution. *Murder.* Grayson's heart wrenched at the difference.

"Please, no!" the man cried. "Mercy—!"

Grayson jerked the blade and blood sprayed. The pleas stopped. The entire room went silent.

Grayson dropped the limp head and rocked back on his heels. Droplets of blood speckled his chest, arms, and face. Crimson blood pooled and rolled over the blue carpet, leaving the dead man and spreading toward Grayson's boots.

Henri's voice crawled from behind him. "Perhaps you *are* ready to kill Princess Serene."

Grayson's lungs clamped and the dagger shook in his hand. Sharp pain dug into his skull, radiating from his temples. The droplets of blood were already cooling on his face.

"You should go to her," Henri said quietly.

The back of Grayson's neck prickled and he twisted slowly toward his father.

Henri's chin lifted. "You needed a reminder you wouldn't soon forget, not even in Mortise."

Grayson's heart tripped. "What have you done?"

His father's voice was flat. "I sent Tyrell to her."

Hatred. Terror. Rage. They blinded him. His hand spasmed around the bloody dagger, but he didn't have time to plunge it into his father's heart—if the king even had one.

Tyrell was with Mia.

Grayson bolted from the room.

CHAPTER 40
CLARE

KING NEWLAN SPARED NO EXPENSE FOR Princess Serene's farewell banquet. The vaulted dining hall was lined on three sides with long, dark wood tables, leaving the center of the room open for the entertainers. Musicians, dancers, acrobatic tumblers—colors swirled as they danced about the space, doing tricks and playing loud music that relied on strings, flutes, and drums.

Each table was decorated with garlands and flowers. Elaborate iron candelabras were spaced evenly between the spread feast. Cut fruits were arranged artfully on trays, ranging in colors of yellow, orange, green, blue, and red. Platters with fresh wheat bread sliced around bowls of golden honey, tinged crimson with the candlelight. Spiced drinks and meats scented the air along with buttered carrots and roasted potatoes. Every seat was filled, mixing the cloying smell of perfume with the savory and sweet scents of the food.

The king sat at the head table, his guards poised behind him. Seeing his face cast in the glowing candlelight, smiling and drinking, Clare wondered at the evil inside him. Despite everything he'd done to her personally, she never would have guessed he'd murdered his wife. He laughed at something one of the nearby lords said and Clare wondered how Serene had stayed sane the past two years.

Clare sat at one of the long side tables, about midway down the room. Grandeur was seated at the opposite table, across the room from her. Newlan wanted them to mingle with the nobles in an effort to help them feel the excitement of the coming alliance. Grandeur seemed to be doing his part; he had the nobles around him enthralled as he talked and they all laughed together. His charm was almost palpable. As if he could feel Clare's gaze, he glanced up and shared a conspiratorial smile. She couldn't quite manage the same before looking away.

She knew the conversation at her table wasn't as lively as the king wanted, but he'd placed the Mortisians beside her, which rather killed conversation with the surrounding nobles. Clare understood the king's reasons—Serene needed to be seen beside the Mortisians, openly displaying trust in them. But Clare didn't trust Amil or his father. Bahri Havim sat on her left with his son beside him, so at least Amil wasn't right next to her. He hadn't sought her out since their encounter in the stable, but the covert threat in his final words lurked in her mind.

Clare knew Bennick, Venn, Dirk, and Wilf were all gathered somewhere behind her, watching the Mortisians closely. It made her feel a little better.

Applause burst around the tables as brightly costumed entertainers scrambled atop shoulders until a pyramid of ten men was built. The top man launched himself into the air, rolling toward the hard stone floor. Clare sucked in a breath with the rest of the watching crowd, but the man landed in a crouch, a grin splitting his face. Clare clapped with the others in the room.

Dancers milled around the tables, presenting flowers or other small trinkets to the guests with an entertainer's flair. Many were young children and they seemed to thrive on the attention. A blonde-haired girl—maybe seven—grinned as she spun to a stop beside Clare's chair and drew out a long-stemmed daisy from her sleeve. "For you, Princess."

Clare took the simple white flower with a smile. "Thank you."

The young girl beamed and danced away.

Clare lifted the flower to her nose and shot a quick look over her shoulder. Her guards stood along the wall behind her and Bennick caught her eye. He sent her a short smile, which she returned almost shyly. Clare treasured each stolen kiss they'd shared this week, though she longed for more. Perhaps once out of the castle they'd find a little more time alone.

Before she turned back in her chair, she saw Gavril sidle up to Bennick. The man's head was down as he spoke in a rush to Bennick, the ridged scars along his face and neck catching in the flickering torchlight.

Bennick frowned at whatever Gavril told him, then signaled for Dirk to follow him and Gavril toward the doors, leaving Venn and Wilf to stand guard over Clare.

"Daisies don't grow well in Mortise, Princess," Ser Bahri said suddenly.

Clare laid the flower beside her plate. "Is that a threat, Ser Havim?"

With the loud music and pounding applause, Clare knew no one could hear them—probably not even Amil, since his father had angled toward Clare, putting his back to his son. The crowd cheered when men stepped out onto the floor, juggling daggers until they blurred in the air.

"Not a threat," Ser Bahri said carefully, swirling the red Zennorian wine in his glass. "Merely an observation. Serjah Desfan is making a mistake in bringing you into his court."

"Then why did you come as his emissary?"

"I couldn't refuse a royal order." He leaned in until his sour breath fanned her face. She eased back on instinct; the sudden light in his eyes was nearly manic. "Desfan's rule is temporary. The serjan will recover from his illness and he'll undo all of this. There will be no wedding. There will be no peace—" Ser Bahri jolted back against his chair with a startled cry, a dagger buried in his chest.

Clare recoiled, slicing a look to the main floor.

Entertainers were hurling their daggers into the crowd. A woman shrieked, the sound ringing sharply against the stone walls.

Clare shoved from her chair, lungs burning as she watched Amil grasp his father's shoulder, screaming for aid.

A hand slammed down on Clare's shoulder and she spun to see Venn towering over her, his expression locked. "Stay low." He didn't give her another choice as he hauled her toward the servants' passage behind the head table, one hand pressing between her shoulder blades. The king was also being herded to the narrow passage and so was Grandeur. Chaos had overthrown the room. Everyone was running, and—

Bennick.

Clare nearly stumbled. She threw a look toward the main doors, which had been shut, and her blood ran cold. Guards wearing blue uniforms were piled on the floor, their bodies unmoving. They'd probably been among the first killed.

Her heart wrenched. Was Bennick one of them? Dirk? Gavril?

She tripped on her own feet but Venn held her up and propelled her forward.

The nobles screamed as they darted for safety. Some cowered under tables while others dashed toward the shadowed corners, and others still pushed to follow the king's retreat. Beside Clare, a middle-aged woman wearing a beautiful violet dress suddenly fell, a crossbow bolt buried in her back. The snap and twang of firing bolts seemed louder than the screams. A flash of heat scorched inside Clare, a mix of fear and panic. Sweat coated her body, sticking her dress to her back.

Venn cursed and dragged Clare to a stop. His grip bruised her arm, but that throbbing pain was nothing when she saw what he'd seen.

The king's guard was being cut down by men with swords who poured from the servants' passage. Three, five, ten—too many attackers to count. Screams of alarm, pain, and death lit the writhing room.

Venn shoved Clare against the stone wall, his arms landing on either side of her head as he caged her in, shielding her with his own body. His throat jumped as he swallowed. "There's another passage across the room," he gritted out. "We'll—"

He slammed against her and Clare choked on a scream. Her arms came around his waist on instinct, though he was far too heavy for her to hold.

Clare crashed to her knees with him and when he slumped against her, she saw the bolt buried in his back. Blood bloomed, spreading between his shoulder blades. It only took seconds for the blood to reach her gloved hands, soaking into the white material. Panic exploded in her gut. "Venn!"

He didn't move.

A sob caught in her throat. Her arms trembled as she tried to lift him. From the corner of her eye she saw Wilf charge toward them, shoving people aside. She opened her mouth to scream for his help, but her muscles locked at the snarl on his face.

The darkness in his eyes was a physical attack and Clare's breath caught when he drew a knife from his belt and threw it, spinning it through the air—right at her.

Clare couldn't move, pinned beneath Venn's weight. Her arms tightened around Venn, as if that would somehow protect them.

The dagger thudded into flesh and she flinched. A gurgled cough sounded beyond her and Clare whipped around. An attacker crumpled, Wilf's dagger lodged in his chest. His outstretched hand fell so close to her, his curling fingers brushed her skirt.

Wilf dropped into a crouch before Clare, his large hand braced against the nearby wall. "Are you hurt?" he demanded.

She stared at him, heart thudding. Wilf had saved her life.

He vented an irritated breath. "Are you hurt?"

"No." She tightened her hold on Venn. "But—"

Wilf dragged Venn off her and made a quick study; the bolt was angled and had impaled closer to his shoulder than his heart.

Clare's eyes darted to movement over Wilf's shoulder. Another attacker was coming up behind him. Clare stiffened. "Look out!"

Wilf spun. His massive body slammed into the attacker, sending them both crashing to the floor.

Clare's heart thundered in her chest, deep and aching. Forcing herself to think past her fear, she dragged up her skirt and drew out Eliot's dagger. Clutching it in her bloodstained hand, she darted a look over the room. It was pandemonium. The attackers weren't obvious at first glance, though most seemed to wear the bright costumes of the entertainers. Not all the entertainers were attacking, though—Clare could see their bodies on the ground, too, some of them so small . . . the children who had handed out gifts and flowers.

It was too much. The death. The screams. The terror. Clare couldn't drag in enough air. She couldn't think. She couldn't leave Venn, even though instinct cried for her to seek shelter. Feet pounded the stone floor and screams stabbed the air.

Beside her, Venn groaned.

"Venn?" She bent over him, her free hand touching his right shoulder—the furthest from the bolt. "Don't move. You've been hit."

"You don't say," he gasped, hissing out a sharp breath.

Tears burned her eyes. "You'll be fine."

He shifted a little and his entire body shuddered. He swore hoarsely, hands curling against the stone floor. Swallowing past the pain, he ground out, "You have to get out."

"But the passage—"

"Then hide," he cut in. "Get under the table. The palace guard will come, but you need to hide until then."

"I'm not leaving you." A glance revealed Wilf was fighting yet another attacker. Her skin crawled and the dinner she'd just eaten swam uneasily in her belly.

Venn tried to push himself up, but his shaking arms couldn't manage it and he cringed.

"You need to stay down," she told him. "It's a fates-blasted miracle that bolt didn't pierce a lung. You need to—" She cut herself off the moment she locked eyes with a man standing mere feet from her. He was one of the entertainers, dressed in a bright red costume. He held a knife and the second he saw her, he stalked forward.

Clare surged to her feet, gripping her knife. Venn cursed as he struggled—and failed—to rise. Clare stepped over him. She tried to think past the panic swelling inside her. There was nowhere to run and she refused to leave Venn.

The approaching attacker grinned at her fighting stance and flipped the blade in his hand. She realized too late he wasn't going to fight hand-to-hand—he'd only come closer so he wouldn't miss.

Clare tensed and the man drew back his arm, prepared to hurl the knife.

A soldier plowed into him, toppling them both to the ground. The movement was a blur, but Clare knew it was Bennick. Her chest squeezed painfully as Bennick and the attacker rolled on the hard floor, Bennick ending up on top. He cocked back a fist and slammed it into the man's face.

Dirk skidded to a stop in front of Clare, blocking her view. "Are you all right?" She jerked out a nod and some of the strain left Dirk's face. He grasped her arm. "We need to find cover."

"But Venn—"

"The others will get him."

Arguing would only prolong the danger for all of them, so she moved with him, Dirk sheltering her as they ran to the nearest table. Clare crawled underneath it, jostled by others seeking safety. Elbows caught her ribs and back but she pushed against them to create more space.

Dirk didn't join her, though. He crouched beside her, one hand grasping the table's edge. For the first time she noticed the drawn sword in his hand. The blade was streaked red.

Though it felt like an eternity, it was only a few moments before Dirk lurched away so he could help Bennick haul Venn under the table.

Bennick breathed hard, his face slick with sweat. He knelt beside Venn, but his eyes tracked over Clare, catching on her bloody gloves.

"It's Venn's," she said before he could ask. She made her own quick study of Bennick; he seemed unharmed, except for some swelling on his jaw where he must have taken a hit.

A vein in his temple pulsed as his attention dropped to Venn and the bolt stuck in his back. Without warning, Bennick gripped the bolt and tore it out.

Venn howled. Clare jumped, nearly hitting her head on the table.

Bennick snagged a linen napkin that had fallen to the floor and pressed it over the wound. "You're going to be fine," he told Venn, who was trembling.

Clare set a comforting hand against Venn's head.

"I hate you so much right now," Venn rasped at Bennick.

"I'm saving your life."

"If you really cared, you could've let him shoot you instead."

Bennick ignored him and darted a look at Clare. "Can you keep pressure on the wound?"

She nodded, though her stomach knotted. Bennick backed out from under the table to rejoin the fight. Dirk remained beside her, though the way he kept shifting his weight told Clare he itched to help the others.

Shrieks and yells continued as people fought and died. The clash of longswords rang out in the vaulted hall and the thud of bodies falling always seemed to follow the snap of a crossbow. The crash of the main doors flying open made Clare jump and she pressed closer to Venn as new shouts rose above the roar of the fight. Footsteps pounded the stone floor—more palace guards had arrived.

Clare murmured soothing words to Venn, ignoring the strange looks of the nobles huddled nearby. If they thought Serene wouldn't help Venn, they didn't really know her.

The fighting was brutal, but after another couple of minutes it was over. Weeping and pained cries filled the room and soldiers shouted orders as they rounded up the surviving enemies.

Bennick ducked under the table. Seeing him safe swept a wave a relief over Clare. He darted a look at Venn. "How is he?"

"I'm not dead," Venn grunted. "You don't have to talk over me."

Wilf and Dirk crouched on either side of Bennick. Wilf eyed Venn and grunted. "You're supposed to dodge them, idiot."

Venn growled low in his throat.

"He needs a physician," Dirk said.

"Wilf," Bennick ordered.

The pox-scarred soldier nodded and sheathed his weapons.

"Not him," Venn groaned.

Bennick ignored his friend and wrapped a hand around Clare's fingers, easing her hand away from Venn's wound so Wilf could drag the young soldier up into his arms and carry him off.

Bennick's thumb brushed over her wrist. "Are you all right?"

They were alone under the table now. The nobles had scrambled out, and Dirk stood beside them. Clare's hands felt weighted with Venn's blood and she was still trembling. She was alive—all her guards were, but . . . "I thought you were dead," she whispered, voice roughened with emotion. Bennick stiffened beside her, but she forced herself to continue. "I saw you and Dirk walking toward the main doors with Gavril, and when I saw the soldiers lying there . . ."

Bennick's eyes softened. "Gavril had a feeling he couldn't shake. He asked me to come with him to search the nearby servants' passages, but we didn't even make it out of the room before the strike happened." His jaw flexed, his eyes focused on her. "When I saw that man coming for you . . . Fates, I didn't think I was going to make it."

Clare swallowed. "Maybe my next lesson should be in throwing knives."

He huffed a weak laugh and helped her out from under the table. He let go of her arm but remained close at her side.

Clare scanned the room, taking in the damage. Tables had been overthrown, dishes, chairs, and food scattered. Bodies were stretched out on the ground, loved ones kneeling beside them, crying. Guards carried the wounded from the room, leaving the dead on the floor. Clare's attention lurched over all the bodies, trying not to see the details, but then her eyes snagged on Amil. He was hunched over his father's body, his shoulders shaking with sobs.

King Newlan stood near the head table, his face flushed and his eyes livid. Grandeur stood at his side as they watched the guards gather the entertainers and force them to kneel in the corner. The men and women clung to their small children, their eyes darting to the soldiers standing over them.

Newlan's attention sliced to Clare, relief momentarily pushing through his rage. He motioned for her to join him as he moved toward the entertainers.

Dread curled inside her, but she couldn't disobey. She stepped forward, Bennick and Dirk moving with her.

One entertainer shuffled forward on his knees. He had gray hair, his colorful cape a horrible contrast to the panic carved into his upturned face. "Your Majesty, I assure you, we're innocent. The attackers are not from our troupe. We joined with them for this occasion only, by your order—"

"Silence!" Newlan towered over the man, his jeweled hands fisted at his sides. "You consorted with killers. You took part in this attempt to destabilize my court. You helped attack my royal person!"

The children shook before his wrath, tears streaking their faces. Clare's eyes skipped over them, past the weeping parents to the guards who corralled them. They still had their weapons drawn, mostly swords, but one held a crossbow—Gavril.

Clare felt a blast of relief at seeing him unharmed.

His gaze shifted, and his eyes met hers. She gave a small smile, not thinking about the fact that Serene probably wouldn't have done so.

Gavril's scarred face tightened. In one fluid motion he lifted the crossbow, aiming it at her.

Clare sucked in a breath.

Bennick cursed when Gavril discharged the crossbow. The small bolt cut through the space between them, shooting at Clare's chest.

Chapter 41

Grayson

TYRELL WAS WITH MIA.

The knowledge stabbed through Grayson as he ran, jarring him with each step. He shoved servants and nobles aside as he tore down the hallway, his breathing ragged and his pulse riding high. The bloody dagger was still clenched in his hand, the spray of blood still on his skin. His whole body shook and the knot in his core burned.

Tyrell was with Mia.

Grayson's nostrils flared and the dagger in his hand suddenly felt more solid than the stones flying beneath his feet. His father had sent Tyrell to hurt Mia. All to control *him*.

King Henri wanted Grayson to be cruel. Cold. Merciless.

In this moment, he was.

Fletcher stood before the cell door. He snapped to attention when he saw Grayson charge down the narrow corridor. He didn't even have to give an order—the old guard was already grabbing his keys.

Grayson skidded to a halt before the cell. Every muscle in his body jerked, willing him to keep moving, to break through the thick door even though that was impossible. Rage flexed his throat and his hold on the dagger was strangling. "How long?"

"Several minutes," Fletcher ground out.

Beyond the closed door, Mia screamed.

Grayson roared.

When Fletcher's hands fumbled, Grayson snatched the keys and grabbed the longest one. He thrust it into the lock and twisted harshly. There was a solid click and he kicked the door in, eyes cutting over the room.

Mia knelt on the floor, her wrists tethered to a post at the foot of her bed. Her shoulders were hunched as she cried, unable to escape Tyrell's folded belt. It flew even as Grayson watched, the leather striking her back with a violent snap. Mia shrieked, her ragged breaths catching on a sob.

Grayson's vision hazed.

Tyrell's eyes rounded when Grayson lunged. He tensed a split second before Grayson's shoulder punched into his middle and slammed the air from his lungs. They crashed onto Mia's bed and Grayson knocked Tyrell's hands aside as he straddled him. Clutching the bloody dagger, Grayson used the added weight in his fist to pound Tyrell's face.

His brother grunted and hissed, bucking beneath him, but Grayson kept him locked against the bed. He kept hitting him. The need to make Tyrell bleed controlled every brutal movement. Scarlet blood streaked his brother's pale face and it coated Grayson's knuckles, but the beating didn't slow. It escalated. Because he could still hear Mia crying and the snap of the belt hitting her body was trapped in his head.

His chest exploded and he vented a wordless scream. He raised the knife, blade aimed down.

Tyrell's breath caught, dark eyes flaring with fear.

"No!" Mia's shout ripped through Grayson, halting the knife. From the corner of his eye he saw her, still on her knees, wrists tied to the bedpost. She trembled, brown curls spilling around her tear-stained face.

Grayson's blade wavered.

His hesitation cost him. Tyrell kneed him in the back and Grayson pitched forward. Mia cried out as Grayson landed hard on the stone floor. He rolled with the impact and sprang to his feet. He slid in front of Mia as Tyrell levered up, shoulders squared, his face already swelling and his nose and mouth dripping blood.

"You'll suffer for this," Tyrell sneered. "I obeyed father's orders. I did nothing wrong!"

Grayson snarled and dove for his brother. Tyrell fell back, hands flinching to the knife belted at his waist.

He didn't get to draw it. Grayson's fist plowed into Tyrell's temple and he crumpled to the stone floor.

Breathing hard, Grayson stared down at his brother's unconscious body. He wanted to rip him apart for what he'd done to Mia. He wanted him to suffer as much pain as Mia had—a thousand times more. Rage filled him and he needed to get it out.

Mia's shuddering breaths were behind him, breaking the silence in the cell.

She needed him more.

Clenching the knife in his hand, Grayson twisted away from Tyrell and dropped to a crouch beside Mia, murmuring useless words of comfort as he sawed through the rope binding her.

Her wrists were red, the soft skin horribly abraded. Her sleeves ended just below her elbows, revealing already-forming bruises on her forearms where Tyrell must have grabbed her.

His fury swelled.

The moment Mia was freed she threw her arms around his neck and he fell back onto his haunches, pulling her with him. He tried not to grip her too tightly because he didn't want to cause her more pain, but she crushed herself to him.

The cell door prodded open. Grayson tensed, though it was only Fletcher. The old guard's focus lingered on Mia's shaking form and his mouth tightened. He shot a look at Tyrell. "Is he dead?"

"No." Grayson firmed his hold on Mia when she shuddered against him. "Remove him before that changes."

Fletcher grasped Tyrell's wrists and none-too-gently dragged him from the room. He paused in the hall to close the cell door, sealing Grayson and Mia inside.

Mia's hands fisted Grayson's shirt and her tears splashed against his throat. Each one cut him like a blade.

"I've got you," he whispered, his voice too rough to be comforting. "I'm here." He kept repeating the words, but they weren't enough. They'd never be enough. Because the horror she'd just gone through was his fault. *All* of it was his fault, because she wouldn't even be here if it weren't for him. Henri never would have locked her in this cell if Grayson had just embraced what he'd always been destined to be—a fates-blasted demon.

Mia clung to him as if her welts and bruises didn't hurt at all, though he knew they must cover her body. It was clear she had fought Tyrell. Fought so furiously he'd had to tie her up.

From the corner of his eye Grayson saw the belt, still curled against the floor. As a child, Mia had been struck with a belt. Had Henri told Tyrell that?

He tightened his hold and Mia stiffened. He froze, fearing he'd hurt her.

"Oh, fates," she breathed. Her fingernails dug into his arms and she pushed away. Her eyes fastened on a point beside them on the floor and he followed her gaze to the bloody dagger. He must have dropped it.

Mia's mouth trembled. "Did he stab you? Where?" Her hands smoothed frantically over his chest and sides, and though her fingers found specks of blood, she couldn't find a wound that accounted for the blood on the dagger.

She wouldn't find any.

Grayson's ears rang with the pleas of the old man he'd killed. "He didn't stab me."

Confusion sparked in her eyes. "But—"

"It's not my blood."

Mia stared, chest rising and falling. An angry welt rose on her cheek and a muscle in his own cheek jerked. He reached out, fingers running along the edge of the red line. Mia shivered at the ghosting touch and Grayson's hand dropped, his fingers curling against his knee. "I'll kill him."

Her hands tightened around his biceps. "Grayson, where did that blood come from?"

Adrenaline still coursed through his veins and broke through the shields he normally held in place for her. "I'm the Black Hand," he said, his tone dark. "I don't even know how many lives I've taken. I enforce every law my father makes and everyone outside this cell is terrified of me. And they should be."

Mia was pale, making the welt on her face stand out vividly. Her voice trembled a little, confusion in her eyes. "You only do what you have to do. You don't have a choice."

Grayson's skin felt too tight. Everywhere she touched him, he burned. He tried to pull away but she clutched him tightly.

"Don't do this." Her voice wavered. "Don't pull away. I love—"

"Don't say that!"

She tensed, no longer breathing.

He looked right at her, ignoring the flash of pain that came when he saw the wetness in her eyes. "You don't want to love me, Mia. The blood on that dagger? It's from a man I just killed. He was defenseless. He begged me to spare his life but I still killed him."

Mia stared, stunned. Her hands were banded around his arms, but she was frozen.

Grayson bit out a hard laugh, the sound cold and brutal. "I'm a murderer. I've ripped families apart and destroyed lives, but none of that comes close to the worst thing I've done. Do you want to know what that is?"

Her chin wavered. Tears sliced down her face, wariness and apprehension lurking in her gaze.

"My father told me the truth," Grayson said, the words sticking painfully in his throat. "I know why you're here. You were imprisoned as a way to control me. You're in this cell because of me. Everything you lost—everything you've suffered—it's all because of me."

Horror pulled at her features. "You . . . ?" She couldn't even finish.

Grayson's insides hollowed. He had nothing left. The anger, frustration, self-loathing and guilt that had propelled every sharp word was suddenly gone. He'd lashed out at her with the darkest parts of him and she would never look at him the same way again.

This was the end. Everything between them was over. But while it had been necessary to make her understand, he didn't want to see her revulsion.

He moved before Mia could shove him away. He tugged his

arms free, her hands falling without resistance. He slid back, drawing one knee up to his chest with an arm slung over it. He glanced at the blood still on his glove and his fingers balled into a fist. He ducked his head, spreading his other hand over his aching brow. "I'm sorry," he whispered hoarsely. "I swear I didn't know the truth until tonight. If I'd known, I never would have kissed you. I'm sorry."

Silence reigned in the cell and the stillness made his stomach cave. It would be easier if she yelled at him. Ordered him out, or hit him.

Her dress rustled as she straightened on her knees and Grayson dropped his chin further, cringing as he awaited her attack.

One of Mia's hands settled over his fist and the other slid into his hair, her thumb brushing against his aching temple. Her words were weighted with emotion. "There's *nothing* you could do to make me hate you, Grayson. No matter how hard you try to push me away, it's not going to work." Her voice cracked and her hold on him tightened. "I love you."

A fissure cracked open inside him. He sucked in a breath, his whole body vibrating as he struggled to hold himself together.

Mia made a sound in the back of her throat and leaned in, pressing her forehead against his. "I've got you," she whispered, taking his words from earlier. "I'm here and I won't let go." She pressed a kiss to his brow and that simple action wrecked his fragile hold.

Mia held him as he shattered.

CHAPTER 42

CLARE

THE SNAP OF THE CROSSBOW RANG in Clare's ears, mingling with her staggered heartbeat. After everything she had survived, Gavril was going to kill her.

Bennick shoved her, both of them falling. Pain flared as Clare hit the stone floor on her back and the air was knocked from her lungs. Bennick caught his own weight instead of crushing her, his hands and knees caging her in, their faces a breath apart.

The bolt Gavril had shot streaked harmlessly over them and struck the wall.

"Seize him!" Newlan roared.

Clare's body shook. The sounds of a struggle competed with the heartbeat thudding in her ears. Bennick pressed a palm against her cheek, concern carved in his face as he forced her to meet his gaze. "Clare?" He breathed her name so softly, even she barely heard him.

Her eyes brimmed with tears. Gavril had tried to kill her. Shock, fear, denial—it swam inside her, a storm that stole her voice. If Bennick hadn't been beside her, that bolt would be buried in her heart.

A muscle pulsed along Bennick's jaw. His fingers brushed over her skin, a fleeting touch before he pushed to a crouch and pulled them both to their feet. They walked to where Newlan stood, glaring down at Gavril. The scarred man had been forced to kneel, a palace guard gripping each shoulder.

"You attempted to kill Princess Serene." Newlan's voice vibrated with menace.

Gavril sneered, the hatred on his face completely transforming him from the quiet guard Clare had known. "I only regret that I failed."

Clare strangled Bennick's fingers. "Why?" she whispered.

Gavril's narrowed eyes cut to her, animosity shooting from him. "There can be no peace with Mortise."

"It was you all along." Shock thrummed in Bennick's voice. "You wanted to frame Mortise for Serene's death. You're the one who planted the Night Sigh. The Ogai spiders. The poisoned necklace, the attack in her room . . . It was you at the orphanage too, wasn't it?"

Gavril ground his teeth. "I tried to keep you out of it, Bennick."

"I trusted you!" Bennick snapped.

He bit out a snarl, his rippled scars tensing. "I couldn't let the peace happen!"

"Your actions harmed innocents. People are dead because of you!"

"I had to do something!" Gavril's attention shifted to the king. "You stationed me on the border. You told me to protect Devendra from Mortise and I lost my wife and my daughter." His voice broke, but he plunged on. "Mortise took *everything* from me. And now you tell me to embrace them as an *ally*?" His lip curled, tugging at his scarred cheek. "I served you and you betrayed me. You deserve to lose your own daughter." He spat at Newlan's feet.

The king's face twisted. "You are guilty of treason. Attempted murder of a royal body. Dissent and war-mongering. You will be executed at first light."

"No." Amil Havim shoved past Clare. He glared at Gavril with shaking hands, his bearded face tight. "You're the reason my father is dead. You'll pay for his blood with your own." He jerked a dagger from his belt.

Clare gasped.

Bennick lunged, but Amil had already shoved the blade into Gavril's heart.

Gavril went rigid. His lips parted and blood dripped from his mouth. He tried to speak, but failed.

Amil planted a boot against Gavril's front and jerked his blade free. The guard collapsed, slumped on his side, fingers twitching once before he went still. The light fled his eyes. His face was tipped so the torchlight danced across his horrible burns, and that image would be with Clare forever. Her hands clamped over her mouth. Bile scorched her throat and tears bloomed behind her eyes. Gavril was dead. No chance for last words with his father. Nothing.

He was a man tormented by grief. He had killed. He'd nearly killed Clare several times, but . . . he'd saved her, too. And he hadn't deserved to die on the floor, murdered in a fit of rage.

Amil gripped the bloody dagger and turned to King Newlan, his voice terrifyingly level. "In the morning I ride for Mortise."

Newlan's hands fisted slowly at his sides. "The treaty?"

Amil's eyes flashed, his mouth a hard line. "Our emissary is dead, murdered by one of your men. Mortise was accused of the crimes of *your* people. That's what I'll tell the serjah. We'll see what he decides." He turned on his heel and strode from the room, Mortisian guards carrying the emissary's body behind him.

King Newlan's shoulders tensed as he glared at the dead man near his feet. If Gavril wasn't already lying in a pool of his own blood, Newlan would have killed him again. There was nothing the king wanted more than this alliance, and Gavril might have ruined it. "Remove this filth," he hissed. "There will be no burial. His body will feed the crows."

Clare turned her head aside when Gavril was dragged away. She didn't want to see it. Didn't want to face it. She wanted to hide in some corner until the world stopped spinning.

But the horror of tonight wasn't done.

Newlan rounded on the huddled entertainers. "You were hired by that traitor to kill Princess Serene. Your goal was to destroy the peace with Mortise."

"No," the gray-haired man pleaded. "Your Majesty, it wasn't us. Please, I beg a fair trial for me and my troupe."

Newlan's lips pulled back in a silent snarl. "Kill them."

Mothers howled and fathers cried for mercy. Children screamed and clutched their parents as the soldiers stepped forward, wielding their swords.

"No!" Clare moved so quickly Bennick could only curse, his hand snatching nothing but air as she darted into the space between Newlan and the entertainers. She faced the king, heart slamming against her ribs. Gavril's blood streaked the stones near her feet, strengthening the steel in her spine. "You can't kill them." Newlan's gaze sharpened in warning, but even though Clare could barely breathe, she wouldn't defer to his temper.

"Put them on trial," she said. "Find the guilty, but don't punish innocents."

Bennick's eyes burned her, begging her to meet his gaze, but she didn't look away from the king.

A muscle in Newlan's jaw ticked. "You forget your place."

She lifted her chin. "I won't allow you to hurt them."

"You won't *allow*?"

Everyone stared. The frantic whispers ceased, every eye fixed on the drama before them—the princess, defying her father.

That would have been inexcusable enough, but the truth was far worse. Clare was an imposter. She had no power, only the illusion of it. Yet strength coursed through her. Adrenaline and a sense of rightness kept her spine straight and her gaze firm.

"No," Clare said, voice ringing through the room. "I won't allow it."

A vein in Newlan's forehead pulsed and his nostrils flared.

Grandeur stepped forward, placing himself at Clare's side. His voice was low as he addressed the king. "Serene is upset. Perhaps it would be best to defer to her wishes." He glanced at Clare, the worry in his eyes barely veiled before he focused back on Newlan. "She's been through a great deal tonight. Please show leniency."

The king's attention darted between them and the silence stretched.

Clare's pulse roared in her ears.

Finally, Newlan spoke. "Take the vermin to the dungeon. Their fates will be determined in court."

The entertainers were herded to their feet. Men and women shot Clare grateful looks, but fear still smothered them as they kept their arms around their children.

Clare opened her mouth, ready to order that Newlan let the women and children go, but Grandeur sent her a quelling look, his eyes sharp with warning.

"Everyone out," the king ordered.

Nobles and guards made their way to the double doors at once, muttering amongst themselves, some with arms still wrapped consolingly around each other. Bennick moved to Clare's side and grasped her arm. His face was lined with tension, his entire body stiff. Before he could tug her toward the door, the king's glare froze them. "You stay."

Clare's body locked and Bennick's fingers tightened against her wrist. "Sire—"

"Get out," Newlan barked.

Bennick froze, and for a horrible moment, Clare thought he might refuse the king. But then his hand fell from her arm and he backed up. Clare held her breath the whole time he retreated, Dirk following him out.

Grandeur hesitated, but one look from the king and he dipped his head. As he turned, he gave Clare a short nod. She hoped he caught the gratitude in her eyes. While she no longer trusted the prince, she was thankful he'd risen to her defense.

The doors closed, leaving Clare alone with the king.

Newlan's low voice cut through the vaulted room. "You undermined me tonight. I don't tolerate that from Serene. Fates know I won't tolerate it from you."

Her hands fisted at her sides, the blood on her gloves now cold. "Killing them would have been wrong."

Newlan shot forward, eyes flashing. "I am *never* wrong. I'm the *king*." His hand swung and the back of it caught her cheek. Her breath hitched and pain sparked across her face. The gold ring on his finger added a bruising weight and the slap echoed in the empty room.

Clare pressed her palm to her throbbing cheek. She breathed hard, face heated, cheek throbbing as she met his furious stare.

"You are no one," he said through gritted teeth, hot breath hitting her face. "*Nothing*. Your life has meaning only because I say it does. You will *never* forget your place again. You won't be the only one punished if you do. Do I make myself clear?"

Thomas and Mark's faces swam before Clare's eyes and she jerked out a nod.

Newlan studied her, letting the threat settle between them before he dismissed her with a flick of his chin.

But even as Clare moved for the door, her cheek throbbing, she could not regret standing up to the king.

CHAPTER 43

BENNICK

BENNICK STOOD RIGID IN THE CORRIDOR, eyes fastened on the closed banquet hall doors. His body twitched with the need to be inside that room, standing beside Clare, but he couldn't disobey his king. So he stood with his feet firmly planted, spine straight, shoulders locked as he fingered the blood staining his hands. Venn had lost so much blood; Bennick prayed the physicians could save him.

So many had died. Clare could have been killed so many times because Gavril . . . Fates, Bennick didn't even know what to think. He could only feel.

Shock—Gavril had been the assassin all along.

Fury—Bennick had trusted him, given him access to the princess's room, and he'd hurt Clare and Serene, nearly killing them both.

Guilt—Bennick should have known. He hadn't done enough for Gavril. Hadn't realized he was so consumed with hate and grief.

He wanted to shake Gavril. Demand answers. Rage at him for what he'd done. Apologize for not seeing the depth of his pain. But he couldn't do any of that.

He thought of the orphanage attack—Gavril had looked panicked when he came into the alley and had immediately asked about Clare and Bennick's injuries. He hadn't needed to study them—he knew they were hurt, because he'd been the one to do it. He probably hadn't meant to hurt Clare, and he'd been holding back when Bennick fought him, which was why he'd delayed drawing the knife. Even tonight, Gavril had tried to draw Bennick from the room to save his life.

Bennick didn't know how to feel about any of it.

One of the tall doors pushed open and Clare slipped out, her head ducked. Her unbound curls shielded her face as she moved stiffly into the hallway. The king's bodyguards passed her, returning to the dining hall.

Bennick strode to Clare's side, Dirk right behind him. "Are you all right?" he asked.

Clare's head lifted, revealing burning cheeks—one a harsher shade of red.

Bennick's vision narrowed. The king had struck her.

"I'm fine. Can we go see Venn?"

"Of course," Dirk said.

Bennick couldn't speak; his mouth had gone dry.

Dirk led the way down the corridor and Bennick walked so closely beside Clare their arms brushed. Her reddened cheek practically glowed in the dim light of the narrow passage. His pulse snapped and his hands clenched. It was a good thing they walked away from the king; if he saw Newlan now, he didn't know what he'd do.

Cool fingers wrapped around his, startling him. Clare didn't look at him, just held his hand. Her soft glove was damp with blood, but he didn't care. The contact grounded him, loosened some of the tightness in his chest.

Within minutes they entered the physician's ward. The waiting area was filled with noble lords and ladies gathered in clusters throughout the room, some begging physician apprentices to let them into the private rooms to see a loved one. In the back corner of the waiting room, Bennick's eyes locked with Cardon's. The bodyguard wasn't alone. Vera stood with him, chewing her lip as she eyed a nearby closed door. Another maid was beside them, and it took Bennick a moment to recognize Serene in the maid's gray and white dress, wearing a kerchief over her head.

"They've sewn the wound," Serene said lowly as they drew close. "He's going to live."

"Thank the fates," Clare breathed, squeezing Bennick's hand. He should probably let go, but his fingers wouldn't move.

"The bolt broke one of his ribs," Cardon said. "He'll be in some pain for a month or so, but if he's careful he can still come with us to Mortise."

Bennick eyed the princess. "You shouldn't have left the safety of your room."

Serene rolled her eyes. "Please, Bennick. You know me. Besides, everyone is too preoccupied to notice me."

He might have tried arguing, but he was distracted when Clare slipped her hand free and moved to Vera. She wrapped an arm around the pale maid's waist and whispered to her.

Cardon lowered his voice. "Was it really Gavril?" When Bennick confirmed it with a short nod, Cardon cursed. "I can't believe it."

Serene braced her hands on her hips, eyebrows drawn together. "I know he was a friend to you all. I'm sorry."

Bennick couldn't stomach her apology—not when Gavril had put her life, and Clare's, in danger. "I should have realized it was him."

"His pain was an effective mask," Serene said. "You couldn't have known." Her words, spoken so directly, offered a surprising level of comfort. Emotions still warred inside Bennick, but self-blame was no longer the winning force.

The door pushed open and Wilf emerged. His jaw tightened as his eyes swept over them. "Fool's awake."

Vera dove around him, the first to enter the private room. Serene, Cardon, and Dirk went next, and Clare and Bennick moved to follow, but Clare paused before Wilf.

The large warrior viewed her with lowered brows.

"Thank you for saving my life," she said.

Wilf's forehead creased. "Only doing my duty."

Her mouth twitched. "Well, thank you."

Wilf watched as she disappeared into the room, then shot a confused look at Bennick. "What was that?"

Despite everything, the corner of Bennick's mouth lifted. "She once thought you were trying to kill her."

Wilf frowned. "Why would she think that?"

"You're a little gruff sometimes."

The large man only grunted.

Everyone crowded around the small room's only bed. Venn's uniform had been replaced by a thin white shirt and he lay sprawled against a mountain of pillows. "You're all embarrassing me," he said, then coughed. Vera quickly poured him a glass of water from a pitcher on the bedside table and even helped him drink. After a few swallows, Venn tipped his head back and gave her an almost distracted smile. "I'll have an impressive scar."

"You're not in too much pain?" Vera asked, her features

pinched with concern.

Wilf crossed his arms with a snort. "He's so drugged, it's amazing the idiot's conscious."

"That's true," Venn said, grinning at the girl beside him. "Can't feel a thing, Vera m'dear. I mean, Miss dear Smallwood. You're a very small wood, you know. It's in your name: Vera Smallwood." He giggled.

Bennick arched a brow. He hadn't known his friend could make that sound.

Cardon patted Venn's shoulder, his smile pulling at the long scar on his cheek. "You're going to be embarrassed about this tomorrow."

"Never!" Venn scoffed. "I won't be embarrassed because I won't remember it."

Dirk and Cardon shared a grin over his head.

Vera set the cup aside and perched on the bed's edge, Venn's limp hand cradled in both of hers. Serene laughed at something Venn said about Wilf's nursing abilities, and Wilf glowered.

Bennick sidled next to Clare, who stood at the foot of the bed. He set a hand against the small of her back and she sent him a brief smile that shot warmth through his veins. She rested her head on his shoulder and relaxed against him.

His own muscles loosened. The danger wasn't past, not with the road to Mortise stretched before them, but in this room and in this moment, there was peace.

CHAPTER 44

GRAYSON

GRAYSON'S BODY WAS STIFF BUT HE DIDN'T move. He and Mia sat on her cell floor, their backs to the bed, his arm wrapped around her. Her head was tipped against his shoulder and their free hands were joined, fingers threaded together and balanced on his bent knee. She hummed softly, almost unconsciously. It was a lullaby she'd sung to him when they were children, a haunting melody that had always made Grayson long for something unnamable.

Mia had removed his gloves, leaving nothing between them. Hours must have passed since he'd broken in her arms and he knew the welts and bruises on her body must be throbbing. He wanted to take away her pain. Would have done it in an instant, if he could.

He marveled that she was sitting here with him. He'd bared

his soul, showed her the ugliest, darkest parts of him, and she hadn't run away. She'd held him. She loved him. He wanted to memorize everything about this moment; the ethereal quality of her humming voice, the feel of her fingers in his, the warm scent of her, and the wild curls tossed over her shoulder.

Grayson lifted her hand and pressed a kiss to the back of it.

The corner of her mouth rose. "What was that for?"

He kept his lips against her smooth skin. "For everything."

Mia squeezed his hand. "You don't need to thank me."

He'd spend the rest of his life thanking her.

She tugged their hands down and lifted her chin, placing a soft kiss against his jaw. "I love you," she whispered.

A thrill shot through him. "I love you." He traced his thumb over hers, tightening his hold around her shoulders. His throat bobbed as he swallowed. "My father is sending me on another mission."

Mia lifted her head, wariness pinching her features as she sensed the gravity in his words. "This is different from the others, isn't it?"

He nodded.

Worry creased her brow. "Is it dangerous?"

"You don't need to worry about me."

She sent him a pointed look.

His mouth twitched ruefully. "You really don't need to."

Mia bit her lip. "Where are you going?"

"Mortise. Liam and I are both going. We received a royal invitation from Prince Desfan. We leave in a week."

Mia stared. Panic, dread, and fear swam in her brown eyes.

Fates. He shouldn't have said it like that—just announced he was leaving for another kingdom in mere days.

She visibly struggled to find her voice. "H-how long will you be gone?"

"I don't know. A long time. Months." He could feel the tension coiling her body and he tightened his hold on her hand. "You'll be safe, I promise."

Mia glanced away, her grip on his hand almost painfully tight. "What are you doing in Mortise?"

He wouldn't upset her with the truth. "My father is sending us as emissaries to open peace talks."

She actually snorted, her eyes still averted. "Your father doesn't want peace." She shook her head. "I hate this. I hate that you have to do everything he says. I wish I could go with you. I wish . . ."

He lowered his eyes. "I wish things were different, too."

Mia slipped her hand free of his, but only so she could lift her hand to cup his cheek. The ball of her thumb skated across his cheekbone, prompting him to fully meet her gaze. "Promise me you'll come back."

Grayson wrapped a hand around her wrist, his eyes intent. "Always," he reminded her. He didn't want to kill again, but if a stranger's death protected Mia, he knew what choice he'd make. It was the same choice he'd made mere hours ago.

Grayson wouldn't hesitate when the time came, no matter who his target turned out to be.

CHAPTER 45

CLARE

CLARE'S FINGERS TWITCHED AT HER SIDES as she stepped into
the castle courtyard. The carriage waited for her and soldiers
were already on their mounts. The journey to Mortise was about
to begin.

Soldiers and servants bowed as Clare passed, none of them
knowing the real Serene had already left with a limited guard
earlier that morning, taking a different route. For all intents and
purposes, Clare *was* the princess. It felt like her first time playing the decoy all over again. Her stomach roiled and she was
grateful she hadn't forced herself to eat breakfast.

The coming weeks were uncertain. The rebels would have
easier access to her, making them a very real threat. She would
be Serene almost constantly and the smallest thing might trip
her. Grandeur's ring was heavy in her pocket, a reminder of all

the deception surrounding her—the secrets she was a part of. Beside the ring was the dented tin soldier, bringing memories of her family and home. She still hadn't heard from Eliot and she hated to leave before they could reach a full understanding. But she had Bennick, the soldier who would always protect her. And she had all the skills her teachers had imparted. She prayed it would be enough.

Amil hadn't left the castle yet, but he would reach Mortise weeks before the ambling tour did. He'd have plenty of time to sway Serjah Desfan's opinion and jeopardize the alliance. Clare hoped the serjah wouldn't be easily influenced. As much as she hated to agree with Newlan, peace *was* in Devendra's best interest, and she didn't want Amil to destroy it in his need for revenge.

When Clare reached the carriage, she saw Bennick standing beside Master Lank, who was double-checking the harnesses for the horses. The stable master appeared to have aged a decade overnight and Bennick's hand on his shoulder seemed to be the only thing steadying him.

Clare joined them, and the stable master looked into her eyes and kept his voice low so it wouldn't carry to the others. "I'm sorry, Clare." His thin voice cracked. "He wasn't in his right mind."

"You don't need to apologize." Clare settled her hand on his arm. "I'm so sorry for your loss."

Master Lank's throat bobbed. "So am I. But those we love don't always choose the path we wish them to." He gave a final pat to the nearest horse's neck before bowing in farewell and walking slowly away.

Venn passed him, heading toward the carriage. He was bandaged and walking carefully, but grinning and chatting with Vera and Ivonne. Wilf followed close behind, scowling. The sight used to flood Clare with unease, but now that she knew he was no longer a threat, the predictability of his gruffness made her smile a little. Cardon and Dirk had gone with Serene, but everyone else here would stand beside her—a family she'd somehow joined—and with that realization came an inexplicable calm.

"Ready, Your Highness?" Bennick asked, extending a hand.

Clare set her gloved hand in his, the corner of her mouth lifting. "I am."

Bennick's blue eyes warmed as he returned her smile, and Clare stepped into the carriage.

THE STORY CONTINUES IN
ROYAL SPY
BOOK 2 OF THE FATE OF EYRINTHIA SERIES

TURN THE PAGE FOR A BONUS FATE OF
EYRINTHIA SHORT STORY

THE PRINCE AND THE PRISONER

A Fate of Eyrinthia Short Story

HEATHER FROST

THE PRINCE

AND THE

PRISONER

A FATE OF EYRINTHIA SHORT STORY

HEATHER FROST

Grayson is his father's
ultimate weapon—
but he wasn't always.

This prequel to *Royal Decoy* is
the story of how a young Grayson
met the little girl who would
change his life forever . . .

GRAYSON

GRAYSON RAN THROUGH THE narrow corridor, his heart pounding as loudly as his boots. Each impact against the stone floor jarred his nine-year-old body, but he did not slow down.

His brothers had ambushed him outside his room. So exhausted after his brutal training session, he had not paid enough attention to his surroundings. By the time the hairs on the back of his neck rose in warning, it was too late.

His wrists still burned from Carter's crushing hold and the right side of his face ached from slamming into the stone wall. Peter's relentless fists had left bruises across his back and stomach, but he would not let pain slow him down, not now when he had managed to escape.

He heard footsteps behind him.

Peter and Carter were gaining.

Grayson's lungs strained as he pushed through the pain and forced his throbbing body to move faster. He was not even sure where he was anymore. Deep in the bowels of the castle, even servants were absent—not that any of them would help him. They knew better than to become involved in Kaelin family affairs.

He could not run forever. He needed to hide.

A couple more turns in the corridor and Grayson spied a large door. Relief slammed into him almost violently, making his heart kick painfully in his chest. Every tightly wound muscle strained to move faster as he lunged those final steps and grasped the iron handle.

By some blessing of the fates, it was unlocked.

Leaping into the dimly lit sanctuary, he slammed the door closed behind him. His hands shook as he searched for a lock, but there was no key. His pulse pounded erratically, making a horrible roaring in his ears that nearly drowned out everything else.

He forced himself not to make a sound. Clamped down on his breathing until his lungs burned.

On the other side of the door, boots pounded the stone floor, drawing closer.

Grayson was frozen, though the muscles in his legs and arms twitched. If he moved, tried to run, they would hear him. Find him. Hurt him.

Every instinct, every impulse, snapped at him to *run,* but will alone held him in place. His palms braced against the wooden door in front of him and sweat trickled down his back, tensing his spine.

His brothers were right outside. He could hear them, sense them.

Grayson's lungs screamed for air he didn't dare drag in. His pulse jumped in his neck and his fingers curled against the door, preparing to push back if his brothers tried to open the door.

The footsteps rushed past without slowing, continuing to beat down the corridor.

Grayson still held his breath, his body shaking even after the sound of their pursuit died. When he finally sucked in air, the flood of breath rushed to his head and made him dizzy. He sagged against the thick door, his forehead pressing into the smooth wood.

Adrenaline still burned through his veins and his skin felt too tight. But slowly, finally, his heartbeat slowed.

He was safe.

Well, as safe as he ever was.

When Grayson lifted his head and pushed back from the door, the sweat on his back had begun to dry, and a shiver cut through him. Now that his body was no longer locked in danger, he registered the chill brushing his skin.

He must be deep in the castle. Deeper than he had realized.

Glancing over his thin shoulder, he followed the distant glow of light that came from a torch bracketed to the wall. The shadows were thick in this deserted hall and at the end of it, a staircase descended into darkness. Realization hit.

The castle dungeon.

It was not an area he was very familiar with, but he recognized the entrance all the same. And though the prison had sheltered him from his brothers, unease traced down his spine.

He had hidden long enough. It was time to leave.

Grayson reached for the handle but before he could touch it, he heard something.

A whisper. A voice. The soft sound threaded through the cold air and brushed his ears, halting his movements. Even his breath faltered, because the sound . . . it was not what he would have ever expected to hear in a dungeon.

Someone was singing.

The lilting sound was faint, but something about the haunting voice reached into Grayson's chest and clenched around his heart. It was actually kind of painful. But a different pain than he normally felt.

Grayson was moving before he had fully made the decision, his boots scuffing softly over the worn stone floor. When he reached the shadowy staircase, he only hesitated a moment before descending.

He focused on the voice, strained to hear every shifting note. The music became clearer with every step he took, but the ethereal quality remained. It was a gentle song, the kind of lullaby he imagined a loving mother might sing to her child before kissing him goodnight. Things Grayson knew in theory, but had never experienced. Perhaps that was why it sounded so haunting? Or perhaps that was why it haunted him.

He was nearly to the base of the stairs when he realized the song was in an unfamiliar language. But even though he did not understand the words, the emotion in that beautiful voice reached something deep inside him, awakening a pang he had long tried to bury. It was not a pleasant feeling, this almost grief-filled longing that gripped him and made his stomach twist, but he could not stop walking toward that voice.

At the end of the staircase, Grayson found himself in a long hall of the upper prison and he drew up short. In the glow of a flickering torch, a man stood guard outside one of the wooden cell doors.

The old guard eyed Grayson with raised brows, shock etched in every line of his weathered face. The limited torchlight cast shadows over the guard's silver-touched dark hair, and his eyes remained wide as he twisted to face Grayson with a bow. "Your Highness."

Grayson swallowed, his eyes darting to the guarded door.

The voice was coming from the other side, and it was like the fabled siren's call. No matter how much it hurt, he needed to hear it. He needed to get closer. He needed to see who was singing.

The guard frowned. "Is there something you need, Your Highness?" The unspoken question was clear in his tone: *What are you doing here?*

Grayson gestured to the door, his throat strangely dry. "Who is in there?"

"No one, Your Highness."

Clearly a lie, but Grayson didn't press for the truth. The man had probably been ordered to silence by the king.

Grayson moved closer to the door, until one hand tentatively pressed against the smooth wood. The hairs on his arms lifted as the notes of the lullaby climbed higher. The voice was soft and young, clearly female. But despite the softness, there was confidence. She was unafraid to be heard.

Grayson envied that. He had spent his whole life trying to hide.

"What is she singing?" The question just fell out and his cheeks heated. But he didn't try to take the words back.

The guard studied Grayson's profile. "I believe it is a Mortisian lullaby."

"I have never heard a lullaby." The admission was also made without thought, and though Grayson could feel the guard's heavy stare, he didn't turn to meet the look.

Grayson strained to hear each beautiful, mesmerizing note. He was wholly distracted, until the guard stepped closer.

Instinct kicked in and Grayson whipped around, sinking

into a defensive crouch.

The guard's hands flipped up. "Apologies, Your Highness. I was only going to offer . . ." His eyes skated over Grayson's face, lingering on the red line that cut across his left cheek—his newest scar from Tyrell. An emotion Grayson could not name skirted over the man's lined face, and his prominent throat bobbed. "What I mean to say is, if you wanted to look inside . . ." He pointed toward the base of the door, where a thin metal plate could be lifted to push food inside.

Grayson hesitated, and the guard slowly backed away. "I have been meaning to fetch a drink," he said. "I will be just down the hall."

He watched the guard retreat, and only after he had disappeared around the corner did Grayson look back at the door.

He should leave. Not that there was anywhere else to be, but kneeling on the dungeon floor to spy on whoever was singing was wrong, no matter how badly he wanted to.

But then, he was a Kaelin prince. And weren't they all selfish monsters?

Grayson lowered himself to the floor and scooted closer to the food grate, trying to ignore the tension knotting in his gut. His left hand shook a little as he carefully, gradually, lifted the gate.

Slowly, the room beyond was revealed. The floor was the same cold stone Grayson knelt on, though the light was brighter in the prison cell. There were a few lamps lit, rather than just one torch, and he could see the base of a bed draped in a frayed quilt. He saw wooden chairs and a square table—

He saw her.

The girl was small, probably a year or so younger than him. She was sitting on the bed in a faded red dress, her long dark hair spilling over her shoulders in chaotic waves. She was fingering the end of one curl as she sang, her head ducked while she watched the shiny strands of hair play over her fingers. Her small face was round and her dirt-streaked cheeks looked soft in the glow of lamplight. Her skin was a warm brown that would contrast completely with his pale skin.

Her head lifted suddenly, her brown eyes colliding with his gray ones.

Grayson froze.

So did the girl. She stopped singing. Stopped breathing, it seemed. And her eyes flared wide.

Oh, fates. She was afraid of him. And why wouldn't she be? He was spying on her, and he knew his face was . . . hard to look at.

Heat slammed into his cheeks and he wanted to drop the grate, scramble back, and run. But even though his heart raced, he couldn't move. He was pinned by her stare. Completely trapped.

The girl's eyes were dark, and Grayson fully expected fear and revulsion to overtake the shock that had frozen her face. He knew how people looked at him, even if they tried to do it behind his back.

But the fear didn't come. Neither did disgust, or panic, or any of the other things Grayson expected. No, what he saw in her eyes didn't make sense at all.

Relief. Hope.

Excitement.

The girl's pink lips curved up, transforming her pretty face into the most beautiful thing Grayson had ever seen.

His heart thumped.

She scrambled off the bed and dropped to her knees on the other side of the door, lowering her head until she could peer out at him.

Grayson reared back a little, but he didn't drop the grate. He couldn't stop staring at her, even though he wanted to bolt. Even though she . . . unnerved him.

The girl beamed at him, eagerness lighting up her entire face. "Do you want to play with me?"

The words were halting, her tongue clearly struggling with the Rydenic language, but her enthusiasm was unmistakable. Her hands were pressed to the stone floor, as if that was the only thing keeping her still. Her eyes were dancing and energy thrummed from her.

Grayson blinked. He should tell her that princes of Ryden didn't play—his parents didn't allow it. But his throat was dry and his breathing had not quite returned to normal. So he surprised himself by jerking out a nod.

The girl clapped her hands, speaking in a rush of unintelligible words. He could not even tell what language she was speaking.

He just stared at her until finally she paused. She offered a sheepish grin. "Sorry," she said, switching back to Rydenic. "I . . . I've wanted a friend so badly." She glanced around behind her, then pushed to her feet.

Grayson tensed as she walked away and his mouth opened to call her back, but she was already returning, settling into a crouch near the grate. She showed him the small gray pebble she had pinched between her thumb and first finger. Then she set it on the ground and flicked it at him.

It skittered to a stop near his knee. He hesitated, then flicked it back.

The girl grinned, and Grayson's heart squeezed in his chest.

The game continued, the pebble bouncing back and forth between them. Even though Grayson's arm got tired holding the food gate open, he did not ever think of dropping it.

The girl flicked the pebble back at him with more force this time and it hit his knee. She giggled when it bounced back.

Grayson almost smiled, one corner of his mouth rising a bit stiffly—the gesture was unfamiliar. But her laugh was as musical as her singing had been, and the joy in her eyes . . . Fates, it was the most wonderful thing he had ever seen.

Grayson shot the pebble back at her. He was careful not to flick it too hard; he did not want to hit her. She looked so small, he worried even the small pebble could hurt her. But his caution made the pebble fall short in the space between them. He reached for it, ready to flick it again, but the girl was reaching for it too.

Grayson's breath caught when their fingers brushed, his heart tripping violently at the unexpected contact. His fingers were scarred and pale. Hers were soft, warm, and perfect.

The girl did not seem to be breathing, either.

The muscles in his back tensed as he waited for her to recoil. No one liked to touch him. Not the nursemaids, back when he'd had them. Not the physicians, or the servants, or the nobles. The only people who touched him were his brothers, and those hands had only ever hurt him.

She was going to pull away. She was going to cringe back from his scars—from him.

But her fingertips did not move from his. Her gaze lifted and their eyes locked. And then she *smiled.* It was a different smile from before. It was gentle and accepting and . . . loving.

It was like being struck by lightning. Grayson felt a charge go through him, violent and fast, changing him forever. Maybe in ways he didn't even understand yet. All he knew was that this girl was everything—a gift he did not deserve—and he didn't want to ever be without her.

"What is your name?" she asked haltingly.

He wet his lips. "Grayson."

She repeated his name, a slow, exploratory whisper that raised every hair on his body. She flashed another smile, like she didn't realize each one was as brilliant as the sun. "I am Mia."

Mia. It was soft, beautiful, and calming.

It was perfect for her.

The scuff of boots against stone jerked Grayson back from the door. The grate clanged shut and the girl cried out, but Grayson couldn't focus on her distress. He shot to his feet, putting himself between the door and the threat as his hand dropped to the dagger at his belt.

It was the old guard. He stood near the torch, and it looked like he might have been there a while before he had shifted his weight.

Grayson's scalp prickled at the realization that he had allowed himself to become distracted. He had left his back unguarded. A foolish mistake, in his world.

The guard's eyes were trained on Grayson and he stared right back, his hand still on his knife. There was a strange, almost sad tilt to the guard's bearded chin. Grayson could not read the emotion in the man's heavy gaze.

The food gate lifted with a scrape and thump, but Grayson didn't take his eyes off the guard, even when the girl spoke. "Grayson, it's all right. It's only Fletcher. He will not hurt you. Fletcher, this is Grayson. My friend."

Grayson's body stiffened at her claim of friendship. He did not have friends. Friends were a weakness. That is what his father said.

But, in a sudden, desperate wish, he wanted this girl to be his friend.

The guard—Fletcher—eyed them both for a long moment before he focused on Mia. "Do you want him to come inside?"

The question nearly dropped Grayson's jaw. He would not have thought a guard would let people mingle with the prisoner. And he certainly had not expected the guard to *ask* Mia what she wanted.

It also made Grayson wonder why a little girl was a prisoner here, anyway. But those questions faded when Mia gasped *yes*, and Fletcher's focus shifted to Grayson. Waiting. Silently asking if Grayson wanted to go inside.

In all his life, Grayson had never had much of a choice in anything. He followed orders. He fought to survive. He avoided his brothers when he could, but when his father ordered him to face them, he had to.

But now? This moment? This was a choice that was his.

For some inexplicable reason, his chest warmed.

He could walk away, and Fletcher would not stop him. And if he chose to go in there . . .

Grayson knew if he walked through that door, a part of him would never come out. This girl, this place—he would crave it. Every day from now on, coming back here, to her, would be the only thing that mattered.

She would be the only thing that mattered.

It was a staggering realization, and maybe he should have hesitated. Thought through the consequences. But there was no hesitation, because Mia had already stolen a part of his soul the moment she smiled at him.

Maybe she had taken all of it.

He gave his answer and Fletcher fished out his keys. They jangled as they came out of his pocket, and then he fitted the longest one into the lock. With the grating turn of a key, the door swung inward, revealing the girl as she sprang to her feet.

Grayson stepped into the cell and stooped to reach the gray pebble. Curling his fingers around the small stone, he slowly straightened.

Mia was grinning at him, her hands clasped under her chin. Her brown eyes gleamed in the lamplight. "Hello," she whispered.

Grayson's mouth curved and, for the first time, he truly smiled. "Hello."

ACKNOWLEDGEMENTS

These are always so hard to write, because I know I'm bound to miss someone. So many people helped make this book possible. Mom, thank you for always cheering me on. Dad, even though you're not right here with me anymore, I feel your love every day. Thank you both for being the best parents ever! Kimberly, thank you for your incredible design work (the cover and interior look fabulous!) and for always reading whatever I write. Kevin, thank you for designing the map—it's awesome! To the rest of my siblings—thank you for always encouraging me and being my best friends!

A special thanks to Laurie Ford and Anna Brown for reading every version of this book—including the very first one, which started in a totally different place and included characters that aren't even there anymore. Thank you to my other very early readers: Crystal Frost, Rebecca McKinnon, Britney Bird, Stephanie Granado, Alex Essig, Jonnie Morgart, Rachel Wilson, Craig Manning, Michalla Holt, Elyce Edwards, Amelia White, and Cynthia Ford—thank you for your edits, conversations, encouragement, and for sharing this book with so many others!

Thank you to all the reviewers and librarians who helped spread the word about Royal Decoy. And lastly, a very special thank you to all my readers—you are the best people in the world! Thank you for holding this book in your hands, writing reviews, and sharing this book with others. Your love and support keeps me going. Thank you!

Want more books by Heather Frost?

Don't miss the Seers Trilogy

seers are not just **spectators,**
they are also **prey**

When Kate Bennett survived the car accident that claimed her parents' lives, she knew her world would be forever changed. But her life is more dramatically altered than she first realized. Not only is she able to see auras on the people around her, she's even started seeing invisible people with no colors at all. And no matter how attractive the new addition to her American Lit class is, Kate sees what no one else can—the dangerous truths this mysterious boy threatens to pour into her life.

Patrick O'Donnell was killed in the Irish Revolution in 1798. He's here now to try and keep Kate alive, and stop her life from spinning out of control. The one thing he's not going to do is fall in love with her.

But plans change, especially when Demons are involved . . .

Kate is about to enter the world of Seers; where immortals are at war with each other, and unfortunate mortals like Kate are in over their heads.

ABOUT THE AUTHOR

Heather Frost writes mostly YA fiction and has a soft spot for tortured characters, breath-stealing romance, and happy endings. She is the author of the Seers trilogy and the Fate of Eyrinthia series. She has a BS in Creative Writing and a minor in Folklore, which means she got to read fairy tales and ghost stories and call it homework.

When she's not writing, Heather likes to read, travel, and hold Lord of the Rings movie marathons. She owns two typewriters, sings in the car, and dreams of living in a castle someday. She currently lives in Utah, in a beautiful valley surrounded by towering mountains.

To connect with Heather and learn more about her books, visit www.HeatherFrost.com.